**LOVE AND DESIRE SURGED UP IN HIM
LIKE A TIDE THAT WOULD BREAK ANY
BARRIER PLACED AGAINST IT. . . .**

Very carefully, he took her into his arms. She came, not reluctantly, but with a kind of weight, as if pulled against something.

Slowly, very slowly, he bent his head and placed his mouth against hers. Her lips parted, the soft, bruising pressure increasing. Then the restraining silken knot snapped, and they were pressed together fiercely, their bodies crying to be closer.

It was as though nakedness were their privacy; as though clothes had been witnesses, and now they were truly alone with each other. Time held them softly, lapping them like the high tide that is too full for sound or foam. . . .

THE
LONG
SHADOW

Cynthia Harrod-Eagles

A DELL BOOK

Published by
Dell Publishing Co., Inc.
1 Dag Hammarskjold Plaza
New York, New York 10017

This work was first published in Great Britain by Macdonald & Co.
(Publishers) Ltd. as DYNASTY VI: THE LONG SHADOW.

Dell ® TM 681510, Dell Publishing Co., Inc.

ISBN: 0-440-14791-3

Printed in the United States of America
First U.S.A. printing—October 1983

FOR ALLEN
WITH MY LOVE

THE MORLAND FAMILY

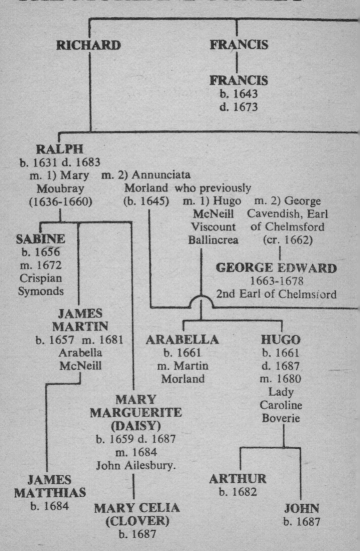

RICHARD

FRANCIS

FRANCIS
b. 1643
d. 1673

RALPH
b. 1631 d. 1683
m. 1) Mary   m. 2) Annunciata
Moubray   Morland who previously
(1636-1660) (b. 1645) m. 1) Hugo   m. 2) George
                        McNeill   Cavendish, Earl
                        Viscount   of Chelmsford
                        Ballincrea   (cr. 1662)

SABINE
b. 1656
m. 1672
Crispian
Symonds

GEORGE EDWARD
1663-1678
2nd Earl of Chelmsford

**JAMES
MARTIN**
b. 1657 m. 1681
Arabella
McNeill

ARABELLA
b. 1661
m. Martin
Morland

HUGO
b. 1661
d. 1687
m. 1680
Lady
Caroline
Boverie

**MARY
MARGUERITE
(DAISY)**
b. 1659 d. 1687
m. 1684
John Ailesbury.

**JAMES
MATTHIAS**
b. 1684

**MARY CELIA
(CLOVER)**
b. 1687

ARTHUR
b. 1682

JOHN
b. 1687

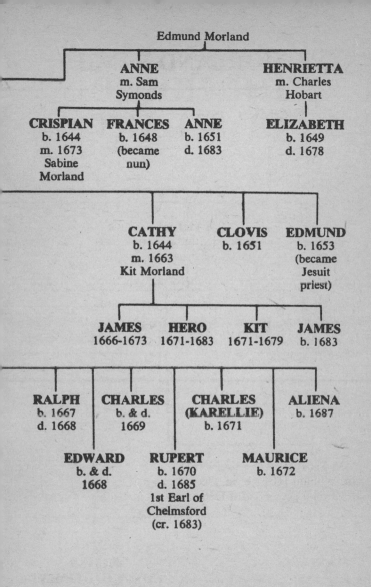

Edmund Morland

ANNE
m. Sam
Symonds

HENRIETTA
m. Charles
Hobart

CRISPIAN
b. 1644
m. 1673
Sabine
Morland

FRANCES
b. 1648
(became
nun)

ANNE
b. 1651
d. 1683

ELIZABETH
b. 1649
d. 1678

CATHY
b. 1644
m. 1663
Kit Morland

CLOVIS
b. 1651

EDMUND
b. 1653
(became
Jesuit
priest)

JAMES
1666-1673

HERO
1671-1683

KIT
1671-1679

JAMES
b. 1683

RALPH
b. 1667
d. 1668

CHARLES
b. & d.
1669

CHARLES
(KARELLIE)
b. 1671

ALIENA
b. 1687

EDWARD
b. & d.
1668

RUPERT
b. 1670
d. 1685
1st Earl of
Chelmsford
(cr. 1683)

MAURICE
b. 1672

THE HOUSE OF STUART

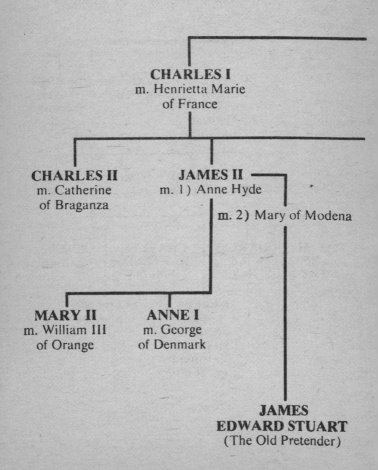

CHARLES I
m. Henrietta Marie
of France

CHARLES II
m. Catherine
of Braganza

JAMES II
m. 1) Anne Hyde

m. 2) Mary of Modena

MARY II
m. William III
of Orange

ANNE I
m. George
of Denmark

**JAMES
EDWARD STUART**
(The Old Pretender)

JAMES I OF ENGLAND
(James VI of Scotland)

ELIZABETH
(The Winter Queen)
m. Frederick, Elector
Palatine

MARY
m. William II
of Orange

HENRIETTA ANNE
m. Duc d'Orleans

RUPERT **MAURICE** **SOPHIA**
m. Elector of
Hanover

GEORGE I

FOREWORD

All historians seem to be prejudiced, and perhaps we should not care to read them if they were not. With this period, as with the Civil War, it is important to read as widely as possible in order to obtain the least biased view, and I will not therefore add the usual bibliography to this foreword, for in order to be useful it would have to be exceedingly long.

For anyone interested in the Monmouth rebellion, I would like to recommend the immensely readable and well-researched *The Western Rising* by Charles Chenevix Trench. For a view of the ordinary life of country people, I cannot too highly recommend *Through England on a Sidesaddle* by Celia Fiennes, who made just such a journey in the reign of William and Mary. For the social life of London I would recommend the works of the Restoration playwrights, particularly of William Wycherley, with the enjoinder to take them all with a pinch of salt.

Life itself is but the shadow of death
. . . and light but the shadow of God.

Sir Thomas Browne:
The Garden of Cyrus

BOOK ONE

PELICAN
IN HER PIETY

The Time that is to come is not;
How can it then be mine?
The present moment's all my lot;
And that, as fast as it is got,
Phillis, is only thine.

> "Love and Life"
> John Wilmot,
> Earl of Rochester:
> *Love and Life*

CHAPTER ONE

Ballincrea House was an old and, of recent years, much altered building which stood on the narrow and muddy King Street, opposite the Palace of Whitehall, and in September 1670 it was the scene of a brilliant gathering: Annunciata Morland, Countess Dowager of Chelmsford, was giving a christening party for her newest-arrived baby.

The circumstances surrounding the birth of the baby were not entirely to the credit of the hostess, who had traveled down to London from Yorkshire shockingly late in her pregnancy and brought on the birth early. But none of the dazzling company who alighted from their coaches before the door worried about that. Everyone had been eager to get an invitation; the countess's close friendship with the leading members of the Royal Family would have been enough to ensure she got no refusals; but, in addition, she was a lavish hostess, and this was not only the first party of the Season but also the first since the Court had come out of mourning. The King's youngest sister, Princess Henrietta d'Orleans, had died tragically in May, and this party would be everyone's first opportunity to display the new Season's colors and styles.

Heavy late-August rains had turned King Street into a black mire, and a bed of wheat straw two feet thick had had to be spread across the entrance to the house, but despite that there was an enormous crowd waiting outside to see the guests arrive. Some of them had been there almost since dawn. Even after the principal people had arrived and gone in, the crowd stayed, though there was nothing to look at but the garlands of flowers and ribbons that decorated the housefront, and the footmen in their black-and-white Morland livery. All the same, the King and the Duke of York were within, and might appear at a window; and it was rumored that there would be fireworks after dark; and besides, there were always a great many broken meats given away at the Morlands' door, and many people in the crowd had brought baskets with them for that very purpose.

The long saloon on the first floor was a beautiful room, light and airy and decorated in the modern style with panels of green and gold silk, and filled with those dainty treasures collected so lovingly by the countess's first husband, Hugo, Viscount Ballincrea. It was a fit setting for Annunciata Morland, who, though she was now twenty-five and had borne six children, was still accounted one of the most beautiful women in the country. Tall, slender, with her mass of black Stuart hair and her dark Stuart eyes, she was the center of attention as she stood chatting and laughing with King Charles II. She was dressed today in emerald-green silk, deeply décolleté, the sleeves opened down the front and clasped with jewels to show the white taffeta of her undersleeves. Her hair was dressed with pearls, and round her neck hung a magnificent emerald necklace, one of the Morland heirlooms and generally known as the Queen's Emeralds. The story was that the gems had been a gift to Queen Katherine Parr from King Henry, and had been given by that Queen to her friend Nanette Morland. If the countess was a little pale and drawn from the birth ordeal, only those who knew her well would have noticed it behind the animation of her face.

"And where is my newest godson?" the King was asking her, smiling down into her upturned face. "Is he not to make an appearance at his own party?"

"Later, sir, when all the guests have arrived," Annunciata said. "Though if it were not for the musicians playing, I think you would hear him expressing his impatience from the nursery."

The King laughed. "Born to take a leading part, that young man," he said. "He struck me such a blow this morning my chin is still tender." The christening itself had taken place that morning in the Queen's closet at Whitehall, with the King and Queen, the Duke of York, Prince Rupert, and Lord Craven as sponsors. The King drooped his head nearer to Annunciata's to murmur quietly, "And of course his entry into the world was somewhat more precipitate than usual, was it not? My dear, what could bring you to risk your health, not to say your life, riding by coach to London when the roads were so bad? I am sure your husband must have been very angry with you."

Annunciata made a moue. "He was," she said succinctly. "But I was so bored, sir, and when I heard that the Court was back I could not stay away any longer. And so I came—and so the baby came. Now, sir, do not be angry with me—you would not have wanted to miss this party, would you?"

The King laughed aloud at that, making those standing nearby stretch their ears to try to discover how the countess amused the King so much. "I could not be angry with you for long, my dear," he said, and took her hand to add, "But seriously, you must take care of yourself. I have lost too many of those dear to me to want to risk you."

Annunciata's eyes filled with sympathetic tears. "We shall all miss Her Highness, sir, though none, I'm sure, as much as you." Annunciata had been a friend and correspondent of the Princess Henrietta, and had spent some time with her and the King during her visit to England that spring.

"Now there is only Jamie left," he said, casting a glance toward his brother, who stood chatting with Annunciata's third husband, Ralph Morland. "And frankly, my dear, he is as much worry to me as joy."

Annunciata cast a startled glance toward the prince and said, "Surely, sir, you do not fear for his health?" The Duke of York had rarely known a day's indisposition. The King smiled grimly.

"Not his health, no, but for his state of mind. You know that I have once again failed to persuade Parliament to the justice of Toleration?"

"I heard, of course, that they had renewed the Conventicles Act," Annunciata said softly. "Naturally, as it affects me personally . . ." The King nodded.

"Here at Whitehall you are safe enough," he said. "As long as we practice our Catholicism discreetly, the country is willing to allow us our little toy. But outside Whitehall there is such an implacable hatred of it among the people, such an unreasoning fear, and James, I am afraid, knows no discretion. He feels it ignoble to hide his religion.''

"They do say, sir," Annunciata said with a glimmer of a smile, "that the convert is always the most vehement. But, sir, my husband tells me that it is time to call a new Parliament. Would not a new Parliament perhaps grant what the old one refuses?''

The King shook his head. "I am afraid not. The mood of the people sways this way and that, and I am afraid that a new Parliament would be far more Roundhead in sympathy, and even more against Catholicism. No, I must make do with what I have, and continue to wear gently away at them, like water on a stone. But you, my dear, you will take care when you go back home? The Conventicles Act—''

"Do not fear," Annunciata said comfortably. "I shall be safe enough in Yorkshire. The North is far more tolerant than the South, and their Anglican service is close enough to our Anglo-Catholic Mass for them to blink at the difference. Besides, Ralph *is* the law in our own small world." They were silent a moment, and then she changed the subject. "Tell me, sir, how fares the Queen? I was sorry that she did not feel well enough to come this afternoon. She looked cold at the service this morning.''

A little way off, Ralph Morland listened with only half his attention fixed on the Duke of York, though the duke had a sweet and musical voice, and though he was more interesting on the subject of ships than on any other. But Ralph's eyes were drawn continually past the duke to the lovely form of his wife, and the sight of her, beautiful and animated, gave him pain as well as pleasure. When he had married her, four years ago, he had felt as if he had at last arrived at the place to which he had been traveling all his life. His life had been a thing of such contrasts: the war had cast its sad and confusing shadow over his childhood, robbing him of both father and mother, and finally of one who was dearer than a mother—Mary Esther Morland, who had raised him. But then young manhood had brought him happiness. He had become master of Morland Place, and had married and fallen in love with his first wife, Mary Moubray, his Catholic bride from the Borderlands.

Ralph was a simple man, with simple desires. A comfortable home, a loving wife, a large family of healthy children, the respect of his peers, and some simple pleasure in the way of good hunting, music, and merrymaking were all he wanted, and for some time he had seemed to have it. That was in the years when Annunciata was growing up, and Ralph, fifteen years her senior, had watched her with affectionate amusement and rescued her from the worst of the troubles her impetuosity brought on her.

But his happiness had once again crumbled. He had been forced to admit that his wife was deeply unhappy; then had come the horror of her lingering illness and death. Then, as if fate were punishing him for his unthinking happiness before, one by one his children had died. He had seemed to wander in darkness, bereft of his God, mourning his dead, purposeless.

Then Annunciata had come home—beautiful, desirable, wealthy, the child of fortune, fresh from the glittering triumphs of her London life, sparkling with life even though she, too, had suffered bereavement and grief. He realized then that he had loved her all his life and she, strangely, marvelously, had said she loved him, too. He had married her, as enraptured and bemused as Endymion abducted by the goddess Diana, and thought that his life was now settled forever. He had all he wanted.

Yet he could not help being aware that Annunciata had been growing restless of late. He had thought it was because of the children—three times she had borne him a son, and three times suffered the grief of bereavement. Little Ralph, little Edward, little Charles, all had lived no more than a few weeks. She had conceived again early that year, and Ralph had urged her to be very careful, remain quietly at home, not excite herself. Yet from the beginning she had seemed to do everything against his advice, almost as if she were daring fate to attack her again. Her latest whim had been the sudden decision to come to Court as soon as she heard the King was back from Windsor. He had argued and pleaded with her, but she had merely laughed—a strange, wild laugh—and in the end all he could do was to go with her and try to mitigate the worst effects of the journey.

He thought sometimes that she had not anticipated just how bad it would be, traveling at snail's pace through the teeming August rain, the coach lurching and jolting, its wheels at times hub-deep in mud, the horses floundering and crying. How could she? She was one of the country's finest horsewomen, and had barely spent ten hours of her life in a coach before. Many a time he saw her, on that journey, grit her teeth, bite her lip, turn her greenish and sweating face from him rather than admit her discomfort. Many an evening he had procured hot water for her from an unwilling innkeeper, bathed her like a child, and put her shivering and silent to bed with hot bricks at her feet. Small wonder, then, that she had gone into labor almost as soon as she reached Ballincrea House. The wonder was that the child, another boy, seemed so well-formed and healthy.

And now she looked so alive and so happy, Ralph thought, as she stood chattering to the King, not in the least shy or overwhelmed, not even displaying a female modesty, but talking to His Majesty as if she were his younger brother instead of his female subject. Ralph still felt faintly ill at ease in these brilliant surroundings, among all these distinguished and titled members of the London *beau monde*. The long saloon with its modern furnishings and fabulous treasures did not suit him as a background as did the solid dark paneling of Morland Place; he knew he looked out of place, and that the rest of the guests thought him merely an up-country farmer, a clod.

And in some ways they were right—he *was* out of place. He didn't like London, with its closeness, its smells, its artificial glamor. He loved the open skies, the sweet fresh wind, the fields and moors, and he came up to London each year with Annunciata only because he did not wish to be separated from her. He wished Yorkshire could be enough for her. He knew that she loved it, as he did, and that she needed to spend part of every year there, to refresh and renew herself; but she also needed the more exotic excitements of London, and it saddened him to see her so at home here, where he felt a stranger.

Ralph suddenly realized that the duke had asked him a question and was waiting for an answer, and he became aware of how rudely he had been ignoring his royal guest.

"I beg your pardon, Your Grace," he stammered in deep confusion. "I fear—I regret I did not quite catch—"

If Prince James was offended, his handsome, impassive face did not show it. He raised one eyebrow and said patiently, "Quite all right, Morland. It is very noisy in here. God in His wisdom must have had some reason for giving women such shrill voices, but . . ." he trailed away, and then recollected himself. "I asked if you and your wife would dine with me tomorrow. The duchess is not well enough to dine out these days, but she would greatly like to see you both. It will only be a quiet dinner, *en famille*, with a few guests. I have asked your brother, too."

"I should be honored, Your Grace. Thank you very much," Ralph said, and hoped fervently that Annunciata had not, in the meantime, accepted another invitation to dine elsewhere with the King. Then a footman came in to announce the last of the important guests.

"His Highness Prince Rupert of the Rhine, Duke of Cumberland." Ralph excused himself to the Duke of York, and hurried over to join Annunciata at the door to receive the prince. Annunciata curtseyed deeply, Ralph bowed, the prince bowed in return, the welcome was spoken and replied to. And then the prince took Annunciata's hands, his grave face softened to a smile, and he stooped to exchange a kiss with her. It was perfectly permissable for women in society to kiss even guests with whom they were barely acquainted, but Ralph could not help a small twinge of jealousy, for it was well known that Annunciata had been romantically attached to the prince some years ago. Though he did not believe the rumors that she had been his mistress, it was true that she possessed a gold locket containing a lock of his hair. Annunciata cast Ralph a glance of mingled entreaty and apology as she led the prince away toward the group round the King, and Ralph, with a small inward sigh, allowed himself to become detached and instead devoted himself to the comfort of Lady Arlington, who had little conversation and was always something of an outsider at these gatherings.

"Please forgive me for being so late," the prince was saying to Annunciata. "I had to call in at the Navy Office, and there was so much business to be attended to that I had much trouble to get away.''

Annunciata stopped to smile at him. ''I knew it could only be important business that kept you away. Do you never rest? You will make yourself ill.''

The prince's expression was tender as he gazed down into her face. The love between them was deep and unspoken—had to be unspoken, for it existed on so many and such complex levels. ''You know that I do,'' he said. ''In fact, I have grown quite frivolous of late.'' Annunciata smiled at the idea of the grave and stately prince being thought frivolous. ''My man tells me he has heard it spoken in the streets that I have been seen to laugh in the theater.''

Annunciata laughed at that. Two years ago the prince had been at Tunbridge Wells with the Court, and had witnessed an entertainment given before the Queen by some actors from the Duke of York's theater. Among the players had been a young actress by the name of Madam Hughes, Margaret Hughes, and Prince Rupert—the grave, stately, dignified Rupert—had fallen quite madly in love with her.

Annunciata had watched anxiously as in his old-fashioned and courtly way he pursued the young woman, who allowed his attentions. He did nothing in haste, and he had taken a year to come to the point, but last summer he had finally made terms with Mrs. Peg, and had installed her in fine style in a house in Hammersmith. Since then he had seemed to be so rapturously happy that Annunciata had with relief concluded that the actress was keeping her part of the bargain. Now she wished to show the prince that she approved of his arrangements, and was anxious to pay appropriate attention to the woman he so evidently loved.

''I am glad to hear it,'' she said. ''And I hear that Hammersmith is lovely at this time of year, when the leaves begin to turn. You must invite me to your house there, so that I may judge for myself.''

He pressed her hand. ''You would come? It would make me so happy, but I hesitated to ask you.''

Annunciata thought how like him that was. In the Court of

Charles II, only Prince Rupert would hesitate to invite a lady to meet his mistress.

"I should be happy to come," she said. "When shall it be? Tomorrow?" She wanted to be sure he knew she meant it.

"I cannot tomorrow—but the day after? Would you come early, and spend the day? And would you—would you think of bringing the children? I should love to have the chance of spending some time with them."

"The day after tomorrow. We shall all come," Annunciata said low and quickly as the King turned round and it was necessary to end their private conversation.

"Ah, there you are," the King said heartily to his cousin. "Come straight from the Navy Office, I warrant, and went there straight from the christening this morning. I'll wager you have neither eaten nor drunk since dawn today!"

"Well, sir . . ." Rupert began apologetically.

Dinner was laid out in the daringly informal French "buffet" style which had become the fashion for the private supper parties that the King so loved. It was typical of Annunciata that she thus made a virtue of necessity, for Ballincrea House had no room large enough to seat all her guests at one table for a formal dinner. As she led the party toward the tables, she heard the interested murmur of comment and, listening carefully, judged that it held no note of disapproval or ridicule, and was able at last to relax. The food she had provided was almost spectacularly lavish, in order to make it evident to everyone that there was nothing makeshift about the arrangement, and while she was still smiling and talking her way forward with the King, her eyes under her drooped eyelids flickered sternly back and forth across the tables and the row of waiting, liveried servants to see that there was no crumb nor hair out of place.

At home in Yorkshire Annunciata liked to supervise every aspect of the running of the household, partly because she could not endure anything to be done less than perfectly, and partly because it helped to pass the long country days. But in town she was kept so busy visiting and being visited, attending plays and parties, walking and riding in the parks, arranging entertainments and ordering and buying new clothes, that she allowed the everyday running of the household to pass out of her hands. When she had married Ralph, her cousin Elizabeth Hobart had been installed at Morland Place as governess to his remaining children, Martin and Daisy. Poor female relations were a boon and a blessing to any large household, for they made very useful unpaid upper servants, and were generally permanent attachments, having little chance to wed and thus leave the establishment. Annunciata saw all the usefulness of cousin Elizabeth, a modest, intelligent, amenable young woman with all the innate taste of a gentlewoman, and also saw that she was wasted in the role of governess, especially when there was a chaplain-tutor attached to the house, and so she set about reorganizing matters.

She found a sturdy, decent young woman named Dorcas, the widow of a weaver who had lived locally, to take the place of nurse-governess, and trained Elizabeth under her own stern eye to the role of housekeeper, to fulfill all those supervisory functions of Annunciata's when she either did not wish or could not find time to perform them. Both Elizabeth and Dorcas were under the unofficial but very effective supervision of Annunciata's personal maid, a sharp-tongued, sharp-eyed Londoner named Jane Birch, who had an air of having witnessed all the folly of the world at some time or another, and not thinking much of it.

So it was that, armed with Annunciata's instructions and Annunciata's recipe books, braced up by Birch's steely glances and the foreknowledge of the tongue-lashing she would receive from Annunciata should anything go wrong, Elizabeth had chivvied the servants and the cooks into a ferment of activity which had culminated in this spread board and the rank of impassive, perfect servants. There was poached salmon with fennel sauce, pike with caper sauce, a whole Morland Place ham smoked to Annunciata's secret recipe; there was spiced tongue, a glazed saddle of mutton decorated with candied oranges, whole lobsters with piquant sauce, a hare pie containing tiny onions, boiled eggs, and asparagus; there were venison pastries and pastry castles filled with crab meat in a cream sauce with cloves and cinnamon; there was a peacock with its tail still on and displayed with a frame of thin wire, and a turkey dressed the same way. There were oysters in sherry with nutmeg, roasted woodcocks, quails in aspic jelly, partridges stuffed with chestnuts, kid boiled in milk, and a dish of delicately stewed eels, of which the King was said to be particularly fond. There were candied fruits and fresh fruits, brandied wild strawberries, blackcurrant junkets, sweet jellies, and the puddings for which Annunciata kept the recipes secret from everyone but her chief cook. And as a final triumph there were ices and sherbets, for which she had had to obtain the King's cooperation, for his icehouse in St. James's was the only one near by. To drink there was Rhenish and sack and the French champagne which was becoming the rage in London society.

Every dish was laid out and decorated to perfection; the cloth was dazzlingly white, every piece of plate was burnished, every piece of crystal glittering like diamond; the flowers and wafers and comfits were laid out as they should be; the servants were as clean and neat and properly attired as if they were painted figures and not imperfect human beings. Annunciata was satisfied. Her eye caught that of Birch, hovering inconspicuously in the background, and she gave the slightest of nods. Birch in her turn passed a look and faint nod to Elizabeth, hovering even farther back from the guests, and Elizabeth relaxed with such sudden relief that her knees almost gave way and she had to put her hands against the wall behind her to support her.

Annunciata also relaxed, as she watched her guests go forward to the table to be served and then move away with full plates and glasses, eating, drinking, and chattering approvingly. It had worked, it was all right, the occasion was a success. This was what she had planned and hoped for when she had made her wild dash for London—to have her baby at Whitehall, to celebrate its arrival with a glittering party. One half of her despised the fashionable mob with its empty-headed gossip and slavish aping of style, and laughed at herself for wishing to compete; but the other half was a restless, hungry thing, an outsider. She was, though an heiress of fortune, and though three times wed to highly respectable men, still born a bastard, a fatherless child of an eccentric mother, and there was some part of her, deeply hidden and angrily denied, for which it was not just an amusement to take on the fashionable world and beat it at its own game, to outfashion

fashion, but a deadly necessity. She was ambitious for her children. This new baby, if he survived, would have every advantage, would be well connected from the very beginning. He should have a title, too—she must begin to work on that problem as soon as she could, for she knew there was great competition to squeeze titles out of the King, and it might take years. . . .

She realized abruptly that she was frowning with fierce determination, and that the King was looking at her with faint, quizzical amusement. She cleared her brow and laughed apologetically, and asked his opinion of the wine. As she listened to his reply she saw out of the corner of her eye that Ralph was looking at her, trying to catch her attention. Dear Ralph! He looked so handsome in his new clothes of peacock-blue velvet and silver-gray silk which she had chosen for him—but she hadn't time for him at the moment, with His Majesty to amuse and the rest of the entertainment to come. She was glad he had come to town with her, but she hoped he would not get too bored, would find something to do to keep him occupied while she was engaged.

When the eating and drinking was almost over, Birch and Dorcas went upstairs to fetch the children, and brought them down to the long saloon to be ready when the company came back in from the dining room. The baby had quieted down at last, and though he was not asleep, he lay silent in Birch's arms in his heavy, elaborate christening clothes, his face as red as a boiled lobster from his recent crying. The rich, lace-trimmed gown had been a present from His Majesty to Annunciata for her first baby, and the silk shawl had been sent from France by Princess Henrietta for her second confinement.

The fruits of those confinements were ushered into the saloon by Dorcas, who smoothed already smooth hair and straightened immaculate clothes and exhorted them to stand still and be a credit to her. Hugo and Arabella, the twins, were nine years old. Hugo, who had become Viscount Ballincrea on his father's death when he was but one year old, had been told many times that he was very like his father in looks and because he had spent so much of his short life being reprimanded for one thing or another he had come to think of that also as a reproof. He was short for his age and stockily built, with a naturally dark skin, tight curly dark hair, and blue eyes. "A veritable little Frenchman," Birch sometimes called him when he was being naughty. His father had been half Irish and half French, and his darkness was due to the French blood in him. Hugo gathered that this was not to his advantage, although he also knew that the King's darkness was due to *his* being half French, too, and in the King's case it was quite permissible.

In his stormy life Hugo had one staunch ally, his twin sister, Arabella. She was taller than he and stronger, and though she was also accounted no beauty by the servants, since she had freckles on her white skin, and a mane of stiff red hair which would not curl by any means, and an uncompromising, unsmiling face, she did not seem to feel their disapproval, nor to care when she was punished, which was often. Birch called her a "queer, bold-tempered girl," and though this was evidently meant as a rebuke, Hugo's quick ear detected an undertone of respect in Birch's voice when she said it. Arabella had been a favorite with Grandmama at Shawes, who had taught both Ara and Hugo to ride and had been a refuge to them until her sad death last year while out hunting. In some way Grandmama's approval had conferred a kind of invulnerability on Arabella as far as their mother was concerned. Arabella strode uncaringly through her troubles, and extended a half-affectionate, half-contemptuous protection to her brother.

The one thing Hugo desired was to be beloved of his mother, and it seemed to be permanently and inexplicably denied him. As he waited now in the long saloon he glanced up at the painting on the wall above his head. It was by Sir Peter Lely, and Hugo remembered sitting for it last year, though he did not know why it was called sitting when it had involved him and Arabella in long hours of standing still and being snapped at angrily when they fidgeted. The painting was called "the Turkish Portrait," for it showed their mother seated at the center in a brilliantly-colored Turkish silk robe and a turban of figured gold-cloth complete with feather. At her feet, gazing up adoringly, were her two brown-and-white spaniels, Charlemagne and Caspar; on either side of her stood Hugo and Arabella; and in the favored place on her lap sat their younger brother George, the cause, so it seemed to Hugo, of his problems.

George was a year younger than the twins—he was eight now—and Hugo stared up at the portrait to avoid having to look at the real live George standing beside him. George was a well-grown, beautiful child, a charming child, beloved of the servants, everyone's pet, their mother's favorite. His skin was clear and fair, his features delicately regular, his hair so pale it was almost silver, his eyes clear gray. He had a sweet smile and a sweeter voice and sang like an angel; and to add insult to injury he was, by *his* father's death, second Earl of Chelmsford and therefore, to the etiquette-conscious household, always took precedence over Hugo, who was only a viscount.

Hugo, who spent much of his time eavesdropping in self-defense, had heard many whisperings about George, most of which he did not understand; but he gathered that there was some mystery about his birth, and about his appearance, for their mother was, of course, as dark as a Stuart princess, and George's father had been a small and indistinguished man whose hair, when it had not been gray, had been dark brown. George did not resemble either of his parents, and there was much wonder among the servants as to why this should be. He did, to Hugo's observation, strongly resemble their stepfather, Ralph Morland, but Hugo could not make anything of this. He stored up the information, however, in case it should ever be of use while he continued hopelessly to strive for what he considered his rightful place in his mother's affections.

"After all," he would say often to Arabella, "George may be an earl, but I *am* firstborn. I should come first. She ought to love me best."

And Arabella, equally unloved, and not caring a bit, would say only, "You're silly. Let's go and play with the puppies."

And now, of course, there was a new rival, the baby, named Rupert after Prince Rupert who was mother's special friend and godfather to them all. But baby Rupert had no title, and to Hugo's eyes was exceedingly ugly, red, and bald, so Hugo had good hopes of keeping his place. Besides, there had been babies before, three times, and they had died, so perhaps baby Rupert would not be around for very long. Hugo's stepbrother, Martin, had lost five brothers to such effect that he was now Ralph's oldest son and eventual heir to Morland Place. Hugo liked Martin. He was thirteen, a small, slight, dark youth with very brown skin and very blue eyes, quiet and scholarly, but with a warm smile and a great fund of good humor. Everyone liked Martin, and Hugo admired him and sought his good opinion and, though he was not aware of it, already modified the worst of his bad behavior because of him. Martin noted this as he did everything—he was a watchful, observant boy—and was lazily amused. He was vaguely fond of Hugo, as he was of everyone around him, family and servants; he made no distinction. All his passion was reserved for his younger sister, Mary Marguerite, always known as Daisy. Since Daisy's birth Martin had been passionately, single-mindedly devoted to her. She was eleven now, fast approaching womanhood, lively and pretty, tall, big-boned, and blonde, and Martin was beginning to fear that he must lose her. He shut his mind to the prospect of her eventual marriage, hoping in some wordless way that it might at last be avoided, that she might stay with him for ever as she was, his pet, his protegée, his love. More and more, lately, she had escaped his grasp, both physically and spiritually, and it made him anxious. His tutor, Father St. Maur, and his father had recently dropped hints about his exclusive love for Daisy. Birch, in her more robust way, had told him that he must let Daisy be and begin looking at other girls, girls he would be eligible to marry. But their words had dropped from him unheeded. For him the world was perfectly divided: there was he-and-Daisy, and then there was everybody else.

At last the dining-room doors were opened, and the party came in, the King leading with Annunciata on his arm. The children, prompted by Birch and Dorcas, made their deepest bows and curtseys, and the King, who loved all children, came to them and spoke to each in turn, and then with a smile took the baby from Birch's arms and turned back to the rest of the company to say, "Here is the young scion who is responsible for our presence here today. May God bless him, and make him the joy and pride of his parents."

There was a murmur of agreement from the assembled company; the principal guests came forward to look at the baby and enthuse over his handsomeness, and one or two of them noticed the other children. Prince Rupert, like the King, spoke kindly to each of them: he was godfather to all Annunciata's children, and they had known and loved him since their infancy. Then the baby began to cry again, and Annunciata hastened to dismiss the whole nursery so that the entertainment could continue uninterrupted.

Late that night, when Annunciata and Ralph were alone together at last and preparing for bed, he asked her, "Were you pleased with the party?"

Annunciata, sitting before her mirror and combing her hair, smiled at her reflection in the glass and said, "The fireworks were good, I thought."

Ralph came up behind her and took the comb from her and continued to draw it slowly through the long, thick coils. She submitted under his hands, her mind evidently far away. She crossed her bare feet and folded her hands in her lap; undressed, and with her hair loose, she looked to him barely more than a child.

"Is that all you have to say," he asked with a smile, ". . . the fireworks were good?"

"What else should I say?" she asked, gently puzzled.

"Here you have entertained the highest in the land, the King of England and his brother and his cousin, and yet you are no more excited than if it had been a family party," Ralph said.

"They are like my family to me," she said simply, but she met his eyes in the glass, returning back at last from her reverie. "Did you enjoy it?"

"Yes," he said, "but I enjoy more being alone with you." And he bent his head to kiss her white neck just behind the ear. She shivered pleasantly.

"You looked very handsome in your new clothes," she said, as he slid his hands about her neck and, still holding her gaze in the mirror, ran them down over her collarbones towards the softly moving shape of her breasts.

"Handsome enough to be your lover?" he asked her.

"Handsome enough even for that," she said. He cupped his hands over her breasts, feeling their ready response, and rested his cheek next to hers. Her mouth smiled, and he reached to kiss the corner of it.

"Shall we go to bed?" he whispered. She continued to smile, and he said, "You look too young to be a wife and mother. You look no older than that wild girl who followed me on horseback one night to let Makthorpe's sheep out of the pen." She turned her head toward him so that her lips were on his, and he kissed her lingeringly. When she was alone with him, like this, she was entirely his, and the world could not take her from him. He released her and said, "Come to bed," and she stood up, slender in her white bedgown, and he took her in his arms and held her small girl's body against his big, strong man's one. She smiled up at him, her hands going up to his chest. "Do you want me?" he asked.

"I want you," she said, but then she added, "but I don't want another baby yet. We must be careful."

A shadow came over him. It was reasonable for her to say so, when she had so recently given birth, but it made him feel she was holding him away. He searched her face anxiously.

"Do you love me?" he asked.

"Of course I do," she said. But already she sounded faintly irritated to be saying it.

CHAPTER TWO

Despite their late night, the Morlands were up early the next morning, of what might have been deemed shockingly rustic habit, had not the King made early rising respectable, if not popular. At six the whole family and all the servants were gathered to hear Father St. Maur say first Mass, and at seven the business of the day began as a little bread and ale was brought for the master and mistress for their refreshment while they interviewed the servants and gave them their orders. Dorcas and Birch brought in the children to receive their father's blessing, and as each in turn knelt before Ralph, they received the sharp critical appraisal of their mother's eye.

"Birch, what is that dress that Daisy is wearing? It surely cannot be the one she had new on St. Anne's Day?"

"It is, my lady," Birch said impassively.

"I vow and swear, that child has grown again," Annunciata said, half amused, half exasperated. "It is full two inches too short. Child, you look like a scarecrow. You must leave off this growing, or you will be two yards tall before you are fifteen."

"She can't help it, madam," Martin broke in anxiously, before Daisy had a chance to reply. "She takes after our father."

"Well, she must stop it all the same," Annunciata said, smiling at Martin to show him she was only joking, "or her future husband will have to stand on a mounting block to propose to her. Dorcas, you had better find something of mine to make over for Miss Daisy. Birch will show you something I don't wear much."

Then the other children came forward. George was embraced, and exhorted not to study too hard, because he looked pale. ''If you have the headache you must be sure to tell Father St. Maur at once, and not go on reading.'' Hugo was told to stand up straight and not slouch in that disagreeable way. Arabella was chided for having untidied her impossible hair already. ''If you would move in a more ladylike way, and not rush about like a hoyden, you would stay neat.'' And as Arabella rose and stepped back with the others, Annunciata asked how the baby was. ''I thought I heard him crying again.''

''You did, madam,'' Dorcas said anxiously. ''I'm sorry to say the poor little man has the colic again. He's not at all well, madam.''

''It is nothing but wind, my lady,'' Birch asserted, cutting in on the Yorkshire woman. ''He will be better by and by.''

''Good,'' Annunciata said dismissively.

Then Dorcas stepped impulsively forward and said, ''Madam, pardon me, but that child is ailing. He cannot eat the gruel—he cannot keep it to his stomach, madam, and that's the truth.''

Birch glared at her, and she faltered to a stop. Birch was a Londoner and as anxious as Annunciata that the children should be brought up in the correct ways of fashionable society. One of those ways dictated that the babies of rich folk were fed on thin gruel, for breast milk was held to be bad for them. Only paupers' children were fed at the breast, and Birch was furious that Dorcas, a simple countrywoman, should suggest it.

''Nonsense,'' Birch said. ''The baby had a trifle of wind. He has stopped crying already.''

Annunciata looked from one to the other, and then nodded. ''I'm sure you are right. Take the children away, Dorcas. I will try to come up and see the baby by and by.'' Dorcas bit her lip, curtseyed, and hustled the children away, the boys to do their lessons with Father St. Maur, the girls to do their sewing under her eye. But as they reached the door, it was opened from the other side, and Annunciata's footman Tom announced and ushered in the day's first caller, Ralph's half-brother, Clovis Morland.

He was a slender and handsome young man with his mother's delicate features, which lit into a welcoming smile that embraced

the whole room, for this was now his family. He had lost his
parents in the Great Plague, and Annunciata had taken him and
his brother Edmund into her household and cared for them and
advanced their careers. They had both been choristers of the
Chapel Royal, and two years ago Edmund had come under the
influence of the Duchess of York and had embraced the Roman
church.

Through the duchess's good offices he was now at St. Omer
studying with the Jesuits. Clovis had been provided with a minor,
but useful, position at Court, and now, at nineteen, he combined
those duties with the task of being the family's factor, as had his
father before him. His delicate appearance was wholly deceptive:
he was enormously energetic.

"Have I called too early?" he said as he bowed over
Annunciata's hand and then clasped Ralph's. "I know I keep
shockingly unfashionable hours, but in the city. . ."

"I know," Annunciata said with a laugh. "You city princes
see the sun rise and set at your labors. Come and take some
refreshment with us. But bid the children farewell first, for Birch
is anxious to get them away."

Clovis greeted them all affectionately, asked after Martin's
cough, kissed the two girls—Daisy wriggled with pleasure, but
Arabella endured it like a horse being groomed—and warmed
Hugo's heart by shaking hands with him before George, but as
they were led away he said, "I had better not stop to eat with
you, for there is a great deal to be done today, if I am to finish it
before dinner."

"Ah, yes, you dine with the duke today," Ralph said. "As do
we."

"And that means we shall get nothng more done, so. . ."

"You are right. I shall come at once. Did you ride here from
the city?"

"No, I took the last of the tide, and there is a pair of oars
waiting for us at Whitehall steps. We can be at St. Katherine
Dock within the half hour," Clovis said, all eagerness as Ralph
stopped to kiss his wife.

"You see how this brother of mine even has the tides working
for him?" he said. Annunciata received the kiss on her cheek and

observed, "By my reckoning, then, the tide will turn again at noon, and will bring you back here in time to change for dinner. How well you have arranged it all, Clovis. Take him away, then—and don't be late."

"What shall you do this morning?" Ralph asked her, lingering. She looked so lovely in her silk and lace *déshabillé* with her dark hair carelessly knotted at her neck.

"I shall call on the duchess, if she is receiving. Go on, now, I have much to do."

Before the door had even closed on the two men Annunciata was up and doing, dispatching her man Tom to St. James's Palace with a note for the Duchess of York, calling Birch to come and dress her and Elizabeth to receive the housekeeping orders for the day, writing a letter to be sent off to Clem, the steward at Morland Place, regarding the rebuilding of the dovecote. Before Tom had returned the tradesmen had begun to arrive downstairs with their fancy goods that they hoped the countess might be persuaded to buy. They knew that she kept early hours, and so made use of the early morning to call on her when the rest of the fashionable world was still abed and asleep. Annunciata had remarked once or twice to the King that her country habits were useful to her, since they ensured her first choice of the new cloths and the least distorted version of the new gossip.

Tom returned with a very cordial note from the duchess, inviting her to breakfast at St. James's, and so at a quarter before nine o'clock Gideon brought the coach to the door, and the countess descended with her footman, her serving woman, and her two spaniels—all the accoutrements of fashion—to be driven slowly to the little palace. It was but a step across the park, and one part of Annunciata wished to be walking with a long free stride across that dew-damp grass; but the rest of her enjoyed the trapping of consequence, and she had Tom put up the window-shades so that the people could see her better, and know who it was that was so intimate with the Yorks as to call at the palace at the hour of breakfast.

Anne Hyde, Duchess of York, had never been a beauty, but her wit had never been denied. In the days when she had capti-

vated the young Duke of York she had been allowed to be well
enough, with a stately figure and fine eyes. Annunciata had first
met her ten years ago, just before the secret of her marriage to
Prince James and her pregnancy had broken upon the world.
Annunciata, newly at Court, had been appointed to the duchess's
household, and since then through her rising fortunes had maintained a respectful friendship with her former mistress. Now
pregnancies and overindulgence at the table had made the duchess
very fat, and continual disappointment and ill-health had removed any prettiness she had had and made her look older than
her years. With her wide mouth, heavy jaw, and watery eyes she
looked far more than six years Annunciata's senior.

She received Annunciata *en déshabillé* in her private chamber,
and when the countess had curtseyed to her she extended her
cheek to be kissed, inviting her to sit in a chair placed close by
the chaise longue on which she was reclining. With a fat, beringed
hand she waved the servants off, and said in her pleasant,
well-modulated voice, "There, now we may be comfortable. It
was kind of you to call, Lady Chelmsford."

"How does Your Grace?" Annunciata asked as she seated
herself, pleased with the attention. "I was so sorry that you were
unable to come to the christening yesterday."

"I was sorry for your sake that I could not," the duchess said,
"but for my own sake—I find these parties very tedious, you
know. I had far rather a good conversation and a private supper.
But good conversation is hard to come by, at our frivolous Court.
I do not envy you your parties and balls, you know. I wonder
you can bear it—you, after all, have a brain."

Annunciata smiled. "So have you, Your Grace, but it is not
fashionable to admit it. Eccentricity is only permissible among
the truly powerful."

Anne Hyde grimaced with pain and eased her position on the
chaise as she said, "You jest with me. Since you first came to
Court you have paraded your eccentricities with impunity. I well
remember your early-morning walks with the King and my husband and Prince Rupert. And did you not make horseback-riding
fashionable? Even now, it is said you discourse with His Majesty
as freely as a man."

Annunciata saw that she was only pretending shock, and said, grave-faced, "I hope Your Grace will give no credence to the latest scurrilous report concerning me. Lady Castlemaine has put it about that she called upon me last week and came upon me *reading a book.*"

She had made the duchess laugh at last, and was glad of it, for she felt that Anne Hyde had few pleasures in her life now. The duchess called for refreshments to be placed on a low table before them, and then ordered the servants away. "I should like to talk freely to you. I am sure you will trouble yourself to hand my plate and cup, will you not?"

"Of course," Annunciata said. The breakfast was simple, but elegant: a pint of chocolate in a long-spouted, silver pot, a pressed tongue, a plate of white bread cut very thin and buttered, a silver bowl full of polished apples, and a crumbly white cheese. Annunciata filled a plate and cup for the duchess, served herself similarly, and settled back in her chair with Caspar and Charlemagne sitting at her feet, their eyes fixed unwaveringly on the tongue.

"Now we may talk," Anne Hyde said. "Tell me your news—how does your family?"

Annunciata talked while the duchess ate, telling her everything that had happened since May, and coming eventually to the birth of the new baby.

"You called him Rupert, I believe?"

"Yes—the prince has consented to stand sponsor to the baby."

"Most gracious of him," the duchess said, her eyes gleaming with amusement. Annunciata had the feeling that Anne Hyde knew everything that had happened between her and Prince Rupert, including the secret of their relationship; but if she did, she would never speak of it, knowing the value of discretion. "But tell me, what made you come to London so suddenly, and so late in your pregnancy, and in such terrible weather? You might have died, you know."

Annunciata told her, painting a clear picture of Morland Place in August in the rain. "There was not even any society in York, all the best people having being away on their estates. It was a clear choice between the risk of death on the roads and the risk of death from boredom at home.''

"Boredom—ah, yes! I can enter into your feelings," the duchess said, her eyes distant. "Lying here, confined to bed or couch by my various ailments and pains—strange, is it not, how our faith teaches us how to endure pain and suffering, but never mentions boredom." Annunciata was not sure how to answer, but was saved from doing so by the opening of the chamber door. A frown of anger crossed the duchess's face at the interruption, but cleared as she recollected. "It is only the children—their morning visit. You will forgive me?"

"Of course."

The two princesses were brought in by their governess to greet their mother with a curtsey. Mary, the oldest girl, was eight years old, already tall for her age, a pretty girl with the Stuart looks, dark eyes, and black curling hair, a sweet-tempered, chattering, sentimental child who was a general favorite with her father and her attendants. Five year old Anne was a different proposition: short, solid, stout, and silent, she was overshadowed by her sister and by any other children she ever met. She was desperately shy and felt her inadequacies with an unexpected keenness. She had a chubby, solemn face, reddish hair, and no beauties, except for an exceptionally sweet voice. The prince had had his daughters taught elocution by an actress, and both could speak and sing charmingly.

Annunciata thought them deplorably ignorant, for apart from the feminine graces of needlework, music, and dancing, they had been taught nothing. It was not fashionable, particularly among Protestants, to educate women. During Cromwell's time the Puritans had laid it down that to educate a woman was merely to make her unfit for the position God had ordained for her—that of performing domestic labors and bearing children. The princesses, despite their parents' conversion to the Old Faith, were being brought up as good Protestants, in deference to the public prejudice.

But Annunciata came from Yorkshire, the cradle of education, from a family which had a tradition of female scholars; and from a family with a long tradition of Catholicism. She had received as good an education as any man, and she wondered that Anne

Hyde could endure her daughters to be so ignorant. She thought she detected a lack of enthusiasm in the duchess for her daughters, and wondered whether she had had any choice about their upbringing. Had her sons survived, perhaps it would have been different, Annunciata thought, and as the princesses were led away she reflected on Anne Hyde's sad history of lost children. The son whose conception had led to the secret marriage with the Duke of York had lived only six months; the birth of Mary had been followed by that of James, Duke of Cambridge, who had died when he was four years old. Then came Anne, and then in sixty-six a son who had lived a few weeks, and in sixty-seven another son who had lived only a few hours. In sixty-eight there had been a daughter who died before she was a year old, and last year the duchess had borne another daughter, who died within days. Eight pregnancies in ten years, with so little to show for it; and though she had perhaps eight more childbearing years ahead of her, it was well known that it became harder to produce healthy children as one grew older. A shiver of foreboding came over Annunciata and she made a silent prayer to the Blessed Virgin and St. Anne to protect her own children.

Anne Hyde watched the children's departure, and when the door had closed behind them she said quietly, "I do not envy them their fate. King Charles will find them each a German prince to marry, and they will be led meekly off like oxen to their fate. At least I chose my own future, for good or ill."

She was silent a moment, and her eyes grew distant and misty. "James was different in those days, you know. He was very beautiful—he is beautiful still, but it is a cold beauty now. Then, he was young, and witty, and charming. At the Hague he would dance all night—he danced so beautifully. People preferred him to his brother, you know," she added, glancing at Annunciata. "You may not think it, but in those days Charles was accounted dour and gloomy. His wit was too sharp. He had seen too much, suffered too much. James laughed a lot, and he had such perfect manners. Everyone thought him charming."

Annunciata nodded, not wishing to break the duchess's mood by speaking. After a while the duchess said, "I fell in love with him the moment I saw him. I never thought—I was nobody, merely

Master Hyde's daughter, but I was clever, in a Court of clever women. And he fell in love with me. They say now that I tricked him. Well, I was never beautiful, and now they look at me and wonder how he could ever have wanted me. But he did—he did. And so we married.'' She was speaking so quietly that Annunciata thought she was speaking to herself, hardly aware of the other's presence.

"He was never faithful to me, of course, not even in the early days before our first son died. But he listened to me. He loved me, and he came to me for advice. It was like that with the Faith—we talked, he asked me questions, he thought about it— and then he took it, too.'' Her eyes filled suddenly with tears, and she turned to Annunciata and cried, "Oh, but is all *wrong*! For me, it came like a flame to my heart, and great sudden light! But not for him. He thought and pondered and questioned, and then, with all the force of his dry passionless brain, he accepted it—accepted it absolutely and without question. But he has no joy of it, that I know.''

She became aware of her tears, and wiped them from her eyes almost with an impatient gesture, as if they distracted her. "He accepts with his mind, but he does not know with his heart. For him there is no joy, no passion. He does not hear the music, see the colors, perceive the glory. He is not pierced with ecstasy. There is no sacred mystery, no dread, no terror, no exultation. Oh, he is cold, cold!''

She wept a little more, and Annunciata watched her in silence, with compassion, and remembered her own light words of the day before, "They do say the convert is always the most vehement.'' Yet though she never needed to speak of it, she knew what Anne Hyde meant: the Faith was more than an intellectual belief; it filled you so that you were like a vessel brimming with water, and the celebration poured yet more into you so that it brimmed over into song, joy, exultation. But not for the duke. She tried to imagine him young and charming, laughing and dancing, and failed entirely.

The duchess wiped her tears again and said, "Not that I have any doubts about his sincerity, you mustn't think that. In fact, if anything, it's the reverse. The King and I cannot even persuade him to be seen in the Chapel Royal, just for form's sake. He thinks it dishonorable to dissemble. He will not compromise. God knows what will happen if he outlives Charles and comes to the throne. He will go too fast for his people.''

Annunciata nodded, reflecting on the one facet of Roman Catholicism that made it intolerable to the English people: that it was every Papist's solemn duty to lead his fellow men back to Rome. And the English people would never submit to being ruled by a foreign prince, especially a prince of the church.

"You think, then, that the Queen will not . . ." she began hesitantly.

Anne Hyde's mouth hardened. "In eight years she has never even carried to term. No, most assuredly the Queen will not. And the King will not even consider divorce."

"Perhaps, if she should—she is frequently unwell. . ."

"She has fainting fits and vapors and more temper than you would credit her for, but she's as strong as a horse, that one. She will outlive us all, make no mistake. And so *I* must get a son. Not that the getting is hard—it's the keeping of them, as you very well know."

Annunciata nodded. Three dead sons, and now the new baby was ailing, so Dorcas said. A pang turned her heart. So few babies survived. Perhaps she had been wrong to do what she did, to come to London and risk his life and his health. Perhaps she should send him back to the country.

"We are all in His hand," Anne Hyde said softly, and Annunciata looked up to realize that the duchess had been watching her thoughts flickering across her face.

"Yes, Your Grace," she said. How often had she comforted Ralph with those words. If God wanted her child, He would take him, and if He wanted him to live, He would send the means.

The duchess evidently thought it time to change the subject. She eased herself again on her pillows and said, "Might I trouble you to pour me some more chocolate? And tell me what news you have on Edmund. Have you heard from St. Omer lately?"

The baby continued to ail, and on the morning after Annunciata's day at Hammersmith, Dorcas sought an interview with her. She waited until the children had paid their morning visit to their parents and had gone to their lessons, and bribed Tom to let her know when Birch was safely out of the way, for she could never speak with Birch present. Finally Tom poked his head round the door and jerked it significantly, and Dorcas, her palms moist with anxiety, bade her charges be still and silent until her return and went out after him.

"You needs be quick," Tom said as they pattered down the stairs. "She's only gone to look for the mistress's muff, so you'll have but a few minutes. They're going to the 'change, but she'll not find the muff where she left it."

"How do you know?" asked the distracted Dorcas.

Tom grinned. " 'Cause I hid it. I listened outside the door, and when I heard the mistress say she wanted it, I ran on and stuck it under the bed."

"God bless you, Tom," Dorcas said fervently.

"Go on with you," Tom said, embarrassed. "It's a bonny bairn, and don't deserve to die."

Annunciata was in a cheerful mood, for she had thoroughly enjoyed her visit to Hammersmith. She had found Mistress Hughes a lively, intelligent girl, sharp witted and evidently enjoying her power over the great Prince Rupert, but an affectionate and good-hearted person for all that. The prince evidently adored her, and Annunciata had stifled a wistful pang when she thought how once he had idolized her in the same manner. But it was wonderful to see his happiness, and to share in it, and to observe his tender delight in her children. The poignancy of the situation had brought her close to tears once or twice, just as the nervousness of their escape gave her a frisson of horror from time to time. He might so easily have become the father of her children! When he touched her hand or caught her eye, the expression on each of their faces mingled relief with regret.

She swung around as the door opened, expecting Birch. "I was thinking we might look for some scarlet ribbon for—oh, Dorcas! What do you want? I am just going out."

"Madam, might I speak with you privately a moment? Madam, it's about the baby," Dorcas said nervously, twisting her hands together.

"What is it? He is not—" Annunciata was startled.

"Oh, madam, please, I beg you to let me get a wet nurse for the child," Dorcas blurted out. Annunciata's eyes narrowed and Dorcas went on before she could speak. "I know what Birch says, but he is so sick, and I am afraid he will die."

"You must not let him die," Annunciata said coldly.

"But, madam, he can't eat that gruel, it makes him so sick, the poor precious. Let me get a wet nurse for him, and he'll—"

"My child, suck like a pauper's child from some pauper nurse? And how will that serve him?"

"If it saves his life—"

"If! And what if it kills him? If he cannot keep down good gruel, how should he thrive on a commoner's milk?" She saw how distressed Dorcas was, and softened her voice. "Come, now, come, I know that you are worried. But he was better this morning, was he not? He hardly cried at all."

Dorcas stared at her hopelessly.

"Madam, he is too weak to cry," she said. Annunciata frowned, and thought, and at that moment Birch came back into the room. Her expression, when she saw Dorcas, said that she knew who had hidden the muff and why, and promised punishment later. Annunciata said, "Go back to your duties, nurse. I shall come up and see you later, when I am at liberty. And I shall instruct Father St. Maur to say a special prayer for the child."

Dorcas could only bow her head and obey. She went back to her duties, but before returning to the girls, she went into the room where baby Rupert lay in his crib and stared down at him with helpless pity. The baby, who had been lusty enough at his birth, had shrunk away to a little skeleton, with eyes sunk back into shadowed sockets. As she looked, he opened his eyes, and gave a faint, mewling cry. "Pauper's milk?" she said aloud. "Why, but you look enough like a pauper's child right this minute." The nursery maid who was keeping watch over the baby looked up, startled, but Dorcas only sighed and went away.

Though it was early in the season, the 'change was crowded, both with those who came to see, and those whom came to be seen, and Annunciata was glad of the size and bulk of Tom to make a passage for her and Birch and carry the dogs. At her favorite stall for ribbons, where she stopped to buy scarlet ones for the carriage horses' manes, she met with one of the King's more permanent mistresses on the same errand. This was a former actress, Madam Gwyn, who had taken the King's fancy much in the way that Peg Hughes had Prince Rupert's, and was said to be the maddest, wildest creature to Court. She was very popular with the common people for her solid commonsense and lack of hauteur, and Annunciata liked her because of her generosity and good-hearted kindness. Madam Gwyn greeted her cheerfully.

"Well, how d'ye do, mistress? I heard you were the lighter of a son. I hope all goes well?"

"Thank you, madam," Annunciata said. "I am very well, but the child, I'm afraid, is sickly."

"Oh, dear, I'm sorry to hear that. I have an excellent recipe for a soothing-syrup. Won't you let me send it to you? I hear you spent the day at Hammersmith yesterday with your—with his Highness?" Nelly said irrepressibly, her round eyes widening innocently. "Why, what a thing it is to be an actress, to be sure! I wonder all women don't try the trade—it seems to be the surest step to advancement. Except, of course, being related to the King." Annunciata repressed her smile, feeling Birch bristling at her shoulder, and Nelly went on, "Why, even the Duke of York has hired an actress as his daughter's governess. Tell me, mistress, what trade will you put your daughters to?"

Birch drew in a scandalized breath, but at that moment a tall and rather beautiful young man came up behind Madam Gwyn and slid an arm round her waist, making her jump like a startled hare.

"How, now, Nelly! Who are you insulting this time? God's day to you, Lady Chelmsford. I vow and swear, you are looking, if possible, twice as beautiful as before your confinement."

"How, now, Jack," Nelly said, firmly removing the arm from her waist and pushing the young man to arm's length. "Are you drunk again? And at this time o' morning?"

It was John Wilmot, the Earl of Rochester, a Court wit and

poet renowned for his wicked way of life and his scurrilous
lampoons of Court dignitaries. He and Nelly respected and even
quite liked each other, for much the same reasons. Annunciata
returned his greeting with suitable coolness, but did not withdraw.
She liked witty conversation, even when it was ribald.

"I'm always drunk, Nelly, you know that. I haven't been
sober in five years. But it doesn't make any difference to me."

"If you'd stayed sober for long enough, you might have got to
be poet laureate instead of Master Dryasdust." That was Madam
Gwyn's name for Court poet John Dryden.

"And if you'd stayed virtuous for long enough," he countered,
"you might have got to be Queen. The one's as likely as the
other."

"Ah, well," Nelly said cheerfully. "if I'm a whore, at least
I'm a Protestant whore, not like that weeping, spying Madam
Kerwell."

"Mademoiselle de Kéroualle," Rochester corrected firmly,
"is not a spy. She was left behind for His Majesty as a penance."

Nelly shrieked with laughter. "In that case," she said, "Charlie
will have to watch out that Dismal Jimmy doesn't steal her away.
He likes his women ugly and miserable—and she won't even
have to convert him!"

Birch was positively radiating disapproval at this reference to
the Duke of York and his strange predilection for ill-favored
mistresses, and Annunciata felt she ought to remove herself. She
smiled at them both and said, "I had better complete my purchases,
if you would excuse me."

"There, have we driven you away?" Nelly cried. "Now,
Jack, you must learn to curb your tongue—but let me send
you that recipe I mentioned, mistress, for your pretty boy's
sake."

"With great pleasure," Annunciata said.

Rochester bowed and said, "No more than *au revoir*, Lady
Chelmsford. I shall see you at the play this afternoon, of course."

"Why, how did you know I was going to the play?" Annunciata
asked, intrigued. Rochester fixed his melting eyes on hers with
great significance. "I know everything, madam. There are no

secrets from me, though there are many that I keep, especially when they concern persons of royal blood.''

Annunciata's gaze remained steady. ''It is not wise to believe all you hear, my lord Earl.''

''It is a wise child that knows its father, my dear Countess,'' Rochester countered solemnly, and as Annunciata began to laugh, he made another bow, and bade her farewell.

They had not been at home an hour when Tom came up to say that the messenger had come from Madam Gwyn with the recipe for the soothing-syrup.

''But she says she must speak with you, my lady,'' Tom said. ''She says it's most urgent.''

''Nonsense,'' Birch said dismissively. Annunciata glanced up at her from a letter she was writing. At times Birch took too much upon herself, and needed bringing down a notch or two.

''Did she say what it's about, Tom?''

''No, my lady. Only that it's urgent.'' He hesitated. ''She looks a rum one, my lady, not like a lady's servant.''

''Do you think she's a thief?''

''No, my lady,'' Tom said hesitantly. ''But there's something rum about her, no mistake.''

''Send her away, and tell her we'll call the constable and have her beaten if she comes here again,'' Birch said.

''Send her up, Tom,'' Annunciata said imperturbably.

Birch folded her lips tight in fury, but said nothing until the woman was ushered in, and then she cried out, ''Why I saw this hussy following us at the 'change this morning! Be off, you wicked creature! For shame to come here like this, you wicked liar!''

''Peace, Birch,'' Annunciata said, even as the young woman flung herself across the room to kneel at Annunciata's feet and cry, ''Mistress Morland, don't send me away, please! Let me speak to you! Only speak to you!''

''Shame girl, it isn't likely!'' Birch snapped.

''Now, Birch, even a criminal is allowed to speak. What is it, girl? Say on.'' And then as the girl flung an anguished glance toward Jane Birch, she added, "Birch, wait outside with Tom. Oh, go on with you, *this* one won't hurt me. By the look of her she hasn't eaten in a week. I could snap her in two with one hand."

The two servants withdrew and closed the door, and Annunciata looked down with interest at the young woman. She judged her to be a year or two younger than herself, and, under the dirt and emaciation of poverty, extremely pretty. The girl had very fine skin, dark red curls, and blue eyes, and, what intrigued Annunciata more, a Yorkshire accent.

"Now, then, you may speak. From your voice I guess you come from my home place. What is your name, girl?"

"Chloris, mistress."

"And how do you come to know me?"

The girl looked embarrassed. "I heard them say your name this morning at the 'change. And about the recipe from Madam Gwyn. I wanted to speak to you, so I followed Madam Gwyn home, and when her servant came out with the note for you, I— well, mistress, I stole it. I ran like a hare, and got here first, though she'll be coming after me, I doubt not."

"Drastic measures," Annunciata said. "You must have some good reason. You *do* come from Yorkshire, don't you? Have you run away?"

"In a matter of speaking, mistress. My father—he works for your master, Master Morland. He's a carpenter. John Moleclough is his name."

"Yes, I know Moleclough. And you—I have seen you before, I think?"

"Happen you did, mistress, for I know you well enough. I used to work at the Hare and Heather."

"Then why did you run away?" The girl looked embarrassed again. "Or were you sent away?"

"Oh, mistress, it wasn't stealing or anything of that sort. I was a good girl—until—"

"Ah, I think I understand. You got with child, and the fellow disappeared, and your father sent you away, is that it?"

"He was a gentleman, mistress, but he said he loved me, said he'd marry me. I came to London to try and find him—but it seemed all I could do here was—well, I'm not like that, mistress, truly I'm not.''

"So you came to me for help? And why should you think I would help you?'' Annunciata said. The girl gazed up into her face, and her large blue eyes seemed to grow larger, to shine hypnotically.

"Because I can help you, mistress. I have the Sight.''

Annunciata stirred uneasily, and though she tried to hide the shiver the words induced, her hand twitched to be crossing herself.

"Have you indeed,'' she said lightly. "And what do you see?''

"That you have a baby, mistress. A little boy-baby. He's sick—awful sick. You are afraid he will die. But he won't die, mistress—I'll save him.''

"How do you propose to do that?''

The girl reached down and pulled apart the front of her gown, showing her swollen breasts under her linen kirtle. "I had my baby, mistress. A boy—he died. A life for a life. I'll feed your bairn at my breast, and save his life, if you will take me in.''

Annunciata jumped to her feet and paced about the room, thoroughly disturbed. Finally she came back to the girl and said, "Get up, Chloris, and listen to me. You know I have a baby, and that he is sick. Well, anyone may know that, without the Sight, for it is common knowledge. I think you have lied from first to last. I think''—this was a guess, but she saw by the girl's expression that she had hit the mark—"that your baby has not died, but that you are concealing him somewhere. Nevertheless, God moves in mysterious ways. I told myself that if He wanted to save my baby, He would send the means. Perhaps that is exactly what He has done. I will take you in, and you shall be wet nurse to my baby. You shall save his life—and you may bring your own bairn, too, to be his companion.''

"Oh, God bless you, mistress! St. Anthony and St. Monica and St. Anne, the mother of Mary bless you, mistress! You won't be sorry, mistress! I'll serve you well, you'll see.'' Chloris seized her hand and kissed it, and Annunciata withdrew it with a wry smile.

"Yes, I think you will," she said. "I always had a liking for actresses, though the line between an actress and a liar is a thin one. But I think you will amuse me if nothing more."

And Chloris's face grew suddenly serious, and she said, "Maybe I do lie, mistress, when it serves me, though I'd never get another into trouble by it. But one thing I said was true—I do have the Sight. And one day it may serve you well."

CHAPTER THREE

The following March—1671—Anne Hyde, Duchess of York, died. The news, when it arrived at Morland Place, affected Annunciata deeply. She had been fond of her former mistress, and the last few interviews she had had with her convinced Annunciata that the duchess was unhappy and disillusioned. Every new scrap of news that came from St. James's Court made Annunciata grieve more. The duchess's last words to her husband were "Duke, Duke, death is terrible, death is very terrible!" at which, so the reports said, the duke was deeply moved, even terrified. He mourned her, but not for long. Soon the news came up the south road that the duchess's household had been broken up, and the two children had been sent away to Richmond, where a household was created for them at the Palace with Colonel and Lady Frances Villiers as governor and governess. Annunciata remembered that the Villiers had a large brood of lovely, intelligent children, and wondered how the princesses, especially shy Anne, would like their new companions.

And the duke began looking for another wife. It was evident now that the Queen would never produce a live heir, and as James, the King's brother, had only daughters, it was essential that he seek another wife at once. But Annunciata chose to interpret it as another sign that the duchess had been unloved, and she wept even louder. Ralph was upset and concerned, but Chloris comforted him briskly.

"Bless you, master, it's nothing—only her condition. If all

this was to happen two months hence, she'd no more than nod gravely.''

Chloris was firmly settled at Morland Place now. Baby Rupert had thrived from the moment he first clamped his hungry mouth around her milky nipple, and he was now a big and bonny child, which caused endless altercation between Dorcas and Jane Birch, for the latter maintained that the baby had been on the mend anyway, and that the breast-feeding had had nothing to do with it.

When early in the year Annunciata had believed herself pregnant again, Chloris had said happily, ''That's good, mistress. I'll feed young Rupert right through until the new baby comes, then.'' Annunciata had been feeling too unwell to want to argue about it, and so the thing was decided without ever being discussed, that Chloris would wet-nurse Annunciata's babes from then on. But her place in the household was not simply that of wet nurse, though it would have been difficult to say precisely what it was. Feeding her babies took up very little of her time. The other tasks about the nursery were done by the nursery maids, and Dorcas was governess with overall charge of the children. Thus when Chloris was not with the babies she was most often to be found with Annunciata, talking to her, attending her, making her laugh.

''I suppose,'' Ralph said once, ''you could say that Chloris is your fool. Queens always have a fool, do they not?''

Ralph liked Chloris, laughed at her antics, and blinked at the liberties she took, and joined in the enthusiasm with the games she organized during the dark evenings when she would suddenly cry impatiently, ''Why, you are all so dull, even the fire is falling asleep! Stir up now, master and mistress, I must make you laugh.''

The children adored her, and found in her an understanding ally and an envoy to their sterner mother. The servants shook their heads in amazement over her, but took their small problems to her. Only Birch disliked her, continuing implacably to disapprove of her, and silently to struggle for the right to attend Annunciata exclusively.

In the summer King Charles signed the Treaty of Dover, which allied England with France against the Dutch, and the following year war was declared against Holland, which pleased Annunciata and worried Ralph.

"The Dutch are not our natural enemies," he said to her as they sat in the long saloon on the first warm evening of spring. She glanced up from her needlework in surprise.

"How can you say so, Ralph!" she cried. "Why, have you forgotten the Medway? They burned our ships under our very noses. We must be avenged for that. And what about Amboina?"

"It was a very long time ago," Ralph said. "Don't you see, these are the things you are meant to think! These are the things they are using to whip up public feeling."

"My grandfather was massacred at Amboina," Annunciata said, "and my grandmother died of a broken heart."

"That is what you are meant to remember," Ralph said. "But nevertheless, it is the French who are the enemy, not the Dutch. They are eating up Europe. They have a huge, almost unbeatable army, and nothing stands in their way except Holland. Once they have swallowed that, they will look toward us."

Annunciata laughed. "Don't be silly!"

"The King is making a mistake—and to combine it with the Declaration of Indulgence—"

"Surely you cannot disapprove of that?" Annunciata said sharply. "So many of our friends released from prison—the shadow lifted—"

"My dear," Ralph said gently, "I do not wish anyone to be persecuted. I would have everyone free to follow his conscience. But when the King makes a Declaration of Indulgence toward Catholics on one day, and allies himself with a Catholic power in war against a Protestant state on the next, he is storing up trouble for himself. You know how the common people feel about Catholicism. They think it is the first step in forcing England back to Rome."

Annunciata put down her needle. "Is that what they are saying?"

"That is what they are saying," Ralph said. "The Duke of York is Lord High Admiral—and he is an avowed Catholic. The chief officers of the army are Catholics. They say Clifford has the King's ear, and he is a Catholic."

Annunciata stared into the fire for a moment. "People are so

stupid,'' she said at last. ''And intolerant.'' A silence fell, and
she looked around the room at her family. The long saloon was
big enough to accommodate many evening pastimes simultaneously,
the quiet and the noisy, and it was filled with pleasant sounds.
Near at hand were the crackling of the fire and the snoring of the
dogs who were lying before it in a tangle like a living rug, the
two great brindled hounds, Bran and Fern, and the spaniels
Caspar and Charlemagne. The dogs would lie before a fire in
the middle of summer, Annunciata thought with affectionate
exasperation.

On the other side of the fire, getting the best light from the
sconces, were Father St. Maur and Clem, the steward, going
over the accounts together, and between them and Annunciata sat
Ralph, helping his man Arthur to mend a piece of harness and
occasionally stirring the dogs with an idle foot. Farther off,
Martin, ever the scholar, was reading a book and occasionally
reciting a passage to Daisy, who was sewing and chatting to
Elizabeth. She was not the least interested in the benefits of
marling arable land but nodded and smiled whenever her brother
interrupted her. Farther off again Dorcas was playing a quiet
game of chess with George, and farthest of all Chloris was playing
a very noisy three-handed game of cribbage with the twins.

It was all so peaceful, she thought, a peaceful family scene. And
then she sighed—it was all so dull! She thought of London, of
plays and parties and feasts, of riding in the park, of new clothes
and gossip. She had not been to London at all this last winter, for
she had given birth in November—baby Charles had succeeded
baby Rupert to Chloris's breast—and the birthing had been hard
and had made her too ill to travel until it was too late in the
Season to be worth doing. It had pleased Ralph no end to have
her home all through the Season, and he had combined with
Chloris to arrange particularly exciting Christmas festivities to
cheer Annunciata up.

She had enjoyed Christmas, and the rest of the winter hunting, and
had looked forward to the coming of spring and all the pleasant
summer pursuits, and in her mellowed mood had been kind to
Ralph. She sighed again. It was her undoing. Now she was
pregnant again, and that meant that she would not be able to ride

and hunt through the summer, that she would be forced into frustrating immobility, and that the next winter Season in London would have to take place without her, too. As if he read her thought, Ralph looked up at her at that moment and smiled, his eyes glancing significantly at her belly.

"I like to see you like this," he murmured softly, so that only she would hear.

"I know you do," she said shortly. You like to see me chained, she added, but not aloud. She thought of his first wife, Mary, who had been married to him for nine years, had endured eight pregnancies, and then died before she was twenty-five. *That* was the fate of dutiful wives! Annunciata's mother, Ruth, had lived without men, had raised Annunciata alone, and been her own mistress all her life. It was not to breed brats like a Puritan's wife that she had educated Annunciata and launched her on a Court career. Ralph was still studying her, but she avoided his eye, concentrating her gaze on her sewing. She felt frustration building up in her against her husband. She had loved him once, when she had fled home from the horror of plague-torn London, seeking a safe warm darkness in which to hide. Then he had been everything to her. But six years was a long time, and she had changed. At forty-one Ralph was still handsome and vigorous, a very attractive man, but she no longer loved him. She found him dull and limiting, and she could not but be aware of the growing conflict between what she wanted from life, and what contented him.

Her attention was claimed by George, who had finished his game with Dorcas and come to her to try to get onto her knee. She put her sewing aside for him and he climbed on, great boy that he was, and put his arms round her neck.

"Well, my darling," she said, "and did my little lord earl win his game?"

"Oh, yes, Mama," he said. "I can always beat Dorcas, even if I give her a pawn." His mother smiled and kissed him, and honesty compelled him to add, "But Father St. Maur always beats me."

He was so beautiful, Annunciata thought, and so clever, this darling of her children. How like his father he looked! She dreamed a little, remembering him—he who had been her best friend as well as her lover, who had understood her as no one else. "We are alike, you and I, Nancy," he had said once. "We are both incorrigible rogues." It had been like being alone, being with him. She remembered his lovely, laughing face, his teasing voice, the name that he alone called her; she remembered him dying, horribly, of the plague, dying in her arms, and she shuddered and clutched George a little tighter.

"What is it, Mama?" George said, and she smiled and shook her head.

"Nothing. A goose walking over my grave." She was so glad she had George, his son, to keep his memory green, her only true friend. But George should not be shut away here in the country like some squire's son! He should be at Court, learning courtly manners and advancing himself. He was beautiful and intelligent, and he had an exquisite voice; he could already have held a position at Court, and have paved the way for the glittering career she meant him to have. She pinned that resentment, with the others, on Ralph.

Hugo saw George leave the chessboard and go to his mother, and as he watched his half-brother leaning against his mother's cheek and murmuring to her, his attention wandered from the game.

Chloris, whom little escaped, felt sympathy for him and, putting down her cards, said, "I am tired of this game. We are all too quiet and dull! Should we not have a charade, perhaps? Yes, let's all play together at charades!" She knew that Annunciata liked charades best of the games they played, liking anything that had to do with acting and dressing up.

Everyone looked up, gauging interest, and then Birch said firmly, "It is too late in the evening; it would excite the children too much, and they would not sleep. Better we should have some music or singing."

"Yes, that would be pleasant," Father St. Maur concurred, for he loved music.

Chloris, not one to abandon a purpose, said, "Well, then, some music. Hugo, you can play something for us on the clavicytherium—"

But Annunciata broke in, shaking her head. "Oh, no, I cannot bear that noise. It jars my nerves so. George shall sing to us, shan't you, my darling?"

"Yes, Mama," George said at once, pleased to be asked, and got down from her lap.

Chloris glanced at Hugo's dark brow and shrugged helplessly as Annunciata said, "Sing me my favorite song, George. Give us 'Oh, the Sweet Delights of Love.' "

And so George stood square, clasped his hands lightly behind his back, and began to sing to his admiring audience. He sang beautifully, and the twins alone were not delighted. Arabella stared indifferently at the ceiling above George's head and thought about horses; Hugo glared at George in fury and thought about revenge.

Annunciata stepped out of the main door into the June sunlight and looked to where Ralph was holding Goldeneye at the mounting block, his face a mixture of pride and anxiety that made Annunciata conceal a smile. He so much wants me to enjoy this day, she thought, and is so unsure that I will. Goldeneye knuckered welcomingly at the sight of her mistress and shifted her small forefeet in a rapid dance of impatience. The mare was sixteen, but had no more notion of behaving sedately than a two-year-old filly, though with age her antics had become more showy than unseating. Her dark eyes shone, and she tossed her head up and down so that the green-silk-fringed turksheads on her browband bobbed and rustled.

"You look beautiful, dearest," Ralph murmured as he handed her up onto the block. "Like a queen." In the interests of a pleasant day Annunciata bit back a number of sharp retorts that occurred to her and merely smiled as she mounted neatly and spread her green silk skirts around her. Sweets for the child, she thought, and remembered how he had arranged special outings and festivities to comfort his unhappy first wife.

Still holding Goldeneye's bridle, Ralph called to her footman, Tom. "Come and take your mistress's bridle, and lead her." Tom's eyes met involuntarily with Annunciata's at the words, and she reached forward and gathered in the slack of the reins with a firm hand.

"My dear husband," she said, "I am by no means a cripple. The day has not yet come when I cannot handle my own horse." Ralph began to make an anxious denial—she was three months pregnant, and Goldeneye barely knew what it was to walk—but she said firmly, with a hint of an edge, "Stand a little off, I pray you, husband," and he could only sigh and obey. He took his own horse, Lion, from Gideon, sprang up to the saddle, and the cavalcade moved off.

It was a large cavalcade, the numbers of the family swollen by the presence of the visitors who had come for the midsummer celebrations—Clovis from London, Francis Morland from Tods Knowe, the family's Northumberland estate, and by the Symonds cousins from Blindburn. Ralph's Aunt Anne had married Sam Symonds, who owned a small estate in the Cheviots. Anne and Sam were both dead now, and their son Crispian was master. He had brought with him his two unmarried sisters, Frances and Anne, whom he referred to irreverantly as Fan and Nan, and Ralph's daughter Sabine, who had been brought up in the Blindburn household.

There was a great crowd gathered in the low field at the upper end of Hob Moor, dressed in holiday clothes and in holiday mood. It was the Feast of St. John, and everyone was disposed to be happy, and this was a new and exciting form of entertainment that Master Morland had arranged for them. The scene was gay with flags, with the striped silk of the open-sided pavilion which had been set up for the ladies of the family to watch from in comfort, and with the bright ribbons and caparisons of the many horses which were being ridden and led about in the crowd. Yorkshire folk loved horses, and men had always tested their favorite steeds one against the other; it was then a logical step for the master of Morland Place to arrange a proper horserace, over a given ground, with prizes for the winner.

After the races there was to be a feast—the cooking pits were already smoking away downwind—and dancing. Only a stone's throw away, on the other side of the great road, was the Hare and Heather, and the landlord had had fetched up to the field a number of great barrels of his best ale, so there would be no lack of mirth. He had been pleased to supply the ale at a very reasonable price, for he expected great trade today, especially in the evening when, for those who could not care too much for horses or women, he had arranged some very exciting cockfighting in the cockpits that stood beside his bowling green, behind the inn and out of sight of the road.

The crowds cheered lustily when the Morlands arrived, a great accolade for Ralph, who was the kind of master they liked, and a more polite, though no less enthusiastic one for Annunciata, who was loved for her beauty and for her intimacy with the Royal Family. Goldeneye boggled and jumped sideways at the pressing, cheering people, and Annunciata sat her leaps with smiling ease, and the cheers redoubled for her horsemanship.

"I believe they'd like to see you ride in the race," Clovis murmured to her as he helped her dismount at the pavilion.

Annunciata smiled. "If this were three months ago, I would have done it," she said.

"And won, no doubt." He grinned. Ralph joined them, having been delayed by the press of bodies from handing Annunciata down himself. "I'm looking forward to seeing how your horses compare, Ralph," Clovis went on. "They are all Kingcup's progeny, are they not? He is a great stallion."

Ralph's face lit up. There were few things he liked as much as to talk about horses. "The best we've had," he said. "Better perhaps than the great Prince Hal, though he sired some fine animals. But they are still too heavy in the leg for the greatest speed. What I want is some lighter, faster blood to mix with our native stamina. Now, I've heard that some of those Barbary horses—"

"If you start Ralph on breeding you will never stop him," Annunciata warned Clovis. "He is quite set on going to Africa to bring one back, so I pray you don't encourage him."

"But think how it would improve the stock," Ralph cried, and then, seeing their amused faces, he stopped. "Very well, very well. I see there are people clamoring for my attention. I had better go to them. Clovis, will you see the countess seated?"

"Of course," Clovis replied.

Ralph turned away to be beseiged by carpenters, cooks, grooms, riders, friends, admirers, and beggars, and Clovis said, "I had sooner my part than his today," and led Annunciata into the tent. He settled her in the central chair and saw politely to the seating of the others—Elizabeth Hobart on Annunciata's right, Frances and Anne Symonds on her left, Sabine and the other children to either side, and the servants along the benches behind, Chloris and Birch fighting steadily for the place directly behind their mistress. Then, obeying Annunciata's glance, he took a stool at her feet, moving the spaniels gently to one side, and prepared to entertain her.

"Now," she said, "as we have some time before the race begins, and I have barely had a chance to speak to you, tell me all the news. You have been to St. Omer? You have seen Edmund?"

"Yes, and he is very happy. He takes his orders this year, at Michaelmas. I think he would almost sooner have been a monk, you know, he is so . . ." He paused, looking for a word, and went on, "His eyes look always inward, at some quiet garden in his soul."

Annunciata smiled gently. "You have lived so long at Court, and still believe men have a soul?"

He looked up at her peacefully. "Call it what you will, there is something that keeps men to run on two legs instead of four."

"And what news of the war?" she said after a moment.

"Bad, all bad. News of wars must always be bad. Our navy achieves nothing at sea, and the French army moves little by little toward the Dutch as they move little by little backward. Now they have cut the dikes and are standing looking at the French across the floodwater."

"Will the French cross?" Annunciata asked.

"I think not," Clovis said. "Things are afoot. There are rumors—more than rumors—that the Dutch people are angry with their leaders for allowing things to come to such a pass. They want peace with the English, just as most of our folk want peace with the Dutch, and they think their ministers have sold that peace for their own ends. There is a move to bring back

William of Orange to his birthright—to make him once again hereditary Stadholder."

"What is that? Is it like to be king?" Annunciata asked. William was King Charles's nephew, son of his sister Mary.

Clovis nodded. "It would become so, although his powers would not be absolute. He would have to seek agreement always with the Dutch parliament, but yes, in effect he would be king."

"And what then? What would we do? I suppose the King would not care to make war on his own nephew?"

"I do not know," Clovis sighed. "I do not know what our King would be about. It passes me that he made war on the Dutch in the first place. But I think you are right, that with Prince William as Stadholder he would sooner ally with him against the French. He would be a more reliable friend than King Louis."

Just then Crispian and Francis, who had been looking at the horses, joined them. They were close friends as well as cousins, having marched together with Monk's army to take London and call back King Charles to his throne, but they presented a very different appearance one from the other. Crispian was short, bullnecked, and stout, having grown stouter than ever since he had become his own master with no disapproving father to watch over him. He ate and drank enormously, and had a fondness for wine—Northumberland being close to Scotland, and with a direct trade-link with Edinburgh, it was easier for Northumbrians to get good claret than for anyone farther south—and his habits had not improved his looks. His fair hair was growing thin, and his sharp features, so like his mother's, were disappearing under fat, while the drink was making his face redder and his blue eyes more watery day by day.

Frank, on the other hand, was thin and brown and as hard as a nut. He lived a Spartan bachelor life at Tods Knowe, running his own estate there and also overseeing Emblehope, which belonged to Ralph, his first wife's dowry. He was a small, slight man, his thin legs slightly bowed by riding, his carriage very upright, his face, though very brown and much lined by exposure to weather, pleasant and alert. He had a high-cheekboned, fine-drawn face, very blue eyes, and dark curling hair just beginning to be threaded with silver.

They ambled up together, Crispian's meaty arm over Frank's shoulder as he talked.

"I like the look of that big bay devil," he was saying. "He'd carry you all day and come in with his head up, and I liked the look of the yeoman who's riding him. He's my sort of fellow—plenty of spirit."

"If he goes on accepting drinks from his admirers," Frank said, "he's going to fall out of the saddle before he gets to the starting place. And that bay is too heavy to be fast. He had legs like oaks."

"Damn sturdy legs," Crispian said. "Go through anything."

Frank caught Annunciata's eye and smiled, giving half a bow to her as he said patiently, "He'd carry you through heavy ground, I grant, but he won't be fast, and this race will go to the fastest."

Crispian changed his ground. "Well, I didn't say I thought he'd win. I said I liked the look of him. How, now, ladies are ye comfortable? They'll bring the horses over to parade for you soon. Now, Fan, now, Nan, move a little over so that we can sit by the countess."

Frances and Anne began automatically to obey him, but Frank put out a hand and said gently, "By no means, Crisp, we cannot put the ladies to such pains. Cousin Fanny, please sit and be easy. We'll sit at the ladies' feet, cousin, and entertain them."

Crispian looked doubtful. "Damn all, Frank, if I get down there I may never get up. Fan don't mind standing a little, do you, Fan?"

But Frank wouldn't allow it, and with a smile at Frances he sat down firmly at her feet making it impossible for her to obey her brother, and Crispian, with a shrug and a thump, eased himself down on the ground between Anne and Sabine, grumbling under his breath, though not in an ill-tempered way, for nothing Frank did was wrong. Annunciata, exchanging an amused glance with Clovis, noted out of the corner of her eye how Frances blushed when Frank championed her, resettling her skirts, flustered with more happiness than the small service merited.

Frank leaned toward her and chatted easily, and Annunciata wondered if he realized the effect he was having on his cousin. Poor Fanny was twenty-four and should have been wed long since, but her father had been many years an invalid, and Crispian was too idle to trouble himself to find her a match. Besides, since their mother's death four years ago, she had been the woman of the house, and he had probably stopped thinking of Fanny as potentially marriageable.

Anne was a different proposition. She was plump, plain, placid, and agreeable, and though she was twenty-one and unlikely now to be wed, she was happy enough living at home, devoted to her brother and sister, and not curious about the rest of the world. Clovis, catching the direction of Annunciata's glance, excused himself to her quietly, and moved himself to sit by Anne and amuse her, an act of kindness that Annunciata applauded, though it left her temporarily without company.

Bran and Fern came thrusting through the crowds and pushed up to Annunciata, poking their hard muzzles into her hands before flopping down beside her, taking up far too much room, and filling the tent with the smell of horse dung, in which they had just been ecstatically rolling. Ralph appeared close behind them.

"Husband, send those hounds away, do," Annunciata said sharply, and with a sigh he grabbed their collars and hauled them away from her.

"May I sit?" he asked, with faint impatience. "They are bringing the horses."

Those who were riding in the first competition came up to pay their respects to the countess and the other members of the family, and to allow them to see the horses. Outside the tent the gambling was already going on at a fevered pitch, and everyone, even the servants, was going to want to place a wager on one horse at least. The people who were competing were as varied as the horses—there were friends of the family, gentlemen from the city and gentlemen's sons, squires from the estates round about, yeomen farmers and tenants, and even some gypsies, who would not come very close to the tent, but made signs of obeisance from a distance, keeping their hands firmly on the rope bridles of their rough-looking mounts.

As to the horse, they ranged from saddle ponies to plow horses.

"I drew the line at mules," Ralph murmured to Annunciata as the strange parade went past, "and there was one mad old man from Galtres who wanted to enter his plow ox with his little daughter riding it."

Annunciata laughed. "I don't believe you. Ah, here are your horses—and I must say, they look magnificent."

Clovis heard her and called across Frank's head, "He will be thought miserly, giving a prize knowing he is going to win it back. Now, truly, Ralph, this was all arranged for your own display, was it not?"

Martin was to ride Ralph's young gelding Oryx, and he came up now to bow to his stepmother and show her the horse. Behind him was Hugo, almost bursting with pride and excitement, because he was to ride Lion in the race. He waited his turn for his mother's attention, and saw with a pang of jealousy that she pulled one of the green ribbons from her sleeve and gave it to Martin to tie around his arm.

"Wear my colors, Martin," she said, "and be sure to win."

Martin thanked her and moved away, and Hugo tugged at Lion, who towered above him, to bring him forward. But even as he did so, George came slipping in through the back of the tent to join the group, and came up behind his mother to lounge gracefully on her shoulder, and she turned to smile at him. Hugo, knowing how badly he was presenting himself, could not prevent himself from glowering sullenly as he led Lion forward. His mother frowned at him and said, "For love, Hugo, stand up a little straighter, and try to look more pleasant. Lion looks too good for you as you are."

Hugo turned and dragged Lion away, the tears burning in his eyes. I won't cry, I won't cry, he said fiercely to himself. He would not let anyone see tears. But the image of his half-brother's fair, beautiful face burned in his mind, gazing across his mother's shoulder, his straight pale hair touching her dark curls. Now the menfolk were getting up, for they had to fetch their own mounts, Francis to ride in the race, just for fun, and the others to follow it on horseback, as would many of the spectators. The women began hastily to arrange their bets with anyone who would exchange a coin or two. Annunciata wagered lavishly on Martin and Oryx, exchanging fine odds with a fellow magistrate of Ralph's through the discreet medium of Tom, and then took bets with other members of the family. Frances bet all the money she had with her on Frank, and then sat, hands gripped together in her lap, scarlet faced with embarrassment that anyone should notice her preference, and determination that he should win.

There were three races altogether, and they took all afternoon to run, for it was difficult to gather together the runners all at the same time and the same place, very difficult to keep them there for the start, and almost impossible to get them all to start at the same time. Once they were away, however, running a wide circular course around the field so as to come back to the same place at the finish, the excitement was enormous, the spectators cheering and shouting on their favored riders, and the mounted spectators flogging their horses along beside the competitors, shrieking and waving their whips, drinking deeply from the flasks and bottles they carried, and frequently falling off or being bolted with. Several spectators got trampled, though none was seriously hurt; one very fat squire fell quietly off his horse under a tree and knocked himself unconscious, and lay there serenely all afternoon, everyone who passed thinking he was merely drunk and asleep; and a pregnant villager was overcome with excitement and gave birth near the cooking pits to a fine son.

The first race was extremely confusing, for the horses were very excited and milled about so at the start that when Ralph finally dropped his handkerchief many of them were facing the wrong way. Hugo was among these, and by the time he got Lion around and found a gap to put him through, the leaders were halfway round the course. It was won by a yeoman called Franklin riding a big gelding which he had bred himself out of his own plow mare, using the services of the Morland stud. He, like many of the forward-thinking farmers, was interested in improving his stock, and he had saved the money to have his mare put to Kingcup in order to get a good strong working horse.

He had had a lucky start in the race, and his gelding, having a calm temperament, was not as upset by the crowds as some of the other horses. Ralph, who had bet heavily on his own horses, shrugged ruefully and said, "At least it was one of Kingcup's colts that won, though it was the wrong one."

The second race was won by one of the gentleman of the city, although Hugo, who was beginning to get the measure of Lion, was not far behind him and felt he might have won had the race been longer. He was quenching his thirst on a piggin of ale when Martin came up to him, without Oryx and holding his left arm in his right hand, supporting it across his chest.

"Why, are you hurt?" Hugo cried. Martin grimaced.

"Poor Oryx got between two drunkards on plow horses, and panicked and threw me. I've sprained my arm. Don't worry, it isn't broken. But I cannot ride in the next race. Would you like to take Oryx? He's faster than Lion." Hugo stared in amazement. "It's all right." Martin grinned. "I've asked my father, and he agrees." Hugo grabbed his hand in wordless delight, and then apologized as Martin winced. "Here, you'd better have the ribbon, too," Martin said, fumbling awkwardly with it. "Take it off—I can't use this hand properly."

"But my mother gave it to you," Hugo said.

"It goes with the horse. Come, now, take it, hurry. You must get mounted."

Almost dazed, Hugo found himself a few moments later riding to the starting place on Oryx, who had settled down, his pricked ears saying that he understood what was expected of him now. Tight about Hugo's upper arm was the green ribbon, the ends fluttering away on the light breeze. He imagined he could smell his mother's scent on the ribbon. His heart was full as he felt the spring of the horse gathered beneath him, light mouth against his hands, taut muscles between his legs. He imagined his mother's face, imagined her looking at him with pride and pleasure as she gave him the prize for the third race and stooped to kiss him in front of everyone.

Martin's words rang in his ears. "Get a good position at the starting place. Keep in the middle, away from the spectators. Get away fast then keep him in front, so that the others don't foul you. He's the fastest horse—he only needs to be allowed to win.''

His eyes fixed on Ralph's white handkerchief in his upraised hand, Hugo pressed his legs to Oryx's sides, holding him against himself with his hands. Oryx gathered his hocks under him, and as the kerchief fell he sprang out from the press of horses with the give of Hugo's hands. Now all was concentrated into the thundering of hooves, the whip of wind past his cheeks, the smell of hot horseflesh, and the ears and neck of Oryx before him. Below the ground seemed to flash past the hard slamming hooves. Hugo was unaware of the yelling of the crowd—it seemed distant like the wash of the sea—he heard only the hooves and his mount's harsh breathing. ''Don't look around you,'' Martin had said. ''Just concentrate on keeping to the center of the track.'' That was easy enough. It had been worn almost bare of grass now, a gray-brown line curving away before him, and he fixed his eyes on it, leaning forward and breathing encouragement in Oryx's ear. And then he saw ahead of him a group of horsemen, right across his path, holding their horses in position and waving and yelling at him. What were they doing! They were in his way! He would have to stop; there was no going round them in the crowd. What had he done? Why were they trying to stop him?

And then as Oryx jerked his head back and skidded to a halt in three sliding jumps, the press of cheering burst through into his brain, and he realized with a shock of delight that it was Ralph in the center of the horsemen, that this was the starting place and therefore the finish, that he had won. Dazed, amazed, his mouth filled with dust so that he could not have spoken even had he words to say, he slid to the ground and stood patting the trembling, heaving Oryx while all around him people cheered him and pounded his fragile shoulders until they felt bruised.

''By, he's a reet plucky 'un, and no mistake!''

''Good for thee, young master!''

''Youngest int' race, and he beat th' old 'uns proper!''

And then, from a tall graybeard on a saddle horse, one of the competitors from the city, ''Well done indeed, your lordship. Well ridden indeed!''

Your lordship! I am Viscount Ballincrea, Hugo thought with

rising exultation, and I have ridden my stepfather's horse to victory, carrying my mother's colors. He staggered under the congratulatory pats, but his face split in a great grin of delight.

Now Martin was pushing through the crowd, his arm in a sling made from his kerchief. With his good hand he took Oryx's bridle, grinning in his pleasure.

"Go on, then, go on," he cried. "I'll take him, and see him rubbed down. Go to your mother."

Dusty, disheveled, his clothes awry, Hugo reached the pavilion. Annunciata, with a rueful smile, was collecting her winnings from Clovis, who had taken her final bet from kindness and because by that time it was small enough for him to meet.

"Too little, and too late," she said with a laugh. "I am twenty pounds the poorer by this day's sport." Then she caught sight of Hugo, standing before her, and she frowned. "Why, Hugo, what a state you are in. Could you not tidy yourself before coming here? And what are you doing with my ribbon? Give it to me—Birch, tie it on again."

"It was me, mother," Hugo managed at last to say, feeling the traitor tears welling up and forcing them back. "It was me—I rode Oryx."

"You?" his mother said in disbelief.

"Martin hurt his arm, and said I should ride Oryx. It was me—I won." Birch looked up from threading the ribbon back through its holes and gave a little tug to the ends as if she wished she were tugging Hugo's hair. Annunciata's frown did not lighten. Hugo's lips trembled—this was not how it was meant to be.

"It would show a more becoming modesty," she said sternly, "if you were to say that you had the fastest horse. If anyone won, it was poor Oryx, whom you seem to have abandoned. A good horseman always sees his horse well cared for. You had better go and do that, had you not?"

When he had gone away and the women were all up and moving, preparing to go and refresh themselves, Chloris came up to take charge of George and used the opportunity to murmur to Annunciata, "Eh, madam, but you were a mite hard on his poor little lordship."

Annunciata paused, startled. "Hugo? Hard? What on earth can you mean?"

"Well, he came up so pleased that he had won for you—"

"You are too soft with that child," Annunciata said. "He has won his prize; what more do you think he wants?"

"Why, madam, your love perhaps."

"Hugo is like his father," Annunciata said. "He loves only himself. My lord earl is looking a little grubby, Chloris. You had better take him away and wash him." And she turned away and took Clovis's arm and bent her head to him with a teasing smile.

"I am looking forward to the dancing," she said. "I hope you may dance with me, if you can spare your attention from Miss Nan for long enough."

"I am your servant, my lady, as always," he smiled back.

"I applaud your kindness," she said, pressing his arm. "The poor girl wants attention. I shall speak to Ralph tonight to see if he can't persuade Crispian to do his duty by his sisters—and by his daughter, too, for that great girl is past sixteen now," she added as Sabine caught her eye, a tall, big-boned, blond young hoyden, the image of her father, "and if he doesn't get her wed soon, there'll be trouble. Now, Clovis, you are unwed, and you could do worse for yourself."

He raised an eyebrow. "Marry my own niece—what do you say, my lady?"

"Not Sabine," Annunciata said, pinching him. "What do you say to Miss Nan?"

"Or Miss Frances?" Clovis said. "Or both. Why should you plan half-measures, madam?"

"Oh, not Miss Frances—she's in love with Frank, didn't you notice?"

"No, I had not remarked it."

Annunciata looked pleased. "You see, a woman's discernment passes a man's. I notice everyone's expression, and judge accordingly."

At which Chloris, walking behind holding George by the hand, shook her head sadly.

CHAPTER FOUR

When the Season started in September, Ralph refused to go to London, saying that since he had seen him so recently, Clovis could perfectly well handle business matters himself, and that there was nothing else to go to London for. Annunciata was furious, for she was too far advanced in her pregnancy to go alone without outraging propriety, and so she had to stay in Yorkshire, grumbling that everyone else would be in London, and that there was nothing to do. In fact, although York had gone downhill sadly since the Civil War, it was gradually being rebuilt, not as a manufacturing center, but as a center of fashion, and a large number of good families were living either in the city or nearby. The regular Assize Courts and markets attracted people to the city, and throughout the Season there were assemblies and concerts and balls. Had she wished, Annunciata could have been a leader of this society.

But, frustrated and sulky, she stayed home, complaining about the weather, the dullness, and her inability to hunt. Ralph tried continually to please her and to make her confinement to the country less irksome by arranging parties of various sorts, and by ordering for her from the best carriage-maker in York a delightful little calèche in which she could drive around the estate. But she only gave him a hard stare and said that the tracks on the estate were so bad that bumping over them in a calèche would be more dangerous for the unborn baby than riding.

Ralph was always very busy in the early autumn, with all the farming matters to oversee as well as the numerous duties as lord of the manor and justice of the peace, and he was from home as much as he was there. Annunciata also had her business to attend to. She had not only the Shawes estate to run, including all the city properties she had inherited from her mother, but the Chelmsford estate, which lay in trust with her for George. The day-to-day running of the household at Morland Place she tended to leave more and more to Elizabeth, and so when she was not occupied with her financial affairs, she was at liberty to spend more time with her children.

The girls found this a mixed blessing. Hugo and George, because they were taking lessons with Father St. Maur, were protected from too much notice from their mother, and Martin, who was now fifteen, when not at his lessons was frequently with his father learning about his future inheritance; but there was nothing to stand between Daisy and Arabella and the necessity at last of learning, by compulsion, a few accomplishments. At other times Annunciata amused herself in playing with baby Rupert and his foster brother Michael; Charles was still too young to interest her. And when the weather was fine she walked out of doors, in the gardens and grounds of Morland Place or, when she was more than usually restless, farther afield, accompanied only by a servant whom she instructed to follow her at a distance so that she might feel alone.

The evenings were the most frustrating, when darkness confined her to the house and Ralph was often still away from home. It was in those months that she began to discover the real value of her stepson, Martin. He was an intelligent boy, and had already begun a collection of books in preference to the toys of youth. He was sensitive to her moods and always eager to please her, and she found him very conversable. His education under Father St. Maur had been sound, and often the three of them would conduct an earnest discussion into some point of philosophy, or literature, or astronomy. Martin shared with her an interest in architecture, and some of the long dark evenings were spent in drawing up plans for the rebuilding of Shawes, which Annunciata intended to carry out as soon as she was free of her present encumbrance.

When all else failed, there was music. Martin could play

sweetly on the hautboy, though he had no singing voice, and
when she wanted singing she could always call on her angel-
child, George. And often while they played and sang to her, she
would cross her hands in her lap and stare into the fire, and see at
its heart pictures from the past, from her crowded life: of her two
former husbands, of her almost-lover, the forbidden Prince Rupert,
and all the other friends and acquaintances of her Court life; and
farther back of her gaunt, silent, unbending mother; of Aunt
Hero, the Haltling, with her fading, damaged beauty; and of the
three young Morland men who had loved her and dominated her
youth—Ralph, Edward, and Kit.

Where do I go from here? she wondered. What happens next?
She searched the flames for images of her life from now onward,
the direction it would take, the love she hoped to find, but found
nothing in the red heart of the fire to allay her fears that the
future would bring her nothing new, only a continuation of
maternity and boredom.

The baby was born on St. Stephen's day, a lucky omen, the
servants said. It was a boy, and the unfortunate child precipitated
a quarrel between his parents the moment he arrived, for Ralph
wanted to call him Stephen, after the martyr, his birth-saint, and
Annunciata wanted to call him Maurice, to please Prince Rupert.
They argued at first politely, and then with increasing rancor
until finally Ralph cried out in anger and exasperation, "You
think more of the Prince than of your own husband. It is lucky
that you did not go to London last Season, or I might wonder if I
was the boy's father after all!"

Annunciata went white. "How dare you!" she hissed. "How
dare you speak so to me." Inside she was trembling with more
than rage, remembering the quarrels she had had with her first
husband, Hugo. But Ralph was no Hugo; he grew pale in his
turn, realizing what he had said, and fell to his knees at the
bedside, taking her hands in his.

"Oh, forgive me!" he cried. "My dearest—I am so ashamed!
I did not mean—you know very well—I spoke in anger, and I am
sorry from my heart. Say you forgive me, please." He kissed her
hands, first one then the other. "To lose my temper with you

when you are still exhausted from the birth ordeal is doubly reprehensible. You shall call the child Maurice if you please— whatever you want.''

After a while Annunciata relented, and since she had her way in the matter of the child's name, they were friends again for a few days.

The next quarrel came about as a result of what had passed at the midsummer races, for in January Ralph announced that following the negotiations he had been making throughout the winter, his daughter Sabine was to marry Crispian Symonds in the spring. Annunciata thought it was a poor match, and said so, and was angry also because Ralph had not spoken to Crispian about marrying off his sisters. He had determined that it was not his business to interfere in something so delicate, and on that and on the betrothal of Sabine he stood firm and refused to allow Annunciata her way.

''The match is good enough, and dear to my heart,'' he said. ''It binds the Blindburn estate closer to us; and the girl is content. It was for that I sent her there years ago, to grow up where she would live. As to the other matter . . .'' and he shrugged dismissively.

But only the next week came news that made Annunciata feel that on the latter head she had been right at least. A letter came from Crispian, which Ralph assumed would contain details of the betrothal; instead it gave the shocking news that Francis was dead, had been killed by a fall while out hunting in the Keilderburn Ravine. Annunciata was deeply shocked. She had known Frank well in London, and had liked and admired him, and she had deplored his solitary and Spartan life. In his letter Crispian said also that Fanny was in a state of collapse after hearing of his death. ''It seems,'' he said, ''that she has been in love with him all these years and has been hoping that he would ask her to marry him one day. Well, it is too late now, poor Fan.''

''You see,'' Annunciata cried, her eyes red from weeping, ''if you had spoken as I asked you none of this would have happened. He would have married Fanny, and then he would have been safe at home with her instead of out scrambling around ravines.''

It was illogical, and Ralph knew that she knew it, but though he soothed her and petted her, he would not allow to her that he had been wrong in not broaching the subject with Crispian, and the breach between them widened.

The final blow came in February, when the news came that Parliament, assembling after the recess, had reversed the Declaration of Indulgence toward Catholics, and, what was more, had passed a Test Act to exclude Catholics from office.

Clovis, who rode up from London as soon as the implications were known, said, "Shaftesbury and Arlington are behind it. They are aiming a blow at Clifford because he is the only Catholic member of the Cabal, and has the King's ear. He will have to resign, of course. And as far as Parliament is concerned, it strikes at the Duke of York. He will have to resign as Lord High Admiral. It won't make much difference to the navy, of course—Prince Rupert will take over for him, and the prince and the duke are as one on naval policy—but it will make a deal of difference to the duke."

"But I don't understand," Annunciata said. "Why will the duke have to resign? Everyone knews already that he is a Catholic. How will the Test Act make any difference?"

"Because, my dear Countess," Clovis said gravely, "the Act demands that anyone who holds public office will have to take the Communion in the Anglican form, which involves denying the Transubstantiation, and Prince James will never do that."

And Clovis turned his eyes thoughtfully on Ralph, who nodded, and said quietly, "Of course, a justice of the peace would have to do it, too, would he not?"

"Then you will have to resign?" Annunciata said.

"I will have to think about it," Ralph said.

He did think about it. He also consulted Father St. Maur, and spent no little time in the chapel, meditating, and in the steward's room, reading, and in the end he announced that he had decided not to resign, but to take the Anglican Communion when he was put to the test. It was the last straw for Annunciata, and they quarreled furiously. Ralph's faith had never been as firm as hers, and now he said, "I do not wish to give up public office. More, I do not wish never to be able to be offered other offices; and I do not wish to place my children in an undesirable light. It is a practical decision, nothing more. You will see—lots of Catholics will take the oath for the same reason."

"Other men are not you," Annunciata said bitterly.

"You want me to be a saint, Annunciata, but I am only a pragmatist. It does not seem to me such a big thing."

"Your faith does not seem to you a big thing? To deny the Transubstantiation, which is the very heart of faith, the heart of the Sacred Mystery."

Ralph stirred uneasily. "You women always regard the mystery more than men do. But have we not always been taught that God more regards the thoughts of the heart than the words of the mouth? So I shall say the words with my mouth, but think otherwise with my heart, and God will know."

"And how, then, is God to distinguish between oaths that you mean and oaths that you do not? And what is an oath but words spoken, mouth and heart, to God? What value is it if it is a lie?"

"The men to whom it is spoken will not know—or care—that it is a lie. And so I will keep my position."

Annunciata opened her hands despairingly. "And if you lie to God, you lose your soul. It slips through your fingers like grain—and what then?" And she remembered Clovis's words—"The soul is what makes men to go on two legs instead of four."

She argued with him and prayed for him, but when the time came, he took the oath, and something snapped in her, some invisible cord which had bound her to him before, however unwillingly. She looked at him that day with cold eyes and thought, Now you are nothing to me. She did not yet know where that thought would lead her, but behind the anger and grief she felt the stirrings of relief, and of anticipation.

Ralph sat by the fireglow in the steward's room, Bran and Fern snoring softly at his feet. The rest of the house was dark and silent: family and servants had long since gone to bed. Ralph could not have slept—he felt restless, dissatisfied—and so he had sat up watching the flames until they died down, and now he sat motionless watching the wavering film of ash over the embers. The local people called it "visitors," that strange cobweb, and believed it foretold the arrival of strangers. He got to his feet without disturbing the sleeping dogs and went quietly through to the chapel, seeking some palliative for his mind.

The chapel was dark but for the sanctuary lamp, and by its glow Ralph made his way to the master's seat, the place on the front bench where by tradition the Master of Morland Place sat for the twice-daily celebration. It had been his seat for fifteen years now. He stretched out his long legs and reached out his hand to the wall, his fingers discovering blindly the shape of the little bear that some long-ago Morland had carved in the stone. So often he had sat there, his fingers going over and over the rough shape as he paid his dues of devotion to God. Here he had always felt the strong ties of tradition, the weight of his ancestors, the heavy cloak across his shoulders that was the rights and privileges and responsibilities of being the master. Here before him, generation after generation, had sat those who had worn the cloak before him, and the celebration of the Mass had always seemed central to being master. But never until now had he wondered what it had to do with the Faith.

It occurred to him that the Faith had never meant much to him. His womenfolk and the servants, he knew, had had that blind devotion. He had seen their faces transfigured by it, witnessed their ecstacy and their peace. To him it was a tradition, but he had no comprehension of the mystery. His own faith was more commonplace: he did what he thought best, and trusted that God would do the same for him. Why, then, had he been betrayed? He had done what was best for Morland Place, for his children, for his wife, and yet she had turned against him. He believed that God would understand what he had done, but she had stared at him with eyes full of shadows, eyes that looked beyond the daylight into the ancient dark mysteries. It was, he thought with sudden irritation, like the common folk believing in fairies: once the sun went down and the world of darkness gathered round them, they abandoned common sense and reverted to the beliefs of their ancestors, performed simple magics, consulted wisewomen, placated pagan gods and feared demons.

He remembered his grandfather, Edmund, who had refused to fight for the King during the Civil War, in order to keep Morland Place safe. The servants told the story of how the statue of the

Blessed Lady, which was older by far than the house, had wept real tears when Edmund opened the gates to the rebel soldiers. Some of the older ones claimed to have seen it. But what had Edmund done that was so terrible and what had he, Ralph, done? If Edmund had resisted, Morland Place would have been battered down by cannon, many people injured, perhaps killed, the family ruined, perhaps forever. And if Ralph had not taken the oath, he would have been barred from public office, and the family placed under the displeasure of the law. He moved restlessly, seeking answers to unanswerable questions. He remembered his first wife, Mary, and her unhappiness, and yet he had done nothing to her to make her unhappy beyond marrying her in the first place, and how could he ever have thought that that was wrong?

Father St. Maur had been no help to him. When Ralph had put his case to him—badly, because he was not good with words, because, finally, he did not really know what it was he wanted to ask—the priest had only said, "A man must do his best, and that's all he can do."

St. Maur was Annunciata's priest, he thought angrily. To *her* he would have given answers. A slight sound made him turn his head, and he stiffened as he saw the chapel door opening. It was Annunciata. He thought at first she had come to look for him, but he quickly saw that her steps were purposeful, and she looked neither right nor left but moved straight toward the Lady Chapel. She had not seen him, for he was in shadow, and he kept quite still, waiting to see what she would do. She had brought the night-light from her bedside, and its small flame lit her white face and threw fantastic shadows leaping behind her to the roof like giant bats.

She went to the altar in the Lady Chapel, and lit two candles, and then she knelt on the prie-dieu before the statue of the Lady and folded her hands, lifting her face to the Blessed Mother's still gaze. Ralph watched her, and his mind ached with her beauty. The sleeves of her white bedgown fell back from her long wrists and slender hands, her tumbled black curls fell back from her face, leaving the line of her profile clear-cut and fragile against the surrounding darkness. Her dark eyes shone, her lips moved in prayer. What was she thinking, he wondered. What was she asking? Her face seemed sharpened with some emotion, but he did not know what it could be. He wondered if she had come down to look for him, if she missed him, was sorry for her coldness. As he watched he saw the shining diamonds of tears on her face; he watched one drop make a slow, sliding curve down her face to the corner of her mouth, watched the tip of her tongue come out involuntarily to catch it, and he wished frantically to have her in his arms, to have her bring her tears to him, so that he could lick the drops from her cheeks, press her close, comfort her as he had done so often. He had cared for her and protected her all her life, and he could not endure her tears. He got up quietly and moved toward her, and she had crossed herself and stood up before she saw him.

For a long moment they looked at each other while he searched for words to reach her. Her proud, beautiful face grew distant even as he watched, drawing away from him. He said, "I couldn't sleep, so I . . ." He let the sentence die with a mild gesture toward the chapel. She watched him impassively. "You were crying?" he said, still hoping she might fall on his neck and let him stroke her hair. But she said nothing, and finally, in desperation, he said, "I was thinking I ought to go to Northumberland soon. There is much to be done there." He wanted her to ask to come with him, and he waited for her to speak, but she seemed only to withdraw a little more. And now, how could he ask her? "I should go soon. Perhaps I should go tomorrow," he said at last, hoping the suddenness would provoke something in her.

But she said only, "Perhaps you should," and he watched her in miserable silence as she walked away. Why had she been crying? he wondered. But he knew that, even if it was their estrangement that made her unhappy, her tears were not for him. The next morning he made his arrangements, and within the week he had set off for the north.

Ralph saw enough in the first two days of his visit to Blindburn to convince him that he had been right to betroth Sabine to Crispian, and he agreed that their wedding should take place at once. Sabine had been a wild, unladylike, hoydenish child, but she had never had any ambitions beyond the securing, ultimately, of a good establishment where she would be able to indulge her favorite pastime of hunting. She had resisted the efforts of her father and priest to educate her so successfully that though she could read and write, she never exercised either power unless forced to, and her accomplishments were as few as her ambitions. She had no nonsense about her regarding romantic love: she had read too little to have absorbed such notions, while spending her time among animals and grooms had given her a thoroughly practical outlook on marriage. She was well contented with Crispian: he would give her the right number of horses and servants, and since she had grown up with him she had no fear of him, and enough affection.

As for Crispian, his feelings about the match were even more simple. He knew he must marry sometime, in order to have a son to whom to pass on his estate, but he was lazy and self-indulgent, his two chief vices, and to have a wife presented to him without his having to take any trouble over the matter was pleasant to him. She was a wife, moreover, whom he knew and already commanded—he would not have to get to know her, or take pains to please her. He liked Sabine well enough—as much as he liked most people, in fact, neither more or less. The only person in his life whom he had ever cared deeply for, the only person who had ever stirred him from his lethargy, had been Francis. For Frank he had marched through the depths of winter to join General Monk's forces, suffered blisters and chilblains and hunger and weariness, left his warm fireside and regular meals to follow an ideal. But Frank was dead, and nothing would ever again stir him thus. He smiled genially as he allowed Ralph to marry him to Sabine, and allowed Anne to arrange the wedding feast and teach his bride her new duties.

The other arrangements were made satisfactorily. On Frank's death the Tods Knowe estate had passed back into Ralph's hands, and would need either a tenant or a steward to run it. There was also the Emblehope estate that had come to Ralph through his first wife, Mary, which Francis had overseen for him; it was mostly moor and rough grazing, but it had a good, solid, stone-built house, the house in which Mary had grown up. Ralph decided to give the Emblehope estate to Sabine for her dowry, retaining the reversion of it and a rent-charge on its produce, and after talks with Crispian it was decided that the young couple would live at Emblehope, as the house was better than the one at Blindburn. Ralph would find a tenant for Tods Knowe, Crispian would find a steward for Blindburn, and he would oversee both estates in addition to running Emblehope.

"It will be much more pleasant at Emblehope," Sabine confided to Anne as they and Frances sat sewing in the last of the daylight, finishing off her wedding clothes. "The hunting is good here, but we are snowed in for so much of the time. The house is much bigger, too, and we'll have lots more neighbors to visit. Why, I'd be surprised if we didn't have visitors every day of the week!"

"It's close to the road, too," Anne said. "There will be no trouble in getting supplies, anything we want—the main road to Edinburgh passes only two miles from the house, so Crispian says."

Frances looked up and said sharply, "Crispian will be happy then—he will be able to get all the claret he wants."

"Of course, a bigger house will take more running," Anne said thoughtfully, and Sabine leaned across to pat her hand.

"But you'll manage. You could run ten houses, you're so clever." It was blatant flattery, but Anne was too pleased by the assumption that she would go with them to mind that. She did not doubt that Sabine would leave everything to her when it came to running the household, but the idea of all the visitors they would receive at Emblehope enchanted her. She still had not quite despaired of marrying. She and Sabine continued to chatter as they worked, looking forward to the new life that would open up to them, and Frances continued to work in silence. She had her own plans, though the time to reveal them was not yet right.

A fortnight after the wedding they all rode over to Tods Knowe, there to hold a memorial service for Francis, for the weather had been too bad at the time of his death to hold as grand a funeral as Ralph thought fitting. The ceremony was conducted in the little turf-roofed church which stood at the edge of the moor just above the cluster of buildings that made up the Tods

Knowe steading. The service was well attended, and afterward there was a banquet in the great hall, which was hung about with wreaths of bay and rosemary, black banners, and Frank's arms, the Morland achievement with his cadency mark, a martlet, in chief. When the feast was well underway, Ralph slipped out alone and walked back up the hill to the church.

The day had been sunny to begin with, but now the gray clouds had swept across, bringing an unseasonable darkness, and fine, penetrating rain was beginning to drift in, shrouding the tops of the hills around with mist. The little church stood in its small, ancient graveyard, divided from the moorland only by a dry-stone wall which had collapsed in places, letting the wild in. In one corner was a wild plum tree, twisted and bent with age and fierce weather, its black spiky limbs beginning to break into blossoms, and it was here that Ralph had buried his first wife, thirteen years ago.

The stone had settled now, and was beginning to moss; ferns were growing in the damp place between it and the wall, and ivy had come over the wall to embrace it. Ralph stared down at it, and thought, it seems so much a part of the place, that you would think it had been there forever. He tried to think of Mary, but he could not make her real in his mind; she was too far away. Five of her sons he had seen buried, too, and they did not seem real to him, either. Only his own grief he remembered. He stared away across the broken wall, across the soaking bracken to the wall of mist, the blankness that was the sky grown low. Somewhere near a sheep coughed, invisible in the murk; water dribbled along the black knotted spine of a branch and dripped onto his shoulder. He looked up, and saw with wonder how a blossom, white and tiny as a star, had broken from that dead-looking limb, fragile in the delicate rain. The enormous complexity of life depressed him. He did not know whether things happened to him as reward or punishment for his deeds, or whether events were random and without cause, and either possibility seemed equally frightening.

A shiver ran down his spine and he turned in terror to see a gray figure coming silently toward him out of the misty rain. All at once the rational man in him fled, and he was as superstitious as any peasant. His hair rose on his scalp and he made the horn sign against evil without a thought, for surely it was Mary's ghost come to haunt him, the nebulous figure of a woman in a gray cloak and hood, drifting over the wet grass without bending its stems. But the terror lasted only a moment, for as she came nearer he saw the raindrops clinging to the thick oiled wool, heard the hiss and rustle of her movement, and then she lifted her head and he saw within the hood the face of Frances.

"What are you doing here?" he said. "You will catch cold. Go back to the feast."

Frances stopped beside him and looked down at the grave, and as if she had been a party to his thoughts earlier, she said, "It looks so old, it's at peace with the ground. His is like a new wound." She nodded her head toward the open moor. "I wish someone had taken him away and buried him and not told us where. Then we should not see his grave grow more and more at one with the ground, taking him further from us, year after year, until he belongs there." She looked up to see if Ralph had understood. "As she does now—don't you feel it? She is not yours anymore."

"I was trying to remember what she looked like, but it won't come," Ralph said.

Frances nodded. "I shall not see it, at any rate. I shan't be here."

"Where are you going?" Ralph asked, more sharply than he meant to, for he was afraid she meant that she would kill herself. He had seen for himself how strange and withdrawn she was.

"I need your help—that's why I came to speak to you. *They* will try to stop me." She gestured towards the house where the rest of her family were gathered. "I want to go to France. I want to take orders."

"You want to become a nun?" he asked in astonishment. She did not seem to hear him. She was staring down at the grave again, seeming to forget it was not Frank's.

"He was never mine, not alive nor dead, but he was everything to me. While he lived, I could live, knowing I would see him from time to time. Now he is dead—no one has ever wanted me. I will give my heart to Jesus, if He will take it. It's no prize, but . . ."

She stopped for a long while, and Ralph searched around for things to say, something to comfort her, even to make contact with her. He could not begin to imagine what she was thinking. At last he said, "You loved Frank," and hoping to comfort her, he blundered on. "He was a fine person. Perhaps if he had lived—he never married after all. . ."

"He didn't want me," she said blankly. "It was *her* he wanted, always, ever since he met her in London. I knew, but it didn't make any difference. I couldn't have stopped loving him, just as he couldn't stop loving her. He never told her, of course. How could he? He would never have told anyone, but once when he was very low he broke down and told me." She lifted her face to Ralph's, and he saw the anguish of old hurt in her eyes. "He told me—he said—he said that she came between him and God; that when he tried to think of the Blessed Virgin, it was her face he saw."

"Who?" Ralph asked, but she did not hear him. She went on as if he had not spoken.

"He would have died for her, he told me so. And when she married you, he nearly did. But he had enough blasphemy on his soul already, and so he endured. And now he's dead. I would like to die, too, but I haven't deserved it yet. I must wait my time. You must help me—you do see that you must help me?"

"Yes," said Ralph slowly, his eyes wide and distant, "yes, I do see. I will help you."

She seemed satisfied with the answer, and turned and walked away, seeming to shrink rapidly into the growing murk. Ralph remained where he was for a long time, staring after her when she had long disappeared.

CHAPTER FIVE

Annunciata stood by the unlit fire in the steward's room, one elbow leaning against the chimney breast, one foot up on the end of the firedog, as she chewed a finger of her lavender gloves and tapped the side of her boot with her long-lashed crop. She was dressed for riding in one of her elegant habits of dark blue Morland broadcloth. Her hair was knotted up, falling in a long, thick tail of curls behind, and her much-feathered hat lay on the table at which Martin was sitting reading a letter. He read quickly, but when he had finished he turned the letter and read from the beginning again. Annunciata tapped her boot faster and eyed him with impatience.

"Well?" she asked, and when at last he lifted his eyes to her she said again, "Well?"

"My father has arrived at Birnie. He intends to stay there for some weeks, and then escort Cathy and Kit to Edinburgh, and stay there for a while."

"Is that all?" Annunciata raised an eyebrow. "So much paper and ink for so little to say?"

Martin smiled at her impatience. "Most of it is about their plans to rebuild Aberlady. Their fortunes have improved, Aunt Cathy says, and Kit will go to London in the autumn to try to borrow money. I suppose my father will return then, but she does not say so."

"Cathy, living in a castle," Annunciata mused, and then she laughed. "It does not seem possible. When I think of her—Ralph used to call her Caterpillar! I suppose Kit goes to London to try to get the Hamilton title granted him. Cathy would like that, to be Lady Hamilton! Does she mention such a plan?''

"No," Martin said gently, "just about the rebuilding of the house, and about the children: her son born in spring has died.''

"Ah!" Annunciata cried with quick sympathy. "And she has lately lost her firstborn, too—he must have been seven or eight. How terrible for her. But the twins are well, I hope?''

Martin glanced down at the pages. "She does not mention them, so I suppose they must be. Now, madam, what will you do today, may I ask?''

"You may not only ask, you may accompany me," Annunciata said, and as Martin gave a protesting glance at the table, littered with business he ought to attend to, for in his father's absence he had to run his father's estate, she caught his wrist and tugged it laughingly. "Come, now, Martin, you must! The day is too fine to be indoors, and you must learn to do business when it rains and pleasure when the sun shines, as I do. Why, I have an estate to run quite as large as yours, and you don't see me within on a glorious day like this, do you?''

"Where would you go?" Martin asked, amused. At sixteen he was a man, there being nothing boyish about him but his slender build. He reminded Annunciata a little of Frank, with his dark-haired, blue-eyed good looks and his weather-browned skin.

"I want to ride about and be seen, and harry people, and make a nuisance of myself, so that no one will be able to be unaware that the countess is at Morland Place. I want to go over to Micklelith and see John Moleclough about the carving on the staircase at Shawes, and to worry Ben about the dovecote—I'm sure he could have had it done by now.''

"It is a very large and elaborate one, you know," Martin reminded her gently.

"Five hundred holes is not so very large," Annunciata replied, whisking away the objection.

"But the shape, madam, is difficult—that dome, for instance. Master Wren may be a fine architect, but does he understand about pigeons?''

Annunciata's brows drew together as she prepared to defend the man whom, in common with the Royal Family, she had chosen to patronize as lavishly as possible, and then she realized that Martin was teasing her. She laughed and drew her hand through his arm and made him walk with her toward the door.

"Now I know you will come with me—you cannot refuse."

"I could refuse you nothing," he said gallantly.

She tapped his cheek with her forefinger and reproved him. "No court manners, sir, with me! I know that you have many good reasons for wanting to go yourself to Micklelith."

"But it's true," Martin said, opening the door for her and letting the spaniels out like a small furry flood. "Besides, my father left me in charge, and that means that I have to take care of you as well as of his estate."

Annunciata entered the passageway and relinked her hand to his arm. "It is strange," she said musingly, "how peaceful it seems without him here."

"Peaceful?" Martin queried. Annunciata glanced at him.

"I don't mean, of course, that your father disturbs the peace, but—I don't quite know how to express it. You manage everything so well, and the servants all seem in a good temper, and the children are quieter, and the beasts feed well and the sun shines." Martin was laughing now. "I know, I know, it sounds foolish, but Morland Place seems to fit you so well. I don't miss him at all."

"Oh, Mother!" Martin cried, shaking his head with mirth.

She gripped his arm sharply. "Don't call me Mother," she said. "I am not your mother."

His smile faded with slight surprise. "I'm sorry. Madam, then."

"Or my lady?" she suggested lightly, sorry to have spoken so shortly. He looked at her seriously for a moment.

"Yes, my lady is good. You are my lady, and I am your liege man, of life and limb."

They passed into the great hall, and Clem's grandson Clement was there, waiting at the great door, which was his station, to be called for duties or messages.

"Ah, Clement, will you have Goldeneye and Queen Mab saddled and brought to the door?" Martin said. "The mistress

and I will ride out to Micklelith. And send to ask Father St. Maur
if he has any messages for the school or the hospital—we will
ride that way back.''

It was some hours later that they rode back through the barbican into the courtyard, threading their way through the peacocks,
who were displaying themselves with ponderous magnificence to
their indifferent hens, and were far too engrossed, as well as too
unwieldy, to get out of the horses' way. One old, superseded
cock was sitting on top of the stable block, making the day
hideous with his shrieks, as if he hoped to spoil the romance
from which he was excluded.

''And we must have the races again at midsummer,'' Martin
was saying. ''Since my father is away, it will be for me to
organize it. Hugo can help.''

''Hugo? What use will he be?'' Annunciata asked in surprise.

''A great deal,'' Martin said firmly. It was not for him to
criticize his stepmother, but he hoped that he might gently awaken
her to his stepbrother's good qualities. ''He is very sensible, and
an able messenger, too. I hope he will ride Oryx in the races
again. He is such a good horseman.''

''It would be better if he paid more attention to his lessons,
and his manners,'' Annunciata said. ''I shall have great difficulty
in getting him a place at Court if he slouches and scowls all the
time. Now George—''

But as she halted Goldeneye at the mounting block where
Gideon was waiting to take her bridle, Clem came out from the
house holding a sealed envelope in his hand.

''Madam,'' he called, ''this came for you just after you had
left. It is an express, madam—''

''From Scotland?'' Annunciata asked abruptly, her hand going
nervously to her throat.

''No, madam, from London. With His Highness's seal.''

Martin had jumped down and handed Queen Mab to a boy,
and now he came to help Annunciata from the saddle, and to take
her gloves from her, as she pulled them off to open the flap of
the letter. He watched her face as she read it. She had not
anticipated bad news from that quarter, but as she read her

expression changed from one of contented pleasure to shock. She grew white, and her lip trembled, and she caught it between her teeth. She read the words several times, and then crumpled the heavy paper together between her two hands, carelessly.

"Madam, what is it? Not bad news, I hope?" Martin asked her.

She looked up slowly, as if coming back from a long way away, and did not seem at first to understand his words. Then she licked her lips and said, "No—no, not bad news," Yet she was clearly shocked. "Not bad news." she said again, and then collecting herself with a visible effort she said, "You must forgive me—I have need of quiet. I will walk a little in the rose garden."

Martin watched her go with consternation, and then his eye met that of Clem, and the two men exchanged agreement.

"I think," Martin said diffidently, "that one of her women ought to go with her. Where is Birch?"

"Mrs. Birch is over to Shawes, master," Clem said. His ready acceptance of Martin in Ralph's absence was indicative of the way the servants viewed the young man. "Miss Elizabeth is resting, but I could call her."

Martin thought for a moment. Whom should he send? And then the answer came clearly. Someone who could reach his stepmother, if she needed help. "Send Chloris to her. Tell her to be—"

"Discreet, master?"

"Subtle."

Chloris took some time to find her mistress, for Annunciata had retreated, like a wounded animal, into the shelter of one of the arbors, and the roses grew so thickly there that the arbor was almost sealed by trailing branches of white flowers. When Chloris found her she was sitting in the very center of the white marble bench, her hands in her lap still folded round the crumpled letter, her head bowed so that her face was hidden by the fall of her hair. Caspar and Charlemagne, already exhausted by their exercise, were sleeping in the grateful coolness of the rose-scented shade behind her.

She looked up when Chloris appeared, but took no other note of her. She had been crying, and Chloris hunkered down in front

of her mistress and drew her handkerchief from her sleeve and
dabbed away the tears in silence, knowing better than to speak.
Annunciata allowed the attention, and gradually became aware of
her maid. Chloris had grown handsome of late, she realized
dully. Good food and security and good converse had given her
the glow of a fit, well-groomed horse; her skin was pale and
clear, her eyes bright, her hair a mass of glossy red-gold curls.
Far too handsome for a nursery maid.

"Chloris," she said at last, and her voice sounded dazed.

"Yes, madam. Yes, my poor lady."

"Where's Birch?" Birch would understand. She could tell
Birch.

"You sent her over to Shawes," Chloris said gently. "Shall I
send for her?"

"No." No matter. She could not explain to Chloris. But then
the words seemed to burst from her. "I should have expected it,
but still it came as a shock. I knew all the time it might happen,
but I shut my mind to it."

Chloris's luminous blue eyes drew her on, limpid with sympathy.

"It _hurts_, Chloris. I know it's foolish—even impious—but it
hurts."

And Chloris, knowing from Clem that the mistress had had a
letter with Prince Rupert's seal, and knowing a little from Birch
and something from other servant's gossip, made one of those
leaps of understanding that gave her a reputation for having the
Sight.

"I know, my lady. But you knew it had to happen."

"You know? You know what is in this letter?" Annunciata
asked, still dazed.

"Madam Hughes has had a baby," Chloris said quietly.

Annunciata stared. "How did you know?"

"I can read it in your face, my lady. I just know, that's all."

"A girl," Annunciata said, looking down at her hands as if to
read the words there. "Born on June the ninth. They have called
her Ruperta." She looked up. "I don't know why I should care
so much, but—"

"It makes it all seem real, and it has never been real to you
before," Chloris said.

"You do understand," Annunciata said, catching Chloris's hand. "Do you think me wicked? But it's true, I never allowed it to be real in my mind. As if I could always turn the page back, and make the story come out right after all. And now—it's like losing him." She began to cry again, taking back her hand to press her fingers to her eyes to try to stop the tears.

Chloris stared at her in pity. "Cry, my lady," she said. "There's healing in tears."

Annunciata put her hands over her face in protest, and her voice was muffled. "I want my mother. I want Ellen," she cried. But her mother and her governess were both long dead, and she had turned away from Ralph. There was no one now who could make things right for her. She must suffer her pains alone. "I am being punished for my wickedness."

Knowing by instinct the time was right, Chloris went forward onto her knees and drew her mistress into her arms, and Annunciata yielded and sobbed on her maid's shoulders.

"Cry, mistress," Chloris whispered. "It's right to cry. It was none of it your fault, and you are the only loser by it. Cry, and then come in and make your peace with Our Lady. She always understands."

The white roses gave up their scent, powerful and sweet in the hot June air. Annunciata remembered the scent from the garden at Ballincrea House, the summer of the Great Plague, when she had dwelt with death.

"I shall always hate the smell of roses," she said after a long while. "Take me in, Chloris."

The year fattened and the harvest came and still Ralph did not come home. On looking back it seemed to everyone a strange but happy summer, full of long sunny days, rides and picnics and water pageants, fowling and hunting and balls in the evenings, and fireworks, and horse racing, and games of pall-mall on the Long Walk in the summer twilight with the swans motionless on the moat, kissing their own still reflections. For the children it was especially happy, for their mother, subdued, seemed gentler and more kindly than before. George, who was a sensitive child, worried that his mother sat and gazed at him so mournfully sometimes, but to Hugo the change was like a miracle. His mother no longer snapped at him or ignored him, and sometimes seemed even to approve of him, or be amused by him. He basked in the unexpected sunlight, and grew gentler himself, smiled more, scowled less, quarreled less with Arabella.

Arabella, though indifferent to her mother's approbation, enjoyed the freedom that summer that she had never had before, with the whole family being out of doors all day in pursuit of pleasure. Annunciata thought Arabella had a look of Ruth, Annunciata's mother, about her from time to time, something in her rather bony white face, and that stiff mane of reddish hair, and the thought made her less critical than usual of her unruly daughter.

She took time to play with her babies, too, and when she sat by the moatside or riverbank with Rupert and his companion Michael, and little Charles and Maurice playing near her, she often thought back to that sweet summer she had had at Hampton when the twins were only babies and George newborn. The last summer before she had fallen in love with Prince Rupert, changing her life forever. Edward had been alive then. Edward had saved her from committing the horrible sin, but not even Edward could change what was in her heart.

Letters continued to come from Ralph at intervals, saying little, dealing with one or two items of business and asking after the state of the harvest or Kingcup's swollen hock. He never wrote any private messages to Annunciata, and, unreasonably, it worried her. Did Cathy and Kit know about their quarrel and estrangement? She imagined Ralph discussing her with Kit, and the idea horrified her. And she became, in self-defense, convinced that he was staying on in Scotland for no good reason, that he had fallen in love with some young Scots lady from Edinburgh's high society and was having an affair with her. She tormented herself with the idea, without stopping to wonder why it should torment her.

Then suddenly in October he was home, without warning, riding in one closing afternoon, looking pale under his weather tan and thinner and older than before. He came in a hurry, having many orders but no smiles for anyone, and his first words were that he was to be off again on the day after next.

"I have heard of a horse," he said. "A gentleman in Edinburgh, who has many friends in far places, told me of a horse, a magnificent Barb stallion, on an estate in Genoa. He has arranged the sale for me. I go at once to bring it back."

"But must you yourself go?" Annunciata asked in astonishment. It was surely a servant's task. Ralph's eyes glittered strangely.

"I want to go," he said, and that was all. She did not understand, he thought: he must have this horse, and he could not entrust so fabulous a prize to any underling. The day of his presence at Morland Place seemed afterward unreal, and when he had gone the house seemed to settle down like leaves whirled up by a wind settling gently to earth, and the peace of the summer flowed on as if he had never been.

In November the Duke of York's new bride was brought to England amid some controversy, for she was a Roman Catholic Italian princess, a bad choice, many people thought, for an avowedly Roman Catholic heir to the throne.

"They say, my lady," Birch reported, "that she is so pious she was determined to become a nun, despite her rank, and that it was only with great difficulty that her father persuaded her to accept the marriage."

"They also say, my lady," Chloris said, mimicking Birch's style, "that her father is not her father and that she is the natural daughter of the Pope himself."

The two women were helping Annunciata sort through her gowns, and as always their presence together bred that faint rivalry for their mistress's attention.

"Well, no matter about that," Annunciata said imperturbably, "she is to be the new Duchess of York, and I have to go to London to pay my respects to her."

"Without the master, my lady?" Birch asked disapprovingly.

"Evidently, without the master," Annunciata said sharply. "It would be extremely discourteous not to present myself to the new duchess as soon as possible and since neither I nor anyone else has any idea where the master is . . ." She examined the dress that the women were holding up between them. "No. We'll have that one made over. The color is pretty: it will make a nightgown.

Birch, go see if I still have that pink scarf that was the same color.''

When Birch was out of the room, Chloris said, ''It would do no good, my lady, to say it will look strange for you to go without the master?''

Annunciata frowned, and then decided against anger. She needed to be able to confide in Chloris. ''None at all. You are right, of course, it is only an excuse to go. But that is my business, and it is your sad fate to have to keep such knowledge to yourself.''

''Aye, mistress. Like your quarrel with the master—that was only an excuse, too, wasn't it?''

''What do you mean?'' Annunciata was shocked, and turned fiercely on Chloris, who only shook her head sadly, unmoved.

''If it had not been that, it would have been something else. Come, mistress, you know it's true. And you know it's no use being angry with me, because you need me now.''

Annunciata stared at her, and then slowly nodded. ''Yes, yes, it's true. And I do need you. My clown—that's what Ralph called you.''

''Clowns may speak the truth when no one else dares. Will you take me to London, mistress? I'll serve you well.''

''What about your duties here?'' Annunciata said.

Chloris made a wry face. ''I've fed your babies, mistress, and I'm well satisfied. Three years of wet nursing, three years in milk—it's enough for anyone, wouldn't you say, mistress? I'd like to go to London and be your waiting woman and have a little fun into the bargain.''

Annunciata considered. ''You would make a handsome waiting woman,'' she agreed. ''And that would reflect well on me. It is time Maurice was weaned, I suppose.''

Chloris's face grew more tender, and she said softly, ''And after all, my lady, you won't be needing my services as wet nurse anymore, will you?''

Annunciata's eyes filled with tears, and she clenched her fists. Chloris thought she was only crying for the loss of her love for her husband, but the truth was evident a moment later when she whispered in a terrified voice, like a child afraid of demons in the dark, ''I don't wish him dead, I don't, I don't.''

Chloris, sorry for what she had stirred up, dropped the dress she was holding, and took her mistress's hands and gently unclenched them.

"There, my lady," she said. "Sin is all around us all the time. We only have to be careful it doesn't creep up on us. The master will be back by and by, when it pleases him. Menfolk do as they please, without consulting anyone."

The wedding of Princess Mary Beatrice d'Este to the Duke of York was carried out very quickly and quietly, the same night she arrived in England. There were riots in London all the same, and effigies of the Pope were carried through the streets and burned, and some of the city's leading Catholics had their windows smashed. The people thought Princess Mary was the Pope's daughter and was marrying their duke in order to lead England back to Rome. The King did not seem at all perturbed when Annunciata presented herself to him on arrival at Whitehall, but he revealed his anxiety when he said, "I have arranged for an apartment to be made free for you, madam, here in the palace. You will be safer so. Ballincrea House is not any easy place to guard."

"You think there is danger, sir?"

Charles shrugged. "A little, perhaps. I would sooner have all those dear to me safely under my eye, until the streets are quieter. It won't last long. London fires burn up brightly, and die down quickly."

So it was at Whitehall she lodged, and there was presented to the new duchess. Mary Beatrice was a strikingly beautiful young woman, tall, dark haired, and dark eyed, and just fifteen years old. Just as I was when I first came to Whitehall, Annunciata thought. And she wondered if this beautiful creature with the passionate eyes would stop the duke from philandering; and whether this young and vigorously healthy creature would give the duke the son he desired and the common people feared. Either way, Annunciata thought, there would be troubled times ahead. The duke's eldest daughter Mary would most likely be married to Prince William of Orange as soon as she was old enough, and if the Catholic duke and duchess had no Catholic son to take the throne, then Princess Mary and her Dutch husband would do so. She made her curtseys, and thought abruptly of Anne Hyde, who, though she had converted her husband in the first place, must have died knowing the difficulties that would bring in its train.

After the formal presentation, Annunciata was making her way back to her apartment to change for the supper party the King was giving for the new duchess, when a servant in the duke's livery overtook her and asked her to attend the duke at once in his audience chamber. The duke greeted her courteously, and Annunciata noticed that there was on his normal expressionless face a shade of something like embarrassment.

"I wondered, Countess, whether—that is, I suppose—you will have heard the news of your husband?"

Annunciata composed her face to gravity and said calmly, "I beg Your Grace's pardon, but I have had no news of my husband these many weeks."

"Ah, I see," the duke said, and took a turn up and down the room in order to be able to face her again and say, "The King said something of it—I hardly liked to assume—but, my dear madam, you will be happy to know that your husband took passage on one of the ships that accompanied my wife's vessel. It was, in fact, a horse transport." The duke's voice betrayed his embarrassment. "I understand that he is proceeding at once to Yorkshire, on account of the difficult nature of the beast he has been bringing home."

"He got the stallion, then, Your Grace?"

"So I believe. It was fortunate that the princess's flotilla was leaving at the time when your husband was seeking some means by which to get the beast back to England." A flicker of emotion passed through the duke's eyes. "I understand that the journey was a particularly difficult one, and that some parts of the ship have sustained a certain amount of damage. No one was hurt, however. I am glad to have been able to bring you good news."

Annunciata thanked him and left, and by the time she reached her apartments Chloris had received the news in more colorful form from other sources.

"The horse made the journey a nightmare, my lady," she told

Annunciata as she helped Birch undress her. "It acted like a demon from the moment it set its foot upon the quay, and the master had to sit up with it night and day, he couldn't leave it for a second. And the devil horse kicked the ship nearly to bits, and the Italian sailors fell to crossing themselves and praying, thinking it was some night thing sent to sink them. And then when they got to England and managed to land the animal, without killing anyone in the process, which was a miracle, the ship's captain presented a bill for the damage—to the duke himself! It seems the master's Italian was no better than the captain's English, and he thought the horse was for the princess. He said he wished the duke joy of a woman who could ride such a monster!"

Annunciata laughed, seeing now why the duke had been so embarrassed. But Birch broke in on the amusement with the observation that since the master had gone straight home to Morland Place, the mistress would presumably have to cut short her visit and follow him.

There was a silence, and the three women looked at each other. It was a turning point. Annunciata swallowed tensely and said, "I will stay. It would not be seemly to hurry away. I will write to the master and ask him to come back as soon as he has got the horse home. And in the meantime—I will stay."

Martin was so shocked at the sight of his father he could not speak. Ralph laid a hand on his shoulder and tried to smile.

"Be easy. It is mostly lack of sleep. I shall be well enough by and by, when I have bathed and eaten and rested. Where is your stepmother? I must show her the horse. I did it, Martin, I did it, though there were times—such a journey, dear God! But what a horse! Come, you shall come and see him. He is the most beautiful—but words are not enough. You must see him. Fire in his eyes and the south wind in his loins, and he shall sire such horses as will make our name famous throughout the world. Come, come and see."

He led his son toward the yard as he spoke, and Martin went meekly, seeing his father was half delirious with exhaustion. The horse was standing in the yard, with two grooms holding the ropes on either side of him, and though he was almost as tired as the man who had brought him here, he trembled and shook with rage and fear, ready at any moment to rear up and strike out if offense were offered him. His ears flickered back and forth, his nostrils strained to understand the strange air about him, his eyes rolled whitely, seeking danger. Ralph walked straight up to him, holding out his hands, and the horse bared his teeth and laid back his ears, and then stood quietly, surveying his new master. And despite all his other worries, Martin stopped still and gazed on a horse whose equal he had never seen. The power of the crest and loins, the depth of heart, the great swelling quarters, together with the delicacy of the head, the fineness of the legs, made a combination of strength and beauty that moved him so deeply he almost wanted to cry. Ralph was speaking, a slow crooning like an incantation as he stroked the wet neck of the great horse.

"As black as night, as fast as the wind, as strong as the sea, oh, you will father horses so swift and light they will seem like lightning bolts let loose. Sha, sha, my black one, my beautiful. I have no stable fit for you, but I will house you as best I can, until I build you a palace. Come, then, come, then."

"Father," Martin said at last, "will you not leave Gideon to bed him down, and come in? I am afraid for you, you are so worn."

"I shall call him Barbary," Ralph said, still stroking the stallion as if he had not heard. "There is no name good enough for him, so I shall call him only what he is."

Martin could not get him in: he insisted on bedding down the horse himself, and staying with him while he ate the feed that Ralph had prepared with his own hands, and even then, when the horse had eaten and was at last beginning to look sleepy, Ralph stayed, talking half to the horse and half to Martin. Then at last he asked again the question, "Where is your stepmother? Why does she not come?"

There was no help for it, Martin knew. He looked at his father steadily. "She is not here, Father. She is in London. At Whitehall."

"Without me?" Ralph whispered.

He stared at the horse, not at Martin, and at last the boy reached out to touch his arm and say, "Father, please come in."

"Without me," Ralph said again, and he shook his head as if

to clear it. Then he looked at Martin, and the boy drew back his hand, pushed away by the gravity of his father's face. "Go in, Martin," Ralph said quietly. "See that no one disturbs me."

"Father—"

"I will be in, by and by. Go in, I say."

The horse was dozing, fitfully, waking every few seconds in its nervousness, still looking for danger, still in its mind tormented by the terrible noises and movements of the boat.

Ralph pressed his face against the sweet horse-smelling neck and remembered Frank's reported words: "She came between me and God." Ralph also had made her the daystar of his life. "Now you will have to be my pride," he said into Barbary's mane, and then he began to cry.

CHAPTER SIX

Ralph's reply to Annunciata's letter was carefully worded, but left no room for misunderstanding.

"My dear wife," it said, "it is indeed unfortunate that I did not know of your presence at Whitehall at the time of His Highness's wedding. However, there being so many matters requiring my attention here I find it impossible to come to you at present. You have with you enough attendants, and I am not at all afraid for your safety on the journey home, but as the Christmas season approaches I would urge you to make haste to set out."

The letter arrived just as Annunciata was about to leave for the theater at Drury Lane, at which the King would also be present, and so she had thrust it into her muff and read it in the coach. She read it with a furious frown, and when she had finished she thrust it back into her muff with an angry exclamation. "And to think I paid threepence for that!"

Birch and Chloris exchanged a glance and forebore to comment, and Annunciata stared out of the window for the rest of the journey to avoid their gaze. She brightened a little at her arrival at the theater, for her coach was fairly new still, and though the horses were hired, they were good. Her two footmen walking before to clear the way and her coachman and boy were all dressed in livery, and when she stepped down from the coach she was attended by a lady's maid—Birch in her expensive, plain garb—to lift her train, and one of the prettiest waiting women—Chloris in an old gown of Annunciata's made over—to carry her dogs. The crowd lounging outside the theater to see the gentry arrive cheered her sufficiently, and two barefoot boys fought briefly and silently for the right to lay their meager bodies over the rear coach-wheel in order to protect her garments from brushing against the muddy surface.

The play had already started—it was fashionable to be late— and Annunciata's progress was so slow that she was still on the stairs when the King arrived, and so could be invited to share his box.

"All alone today, sir?" Annunciata said with pretended amazement as she took his arm happily up the stairs.

Charles smiled with pleasant malice. "Barbara and Fubbs have two fine colds in the head, so today I may please myself. Whatever one has, the other must have, of course."

"So that's why you gave Madame Kerwell her duchy?" Annunciata said innocently. Louise de Kéroualle had just been made Duchess of Portsmouth—Barbara Palmer had been Duchess of Cleveland for three years and had tormented Madame Kerwell with the fact.

"Of course," Charles said. "Otherwise I should have had no peace."

"You resisted the idea for long enough," Annunciata remarked.

"Because it amused me to see Barbara pursuing poor Fubbs from room to room making her change chairs. Our Court etiquette is such nonsense, but after all it keeps us amused. But people were beginning to say I slighted her, and that would not do, especially since she has lost her figure in the service of her King." Kerwell had never regained her figure after bearing the King a son, and it was since she grew fatter every month the King had begun to call her Fubbs.

"Your Majesty is tender toward women's reputations," Annunciata murmured wickedly as they reached the box door and Charles had to let go of her arm to walk in ahead of her.

He acknowledged the cheers of the audience, waved the actors on with their play, pulled a chair close beside him for Annunciata, and when they were settled he propped his chin on his hand negligently and said, "The reputation of those near me concerns me. You are beginning to be talked about, my dear."

Tears prickled Annunciata's eyes. "I wrote to him, sir, asking him to join me, and he refused and ordered me home. His letter came just as I was setting out today. She pulled it from her muff and handed it to the King, and he read it gravely and passed it back to her.

"What will you do, then?" he asked gently. "You will go back to Yorkshire?"

"No," she said, lifting her head defiantly. "Let him come to me—I will not go to him like—like—"

"Like a dutiful wife?" Charles suggested.

Annunciata looked angry. "Why is duty to be all on the wife's side? All summer long he left me alone, and went off in a ship to Genoa on some mad freak so that I did not even know if he was alive or dead. Where was the dutiful husband? It was his fault that I had to come to London alone, and his fault that there is so much business to attend to now."

The King looked sad. "It is the way of things," he said. "It may be unfair, but a wife has a reputation to lose and a husband has not. My dear, let me beg you to go home. There is already talk about you."

"They have talked about me before, sir," Annunciata said lightly, but her face was strained.

"What they said before was not true," the King reminded her. "And it was only the uninformed who talked. Now there is beginning to be scandal at Whitehall."

"At Whitehall! Who can shock Whitehall?" Annunciata laughed tightly.

The King took her hand, "I know, I know. At my Court husbands and wives may be openly unfaithful to each other, and no one thinks the worse of them. But my dear, even at Whitehall husbands and wives may not live apart from each other."

"What of the Duchess of Cleveland?" Annunciata said.

"Barbara is a little different," Charles said, "but even she does not live officially apart from her husband. Their home is at Whitehall, and Roger has to spend a lot of time away on business."

But Annunciata was adamant. "I will not go back," she said, sticking out her lip like a defiant child. "I will not crawl back like a whipped dog to a husband who so little regards his own duty.''

The King sighed, and they watched the play for a while in silence. Then he said, ''Well, if you will not go, I suppose I must do something about it.'' She looked at him inquiringly, and he smiled suddenly, his teeth white beneath his dark moustache. ''You said I was tender of women's reputations, and I must be doubly so when it is a member of the family. I seem to remember I had to rescue your name once before, little cousin, so it will not be without precedent if I do it again.''

Annunciata stared at him gratefully. ''I was never entirely sure if you knew,'' she said.

''I won't tell you what the Whitehall Whisperers are saying,'' he said. ''You'll find that out soon enough.''

The King was indolent, but when he decided to do something he did not delay. Within days the official letter had gone out appointing the Countess Dowager of Chelmsford Lady of the Bedchamber to the Queen, and allotting her quarters at Whitehall, thereby giving her an excuse not to go back to Yorkshire. Annunciata wrote back to Ralph, couching her refusal to return in less defiant words, and settled down to enjoy herself. Christmas was always the most riotous of the year's holidays, and at Whitehall it was a feverish round of gaiety that prevented her from once thinking of Morland Place, Ralph, her children, or her duty. At New Year when gifts were formally exchanged with the King, she gave him one of the curiosities that her first husband Hugo had collected. It was a gold statuette from Persia of a naked boy holding a wine jar on his shoulder. When the wine jar was filled with wine it passed through conduits inside the hollow statue and trickled out through the boy's penis, and the idea was that the recipient was expected to catch the wine in a cup and keep draining it without losing any. It caused great comment and amusement, and several of the court gallants drank themselves insensible trying to beat the statue.

The King's gift to Annunciata caused even more comment, not because it was curious, but because of its value. He gave her a diamond collar, said to be worth more than a thousand pounds, and it gave rise at once to the old rumors that she was his mistress. However, none but the real outsider could believe that for long, and soon both Court and town settled down to another old idea, that she was in fact the most youthful of all his youthful indiscretions. The King was only fourteen when Annunciata was conceived, but no one any longer put it beyond him, and neither he nor Annunciata made any attempt to kill the story. It conveniently explained his enigmatic relationship with her, and gave her a good reason for being at Court, even without her husband. In February the peace with the Dutch was finally signed at Westminster and Parliament was dismissed, and the King made Sir Thomas Osborne his Lord Treasurer, and created him Earl of Danby. Osborne was a Yorkshireman and a family friend of the Morlands, and some of the Whisperers determined that it was done as a compliment to Annunciata, for no better reason than, at the same time as ennobling Osborne, the King granted Annunciata certain revenues from the port of Hull. To the gossips it confirmed for good that Annunciata was the King's natural daughter, and her presence at Court was thus so well explained that it was quite forgotten she had come there without her husband and refused his request to go home. Once again the King had saved her.

Hugo had enjoyed Christmas at Morland Place more than any he remembered. At Martin's instigation Ralph had named Hugo Lord of Misrule for the twelve days, which meant that everyone had to obey him, whatever he told them to do, and he and Martin had a great deal of fun thinking out absurd orders. He was also master of ceremonies in all the games and festivites. Martin and George between them wrote a masque with music, and Hugo had the direction of it, which pleased him so much he even accepted it as reasonable that George should have the principal part. There was all the traditional feasting—the boar's head, the gilded peacock, the plum porridge, the mincemeat pies—with the poor at the gates coming in every day for the open table, and tenants and villagers bringing seasonal gifts for the master and staying for good ale and good fare.

There were mummers and jugglers and traveling players and

carol singers forever at the door, and they, too, were brought in to the great hall, made festive with boughs of bay and rosemary and holly and ivy, to entertain the gentry. There was singing and dancing every night. At the Boxing Day hunt Hugo was in at the kill and Ralph awarded him the antlers, and when the Twelfth Day Cake was cut, Hugo got the King's token and Daisy got the Queen's token, and he got to kiss her, which he did with a flourish that made everyone laugh. For the whole season everyone was kind to him and no one slighted or despised him, and he was gloriously happy. His one regret was that his mother was not there to see what a fine and popular person he was.

He was aware, all the same, that everything was not right. His mother's absence did not surprise him, for to him she was a goddess and her actions were therefore beyond question, but he was aware on the periphery of his senses of a certain constraint among some of the servants. His stepfather, too, was not entirely happy. Hugo thought he had a tucked-up look, the way a sick horse has sometimes, a cautiousness about his movements as if to move freely might jog some pain into sharpness. He thought Martin probably knew what it was all about, partly because he thought Martin knew everything, and partly because of the way Martin watched his father sometimes, with a sad and knowing look. But he did not associate any of this with his mother's absence. He only hoped that she would come back with the good weather, like a swallow, so that he could enjoy another summer like the last one.

Hugo's reading of his stepfather's condition was surprisingly accurate: Ralph was too shocked to know how unhappy he was. He had not expected for a moment that Annunciata would refuse to come home—how could he? When her letter came he read it over and over again, thinking he must have misunderstood it, and when he was sure he had understood it he was still certain she would come for the Christmas season. Not to come would be monstrous, for it was the time when the whole world was at Morland Place—at least, the whole of the world that was important to Ralph. All their friends and neighbors, all the important people from York's society, their tenants, the villagers, their dependents, everyone right down to the destitute women from St.

Edward's Hospital, all flocked to Morland Place at Christmas to pay their respects and share the season's pleasures. For the mistress not to be there was monstrous.

But she did not come, and Ralph had to face his world's surprise and, he imagined, censure. Annunciata's appointment as Lady of the Bedchamber to the Queen gave him at least something to say in reply to the inevitable inquiry, but it did not stop people shaking their heads doubtfully or whispering when they thought he could not hear. Had he been able to make the excuse boldly they might not have thought so much about it, but his bewildered look gave the truth away.

Martin stepped into the breach as he had done before, and in the subtlest way he made all the arrangements, gave the servants their orders, organized the festivities, and entertained the guests, while managing to appear to be doing no more than following his father's directions. His sympathy, he knew, would have been offensive to his father, and so he hid it and did his best for Ralph by pretending that nothing was amiss. It was left to another member of the family to provide comfort.

It happened on Boxing Night, the Feast of St. Stephen. There had been the traditional hunt in the morning, the huge and lavish dinner, the masque in the afternoon, and dancing before supper, and when everyone had retired to bed Ralph had called Clem to bring him a jug of mulled claret to the steward's room. Clem had done so, finding his master sitting by the fireside, chin in hand, brooding. With a sad shrug, Clem put down the jug and glass, made up the fire, let in Bran and Fern, who were whining at the door, and with a quiet good-night left his master to the best comfort he could offer. Ralph sipped slowly at the claret and watched the leaping flames and brooded darkly over the past year. This day was baby Maurice's first birthday—his health had been drunk at dinner, and the health of the child's sponsors, in whose company, Ralph supposed, Annunciata was enjoying *her* Christmas festivities.

A year ago, he thought, she was upstairs in my bed, giving birth to my son. The candles burnt out, but the fire spat and crackled, giving as much light as Ralph wanted. The dogs fell asleep, and snored, and dreamed, paddling their paws after dream rabbits. The claret went down, and he stirred himself enough to go across the hall to the buttery, where he discovered that Clem had thoughtfully left another bottle easily to hand, the cork drawn and replaced lightly. Clutching his booty, Ralph shuffled back across the icy hall to the snugness of the steward's room, filled his glass again, and set the bottle on the hearth to warm.

The tap upon the door was so light that he did not notice it, but at the second knock Bran woke and lifted his head to look toward the door.

"What is it, old fellow?" Ralph asked the dog, and the door opened hesitantly. "Who's there?" Ralph said sharply. "I don't want to be disturbed."

The door opened fully, and there stood Elizabeth with a cloak over her bedgown and wrap, looking confused.

"I'm sorry—I thought you said to come in," she said.

"I was speaking to the dog," Ralph growled. "I didn't hear you knock."

"I'm sorry," Elizabeth said humbly, and was beginning to withdraw.

Ralph was suddenly and sharply aware of his loneliness, and he said, "Don't go. Now you're here, come in. Come to the fire— you must be frozen." He knew how cold it was out in the hall. She looked at him doubtfully, and then as he said, "Close the door—the draught is icy," she seemed to make up her mind, and came in, closing the door behind her, and drew nearer the fire. "What are you doing up at this hour?" Ralph asked. He was aware suddenly of how drunk he was, but his voice sounded amazingly clear and lucid, though very far away.

"I couldn't sleep," Elizabeth said, holding out her hands to the fire. Ralph stared at them, and thought how fine they were, thin little starfish hands, the firelight shining through them in a delicate nimbus, showing the shadows of the bones. "I came downstairs to get something to make me sleep and I saw the light under the door, so I came to see who it was." Ralph accepted this, though he knew it was a lie. It was impossible to see the door of the steward's room until you turned into the passage, and the passage led nowhere but the steward's room and the chapel. He didn't mind why she had come here—he was simply glad she had.

"You had better have some wine. Here, sit here, and put your feet in the fender. Come on, dogs, move yourselves." He thrust the dogs, groaning, aside, and pulled a chair to the fireside and sat Elizabeth in it, and poured her some wine into his glass. "Take it," he said, and seeing her hesitation, added, "It's all right—I'll drink from the bottle. Come, it will make you sleep."

He fussed over her, enjoying the sensation—it was long since Annunciata had allowed him to fuss over her. She sipped her wine in silence, and he saw the flush of warmth return to her cheeks—or was it a flush of shyness? She kept her eyes modestly down as she sipped, and there was something unprepared about her mouth. Ralph returned to his seat, and drank some more wine, and observed her in agreeable silence. In his way he had always been kind to her, but he was aware that he had never really noticed her much. She was the daughter of his youngest aunt, who had married a young squire from Essex, one Charles Hobart, who had had the misfortune to be on the wrong side during the war. She had been brought up at Morland Place from childhood, and hers had been the lonely fate of the poor female relative—to be slighted by the servants and treated as an upper servant by the family.

Elizabeth had always thought too lowly of her deserts to be offended by her treatment, but there had been times, long ago, that Ralph had noted how Annunciata as a young girl had used Elizabeth as a foil, a dark background against which to scintillate. And yet, he thought, looking at her now, she was so pretty in her own right that a little animation would make her quite beautiful. She had a delicate face, round and sweet with a pointed chin, large dark eyes, and a gentle, shy mouth, and her brown hair was thick and curling, and, just now, pleasantly disarrayed. She was a few years younger than Annunciata—he screwed up his brow and worked it out—just twenty-four, and for ten years she had performed vital functions within his household, first as governess to his children, and latterly as housekeeper to Morland Place. In her quiet way she had done much to hold things together; yet she ought to have been married and had a household of her own. The wine, warm in his blood, loosened restraints in Ralph, and he said abruptly, "Elizabeth, do you ever feel you have been wronged?"

She glanced up, startled. "What do you mean?"

He found it hard to put into words, and said at last, "You must have wanted to be married?"

"I never thought about it," she said quietly before turning away. "I never saw anyone that I wanted to marry among those who would be eligible."

"Who?" Ralph asked, puzzled. "I mean, who was eligible?"

She pasued for a moment, and said, "I had no dowry, you see. So no one I might have wanted would have taken me."

He was not sure what she meant. Had she seen someone she wanted, someone who would have taken her had she *had* a dowry? Or did she feel ineligible in some other way? He did not feel able to ask. Instead he said, "I ought to have taken better care of you."

Now she looked up at last. Her eyebrows lifted in surprise, and he found himself notcing what delicate, fine cyebrows she had, as if they had been painted by the finest brush and the steadiest hand. "You?" she said. "You have always been so kind to me. Did you think I was ungrateful?"

The question confused him. He picked up the bottle and drank a great deal of claret in the hope that it would clear his mind, or at least free his tongue again. Elizabeth continued to gaze at him, and her hands, folded in her lap around her glass, seemed to him the essence of repose.

He said after a long pause, "But then, you must have felt she was unkind to you. She never—she always—she secmed to see you as a—*convenience*."

Elizabeth seemed to know who *she* was. She tilted her head a little, as if thinking about it, as if eager to be scrupulously fair. "If she wronged me," she said at last, "it was not in that way. In fact, it was not in any way she could have known about, or meant to be. No, she was not unkind. It is just the way things are."

And she drank from her glass, and seemed about to end the interview. But Ralph did not want her to go. All sorts of ideas were breeding in the wine-warmth of his brain. Without the least justification he suddenly felt a party to her thoughts and feelings. He set the bottle down and stood up, and took a step toward her.

"I'll make it up to you," he heard himself promising, and he was surprised at how urgent his voice sounded. "I'll do anything I can. . . ."

She stood up, too. She was small, much smaller than Annunciata, and her shoulder fitted neatly under his armpit, taking his weight as if she had been built specifically for that. She turned with him to the door, and he went, leaning on her, rubbing his cheek against the soft nest of curls on the top of her head.

"You have the most downy hair, you know," he said conversationally. "*Hers* is like a horse's mane—you could comb sparks out of it."

"Hush," she said. "Don't make a noise."

His brain was divided quite astonishingly in two, one half drunk and babbling, the other half as clear as a frosty night. It was as if he was standing back and watching himself as he turned her firmly away from the staircase hall and toward the privacy of the old spiral stairs that led directly to the dressing room of the great bedchamber. In the dressing room he detached himself from her shoulder, turned to face her in the dark, drew her against him, and kissed her. She came with only a slight hesitation, and when he found her lips they were warm and soft and ready. He kissed her for a long time, and then rubbed his mouth and cheek all over her face and hair, sighing contentedly.

"You should have been married," he said. "Mam used to say that all sin could be defined as waste."

She did not speak, but stood, not precisely passive, but unmoving in the circle of his arms, and he could feel the light rapid movement of her breathing stirring her breasts against him. Keeping his arm about her shoulders he led her into the bedchamber, and they made the short journey like old friends. He put her into the bed, and undressed himself quickly, afraid she would slip out of the other side and disappear before he could get in, but she was still there, warm and soft, when he got in between the sheets and pulled the curtains round. He took her in his arms again and snuggled down with her, tucking her in against his body and resting his chin on the top of her head. It was a long time, more than a year, since he had had sexual intercourse, and yet he felt more friendly than aroused.

Gradually Elizabeth relaxed, and it was then that his body began to stir. As far as he knew she was a virgin, and the clear part of his mind told him that nothing more than had happened already was permissible. But when he took her small starfish hand and guided it, she did not flinch. He kissed her again, thoroughly, and then she said quietly in the darkness, ''Whatever happens—I trust you.''

''Yes, I know,'' he said. He had never felt such huge, overwhelming kindness for anyone.

''What if—what if I should—'' She was having trouble with this sentence.

''It will be all right,'' he said. He felt sleepy now, but his hard organ lay in her hand like the gift of a puppy, that demanded as much care from the recipient as the donor. He moved across her, feeling her following his movement like someone learning a new skill. She knew nothing, of course—he would have to teach her everything. Annunciata had been many men's before him, and never entirely his, but Elizabeth—desire stirred in him. Elizabeth had been no man's before. Elizabeth would be his alone.

''I'll take care of you,'' he said. ''I promise—always, always.''

And beneath him, trusting as a friend, she said, ''Yes.''

The letter was grubby and dog-eared, but no more so than the squint-eyed vagabond who brought it to him. Ralph opened it gingerly, and with some difficulty since the frosty air had numbed his fingers. He was out by the north field's shippon supervising the early lambing, and the man had sidled up to him like a thief and handed him the letter without looking at him—although in justice Ralph had to admit that his squint was so villainous it would be hard to tell when he actually *was* looking at him.

''She will be at Newmarket for race week, at the King's Head, with PR and no other,'' the note said cryptically and in a disguised hand. Ralph read it and crumpled it up and then addressed himself to the squinting man.

"How much did she tell you I'd give you for this?"

"A shilling," said the man indifferently, and then added, "it's a long way, and terrible cold."

But Ralph knew his correspondent. "Nonsense. Why, it's only threepence by His Majesty's mails."

"His Majesty's mails get robbed," the messenger said, and spat on the ground to show his independence.

"She said sixpence, or I'm a Dutchman," Ralph said. The man shrugged and tilted his face to the sky as if testing for rain. "Ah, well, I suppose good news is worth paying for. Here's your shilling."

The man took it, inspected it, and put it away in some recess of his multifoliate clothing. "I pass back that way," he said. "If I should see her, would you send her word?"

It was a concession to truth. Ralph repressed a smile and said, "If you see her, tell her I'll be there."

"Aye," said the man, and strode away. Ralph watched him and then returned to his work, his heart lighter. Race week at Newmarket! It was essential that he and Annunciata should meet and talk, but they were both proud. He would not go to Whitehall and she was too proud to come home. Newmarket was the ideal compromise—no one could doubt his interest in horse racing, he who held races every summer at York, who had traveled half across the world to bring back a Barbary stallion to improve his own stock. And she would be there with Prince Rupert—that was good. Rumor had told him more about her than her letters had these months past, but rumor was unreliable. Much of it said she was the King's mistress, which, he imagined, probably meant she was some other man's mistress. Though the King had, indeed, awarded her an income and an apartment close to his own. If he had lost her to the King he had lost her indeed. He wondered what rumor had told her about him. He and Elizabeth had been scrupulously discreet, but servants had mysterious ways of finding things out, and he doubted not that some of them had traced his new contentment to its source.

Race week was in March. He would go quietly, without ceremony, and find her, and talk to her. He told himself he did not care, for his own sake, whether she came back or not, but

there was the family to consider, the children, reputation. Some
arrangement must be reached; some concession to respectability
made. But he was not telling himself the whole truth. As the time
came nearer for his departure to the South, he found himself
trembling with anticipation. She was the love of his life, and the
gentle contentment he had been finding with Elizabeth was no
more like his feeling for Annunciata than a candle was like the
sun. In the darkness of night a candle is a good, a blessed thing
to have; but no man can help longing for daybreak.

King Charles had made horse racing popular, and horse racing
had made Newmarket popular. Race week was one long round of
gaiety, and the little village seethed with excitement. Every inn
and lodging was packed, and the streets thronged with fine ladies
and gentlemen, their servants, and those who provided the where-
withal of pleasure. Horses were everywhere, and the smell and
sound of them filled the days as music and the sounds of dancing
and merrymaking filled the nights. Tradesmen of every sort
gravitated towards the town like wasps around spilled jam—
saddlers, chandlers, lorimers, farriers, and smiths came because
the horses came, along with grooms looking for a position and
bright-eyed younger sons of good family hoping someone would
pay them to ride their horse in a race.

Peddlers and chapmen, hatters, lacemakers, mantuamakers,
tailors, cobblers, hairdressers and barber-surgeons came to attend
to the world of fashion, together with maids and footmen out of
work, and the shadowy underworld of rooks, sharpers, coney-
catchers, thieves, pickpockets, whores, and pimps who were as
inevitable as lice in a wig. And because all the rest came, the
village filled with vendors of food and drink, and cookshops,
stalls and cookpits were set up on the fringes of the village to
compete with the taverns and inns.

Annunciata loved it all. She adored the noise and crowd and
excitement, the feasting and dancing; she loved to appear daily in
the grandstand between the King and Prince Rupert, and to
advise them which horses to lay their wagers on. She loved the
horses and the excitement of the races, and, having a good eye
for horseflesh and some experience, she was able to place her

own wagers so successfully that both the King and Prince were in her debt before the week was half gone. The King had come informally, which meant the Queen was not with him, nor any of his mistresses, and she loved the consequence of being the only woman close to him. And especially she loved being with Rupert, with no competition from Peg Hughes. At the balls and assemblies they attended, her hand was sought by every gallant, but she danced mostly with the prince. Sometimes as they moved up the set they would talk about horses or dogs or some other uncontroversial subject, but mostly they remained in a happy silence, their hands touching, smiling when their eyes met.

Annunciata noticed that Chloris had an air of suppressed excitement about her, but she was too preoccupied to pay it much attention, and allowed herself to assume Chloris was promoting an affair for herself from among the young captains-about-the-town. But on the fourth day, when Annunciata was lounging in bed late and wondering what to eat for her breakfast and what to wear for her dinner, the door was flung open more vigorously than etiquette suggested and Chloris stood there, looking red-faced and excited, and said, ''A visitor for you, my lady.''

Annunciata frowned. ''So early? Who is it? I can't see anyone,'' she began, but Chloris had already stepped back from the door, and ushered the visitor in. Annunciata had barely time for a gasp of outrage, when the visitor took off his hat and came forward into the light from the window and said, ''You can spare me a little time, I hope.''

Annunciata did not speak for a moment, but her heart fluttered in an uncomfortable way beneath her breastbone, and in that moment's pause Chloris withdrew and closed the door. I'll make her smart for this, Annunciata thought, but in a calm, almost a languid voice she said, ''Of course, Ralph. As much time as you wish. Come and sit down. Can I send for some refreshment for you?''

''Nothing, thank you,'' Ralph said. ''I'm sorry to call on you so early, but I wanted to be sure of catching you in. You have such a full life.''

They were like polite strangers, she thought. He came across to her, and for a moment she thought he would stoop and kiss her, but

he sat on the chair nearest the bedhead and undid the lace of his
cloak and flung it back from his shoulders. Annunciata watched
him, and she was trembling inside. He had brought with him the
smell of outdoors and the smell of horses. He was wearing boots,
and they were mudsplashed, so she guessed he had just ridden in.
His clothes were fashionable, but not overdecked, and they em-
phasized his strong, outdoor body, so different from the pale,
limp bodies of the town gallants, who were like the grass that
grows under floorboards. His fingers were strong and capable as
they tugged at his cloakstrings. He was so real, and too bright,
like strong sunlight to unaccustomed eyes. She tried to look at his
face, but her eyes shied away. He was forty-three years old, the
same age as the King, but she had never before thought of him
that way. Suddenly he was grown-up, and real, and she was a
child, and at play. She felt small and powerless. She felt as if he
had discovered her at some prank, and had come to take her
home and punish her. Real life was back there at Morland Place:
the rest was but a toy.

For a long time there was silence, and Ralph looked at her
while she looked at his hands. Then he said in a voice that was
quiet, and kind, but firm, "Annunciata, we cannot go on like
this."

Her face burned, only partly with anger. "Have you come here
to lay the blame on me?"

"I have come here to make peace with you," he said. "I have
come here to ask you for your terms."

Now she looked at him. "It's over between us, Ralph. Don't
you realize that? After your behavior last year—"

He looked at her with blank incomprehension. "What did I
do?" he asked. It had been like that with Hugo, she remembered,
her husband Hugo whose memory she now hated as much as she
had once loved him.

"Don't make me hate you," she said, as if he had heard her
thought. He still looked uncomprehending.

"I don't want to," he said. "I never wanted that. I don't know
why there is this coldness between us."

"No, you don't, do you?" Annunciata said, and she laughed
harshly. "I suppose you think you are being more generous than

I could expect. I should thank you for being such a kind, thoughtful husband, and beg your pardon, and come home with you to endure my disgrace. That's what you expected when you came here, wasn't it?''

Ralph did not attempt to answer any of this, knowing it was impossible. Instead he said, ''There is talk, and there is scandal. It isn't good for the family name, or for the children. All I want is some compromise with you, for the sake of the family. I don't want to talk about blame, or what is past. There is the future to think of.''

Now she sat up straighter and stared at him penetratingly. ''There's something about you,'' she said, scanning his face, ''something different. You've got a woman, haven't you?'' Ralph made no answer, but his face grew stern. Annunciata said, ''Yes, that's it. You've taken someone else to warm your bed. That's why you are suddenly so generous. You want me back for propriety's sake, to give my seal of approval to your amour.''

''The children wonder why you do not come home,'' he said calmly. ''And there is Shawes to run—it needs your attention.''

Shawes! Homesickness suddenly tightened her throat. In a small voice she asked, ''Did they finish my dovecote?''

''Yes,'' Ralph said. ''And the staircase at Shawes. You were going to rebuild the old house, remember. Come home for that, if for nothing else.''

She turned her head away, sad sickness filling her heart.

''No. I shan't rebuild Shawes. That's finished, too. Let it rot. But I'll come home in the summer.'' She looked at him quickly to catch his look of triumph, but he looked only unremittingly grave, even sad. ''I always meant to—I was never intending to stay away for good. It's my home, too, you know. I'll spend the winter Season at Whitehall and come home every summer.''

''Thank you,'' Ralph said.

''And you?'' she asked harshly. ''Will you extend the cloak of your protection to me in return? Will you come to Whitehall?''

''Sometimes. If you want me to.''

They stared at each other, both secretly aghast at the gulf between them. Yet there seemed no way of crossing it.

"Thank you," Annunciata said quietly. Then, with difficulty, "I hope she makes you happy."

"Happy?" he said. "No, I can't expect that. It helps a little, that's all." He stood up to go, and then looked down at her and said hesitantly, "Annunciata, if you want to—if you want to take a lover—I shan't blame you."

There was a short silence. You should not have said that, she said in her heart, and she thought that perhaps he knew it, too. Some words break things beyond mending. He longed to throw aside this restraint and take her in his arms, break down the barriers she had put up against him, and take her in a flood tide of passion. But that, too, would be unforgivable. He did not understand it in her, that pride, but it was like a man's. She must give freely, of her own will—to take from her was to steal her substance, and she could not endure it. He remembered the moment, long ago, beside the river, when she had come to his arms and rested her head trustingly on his shoulder, and said that she would marry him. He had been grateful then. As the years with her had multiplied, he had forgotten that gratitude, had accepted her as his right—that was his mistake. But there was no repairing the situation now. She might one day come back to him, or she might not, but there was nothing in the world he could do about it.

"I'll go now," he said, drawing his cloak about him. She looked fragile and exotically beautiful in the bed, looking up at him with those alien dark eyes. He wanted to say, I love you. He wanted to say, Come home soon; but those eyes forbade him everything. In the end he could only say, "God bless and keep you," and left her quickly, before either could see the other's tears.

CHAPTER SEVEN

It seemed to Elizabeth that all her life had been spent in a dream. From the moment she first came to Morland Place as a young child (unwanted by her widowed father) the servants, and particularly Leah, the housekeeper-governess, had impressed upon her that she was not the equal of the young ladies of the house, that she was to be grateful, modest, dutiful, and hardworking. The instructions worked upon a naturally pliant nature: she was docile and meek, and beside plain but clever Cathy and the dazzling Annunciata, she had known herself to be of inferior material.

She had been educated alongside the young ladies, but she had learned little besides the basic skills of reading, writing, and reckoning. It was as if her mind rejected those things that would not be necessary to her—the accomplishments of gentility—while she had excelled at the housewifely arts that would earn her her keep within the family. So for years she had kept house—but not her own house. She was neither family nor servant, important but not valued, needed but not thanked. She had not been unhappy, but happiness had been closed to her, like a foreign language she had never been taught: contentment was the best thing she knew.

But this last year, since Annunciata had lost interest in the day-to-day running of the house, she had begun to feel her power a little, and this was reflected in the subtly altered bearing of Clem toward her. He had always addressed her more or less as an equal before, but now he deferred to her ever so slightly in his behavior, and had began to call her madam instead of miss. Her days were busier than ever. She rose at five, for the first celebration was at six or sometimes earlier in the summer. There followed a little bread and ale for breakfast, and then she began her work.

She inspected the dairy, judged the supply of milk, overlooked the making of butter and cheese; she inspected the poultry yard, counted the eggs, scolded the poultry maid about letting a hen be pecked, saw which females were broody, inspected the hen meal and made a note to see Clem about putting down traps for rats, ordered a couple of ducks to be put aside for fattening; she visited the fishponds to examine the stocks of carp and perch; she inspected Annunciata's elaborate new dovecote and talked to the cote keeper about the breeding pairs that were to fill its increased number of nest holes.

She visited the kitchen, perhaps her most important daily duty, to order dinner—or rather, to discuss dinner with as humble an expression as possible with the chief cook, who was a ferocious autocrat with a vile temper—and to inspect the larders and storerooms, make lists of what needed replacing, bully the kitchen maids into cleaning the floors properly and scouring the pewter into a better brightness, and give orders for the making of preserves. Sometimes she had actually to stand and supervise the making of some dish, when the recipe was a secret one from the heavy, leather-bound *Recipe Book* that had been handed down by generation after generation of Morland Place mistresses.

The butteries and cellars she did not visit: that was Clem's kingdom, and he would have resented any interference.

Everything stopped for prayers at eleven, and then Elizabeth had to go and inspect the gardens that were her province: the herb garden, the kitchen garden, and the orchard. The beehives were also her responsibility, and the collecting and storing of honey, and also the feeding and care of the peacocks and swans. Dinner was generally at one, and lasted for two hours or more, depending on who was present, and then came the rest of her day's work. She had to inspect the house to see that it was kept clean, tidy, and in good order, see to it that the beds had been made properly, that the linen was clean enough, that the fires were made up and water fetched. She inspected the linen cupboards and the household stores, ordered flowers to be arranged in various rooms, including the chapel, checked on the stock of candles, which were made on the premises. She inspected the servants' quarters to see they were kept clean and interviewed any servants who had requests or problems. Then she sat down to her endless daily task of sewing, which filled every moment that was not otherwise occupied.

The evening celebration came at six, and then there was supper, a little music or conversation perhaps, and bed. The routine was only disturbed by the variations of the seasons, each of which brought her extra tasks and problems, and by the special days in the year, the feasts and holy days, all of which meant extra work for her, as well as pleasure, and the quarter days, when the house was given its great cleanings and the washing was done.

But now, now there was Ralph! She knew that it was wrong, a sin, that she was wicked, and yet it filled her with such happiness that it seemed like a blessing, and she could not bring herself to confess it as a sin. She went about her daily duties with the same efficiency as always, but with a new energy and a smile of bliss on her face that she tried and tried to repress but that always escaped her vigilance. She felt as if she had been asleep all her life until that night when she had gone down to the steward's room to seek him out.

She did not, even now, know what she had expected that night; quite why she had gone. Yet what happened seemed so *right* that she could tell herself that it was *meant to be*. Father St. Maur would say she was making excuses to herself, and perhaps she was. Since she would not or could not confess the sin and ask absolution, she could no longer take the holy sacrament of the Mass, and this, probably, had been the first thing to alert the servants to the new state of affairs. What they thought about it she did not know but could guess. They were unfailingly polite to her—they were all too well trained to be otherwise—but she had been aware of strange looks and whispered conversations cut short at her appearance. Clem looked at her oddly from time to time—not exactly disapproving, but sad. She thought perhaps he pitied her.

She did not yet know she was to be pitied—her joy was too new. She lived each day in the recollection and anticipation of the night. She did not sleep with Ralph every night, but often, and during the day, on those occasions when they met, he treated her with a new tenderness. He had always been kind to her, but now he behaved as though he actually *saw* her.

She wondered if she would conceive. She would like to bear him a child, although her mind balked at grappling with the problems that would cause. She daydreamed sometimes about marrying him. Divorce was impossible, of course, but if Annunciata should die—people did die . . . She did not wish her dead, Elizabeth told herself hastily, but if it should happen . . . It made another good reason why she could not take the sacrament, those secret thoughts of hers, but for the present being shut out from the Communion did not trouble her. She was in love and rapturously happy, and she was living for the moment. She did not want to look beyond this burst of sunshine toward the shadows beyond, but she could not help wondering from time to time what would happen when Annunciata came home, and hoping and hoping that she would not.

Now that Martin was able to help him so much with the business of running the estate, Ralph had more time to devote to his chief love of breeding horses, and throughout that spring he poured out the passion that Annunciata no longer wanted, on his new stallion. Once he had settled down in his new environment, Barbary proved more gentle and tractable than any of the other Morland stallions Ralph had known. The black horse's intelligence was uncanny, seeming at times almost human, and Ralph found that with time and patience he could train him almost like a dog. And like a dog the stallion attached himself to Ralph. He would consent to be fed and groomed and attended by others, if Ralph were not there, but Ralph alone had his love, and none but Ralph trained or rode him.

It was a new experience for Ralph, to ride Barbary. Kingcup, the older stallion, had been broken to hand, but not to ride, and though he was gentle enough in his stable, no one would dream of getting on his back. But Barbary actually seemed to enjoy being ridden, and would whinny with excitement when Ralph appeared carrying his saddle and bridle. Once out of the gate, he would walk out with his neck stretched and his ears pricked and his eyes going everywhere. He was interested in everything, and while Ralph rode him he kept up a continuous commentary in grunts and whickers, as if he were telling his master what he saw around him.

And he was fast. To gallop on Barbary was like flying, like being carried along by a gale, effortlessly, almost soundlessly. Barbary was so sure footed he could go over any ground, and Ralph loved to take him out onto the moors and let him race the clouds, leaping the burns and dikes and low stone walls as they came, barely breaking his stride. In June, when the mares Barbary had covered were growing heavy with his first progeny, Ralph rode him in the races, and he was so much faster than any other horse, even the fastest of Ralph's own, that he had to decline the prizes and say he had entered just for fun. There was a great deal of talk and speculation among the other horse breeders at that time, and many of them advised Ralph to run the horse in other races, at Newmarket or Windsor perhaps. Everyone wanted Barbary's services for their mares; some warned Ralph to be careful lest the great stallion be stolen.

Ralph was careful enough. Just before midsummer the new stable he had had designed for Barbary was finished, and the local people talked about it in awe and wonder, and called it the marble palace, for never had any horse lived in surroundings of such magificence. But part of the design of the stable was a section containing living quarters for a groom, and from the time he moved into his new home, Barbary was never alone, and a trusted groom slept there within sound of the stallion every night.

Ralph had hoped Annunciata would come back for the midsummer festivities, but his correspondent sent him no good news. She went to Windsor in early June, then to Oxford and Woodstock, and it was not until July that a hurried note arrived saying that they were on their way. Ralph passed on the news without saying how he came by it. Elizabeth quitted his bed and ordered a frenzied cleaning of things already clean, and Dorcas took out the children's best clothes, and finally on the eve of St. Swithin an official letter came from the countess to say that they had reached Wetherby too late to complete their journey but would be home the next day.

Hugo tried to make no sound, but Arabella had ears as sharp as a dog's.

"What are you doing?" she whispered.

"Getting dressed," he replied, hoping she would not ask any more. He knew that she would think him a fool if he told her what he was going to do, and he did not want her to voice her opinion. Somehow things always seemed worse once they were put into words, he thought. Even if you knew what someone was thinking, it was all right as long as they didn't say it.

In the dark room Arabella was merely a white smudge where the thin light from the window touched her face. There was a silence, and then her voice came, low and emphatic, "You *fool*."

"Don't Ara," he muttered, struggling with his stockings. Now he was thirteen his muscles were filling out, especially his leg muscles, and his cotton stockings strained over his calves in a disobliging way. He needed new clothes, but who was to order them for him, with his mother away?

"You *are* a fool," Arabella said quietly. "You're going to meet her, aren't you? Haven't you learned yet—she doesn't want us. She doesn't like us. If she wanted us she would have taken us with her, or stayed home. You'll only call trouble down. And what about school? You'll get a beating."

"Mother will tell them it's all right," Hugo said stubbornly. He and Arabella and George all went to St. Edward's School, and though, in accordance with a policy laid down by the gentle founder, James Chapham, beating was less frequent there than in other schools, playing truant would certainly call down the wrath of the ushers in the most physical way. "She'll be so pleased she'll tell them it's all right."

Arabella was silent in the face of such infatuated folly. "Where are you going?" she asked. "Where will you wait for her, I mean?"

"I'm going all the way. If I hurry, I can get to Wetherby before they set out."

"On horseback? You're going to steal a horse? You are mad."

Hugo wrenched his surcoat on and went back to the bedside, carrying his shoes. "Don't give me away, Ara," he pleaded. He could just make out her face, and she was looking at him with a kind of pitying contempt. She cared nothing for their mother, and despised his schemes to please her. But she was loyal to him.

She said, "Of course I won't. But they'll find out soon enough. I'll tell them you went to school early, and I'll tell them at school you're ill and in bed."

"They'll beat you," Hugo said hesitantly. Lying was a worse crime than playing truant, being a sin as well as a misdemeanor, but Arabella only shrugged.

"I don't care. But she's not worth it, you know."

"It'll be all right," Hugo said, "you'll see. And I'll ask her to make it all right for you, too."

"Go on, it'll be getting light soon," was all his twin said, and she lay down and turned her back on him dismissively.

It was nine miles to Wetherby across the fields, nearer eleven by road, but in any case only about two hours' riding, and he thought his mother, being a Court lady, would not rise very early. Fortunately, as it was summer, there were a number of horses in the paddocks outside, and he planned to use one of those. He could never have got a horse out of the stables and out through the barbican without detection. As it was he slipped quietly out through the back entrance. The dogs knew him and made no fuss, even when he took out a saddle and bridle from the tackle room. It would have been easier to ride bareback with just a rope halter, but he did not want to appear before his mother like a thief.

Martin's mare Queen Mab was in the paddock, and came quietly to his hand when he called her. Martin wouldn't mind, he was sure. He tacked her quickly, led her out of the paddock, and mounted as the first streaks of yellow were appearing in the eastern sky. He decided to go across the fields as far as Walton, and pick up the road there: that would be the quickest way. He

felt lighthearted, and excited. Perhaps he would pick some flowers on the way, and when he saw her, he would leap down from
the saddle and present them to her with a flourishing bow, and
say, "Welcome home, my lady Mother!"

And she would smile and say . . . He drifted off into a dream
of what she might say, and after a while he began to sing in time
with the soft thudding of Mab's hooves.

It was no more than typical of the way fate handled Hugo's life,
that as he was passing through Walton to pick up the more
southerly of the two roads to Wetherby, his mother, with her
attendants, was riding through Bickerton, not two miles away, on
the more northerly road. She might be a fine Court lady, but she
was a seasoned enough traveler to know the value of an early
start.

The sun was high when a dirty and sticky Hugo rode back in
on a tired and dusty mare. Martin met him in the yard with a
mixture of sympathy and exasperation.

"I wish you hadn't taken Mab," he said. "I wanted her today,
and now look at her."

"I missed her somewhere, on the road," Hugo said, barely
hearing him. "When I got there, they said at the inn she'd left. I
didn't think she'd start so early."

"You didn't think at all," Martin said. "Well, it's all discovered,
I'm afraid. Even if I'd known about it, I couldn't have kept it
from her. She sent down to the school straight away, you see, to
fetch you out, and then it was discovered that you were missing.
Arabella told the ushers you were at home, so she'll get a beating
from them tomorrow. She's had one at home already. Your
mother's furious. Why do you do these things, Hugo?"

"Where is she?" Hugo asked, his face pale, his lips trembling.

"In the long saloon. You'd better go straight up—she wants to
see you right away. I'll take Mab. What a state she's in—what
have you done with her?" Hugo dismounted and Martin crossly
took his tired mare's bridle and led her away as Hugo, making
futile attempts to brush some of the dust from his clothes, made
his way indoors.

The interview was as terrible as he could have imagined. His mother, beautiful and furious, lashed him with her tongue, wounding him far more than the beating he was to receive later.

"I only wanted to please you," was all he could manage to stammer in his own defense.

She rounded on him, her lip curled in contempt. "Please me? Look at you! How could the sight of you please me? You look like a clown, covered in mud, red faced, filthy."

Behind her chair, not in the least wishing to be a witness to the interview, young George stood obediently where he had been placed, trying to avoid looking at his half-brother. Annunciata gestured toward him with one long hand, and he shrank into himself even more.

"If you want to know what pleases me, you might look at your brother. And you might do worse than try to emulate him. *He* looks like a gentleman, and he behaves like one, too." George's clothes fitted him, and he found no difficulty in staying clean and tidy, while dirt seemed magically attracted to Hugo. But how could he say these things? He glowered at George, and George longed for the floor to open under him and swallow him, while their mother continued her tirade.

"And if you spent more time at your lessons you might speak and think more like a gentleman and less like a groom. The schoolmaster is less than pleased with your studies. George is far ahead of you in Latin and Greek, though he's a year younger. All you and Arabella seem fit for is riding about the countryside with dirty fingernails."

When it was all over, Hugo was allowed to go, and he stumbled blindly out, trying to hold back tears, sent to get himself clean before being sent back to school; leaving George behind him to enjoy his mother's approbation. George was not going back to school that day, nor for the rest of the week. His mother wanted to have some time with him, and he was well enough advanced in his lessons to be able to quit school for a time.

The last thing Hugo heard before he shut the saloon door behind him was his mother saying to his younger brother,

"Fetch your instrument, my darling, and play to me. My nerves are so upset."

Annunciata had come home in a softened mood, but it had not lasted long. She had been away too long, and everything struck her as strange and strained. The servants seemed to look at her askance; the babies had grown out of recognition; the household had flourished without her, as if it did not care whether she came back or not. The very sun seemed to shine too garishly, and the peacocks shrieked as if in derision. Her awkwardness was compounded with a sense of guilt that she did not feel she ought to have, and it was partly that guilt, and a reaction against it, that had made her send Gifford down to the school to fetch her older children out. The discovery that Hugo was missing had made her feel that she was appearing ridiculous, and the storm of her feelings broke.

Behind it all was something else, senses on the very edge of awareness, something she did not want to admit to her conscious mind. Morland Place was complete without her in a way that she did not want to understand. It ought to be lacking a mistress, and it was not. The mistress was there, and her heart sickened as the knowledge tried to force its way in.

Of course Elizabeth performed all the tasks of housekeeper to perfection, as she always had when Annunciata had been away or otherwise preoccupied. But there was something different in Elizabeth's bearing, something different in the way the servants spoke to her, even in the way they stood before her when she spoke to them. Morland Place was Elizabeth's home, and it was no longer Annunciata's, and she did not want to know why.

The day passed, relentlessly hot, glaringly sunny, and all the things that should have constituted celebration at the return of the mistress seemed only to jar on the nerves. Baby Maurice was fretful because he was teething; the dogs were bad tempered in the heat; Ralph was by turns distant and awkwardly jovial; Elizabeth shook like an aspen whenever Annunciata spoke. When the twins returned from school a fresh layer of awkwardness was added as they both sulked and glowered, and no one was sorry when the last prayers were said and they could all retire to bed.

In the privacy of their bedchamber, Annunciata and Ralph finally spoke. Annunciata, undressed and clad in her bedgown, had dismissed the servants and was combing her own hair, walking up and down the room as she did so and wielding the comb so like a weapon that Ralph was reminded how he had said she could comb sparks from it. He undressed himself in silence, and when he was in his bedgown, too, he sat down on the edge of the high bed and watched her up and down the room with resigned eyes.

"Had we better speak? Or would that be worse?" he said.

She whirled on him so fast he actually ducked in spontaneous reaction.

"Are you trying deliberately to humiliate me? Of all people, to choose her!"

"Who?" Ralph said involuntarily.

"Of all people, that little creepmouse! You could have taken someone from the city, set her up decently like a gentleman, done the thing in style. Or even just taken a dairy maid behind a haystack and said no more about it, had your tumble and be done with it. What do you think people will say? How do you think they will regard it? It's scandalous! You'll make me a mockery. People don't behave like that in decent society. Setting up with your cousin—my cousin—my housekeeper! Living together like man and wife, in my house, for all the world as if I were dead and buried."

She whirled away, walking up and down again as if she could exercise her fury away. Ralph said nothing, there being nothing he could effectively say. At the end of the room she suddenly stopped, and turned slowly where she was as if weariness had descended upon her in that place. "Perhaps that was the next step. Is that why you wanted me to come home, Ralph? So you could poison me? Or an accident out hunting, perhaps—that would look better. And then the heartbroken widower, after a due period of mourning, of course—"

"Don't speak like that," Ralph said gently. "You sould like a madwoman."

She stared at him, her shoulders sagging. "I feel mad. Perhaps I am going mad. Why did you do it, Ralph? For God's sake, why?"

"I never wanted you to go," he said. "It was your choice to leave me. You stayed away, and I—she was a comfort to me, that's all. I didn't choose her to spite you. You must know that."

"I don't know anything, except that you have humiliated me."

"You humiliated me, when you refused to come home. I even came to try to get you back. It was your choice."

Her eyes met his, suddenly penetrating. "But you wouldn't do it now, would you?"

He didn't answer. At last he said, "Do you want me to send her away? She could go to Emblehope. Anne would—"

"No," Annunciata said harshly. "Someone has to take care of the household. I don't care anymore what you do."

She turned away and went to the table and poured herself a cup of wine, and sprinkled cinnamon into it from the silver shaker that stood on the tray with the claret jug. She swirled it to mix the spice, and then sipped slowly, and when she turned again to face Ralph she was composed, and his heart sank, for she seemed so far away from him.

"You have released me," she said, smiling, and Ralph could only stare at her, bewildered, as he had been from the beginning, at what had happened, wondering what he could have done differently. They spoke no more until they were both in bed, and Ralph had blown out the candles and pulled the curtains. He lay down, and was instantly, achingly aware of her body close beside him, feeling it all down his side though he was not touching her at any point. At last, after a long time, he reached out a hand, cautiously as if to a dangerous animal, and stroked her head, comfortably. She lay passive, not moving toward or away from it, and emboldened he stroked her cheek and neck and let his hand drift down to her breast. Her nipple stiffened at his touch. He thought that perhaps their bodies might speak freely and remove the barriers that words had put up between them, He loved and desired her still, and thought she must feel the same. But when his hand moved to her waist she said calmly and unemphatically, "No." He removed his hand, and she added, "I might get pregnant, you see, and I couldn't have that."

They spoke no more, and Ralph drifted into sleep. He woke an hour later to a gleam of light and quiet voices. Chloris had come to rouse Annunciata to tell her that George had been violently sick, and he was suffering from cramps in the stomach.

It was a strange summer, but not entirely unhappy. Outwardly, Annunciata and Ralph were friends, and as the days passed and the tensions slackened, what they assumed for the public gaze took on a kind of reality. They had been friends for all of Annunciata's life, and if at night they lay as far apart from each other as the bed would allow, during the day they rode and hunted together, talked easily, discussed business, and continued that friendship as if neither marriage nor estrangement had disrupted it. Elizabeth faded into the background in a way which would have been difficult for someone who had not had her upbringing, and Annunciata found it easy to push her to the back of her mind and behave as if she had never existed.

She had plenty to occupy her, for Shawes had inevitably been neglected, and business took up many of her hours, and she spent much of the rest of the day riding or hunting, which had always been her main summer occupation. And she wanted, also, to spend time with her children. Rupert, at four, was a delight, quick and advanced for his years in a way that reminded her of Martin at the same age, beginning to grown too tall for petticoats, and having a great look of his royal grandfather about him. Charles at two and a half had the prattling charm of all children at that stage, and was going to be fair like his father; Maurice was yet a baby, and the province of nurses, though Dorcas swore he was going to be the most intelligent of them all. Her first fury with Hugo lapsed into her normal indifference, but she took more of an interest in Arabella, for she was approaching womanhood and would soon be ready for the marriage market. As Arabella grew up, she grew better looking, and Annunciata guessed that this process would continue, for her features were still too big for her face. She looked like Annunciata's mother, and she had been handsome in later life. Thirteen was still too young, of course, but next year, when she was fourteen, Annunciata planned to take her back to Whitehall with her. One could not start too early where there was such competition.

As to little George, her darling, he gave her the greatest cause for concern that summer, though it was not through his own fault. He was everything she had always loved in him, but his health gave her a great deal of worry. That first bout of sickness was followed through the summer by others, and the pattern was the same—sharp pains in the stomach, followed by vomiting, and then a period of sickness and voiding. The doctor came and was puzzled. "Something he has eaten," he said the first time, and the third time he said, "It's almost as if he's being poisoned." But he did not say that to her ladyship, only to the maid. It did not do for a doctor to mention poison to those who were paying him. He gave orders for various physics for the child, bled him at regular intervals, and gave instructions as to what foods he should eat and what avoid.

In September she and Ralph rode up to Northumberland to visit Crispian and Sabine, who was pregnant for the second time, her first pregnancy having ended in miscarriage. They traveled on horseback, and informally, attended only by Tom, Arthur, and Chloris, and away from Morland Place they discovered something like a freedom with each other. At Emblehope they were greeted kindly by Crispian and Anne and ecstatically by Sabine, who was eager to show them in what a great way of society she now moved, and even more eager to show her friends and neighbors the great countess who was a close friend of King Charles himself and lived at Court because the Queen found her indispensible. The flattery was pleasant, and the lack of any need for effort, and though they stayed a month Annunciata remained happy, and would have stayed longer had not the year been running out.

Back at Morland Place Annunciata stayed for Founder's Day— October fourteenth—at St. Edward's School, when there was always a celebration, a day of freedom, feasting and gifts for the children, a special service of thanksgiving at the church, and a banquet for the masters, governers, and sponsors. It was one of Annunciata's own ancestors who had founded and endowed the school, and she was the guest of honor for the day, and all the children came up to her after the service one by one to curtsey and give her a single white flower, and to receive from her the Founder's Day penny.

As soon as that was past, she became restless for London again, and within three days she was gone with her servants, horses, and dogs to take up the other half of her divided life. She had felt kindly toward Ralph for most of the summer, but as she said good-bye to him that sharp October morning, the blank windows of the house behind him seemed to be waiting for her to go, seemed to conceal at each pane the woman who was waiting to step into her shoes. She pulled her fur-lined hood closer about her face, nodded to her husband briskly, and turned Goldeneye with a sharp tap of her heel toward the barbican.

London's welcome was not unequivocal: she discovered on her arrival that Ballincrea House had been flooded during the summer and a great deal of damage had been done, not only to the contents of the house but to the structure itself. Fortunately she had her quarters in the palace.

"It's a dreadful old house," she complained to the King at their first private meeting. "I don't think I can bring myself to spend money on it. I'd sooner pull it down."

"I don't think you need to do that, my dear," the King said, picking up Charlemagne and stroking him idly. He had called in on her on his way back from a tennis match with his brother, and the sharp smell of his sweat was in the room. "If you leave it alone it will fall down of its own accord."

Annunicata smiled. "A good thing if it did. I'm sure it isn't healthy. There are such rats in the kitchen as you never saw. You could saddle them and ride them round Hyde Park."

The King put down the spaniel and picked up his hat. "Why don't you build a new house? Everyone else seems to be doing so. I'm sure Kit Wren is longing to design you something—your dovecote simply whet his appetite."

"Now you are laughing at me," Annunciata said.

The King grinned. "Of course not, sweetheart. It's just that my ministers will have forty fits apiece if I start any more new buildings—but if you decide to build a house, I shall be able to interfere to my heart's content."

The first necessity for the Season was a wardrobe of new clothes, and Annunciata sent word on the morning after her return for her dressmaker, Mrs. Drake, who was still, despite her enormous age, at the top of her profession. From the moment she returned, Annunciata's anteroom was aswarm with people who had things to sell, cloth, lace, garniture, jewels, nonsenses, so all the materials were at hand for Mrs. Drake to practice her art.

"Such colors!" she cried as she swept through the crowds, carving a wake like a ship at sea, and into Annunciata's chamber. "You will be so happy this Season—the colors are going to look wonderful on you, and so dreadful on everyone else!"

It was while she was still closeted with Mrs. Drake that a maid— one of the new underservants of whom a continuous stream passed through every London household—knocked at the door and said, "There's a gentleman here to see you, m'lady."

"What name, child?" Mrs. Drake snapped before Annunciata could speak.

"A Master Morland, m'lady," the maid said, as if it were Annunciata who had asked. Mrs. Drake and Annunciata exchanged a startled glance. What was Ralph doing here? she wondered. Mrs. Drake pulled her samples together and rose.

"I'll go. You will want some leisure to think over your gowns in any case, but I'll have the crocus silk made up at once. Send the gentleman up, child, don't stand there gawping."

Mrs. Drake swept the maid out before her, and Annunciata stood up, smoothed her skirts down, examined her hair in the mirror, and turned to face the door just as it opened to reveal the maid ushering in a tall, dark-haired man in a suit so lacking in ornaments he might have been a Puritan. His blue eyes met Annunciata's startled dark ones. He turned a little pale, and then developed a red patch on each cheek. He seemed indefinably disturbed at being here, and yet his hand that stretched out to her was trembling with eagerness.

"Forgive me for not sending a messenger first," he said. "I thought of it, but I wanted so much to see you that I just couldn't make myself wait."

And Annunciata's astonished face warmed into pleasure, and her eyes sparkled as she took his hand and pressed it.

"My dear Kit, how could I be angry with you? I should have been angry if you had hesitated to come straight to me. It is so long since I saw you, so very long." The maid withdrew, and shut the door. Annunciata and Kit remained as they were, their hands joined as if across the enormous stretch of years since they had last seen each other. "You've changed," she said at last. "You were a boy when I last saw you. Now you are a man."

"And you," Kit said, unable to take his eyes from hers even long enough to take off his cloak, "you are simply more beautiful than ever. Not a day older."

"Don't begin talking nonsense so soon." She laughed, releasing her hand. "Give me your cloak, let me call for some refreshment for you. Oh, Kit, it's so good to see you!"

The last words broke through as if from a younger, more reckless Annunciata who lived still within the formal shell. Kit swung his cloak off and flung it from him, not even looking to see if it landed on the chair it was aimed for, and put his hand back into her outstretched one.

"Is it?" he asked. "I hope it is—I've been wanting this for so long—to see you again." He seemed suddenly embarrassed by what his words implied, and added clumsily. "We have so much to talk about. So many years . . ."

"How is Cathy?" Annunciata asked sweetly. Kit reddened in confusion, and she was sorry—she did not want to upset him like that. "You have come to Whitehall on business, I suppose?"

"Yes," he said, seeming glad of the neutrality of the question. "Business with merchants and goldsmiths—and also with the King. I need help to rebuild Aberlady, and there is the question of the title."

"Then you may have to stay for quite a long time," Annunciata said. He grew serious.

"Does it matter to you, how long I stay?" he asked. Annunciata

was suddenly minutely aware of every sound in the room, from
Charlemagne's muted growling as he worried a slipper under the
bed, to the closer sound of Kit's breathing. Kit, dear Kit, almost
her brother, the third of that trio of young men who had challenged each other for her smiles through the sweet sunny days of
her careless girlhood. Edward had become her lover, was the
father of her beloved son George; Ralph she had married. And
now here was Kit, pressing her hand and gazing at her with those
dark-blue Morland eyes, like Frank's, like . . .

"I hope you have a great deal of business," she said. "I hope
you have to stay a very long time."

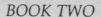

BOOK TWO

PEACOCK
IN HIS PRIDE

Then since we mortal lovers are,
Ask not how long our love will last;
But while it does, let us take care
Each minute be with pleasure past:
Were it not madness to deny
To live, because we're sure to die?

Sir George Etherege:
"To a Lady"

CHAPTER EIGHT

In October 1677, Hugo McNeill gave a most successful party in his rooms at Christ Church College, Oxford. Like most "gentleman commoners," he lodged at Peckwater Inn, whose old buildings had recently been extended to form a quadrangle close by the main college quadrangle—begun so long ago by Cardinal Wolsey, and completed not quite a decade ago by the present dean, Dr. Fell. Dr. Fell had raised a great deal of money from members and friends of Christ Church to complete Wolsey's great design, and it was a source of great satisfaction to Hugo that his mother had contributed to the fund.

For he loved it here at Christ Church. He felt, at last, at home. However much or little his mother loved him, she had not stinted him when it came to sending him to the university, and she had given him enough money and a large enough allowance to set himself up in as much style as even he could have wanted. He had one of the best sets of rooms in Peckwater Inn, consisting of a bedroom, a dressing closet, a drawing room, and a servant's room, and he had decorated and furnished them himself. He had spent three months in Paris that summer, accompanied by Father St. Maur, and had brought back many ideas and some pieces of furniture. The fashion now was for light, delicate pieces, and a great deal of inlay, and in the drawing room he had a number of small tables and chairs inlaid with silver.

The walls of his bedchamber had been bare plaster, and he had had them papered with Chinese paper, which cost a small fortune, but could be taken down and used again when he moved quarters.

The paper was white with a pale blue pattern upon it; his bedhangings and curtains were blue, and on the chimneypiece he had a couple of blue-and-white Dutch roll-wagon vases—so the overall effect was very elegant.

He had not been able to do so much with the drawing room, for the walls there were paneled, but he had bought two thick Chinese carpets which he laid upon the floor, and over the fireplace in pride of place was the painting of his mother by Lely, the Turkish Portrait. She had recently had a new likeness taken, of herself on horseback, and since she had lost fondness for the Turkish she had given it to Hugo, one of those casual gestures which he valued so much more than she intended.

But if he had been restrained in the drawing room, he had made up for it in the dressing closet. Determined to be ahead of fashion if he could, he had furnished this little room with a French close-stool of a delicate wood called mahogany, which was not yet much seen in England, inlaid with silver. The vessels were all silver—the ewer, basins, tripod, and dishes—and he had had his coat of arms engraved upon each item. But the final piece of extravagance was the ebony bath with the silver scrollwork. This had cost so much that he had not been able to pay for it, and with great trepidation he had got it upon credit and told them to send the bill to his mother. She had been furious with him at first. In vain did he argue that she had taught him to be fastidious about his person, that she had told him he might set himself up as fashionably as he wished. There was a limit, she said, to the price anyone should pay for a bath. But when she saw the article, she "soothed down wonderfully" as Hugo put it to a friend. It was *so* elegant, *so* modish, so much better than anything anyone else had, that she agreed to pay for it and to let him keep it for the term of his residency at Oxford, provided she should have it for her own use when he moved on.

Having capitulated over the bath, Annunciata made no more restrictions on generosity. She gave him a servant, a quiet, efficient young man called John Wood, who was one of Clement's numerous cousins from Wilstrop, and bought him a carriage and a pair of horses. The carriage was a little light chariot, almost new, in good condition, and with glazed windows and very handsome upholstery within. She paid to have it repainted and the window frames gilded, and at Hugo's request had his arms painted on the door before the final varnish was applied. The paint was black picked out with gold and scarlet, and she chose him a fine pair of white carriage horses, so the effect was very smart. One of the grooms, a lad called Daniel, came from Twelvetrees to be coachman and groom for Hugo, and he took great pride in his position, and never had the horses out without plaiting their manes with scarlet ribbons to match the reins. Thus Hugo was well pleased, especially when Ralph, of his kindness, gave Hugo Oryx for his saddle horse. Hugo rented a stable and coachhouse in Beef Lane, just opposite the college gates, with a room above for Daniel, and these arrangements were the envy of his fellow undergraduates.

That envy was all that Hugo wanted. He wanted, had always wanted, to be admired, accepted, loved, and now that he had come to a world where his half-brother could not step in and take his place in the sun, he settled down to do whatever was required for popularity. Despite the efforts of Father St. Maur and the example of Martin, he had no natural love of learning, but academic excellence was not necessary for popularity. He entertained lavishly, and was invited, in return, to all the best entertainments; he hunted at Risinghurst, fished at Iffley, shot fowl at Binsey, and took part in improvised horse-races at Port Meadow. Though he had never been interested in politics, he frequented the two best coffeehouses and talked politics and complained, as was the fashion, that the land his father and grandfather had sold for the King's cause had never been restored to him. He even took up smoking, though he knew his mother hated it, and it made him feel very sick; and he visited the most gentlemanly of the brothels and lost his virginity, and very shortly his heart, to a pretty young girl called Molly, whom he bought out and set up in a room in Shoe Lane.

Annunciata very quickly got to hear about this, as she did about everything Hugo did. It was not for nothing she had chosen his servant herself. Through Chloris she kept her finger on the pulse of all the branches of her family, and Chloris, without even being asked, had recently set up a system for obtaining information within Whitehall and through the other great residences in

London. So John reported to Chloris, and Chloris reported to Annunciata, who, in alarm, had certain inquiries made. But Molly seemed to be modest, clean, and not more than usually rapacious, and the countess was satisfied. Every young man of fashion had to have his doxy, and to tell truth she would probably have been more anxious if he had not made those early sexual experiments. At sixteen Hugo was still small in size, though his muscular development showed he would never be tall, perhaps never any taller than he was now. He was stocky, thick necked, and with his thick brown hair, curly as a ram's fleece, and bright blue eyes, he had a certain animal attractiveness, though he would never be elegant like his father.

However, in his exquisite and fashionable clothes he did not look materially different from the other young men who were lounging pleasantly in his drawing room that afternoon in October, drawing on pipes and filling the air with acrid black smoke. There not being room for large numbers, Hugo had concentrated on quality, and had carefully chosen and invited the thirty best young men from his own and other colleges, all of them lords or the sons of lords or from otherwise distinguished families, most of them rich, all of them popular.

The food he had ordered from the cookshop in the High that specialized in French dishes, and John had supervised the battery of hired footmen who carried round the dishes and the silver tubs of Burgundy wine and champagne. At the far end of the drawing room a small consort of musicians played quietly; there were no female guests, and so no dancing, but Hugo had provided card tables and dice, and now that everyone had eaten, at least temporarily, his fill, the tables were beginning to fill up, coins were being clinked, and very soon the play would become both expensive and noisy. Those who did not care to play were either watching or merely smoking and conversing, and everyone was drinking; while Hugo drifted from group to group, reveling in the knowledge that the party was already a success.

By the fire stood a group of three particularly elegant young men who were warming their tails and discussing horses, and Hugo was working his way toward them. Arran and Hamilton were two of the richest young men in Oxford; Masseldine was

Hugo's particular— perhaps his only close—friend, like himself an Irish peer who had never been to Ireland, although unlike himself Masseldine owned a large estate there.

"I vow and swear," Hamilton was saying, "I lost a hundred pound if I lost a shilling on those damned three-footed nags. Ah, here's the man who'd tell us, however," he added good-naturedly as Hugo reached them. "Ballincrea must be the only man at Oxford who can pay his tailor with the proceeds of his wagers."

"Tell us how you do it, Ballincrea," Arran said. He was the younger son of a Scottish lord who, having been sent to England mainly for want of anything better to do with him, was revenging himself on his family by being the most furiously debauched rake in the town. "How do you pick 'em out of the bunch? Or are they marked cards, hey?"

Masseldine spoke up for his friend, making room for him before the fire. "Hugo was born in a stable, that's how. Look at him, Willy, can't you see his father was a stallion? He talks to the horses before the race, and they tell him which of 'em is going to run." And he flung an arm across Hugo's shoulder as the others laughed.

"How's that great stud of your father's, Ballincrea?" Hamilton asked. "My governor's best colt was beaten at Newmarket in May by a damn' black beast bred by that stallion. What was its name? The Turk, that was it! Never seen anything move so fast. My governor wanted to send his best mare to Morland Place, but mordee! The price your father wanted!"

Arran emptied his glass of Burgundy and held it out to a passing footman to be filled and said languidly, "Tell your governor, Hamilton, that I'll serve his best mare for him for half what Morland asks—and you'll get noble blood into the bargain."

The others laughed, though Hugo was still somewhat embarrassed by such coarseness, and Masseldine said, "Now, my lads, we're shocking our host. You know how these old Yorkshire families bring up their sprigs—and Catholics into the bargain."

Arran threw a significant glance upward at the portrait of Annunciata over the fireplace. "Oh, I don't know, though. Some of them manage to throw off the shadow of the convent."

Hugo bristled instantly. "What do you mean?" he demanded.

Arran, wanting only to bait him, said, "What do I mean? Come, Ballincrea, everyone knows your intimate connection with the Royal Family. Favors here, pensions there. None but His Majesty's mistresses command such ready patronage."

Masseldine tightened his grip on Hugo's shoulders as he felt him struggle in anger.

"Are you speaking of my mother, Arran?" he said furiously. "I'll have you know—"

"Why, my dear sir, why so angry?" Aaron said, raising one eyebrow in assumed surprise. "It is a great honor, surely, to bed with the Lord's Annointed? And who knows but that—"

"*Taisez-vous*, Willy! Hold your tongue," Masseldine interrupted, still holding Hugo down. "Ballincrea don't like to hear things like that said about his mother, and come to think of it, nor do I. Come, Hugo, peace, he was only joking. Arran's not insulting her. He hasn't got the brains to insult anyone, have you, Willy, you son of a kilted barbarian? Let's drink to the health of a beautiful and noble lady. Come, lift your glasses, lads," he concluded, and lifted his own toward the portrait. The other three followed suit, Hugo smolderingly, Arran with an assumed reverence, Hamilton openly laughing.

"Tell us the latest gossip, Ballincrea," Hamilton said appeasingly when they had drunk. "You get all the Court news first, I dare swear. Who's bedding with whom—no, not that. S'death, what can I ask him that won't offend?"

"How is your mother's new house progressing?" Masseldine came to the rescue. "I hear it is to be the envy of the Court. It must be nearly finished, surely?"

"So I believe," Hugo said. "The shell is completed, and it is the decoration that is wanting now. My mother is getting Gibbons to do all the woodwork. The King says it will be St. Paul's in Pall Mall."

"Pall Mall? Ah, yes," Arran murmured, "many an eminent person has settled there. Does not Mistress Gwyn have a house in Pall Mall? Your mother is well acquainted with actresses, I believe."

Hugo bristled again. "Now look here, Arran—" he began, but this time Hamilton pacified him.

"All he means is that you have your mother's love of the theater, I'm sure. Do stop being tedious, Arran—go and lose some money at the dice, that will put you in a better temper. Parblew, it is hard work being in company with you!"

And Masseldine added, "You are right, Hamilton. We had better keep these two apart or they'll be ending up on the Meadow. Not that I mind—Ballincrea's got to fight his duel sometime, you know— but we'll end up as seconds, and it's too cold at this time of year for standing in wet grass watching other men fight."

Hamilton shook his head sadly. "I truly believe you never do anything other than for your own comfort and pleasure."

"Why, what else?" Masseldine pretended surprise, then glanced at Hugo. "Though our little McNeill is making a small fashionable corner here for Catholicism. What have you planned for us by way of entertainment, when we have eaten and drunk ourselves almost insensible at your expense? Are we to have a celebration of the Mass? That would have the virtue of novelty, at least."

Hugo smiled. "I have an entertainment for you, but I do not think you will guess what it is. You will have to wait and see. John, some more wine here! Shall we watch the cards, gentlemen? We have an hour yet at least."

The entertainment he had arranged, with some of his mother's talent for originality, arrived some time later in the form of four young actresses from a traveling company, who performed a mildly obscene play in dumb show. They proved a wild success, and after two encores they were allowed to fall ravenously on the refreshments before being whisked away by some of the guests. The rest of the young men settled down to get seriously drunk, and the party went the way of all parties, breaking at one point into a plan for a naked dip in the Cherwell, which was abandoned when it was discovered how cold the water was, and finishing eventually with the last few most favored or most determined guests taking breakfast with the host and swearing eternal brotherhood. It had evidently been a most successful party, and Hugo was well pleased, though he had intended to finish the night with his Molly. However, as he saw Masseldine to his own quarters at half past five in the morning, he felt he had made a true friend.

"You're a good fellow," Masseldine breathed into his ear as, one heavy arm across Hugo's shoulder, he trailed the few yards to his own door. "If they don't spoil you, you'll go far, I promise you. S'blood, but I've never met a colt I more liked the look of. I wish you would marry my sister, that's what."

"Why, thank you," Hugo said gravely, realizing that this was a compliment of rare order.

"S'true, my friend. My governor has strange ideas about Caroline's future, but you've got money, blood, and you're a fine fellow. You must come and spend Christmas with us—I mean it. Promise me, McNeill, you young scoundrel! Ah, I see young Molly in your eye, but let me tell you this: every young buck must have his doxy, his dose, and his duel to make him a man. But he has to survive 'em all, and marry a gentleman's daughter in the end. You've got your doxy, and I daresay you'll find your pox one day. When you fight your duel, make sure you win, and make sure you have that splendid fellow, John Boverie, Earl of Masseldine, as your second. And then marry Caroline. Promise me?"

"I promise," Hugo said, not entirely clear what he was promising, and quite certain Masseldine had even less idea. He opened the door to Masseldine's set of rooms and bundled him into the arms of the waiting manservant.

"I'll take him to bed, my lord. Thank you," the servant said firmly. He was a graybeard of great authority, obviously an old family retainer, and Hugo obeyed meekly, backing out and hearing, as he closed the door, the sleepy voice of his friend saying:

"And he's a Catholic, you see, so he has to keep his promises."

The wedding was a small one, private, and not at all jolly, and Annunciata wondered how successful a marriage might be that had such an inauspicious beginning. Princess Mary, the bride, was still red eyed from weeping: she had wept almost nonstop since the King had told her that she must wed her cousin William from Holland, and she looked as though she might burst into tears again at any moment, which would be a bad breach of etiquette. Annunciata, conscious of the problems engendered by undutiful daughters, had no patience with her, and her hands itched to slap the princess when she sniffed and allowed her lip to tremble.

Standing beside her mother, Arabella had only a little more sympathy, for even red-eyed Princess Mary made a strange contrast with her betrothed. The princess was very tall, five feet and eleven inches, even without her heeled shoes—and handsome in the dark Stuart way, with elaborately curled hair that hung past her shoulders; she was fifteen years old, and of an age therefore to be considered beautiful; she was dressed in the latest Court fashion, with some richness, and when not grieving over her fate she was a playful and happy girl.

Prince William, her cousin, was not at all what a young girl dreams of. To begin with, he was twenty-seven years old, and to Arabella, who was sixteen, as to Princess Mary, he seemed an old man. He was not handsome, either—he was four inches shorter than his bride, a thin, high-shouldered man with the careful gait and pinched, pale face of a perpetual invalid. He had asthma, and breathed noisily through his mouth, and his narrow chest seemed to cave alarmingly with every difficult breath. He was dressed all in black, as was the Dutch fashion, and very plainly, and he wore his own hair instead of a wig. His expression was dour: he never smiled, and rarely spoke, and when he did it was briefly and to the point, without any of the verbal flourishes and compliments of the English courtiers. Arabella thought she would certainly not marry such a man, and wondered why the princess did not run away rather than submit. She decided the princess must be a fool, and she shifted impatiently from one foot to the other until her mother gave her a savage look that stilled her.

Bishop Compton was still intoning through the preliminary speech, dragging his words as if in sympathy with the dreariness of the occasion. Annunciata looked around her in a mixture of amusement and dismay, for there was hardly a cheerful face present. The Duke of York looked both sullen and furious—the marriage was hateful to him, and he had only consented because the King in the end gave him no choice. He had wanted to marry

Mary to a French prince, a Catholic prince: he did not like William's religion or his disposition, and it was well known that William had expressed contempt for Mary's low birth on her mother's side. It was also well known that William's mother, the duke's sister Mary, was not remembered with affection by the Dutch, and another Mary Stuart was unlikely to be welcomed in Holland. But the Protestant wedding was wildly popular among the people of England, and the King was, as usual, pursuing some hidden course of his own, so James had to obey his brother.

The rest of the company was hardly more cheerful. The Queen, as always, looked anxious, and the Duchess of York, who was vastly pregnant, looked uncomfortable. This was her third pregnancy, the first two having resulted in miscarriages, and from time to time both the Queen and the duke threw her an anxious glance. Princess Anne was ill with smallpox and not able to be with her sister for this important occasion, and outside the chamber the November rain poured down from a sodden sky as if it would never stop. Annunciata had to bite back a smile of amusement, and as she did so she caught the King's eye. Charles raised one eyebrow and his lips twitched under his dark moustache and Annunciata knew he was contemplating villainy. The bishop droned on, and the Duchess of York moved uncomfortably, and the King gave a cheerful grin and cried out, "Come, Bishop, you had better make haste. If you don't get them wed before the duchess has a son, they'll never be wed at all!"

The bishop looked startled, the duke and duchess and the bridegroom looked shocked, the bride burst into tears again, and Annunciata bit the inside of her cheeks to stop herself laughing. But the speed of delivery was improved, and the couple were wed at last, and with the King hustling them along they were put ceremonially to bed where, sitting up against the snowy pillows, they received the loving cup and the congratulations of the leading members of the Court who filed past as was the custom.

That done, the King himself stepped forward in defiance of ritual and drew the curtains round the bed crying out, "Now, nephew, to your work! St. George for England!"

Annunciata could only hope that Prince William's English was not good enough to understand that, for it would certainly have shocked his steely Dutch propriety. So they left the young princess to her fate and crowded out into the banqueting hall for the feasting and drinking. The duke and duchess did not stay, and their absence improved the atmosphere somewhat.

A while later the King worked his way round to Annunciata and said quietly, "Heyday! That was the gloomiest wedding I ever did attend. I thought it would never be done, and every time the duchess moved I thought it was all up with us. Still, it is done now, and he cannot go back on it, even if she has twin sons tomorrow."

"It should please the people at any rate, sir," Annunciata said. "And it may quiet the Country Party for a while."

"One has to throw them a bone from time to time. Shaftesbury worries at my heels like a terrier."

"It is wonderful to me that he has managed to weld so many malcontents into a party at all. They have nothing in common, it seems, beyond their discontent."

"And their dislike of Jamie, and their hatred of Catholics." The King sighed. "Why are people so intolerant?"

"They have neither your temper, sir, nor your experiences to moderate them."

The King smiled down at her. "You are looking very beautiful today, Countess. Far too young and beautiful to have such a tall daughter," he added, and they both glanced at where Arabella was standing a little way off talking to Prince Rupert.

Arabella's gown was blue silk over a cloth-of-silver petticoat, and the colors set off her pale complexion and fox-red hair beautifully. The hair was a great problem, for it would not curl no matter what was done to it, and Birch had had to devise a style for her to take account of that. But it looked very well, Annunciata thought, the sidepieces drawn back and knotted high with a cluster of white flowers, the back hair hanging loose and straight down Arabella's back. It gave her a sudden pang to realize that the tall red-haired girl was her daughter. She had a daughter of sixteen! Yet it seemed only yesterday that she had been sixteen herself and enjoying her first season at Court. She sighed, and the King took her hand and pressed it.

"Time flees away with us all, my dear," he said gently, as if he knew what she had been thinking. "But you have children to be proud of, at least. That is all time can give us." He glanced at Arabella again, and Annunciata realized how selfish she was to feel sad, when the King had no legitimate child at all. "How is her brother doing at Oxford?" the King asked now.

Annunciata made a rueful face. "He seems to be trying all the vices at once, sir. But he has some friends of good family, so I hope it may be improving his manners, even if it is doing nothing for his mind. I cannot think he has time to study with all the other things that occupy his time."

"He will grow steadier when he has had his fun," the King said soothingly. "But your second son gives you no sorrow, I think?"

Annunciata smiled. "George is an angel on earth, and now that his health is improving he gives me nothing but happiness. I think perhaps it was the summer heat that made him sick. Since the autumn came, and the cooler weather, he has had no more bouts of it."

"Good. Now I must go and start the dancing, and you, madam, had best keep an eye on your daughter. I see Etheredge making toward her, and I do not think you will want her to dance with such a rake."

"Oh, Lord! Thank you, Your Majesty," Annunciata said, and as the King moved away, smiling, Annunciata hurried to retrieve her daughter and guide her toward a safer dancing partner.

November hung so gray over Akcomb Moor that it seemed the world was trapped in someplace between night and day. The cloud had come down low until it touched the tops of the trees and, touching, disintegrated into fat cold drops that ran down the black limbs and dripped sullenly from naked twigs onto the mash of dead brown leaves below. The tussocky grass betrayed the nearness of the bogs, and the coarse blades were rimed with raindrops. Where Akcomb Woods ended the sky was blank, as if it were the end of the world, but under the trees the darkness was cold and menacing.

Elizabeth drew rein, and pulled her cloak tighter about her, and shivered. The place she was heading for was beyond the wood, but it seemed at that moment equally dangerous to try to penetrate the blackness of the wood or the deadness of the gray horizon. She began to wonder, superstitiously, if she had crossed the border out of the real world. The bogs were near, the bogs that were a name for treachery, with the ground that yielded to your feet, and the false bright-green grass that coaxed you on, and, at night, the flickering marsh-lights that called the unwary to their doom. It was a place haunted by spirits, fairies, ghosts, nameless things, and she knew she would have done better not to come. She heeled her pony, and he turned willingly enough, but behind her the misty cloud had come down and the sky was more blankly impenetrable than the way before her. She stifled a little cry of dismay, and her fingers tightened on the reins, and her pony shook his head and gave a sneeze. The sound was so ordinary and equine and even absurd that Elizabeth relaxed, and gave a small laugh, shaking off her foolish fears. She knew this place, she had known it from childhood, she had hunted here a thousand times. She should not be turned into a gullible fool by a little rain and mist. She turned the pony back toward the woods and rode onward.

She had been glad of the darkness of the day when she set out, for she did not want anyone to know where she was going. It was an errand of secrecy: if she were discovered she might be censured, blamed; she would certainly be ridiculed. So she had waited for the quiet time of the day, the afternoon, after the dinner was finished and cleared away. Normally at that time she rested a little in the bedchamber, or sat in the long saloon sewing. Sometimes Ralph joined her in the bedchamber, and those were times she liked, but today he had gone after dinner straight over to Twelvetrees, where he had been all morning, too. Barbary seemed to be going lame, and Ralph could not rest if anything ailed his beloved horse. So he would not miss her, and if she said she was resting, no one else would miss her, either, until the hour of prayers, and so she had slipped out.

She skirted the wood, keeping near the trees but not quite wanting to venture into their darkness, and eventually as she came round the rough flank she saw her objective: a small, low, one-roomed cottage, huddling in a slight dip like a crouching animal. It gave her pause for a moment, for its thatch was low and overgrown with weeds, and it had no windows, only one door, a black square hole, which seemed to snarl at her, like the mouth of some shaggy animal. Surely the mist clung too familiarly to its walls? Even the smoke from the single smoke-hole did not rise from the roof, but dribbled downward, sliding across the reed thatch and slipping over the edge to join the mist. Elizabeth felt very small and very alone, and though her cloak was thick and all-enveloping and smelled reassuringly of new oiled wool, she felt as if she were naked to the mist and its evil possibilities.

But it was foolish to fear. The old woman was no witch. Only poor ignorant folk believed in witches. Most of the servants referred to her as ''the wisewoman,'' and though none of them had consulted her, they all knew someone who had. Elizabeth rode nearer, and in the deceptive light the cottage seemed to grow no closer until suddenly it was only a hand's stretch away. There was no tethering ring in the wall, but near the black door-hole there was a dead stump of tree round which a rope had been fastened for the purpose. Elizabeth dismounted and led the pony forward, and tethered it lightly. It seemed at ease, not nervous, only resigned to the rain that trickled down its ears. She patted it, feeling the sweet warmth of its neck through its wet coat, and walked to the door hole.

The door was ajar, as indeed it had to be to let any light into that low, windowless place, and as she hesitated the rain dripped steadily off the thatch onto her head and shoulders. It was very dark inside. She could not even see a fireglow, and the smell of the place was daunting: yeasty, choking smell of human squalor, overlaid with a pungent, bitter smell of herbs and very distantly, like a breath of fresh air by comparison, the odor of garlic. Then came a voice, very close, making her start so much she ricked her neck.

''Come in or go away. You steal my light when you stand in the door.''

Still Elizabeth hesitated. "I can't see you," she said.

"But I can see you. Come you in, mistress, if you will."

"Are you the wisewoman?" she asked, peering desperately into the gloom. Her eyes could now pick out a gleam here and there, as if some poor light touched a shiny surface, but it meant nothing to her.

The voice was a long time in answering, and then said at last, "Who knows? Some call me one thing, some another. I hardly remember. Come in at all events. Or go away. It makes no matter to me."

Summoning her courage she ducked in under the low doorway, and the smell rose up like a cloud to fill her lungs. Once inside, she began to see a little more. There was a fire, low, red, and smoky, and over it an iron cauldron on a tripod, which obscured all the light it could give. The rim of the cauldron was one of the things that had gleamed. She peered about her, and there came a thin, strange chuckle from close by that made her jump and turn, and she saw, with a leaping thud of her heart, the huddled shape of something more or less human close beside her.

"Why, you start like the mouse that sees an owl shadow," the voice said. It was neither a woman's voice nor a man's voice, but thin and whispery like wind in reeds, and as sexless, and as vacant.

"I did not see you," Elizabeth said defensively, and her voice boomed too loud in that close place.

"I sit by the door where I can get the light for my work. See, my work, mistress—it is very fine. Did you come to buy from me?"

She held something up, something that seemed to be a palmful of mist or cobweb but resolved itself as the light fell on it to a circle of fine lace.

"I did not know you made lace," Elizabeth said feebly.

"That is who I am. The lacemaker. If I ever had a name, I have forgotten it. I am older than anyone knows. What do you want from me, if it is not my lace?"

"Some say—they say—you are a—wisewoman," Elizabeth said. There was a long silence, and she licked her lips nervously.

The dark bundle did not stir, but the pale web of lace turned and flickered like marsh light in the unseen lap. As the silence grew Elizabeth thought the old one had not heard her, and was about to speak again when there was a long, sibilant sigh that sounded like regret, and it moved her suddenly to pity. She said, "Forgive me—" The old woman said at once, "Nothing to forgive, mistress. Some say one thing, some another. You want my help? I have lived so long, I have outlived all my wants, and yet it is good to be sought if it be only for that. Fetch a stool and sit by me. I cannot speak to your shadow."

Glancing about her Elizabeth saw a low, three-legged stool by the fire, and she picked it up and set it in the doorway and sat on it. It was so ill made she had trouble balancing herself upon it, but once she was settled she looked up, and drew a gasping breath, for the old woman was now close to her, her face on a level with her own, and it was a face so incomprehensibly old that it made her feel cold within her thick, new cloak. Like the voice, it had nothing of man or woman in it, and it was so sunken and wrinkled that it seemed barely human, almost devoid of features. Yet it was not an unhealthy face, nor a weak one: it was dark and strong, and deep in the crevices of skin the eyes lived, bright and expressionless as a snake's.

"You stare at me, mistress." The old voice gave another whispery chuckle. "What do you see?"

"How old are you?" Elizabeth asked, wonderingly.

The ancient eyes did not blink nor flicker, and the voice came with barely a movement of the wrinkled gap that was a mouth. "I was a grown woman when the Queen died," she said.

"The Queen?" Elizabeth said, puzzled.

"Queen Elizabeth. Good Queen Bess, of blessed name. I was full grown, and bore all my children while she reigned over us. What do you want of me? They come here, from time to time, the secret ones, some veiling their faces. They come with sicknesses, they come with sorrows. They bring me what ails, and ask me to make it whole. They bring sorrow like a dead child wrapped in rags and leave it on my doorsill and go away, and sorrow gets up and follows them home. What can I do?"

"But—you have the Power?" Elizabeth said hesitantly, staring into the unwavering eyes.

"Everything that lives has power. What is it you want?"

"I want a child."

There, it was said! She felt the tension flow out of her, like water pouring from an unstoppered bottle. The old woman stirred, and her hands moved among the strands of lace as if there was nothing more to be said. At last Elizabeth broke the silence again, anxiously.

"Can you help me?"

"I am older than anyone knows," the old woman said, and her voice was like the whisper of rats' feet under the thatch. "I have seen men born and die, and their children, and their children's children. I have outlived them all. I have outlived even my own life, and yet He will not take me home. There is nothing more that I care for, nothing that I want except to leave the shadow and pass out into the sunshine. Life is the long shadow cast from God's back. I want to see His face. Why should I help you?"

Elizabeth was silent, disappointment rising up in her like bile. "Is there nothing, then, that you can do?"

"I can give you a potion—is that what you want?"

"Will it get me with child?"

The old woman laughed, a stronger, nearer sound than hitherto. "Nay, mistress, it wants a man to do that."

"But will the potion help?"

"If you believe it, it will. Here, in the shadow, we think we know what our senses tell us, but who can see in the dark? There is only what you believe, and what you believe will be. I will give you a potion, and you will get with child, and nothing will be any different. Show me your hand."

Elizabeth held her hand out, palm up, and one of the old woman's brown claws rose from her lap to take the ends of the fingers and bend it toward her. The old woman's fingers felt hard and dry and sharp like a dog's nails. "I knew your mother," she said as she peered at the white palm. "She believed, and waited, and she got everything she wanted, except happiness. So will you. Go outside and say a prayer to Our Lady, and then come back. I will give you the potion."

Elizabeth rose up and stepped out into the gray, dripping world, her mind whirling. Stumblingly she framed a prayer and, not knowing if she was meant to pray aloud or not, she murmured it, hardly moving her lips, afraid to make too much sound in that place. Then she went back to the door, and looked in.

"Here," said the old woman. She was sitting where she had been, as if she had never moved, and she held out a brown claw from which dangled a small linen bag tied by the neck. Elizabeth took it wonderingly. It crunched under her fingers, and from it came the wholesome, reassuring smell of herbs. "Boil it up in water and drink it down, lees and all. You must do it in one swallow, and you must do it exactly twelve days from the beginning of your next flux. Drink it last thing at night before you go to bed. If you are mated that night, you will conceive."

Elizabeth stowed the bag away in the breast of her gown. "What must I pay you?"

"Nothing," said the old woman.

"Nothing? But I must give you something."

"You have nothing that I want. Go now, and speak of this to no one."

Bewildered, Elizabeth left her and went toward the pony, stumbling a little on the rough grass. The pony lifted his head from his doze and whickered as she approached, longing to be home, and though she rode with slack reins he took her back briskly as though he had trod that path every day of his life.

CHAPTER NINE

Four days after the wedding of Princess Mary and Prince William, while the Londoners were still lighting bonfires to celebrate what they thought of as an end to England's subordination to France, the Duchess of York gave birth to a son.

"God's fish," the King exclaimed on the occasion, "it was a close-run thing." Prince William's gloomy countenance grew a degree more gloomy as his new wife was thus placed a step farther away from the throne, and the King, in a fit of malicious glee, obliged the Dutchman to stand sponsor to the baby at its christening. The prince was wild to get back home to Holland, but the weather was too stormy for it to be possible to set sail, for which Princess Mary was duly thankful. She wept continuously, refusing all attempts to comfort her, and eventually reducing the duchess, who was very fond of her, to tears as well. The Dutch party finally set sail on the nineteenth, to almost everyone's relief, and on the twentieth the news came to Whitehall that the wind had turned foul again and the ship was held up at the mouth of the Thames.

"Oh, Lord!" Annunciata cried to Chloris, who brought her the news. "If they come back again we shall all be flooded out. I vow and swear I have never seen so much water in one place as Whitehall this November. If they come back, I think I shall go straight home to Yorkshire."

But it seemed that Prince William had also had enough, and though the wind stayed foul he sent a firm courteous refusal to return to London, and his party lodged at Canterbury until the wind finally came round, and they set sail, in heavy seas, on the twenty-seventh. By that time the Duchess of York's infant son had died, and Annunciata was so tired of the gloom of Whitehall that she decided to move into her new house, even though it was not completely finished. She spoke to the craftsmen still engaged in their work, and they undertook to finish the main rooms in time for the Christmas festivities.

"I shall have Christmas there," Annunciata said cheerfully one morning, as Mrs. Drake made the final adjustments to a new gown on her. Outside in her anteroom the traders were making a cheerful din as they waited to be admitted with their samples, and soon the first visitors of the day would be calling. Birch was hovering nearby with brushes, ready to do her hair as soon as Mrs. Drake finished the fitting and lifted the gown off, and as soon as she was dressed she was engaged to go riding with a young captain of the guard, Lord Berkeley, to Islington, where, after a canter across the fields, they would repair to the Great Cheesecake House with a party of young people for some entertainment.

The door opened, and Chloris came in with the letters, bringing with her the spaniels, who had been shut out because they liked to rummage in Mrs. Drake's basket and upset her pins, and the noise of the crowd in the anteroom. Chloris walked briskly despite heels almost as high as her mistress's, and Annunciata smiled at the sight of her, for she was every inch a lady of fashion, as befitted a countess's waiting woman, her face discreetly painted, her hair elaborately curled, and yet underneath she was as plain and wholesome as new bread.

"How shall you like that, Chloris? Christmas at Chelmsford House?" Annunciata said.

Chloris's face lit in a smile. "Why, my lady, what a good idea! Will you have the children to stay with you?"

"The children? Ah, I understand—you want to see your own son again. Well, you may go to Yorkshire if you like—there is nothing to keep you here."

Chloris shook her head in pretended amazement. "Why my lady, how you run on! I was only thinking you'd like to see your own children again, that's all."

"You were not, you rogue! What have you there?"

"One from St. Omer, my lady, and one from Oxford," Chloris said, sorting through the letters.

"Give me that first. Have you finished, Mrs. Drake? Well, then, help me out of this."

She read the letter from Hugo while stepping into her riding habit as Birch and Chloris held it for her.

"He wants to spend Christmas with his friend Masseldine, at his friend's home. Who is Masseldine, Chloris? I mean, who is his father?"

Chloris, who always seemed to know everything, answered at once. "Eldest son of the Marquess of Ely, my lady. A very old family, but not rich. Lost everything—"

"In the wars, I know," Annunciata finished for her. "What else?"

"The marquess is a mossy-backed magnate, my lady, never leaves his estate. Her ladyship died these ten years since. But there's a daughter, fifteen years old."

"Ah!" Annunciata said. She sat down to allow Birch better access to her head. "Well, no harm in that I suppose."

"The marquess is one of the old-fashioned sort, my lady. He would not allow anything to happen," Chloris said. She gave the information as if she had been born knowing it. Annunciata never inquired how she found things out, but she guessed in this case that a letter had come for Chloris from John by the same messenger.

"He shall go, then. It sounds as if he is making good friends at last. I should be glad to have him settled. And if I could find someone suitable for Miss Arabella—perhaps I shall give a party at Chelmsford House, a very large party, to celebrate my moving in." She turned her head to Birch's hands. "What else is there?"

"I think you'll want this one, my lady," Chloris said, passing a heavy, much-travel-stained letter. Annunciata glanced at the seal and smiled, and broke it open at once, and scanned the few lines of Kit's scholarly script. She looked up and laughed at Chloris's expression of determined lack of curiosity.

"He will be here next week," she said. Chloris tried to look inquiring, and then she, too, laughed.

"In time for Christmas, my lady."

"Indeed. Have I time before the captain calls to write a letter? I must tell Ralph I shall be staying here."

"I'll fetch paper, my lady. If the captain comes, I'll tell him to wait."

"No, no," Annunciata corrected. "Ask him to wait. One does not give commands to friends, only to lovers."

Although Annunciata asked Ralph to join her in London for Christmas, she knew that he would not come, for he would not break so far with tradition as to be absent from Morland Place at that particular time. She did not miss him at all, for she was absorbed in the delights of her new house and her new neighbors, and in the company of her lover. Kit came to London every winter now, drawn like a moth to her flame, coming officially on business, but in reality to see her. This year she persuaded him to remain for the Christmas season, and act as her host in the new house, which he could do with official propriety, being her cousin and adoptive brother. Everyone knew, of course, that they were lovers, and it made a delicious seasonal scandal for the Whitehall Whisperers, but Annunciata cared nothing for that.

She gave her great party, the most lavish, expensive, and memorable one of the Season, on the day before Christmas Eve, and thereafter the house was never empty of guests. Annunciata was glad to see that Arabella was attracting a certain amount of attention, and even more pleased to see her daughter acting with propriety. She rapidly drew a circle of admirers from among the horseguards, who hung round her, wrote poems to her, and discussed horses with her. Her health was drunk in the mess but it was, Chloris's spies assured her, done in the most proper way. Arabella's admirers tended to be the young sons of country squires, and adored her almost as much for her knowledge of horses as her physical attractions. Annunciata scanned them carefully, and saw none that was good enough as a match, but she did not worry, for though it seemed important for princesses to marry at fifteen, Arabella was well enough connected and would have a large enough dowry to last a year or two longer, if that was necessary to find the right match.

"I have only the one daughter to be rid of," she would say to Birch, "so I shall take my time and do it right."

Once the excitement of Christmas was over, however, Annunciata began to feel guilty, and though she fought off the sensation, she kept thinking of Morland Place at Christmas, and of Ralph alone, missing her, and of her children forgetting her, and the sensation grew. Finally she decided that she would go home at Easter, and spend as much of the summer as she could bear making amends, and as soon as she had resolved upon it, her mind eased, and she was able to enjoy herself again. But before the date came upon which she had fixed for her return, Chloris came to her, pale with anxiety, with news she had much sooner keep to herself.

"From Morland Place, my lady. My information—"

"Who is it keeps you informed?" Annunciata interrupted cheerfully. "My belief is that it is Ralph himself."

"My lady, it is bad news," Chloris said.

Annunciata stared, growing pale. "Ralph. The children? Someone is dead!"

"No, my lady. It is Miss Elizabeth—she—"

"No!" Annunciata cried, forestalling her. "No!"

"She is with child, my lady," Chloris said quietly. Annunciata stared at her, her eyes wide with a strange anguish, and then she rushed from the room, into her bedchamber, slamming the door after her. In the silence Caspar ran to the closed door and scratched at it, whimpering, and Birch and Chloris exchanged a look.

"I'd better—" Chloris began, but Birch put a hand on her arm.

"No, I'll go. It's me she'll want," she said. Chloris read the quiet authority in the older woman's face, and then nodded.

Within the chamber all was quiet. Annunciata had flung herself onto her bed, hiding her face. Birch thought she was crying, but when she touched her mistress's shoulder, Annunciata lifted a white, tearless face from the pillow. They exchanged no words. Birch knew the mixture of anger and pain, for she had seen it before. Under her strong exterior, the countess was vulnerable in strange ways. Birch knew she felt betrayed; and she knew also

there was nothing she could say. She held out her arms, and
Annunciata leaned into them, and put her head on Birch's shoulder,
seeking comfort like the motherless child she still was underneath.

After a long time the countess stirred and sat up, her face still
tearless, and Birch saw she had conquered the pain and shut it
away, and she was sad, knowing it would be better if the
countess could weep.

"Well," she said, in a matter-of-fact voice, "I can't go home
now, that at least is plain. I'll have to stay in London. And I'll
take George away—I won't have him corrupted by her influence."

"Will you bring his lordship here, my lady?" Birch asked
expressionlessly.

"I don't know. No, I'll send him to Christ Church, to be with
his brother," Annunciata said. "It's time he went out into the
world. I should have thought of it before. At any rate," she
added through gritted teeth, "he shan't stay there to see his
mother betrayed."

Annunciata did not consider it necessary to tell Hugo of her
decision, and John, who heard of it from Chloris, thought better
of stirring up Hugo's passions ahead of time. He knew, as did no
one else, how Hugo felt about his brother, and seeing Hugo so
happy and settled, John decided that the longer he could enjoy
his peace the better. So the young earl's arrival came unexpectedly to the viscount, shattering his happiness like a stone shattering ice.

George had grown tall in the six months since Hugo had last
seen him, and though his face was still boyish, his body had
filled out and taken on the dimensions of a man. He carried
himself gracefully, and to Hugo's angry eyes he appeared to have
been designed specifically to show up Hugo's deficiencies. His
clear face, his Grecian features, his wide gray eyes, his thick,
glossy, silver-gold hair curling in heavy natural rings over his
shoulders, his tall athletic figure—beside him Hugo felt small
and ugly and ill-formed. And with George's grace of body came
grace of mind, his easy accomplishments, his quick intelligence.
He learned easily and remembered what he learned. He was an
accomplished musician, sang sweetly, danced and fenced grace-

fully, conversed easily, made friends as naturally as he breathed. Everyone liked George; young women gazed at him almost with awe; young men sought his company; older men approved him.

The worst thing of all was that everyone thought Hugo felt the same way, and it was impossible for Hugo to admit to anyone that he did not love and admire his brother as they did. When Hugo was invited anywhere, George was invited as well, as though that would give Hugo pleasure. If Hugo went anywhere alone, people would ask him where George was, and tell him how much they liked him, sing his praises, and Hugo could only grit his teeth and nod and smile. George had lodgings in Peckwater Inn, and did his best to keep out of Hugo's way, for he at least had no illusions about the way his brother felt about him. But the more retiring he was, the more people praised his modesty and virtue.

One day in early summer Hugo burst into George's room without ceremony, his face dark with anger, and as George looked up from his reading, startled, he said, "This is too much! I won't have it, do you hear me? I won't have it."

"What? What's the matter?" George asked in alarm.

Hugo brandished a fist. "You know very well. Masseldine has just been to see me."

"Oh," said George unhappily.

"Oh, you say! You know then, what I am talking about. Masseldine is *my* friend, *mine*! Must you take everything from me? Cannot you leave me one thing of my own?"

"I don't want to take anything from you," Geroge began unhappily, but Hugo would not let him finish.

"You were hardly here a week before you began turning my friends against me, making them love you more than me. I spent Christmas with Masseldine and his family, and he asked me to go there for the summer, too. And now he tells me he has asked you along as well! Now he will be your friend, not mine, and I shall have no one!"

"But, Hugo, what could I do? When he asked me—"

"You should have said no! Why did you not refuse him? Because you want to steal him from me. Go home to Morland Place, leave us in peace."

"I didn't accept his invitation, truly I didn't. But I could not refuse right away. You see, if I do not go there—"

"You can go home."

"No. Not to Morland Place. Our mother—she does not want me there. She has said—she has told me I must go to her for the summer recess."

Hugo stared wildly, the blood draining from his face. "She asked for you—and not for me?" he whispered. George nodded.

"You see," he said miserably, "what was I to do? Oh, Hugo, why must you make us both so unhappy? Why do you hate me so? You know I don't hate you—"

"So you say," Hugo said bitterly. "But you have always taken everything from me. Everything that should have been mine. I am the firstborn, but you always came first, worming your way into everyone's affections, smiling and bowing and nodding like a damned obsequious dog. Well, go your own way, do your worst, what do I care? You have taken everything from me, and I have nothing more to lose."

And he turned on his heel and flung out, slamming the door behind him, leaving George miserably to contemplate the impossibility of his situation.

Annunciata's letter was brusque. "If I had wanted you in London I would have asked for you. You are not in need of more pleasure, but of more study. I have poor reports of you from your tutors. Your brother has done more in one term than you have in one year. I shall send for you when I am more certain of deriving pleasure from your presence than I now am."

Hugo crumpled the letter slowly and threw it onto the fire. Tears sprang to his eyes and he knuckled them away, angry at his own weakness. Then, as he watched the heavy paper blacken and burn up, his face grew thoughtful, then stern, and the tears dried at their source.

The New Spring Garden at Vauxhall was fast becoming the most fashionable place for smart young people to meet for refreshment, entertainment, and dalliance. It was especially popular with impecunious younger sons and up-and-coming gentlemen of the professions, for the entry into the gardens was free, so one could spend as much or as little as one liked, and the dining rooms were much cheaper than Colby's in the Mulberry Gardens.

Arabella understood all these things, but accepted the assignation without comment. For her the attraction of the Vauxhall tryst was that she was unlikely to meet anyone she knew there—or, more accurately, anyone that she met would be unlikely to tell her mother. She only hoped that Berkeley would be there and waiting when she arrived, for she knew that even cloaked, hooded, and masked, she still looked very young, and though she was confident she could both hire and dismiss a hackney coach without trouble, she did not think she could wait alone in a tavern for long without being approached.

She did not need to worry, however. Berkeley was standing in front of the door to the tavern looking anxious. As the hackney drew up, he came forward to peer through the unglazed window, and with a smile called out something to the driver and got in beside her.

"Well, sir, where are you taking me?" she asked as he lifted her hands and kissed them fervently in greeting.

"To the dining rooms. It is better if we go straight there. A tavern is no place for you. Darling, darling Arabella! I am so glad you came. I have been cursing my idiocy for letting you take such risks."

"What risks?" Arabella asked coolly.

"To cross London, alone, in a hackney! Darling, forgive me. I should never have let you hazard it."

"Oh, pish! I don't regard it. The common people are like animals—as long as you show no fear, they will not harm you."

Berkeley laughed. "Oh, Arabella! You are superb—and so young."

"You may be ten years older than me, sir, but I warrant I have a great deal more sense than you," Arabella said severely.

"I don't doubt it. Otherwise you could never have got away. You *were* unobserved, I take it? How did you manage to escape your jailers, my darling?"

Arabella shrugged. "It is easy enough, in the flurry of unpacking. Everyone wants to think I am with someone else. Besides, when we go to Windsor I am never so closely watched. I can ride out in the park alone there quite safely, so they get into the habit of not wondering where I am, and it takes a little while for the London habit to take over again.''

"A whole month you were gone, cruel, cruel mistress!'' Berkeley groaned. "I hope you had a pleasant time while I suffered."

"Suffered—nonsense! I know exactly what you were doing this month past—getting drunk at the Sun Inn and playing cards at the Groom Porter's. I hope you won, at least."

"Enough to pay for your dinner," Berkeley answered with a smile. "But tell me, what was it like at Windsor?"

"Oh, well enough. It is good to be able to ride again, and of course there were the races at Datchet. And I like Prince Rupert. And the prince's son Dudley was there—he's jolly. We went riding together quite a lot. But, oh, the evenings!"

"Dull?" Berkeley asked sympathetically. The hackney drew up outside the dining rooms, and Berkeley helped Arabella out, paid off the hackney, and led her inside. The landlord came forward quickly at the sight of a red coat, for soldiers were free spenders, but often not free payers, but his anxious look cleared as he recognized his customer.

"Oh, yes, my lord, welcome, welcome. I have your room all ready for you, if you would care to follow me. This way my lord. Madam —Your Ladyship, I mean," he corrected quickly just in case, his shrewd eyes assembling what little of Arabella's face was visible and desperately trying to recognize her. He gave it up with a small shrug and led them upstairs. He would serve them himself, and once she had her mask off it would be easy enough. He got good money from various sources for telling of the secret assignations that happened in his rooms.

Arabella was charmed with the room, which was small but one of the best, the walls papered, the windows curtained with thick red velvet, and many mirrors on the walls giving a sumptuous look. It was furnished with a small dining table and two chairs, and dominated by a huge log fire at right angles to which was drawn up an enormous couch on which, after dinner, most of the landlord's customers were inclined to fulfill the unspoken purpose of their meetings. All around the room were sconces containing real wax candles, a touch of luxury that Arabella appreciated. With the curtains drawn and the candles and fire lighting the room it was hard to remember it was broad daylight outside. It could have been any room anywhere, and it gave her a feeling of immunity from consequence, which was exactly what was intended.

The landlord went away, and Berkeley helped her off with her cloak, hood, and mask, and then embraced her properly for the first time.

"Oh, my darling, it's been so long! Did you miss me at all? Even just a little?"

"Just a little, now and then. Come, my lord, you mustn't expect too much. You must recollect I have been in exalted company."

"And you like to be capricious and teasing, to keep me in my place," Berkeley concluded, leading her to the couch, and sitting down with her without letting go of her hands. "I would do battle with any young blood for your favors, but I own myself defeated by Prince Rupert. You are not become his mistress, I hope?"

Arabella jerked one hand away and slapped his wrist. "Come, sir, what a suggestion! He is my godfather, and as good as a relative. Besides, he is so old."

"I thought you enjoyed his company."

"During the day, when we are out riding or at the races or walking— but in the evenings when he got into conversation with my mother—oh, lord! I had much ado not to yawn."

"Your mother— dull?" Berkeley said with disbelief. Arabella looked at him sharply. He used to take her mother riding and hunting, before he fell in love with Arabella, which was one of the reasons she met him in secret. She did not entirely trust his change of sides.

"They talk about my brothers for hours, and my mother goes on and on about Hugo and George and how wonderful George is and how wicked Hugo is—"

"They were not with you?"

"They are both at the Marquess of Ely's, or were until this week. They are gone back to Oxford now, of course. One of them is to marry my lord of Ely's daughter, but I don't know which.''

"Ah, yes, the divine Caroline," Berkeley said thoughtfully. "I had a mind to marry her myself, but of course she has no money, no money at all. Then I fell in love with you, and all other thoughts fled from my mind.''

"I don't believe you," Arabella said sharply, drawing back her hands, and Berkeley laughed.

"She is a pale, insipid thing beside you, darling Arabella. A draught of watered milk beside the finest champagne.''

Arabella cast a look of disbelief and went on, ''And then they would stop talking about Hugo and George only to begin talking about Lord Shaftesbury and his friends, and that was worse. What, pray tell me, are Whigs and Tories? Aside from being the most boring things in the world.''

Berkeley laughed. "My dear ignorant, have you no interest in politics? And you a Court-dweller.''

"Mother is interested enough for all of us. She says a spell in the Tower only served to whet Lord Shaftesbury's ambitions, and that the King would have done better to cut off his head.''

"She is a fierce woman, your mother, but I don't know that she is wrong. Shaftesbury wants power, and he will harness any brute force to achieve it. His Country Party is a collection of everyone with a grievance, a motley crew of malcontents, with nothing but their hatred of Catholicism and France in common. That's why the Court party calls them Whigs, Scots marauders, and they retaliate and call the Court party Tories, Irish rebels.''

"Pretty language indeed!" Arabella said. "So the Whigs are dissenters and Puritans, are they?''

"Mostly," Berkeley said. "Shaftesbury wants an election, to get rid of the Cavalier Parliament and put him into power, and he gathers around him anyone who has hopes in that direction, but he needs civil discontent to force Parliament to dissolve, and at the moment the people are content. Trade is good and the harvest was good and the Protestant wedding cheered them, and they are not in the mood to be angry. So Shaftesbury gathers his motley crew and bides his time, and makes friends with one he hopes will oust the Duke of York as heir to the throne.''

"Who? What are you talking about?" Arabella frowned.

"Why, who else but the King's beloved son, Monmouth? If enough pressure were put upon the King, Shaftesbury believes, he would legitimize Monmouth and make him Prince of Wales. It isn't a bad plan in some ways—Monmouth's very popular with the people, and he's Protestant to the core."

"He's a conceited braggart," Arabella said contemptuously, "and he's only Protestant because it makes him popular. He's the wickedest person I know."

"He did not dance with you at the last assembly, did he?" Berkeley teased.

"That has nothing to do with it. Besides, Shaftesbury is mad if he thinks the King would legitimize him. The King loves Monmouth, but he never forgets he's a bastard."

"I don't know," Berkeley said thoughtfully. "If it were expedient—"

"The King would not do it at any price," Arabella said.

"You seem to know a lot about politics, for one who has no interest," Berkeley observed, smiling. Arabella glanced at him.

"I know the King, that's all."

"Then—you mean it is the King who is my rival?" He made a face of comic dismay. "Then I am undone. I might have challenged Prince Rupert, but to challenge the King would be treason."

"Oh, don't talk such nonsense," Arabella said, but she smiled all the same, and Berkeley took the opportunity to take her hands again and resume his pleading.

"Oh, Arabella, won't you let me speak to your mother? I'm sure it would be the best way. After all, it would not be a dishonorable marriage—"

"She would not approve," Arabella said starkly. "I know my mother, believe me. And once you spoke, I would be watched harder than ever, and we would not be allowed to meet."

"Then—let us elope together. Once we took bold action, there would be nothing she could do to part us."

"Don't be a fool," Arabella said coldly. "Do you think I would part with my virtue for no return? My mother would cast me off, and I would be penniless, and then you would cast me off, too."

"Have you so little belief in my love?" Berkeley said sadly.

Arabella looked at him with eyes that were wise beyond her years. "If I were as penniless as Lady Caroline Boverie you would not be here now with me."

"You are wrong! Of course, I am glad you are rich, but I would love you if you had nothing. I would face poverty with you, Arabella—I would face anything if you were by my side."

"Then you are a fool. There is nothing so important in life as a good establishment. I do not desire you to be rich, because I am, but if both of us were poor—no, I would not face poverty with you."

"Then what hope is there?" Berkeley cried despairingly. She gazed at him, loving him, but knowing that his mind had less bite than hers, was made of a substance that more resembled clay than granite. He was a courtier of long standing, had grown up with ideals of love, read poetry and wrote it, dallied and philandered his life away, dreaming large impractical dreams, like so many of the young men she knew at Whitehall. But faced with the reality of poverty he would quickly melt away with a charming smile and a plausible excuse. Arabella came of firmer stock, and her mind was weathered by generations of battling northerners.

"We can enjoy each other's company, and hope my mother has a change of heart," she said. "Ah, at last, here is our dinner—I was beginning to wonder if you had remembered to order any."

"I ordered everything you like best," Berkeley said, brightening as the landlord came through the door, ushering in three maids bearing loaded trays. "Pike with bitter sauce, oyster pie, those pastries stuffed with goose liver and almonds—I forget everything I asked for, but I'm sure Master Walton remembered."

"Everything exactly as you asked, my lord." The landlord beamed. "And champagne to drink, and also a pot of coffee, which is Mistress McNeill's favorite, so I believe." Mentally, Walton rubbed his hands with glee. Mrs. McNeill, daughter of the notorious Countess of Chelmsford, who was supposed to be the King's mistress and dined intimately with both the Yorks and Prince Rupert! This little tidbit would sell for a high price in the right market, he thought. He'd get a new hat out of this, and a petticoat for his wife, damned if he didn't!

Hugo struggled to wakefulness, turning his eyes fretfully away from the rushlight's gleam.

"My lord, wake up, my lord, wake up."

Someone was shaking his shoulder. Hugo groaned, his mind still bemused by fumes of Rhenish. Surely it could not be morning already. It was as black as the ace of spades, except for that infernal rushlight that was making his head clang like Great Tom.

"Wake up, my lord, wake up."

"John? What is it? Is it morning?" Hugo groaned.

"No, my lord, it is but eleven—"

"Then go away. I want to sleep." He tried to lie down, but John's large horny hand continued to shake him. Damnit, that was no way to serve a gentleman! Hugo sat up, and his head rocked with pain. "What is it? Unless the house is afire, I see no reason to—"

"My lord, it is the earl—he is ill. You must come at once."

"I'm not a doctor. Go away, John, and trouble someone else," Hugo moaned, but he was being hauled over the edge of his bed, and John was already holding out his bed-wrapper to him as his fuddled brain came to life. "Which earl?"

"You brother, my lord," John said severely, "is very ill. We have sent for a doctor, but I think you should come at once."

"Oh." Hugo stood up, wide awake now, and slipped his arms into the sleeves held out for him. "His man is with him?"

"He has gone for the doctor, sir. Oh, quickly—he is very bad."

John's genuine anxiety slipped out past his servant's manner, and Hugo said, startled, "What is it? What is wrong with him?"

"It's the old trouble, sir, he's been vomiting, but it's very bad this time, very bad." Hugo looked at his servant and read the stark fear in his eyes. "I need your authority, my lord, to send word to your mother and send for a priest."

Hugo's eyes widened. "No! Don't say it! Surely he cannot be so ill? Why, only two hours since I saw him, and he was perfectly well."

"Oh, God, my lord, please hurry!" John cried, turning away and leading the way with the light, and Hugo followed him, feeling as if an icy stone were lodged in his chest.

In George's room there were three rushlights, and the smell of burning mutton-fat would have been strong but for the stronger smell of sickness. The landlord and his wife were both there, roused by George's servant Michael as he went for the doctor, and a very tousled maid who was taking away a bowl and cast a terrified glance at Hugo as they passed in the door. Hugo tried not to see what was in the bowl, but in vain. The vomit was blood-streaked.

He pushed past the landlord, who was standing well back from the bed, and said to the landlady, "How is he?"

"Mortal bad, my lord. I swear I never saw anyone so bad." She cast frightened eyes up at Hugo, and whispered, "Should we send for a priest, my lord? I'm afraid—"

Hugo swallowed. "It can do no harm to have one on hand," he said, and finally moved past her to the bed. Among his crumpled sheets George lay, his face green-white and sweating, his silvery hair dark with perspiration, and blue circles under his eyes. He was still, but almost at once began writhing again, a slow, agonized movement, drawing his legs up and then turning, arching his back and twisting his spine in the most unnatural-looking contortion in his effort to evade the pain. His teeth clamped on his lips, and blood began to trickle out from under them, and he made the most terrible sound, a groan so awful it was hard to believe a human being could make such a noise.

"George," Hugo whispered, "George, can you hear me? George, what's wrong with you?" George paused a moment, and then began his terrible twisting again. Hugo began to sweat also, and turned to the landlady. "He was never this bad before. He always tended to these bouts of sickness, but this—" The smell of sickness in the room was terrible, made him want to vomit. He caught John's eye, and swallowed. "You had better go for my mother. I—I think he is very bad."

The landlord caught the gist of this and said, "Don't you want to wait for the doctor, my lord? He may be better by and by, and your mother ought not to be alarmed. Why, his young lordship can't be so bad—he was right as a trivet not two hours since."

Hugo snatched eagerly at the idea. "Yes, you're right! Wait for the doctor, that's the thing. He'll get better—he always has before."

And then George let out another agonized groan, and arched up off the bed so that only his shoulders and heels were touching. The sheets under him were soaked in sweat and diarrhea. Hugo shuddered.

"No," John said, "better I go now." And in his eyes Hugo read the calmness of despair. He nodded.

"Make all haste, then. Take post horses. Take all the money you need from my purse. Go now."

And John was gone upon the word. Hugo turned back to the bed. The writhing creature there hardly looked like George anymore, handsome, strong, clever, likeable George. He was a soul in torment, a twisted wreck of a creature. What would Caroline think of him if she could see him now? The maid came back in with a clean bowl and damp cloths, and the landlady took the cloths to wipe the earl's brow.

"No, give them to me," he said, and as the landlady hesitated, he added more softly, "I will wipe his brow. He is my brother, after all."

The roads were dry, thank God, and there was a good moon—not full, but enough to see by. With the urgency of his mission, much gold, and the viscount's seal to display, John got post horses with no trouble, and he reached Pall Mall just before seven. He was hammering on the door of Chelmsford House at the hour when first Mass was normally just ending and the countess would be preparing to break her fast. Please God she was at home, John thought desperately. His legs were shaking with weariness, and his mind was hollow with fear. The servant who opened the door did not at once recognize him, and it took precious minutes to send for Birch, but Birch, as soon as she saw him, gave a terrible cry and clutched her throat.

"What is it, John? Something terrible has happened!"

"Take me to her ladyship, Birch, quickly. The earl is sick, terrible sick."

Annunciata was sitting at the small table in her bedchamber,

eating bread and butter, and when she looked up and saw John
her apprehensions were as quick to rise as Birch's had been.

"What has happened? Hugo is sick? Tell me, John!"

"My lady, the lord earl—his old trouble—but worse. Oh, my
lady, I think you should come right away."

The blood drained from Annunciata's face so rapidly that
Birch thought she must faint, but after a second she stood up, her
unheeding hands clutching at the piece of bread she held so
fiercely that it crumbled onto the floor. Her lips were bloodless,
but her voice was quite calm.

"I'll come at once. Birch, go and order horses. Chloris, come
and help me dress. John, you had better sit down for a moment.
Finish my breakfast—you must be famished."

"Oh, my lady—"

"Come, you have done everything you can. Eat, while I dress,
and we will be away at once."

It was three in the afternoon before they arrived at Peckwater
Inn, and Annunciata had been driven almost frantic by the delays
they encountered, yet as soon as she arrived she took command
as calmly as, in battles of yore, her father had commanded
hysterical soldiers. In a matter of moments she was at her son's
bedside. The smell in the room was abominable—sickness, blood,
vomit, diarrhea, sweat, candle smoke, burning herbs, burnt flesh—
and it was stiflingly hot, but she did not notice it. The room
seemed crowded—the landlord and landlady, their servants,
George's servant, a priest, the doctor and his assistant—but they
parted before her like the Red Sea and she was beside the bed
looking down at the pathetic scrap of humanity that her beautiful
son had become. Pity and horror wrenched her heart.

"Oh, God, what have you done to him?" she whispered. How
could anything change him so much? She knelt down and reached
her hands to him, but could not touch him. The doctor interpreted
her question literally.

"We have done everything, my lady, everything we could
think of. Purges, enemas, bleeding, hot irons to the feet—nothing
has seemed to help."

Dear God alive! His poor blistered feet! A cry rose in her

throat and was choked off. Sweet Jesu, what could he have done to deserve such torture? "Go away," she whispered, finding a little of her voice. "Go away, all of you."

"But my lady—" the doctor began.

Her voice rose. "Go away! You have done everything to him that you can think of. Now leave him in peace. John, clear the room."

Slowly, muttering, whispering, the crowds left. Her back turned to them, Annunciata did not see them go. George appeared to be in a coma, for which she thanked God in her heart, hoping he felt no more pain. Gently she tried to straighten his rigid limbs. His face was dusky white, his eyes sunk in their sockets, his beautiful hair lank and flattened to his skull with sweat. How could he have changed in so little time? John came up behind her and put a damp cloth in her hand, and she pushed back her child's hair and wiped his face.

"John, can we give him clean sheets and a clean bedgown?"

"Yes, my lady," John said. He went and came back quickly with what was required, and with Michael's help they changed the filthy sheets and soiled gown and lifted his lordship back onto the bed.

"Dear God, he is so light," Annunciata whispered. He was beginning to relax now. She was able to straighten his body. "Sweet Jesu, his poor feet," she said, staring at the blackened skin and raw blisters. She wrapped them in clean cloths, and the pity of it drew tears from her at last. "I'll never call a doctor again, I swear it. Oh, my son, they tortured you!" She looked round for John, and he was standing near, with Hugo behind him. "John, is there any chance?"

John could not speak. He shook his head silently. Hugo was weeping, and since Annunciata could not bear the sight of his tears, she turned back to George. "Did he make his peace?" she asked.

"The priest came," John said with difficulty, "but he was delirious."

Annunciata smoothed the hair again from the cold brow, remembering scenes from the child's life, remembering the triumphant moment when she had brought him to birth, his happy babyhood, his charmed youth. His skin was dark and his eyes were settling, and she knew there was no hope. "He was so beautiful," she whispered. "So beautiful." She took his damp hands in hers and tried to pray, but her mind was numb. She could not believe it was all over, his lovely, bright life.

Then he stirred and opened his eyes. She pressed his hands, and whispered, "George? George, can you hear me? My darling, I'm here." But she knew he did not see her. His eyes stared sightlessly, and as she watched they began to roll upward, rolling up and up horribly, inhumanly, until there was nothing but the white to be seen, and he was a parody, a caricature of her living son. She stared in horror as his body began also to lift, bowing in the middle, his spine arching up off the bed in a way no body ought to be able to, and she wanted to scream. Lord God, stop it, make it not to be! To watch her son being grotesquely contorted like a mannequin, as if wrenched by giant, torturing hands!

"NO!" she cried out, thrusting her knuckles into her mouth to stop herself screaming. "No!"

And then, as if something had snapped, the child's body flopped back to the bed, and moved no more. After a long while she felt a hand on her shoulder, and thought it was John, but it was Hugo's voice that spoke softly.

"Mother—come. Mother—it's all over."

On the bed the body lay still with its horrible white eyes staring upward, but it seemed already shrunken, as if the life passing from it had taken away its substance. Annunciata stood up, dazed. Hugo's face was tear streaked, his eyes red rimmed with weariness and weeping.

"Come, Mother," he said. She leaned on his shoulder, and he turned her gently and led her away to his own rooms, and there sat her down, and brought her wine. She took the cup dully, and he had to order her, still gently, to drink. She drank, and shuddered, and looked up at him, seeming to see him for the first time.

"Hugo," she said. "My son."

CHAPTER TEN

On a fine autumn day, in broad daylight, the journey seemed less mysterious and fraught with unknown dangers, and therefore, to Elizabeth, more guilty. It was ludicrous to suppose that the old woman was a witch (and yet, said her heart, her potion did make me pregnant) and if she was, it was unspeakably wicked to seek her aid (and yet, it was a matter of survival, and all creatures fought to survive). She rode slowly and carefully, for the sake of her belly, and her mind rang with the conversation she had had with Ralph two days since—two days during which she had wrestled with fear against her conscience.

"She is dazed with grief," Ralph said. "She always loved George best. She adored him, and she can't believe he's dead."

"Poor child," Elizabeth said. She had liked George—who had not? But her sadness was perfunctory. Her own child obsessed her mind.

"I am worried about her," Ralph said. "I do not think she ought to be from home at such a time. I am going to try to persuade her to come here to rest for a few months, until she recovers her spirits. London is not the place for a grieving mother."

"But what about me, Ralph?" Elizabeth had asked him, emboldened by fear.

"Oh, that will be all right," Ralph said vaguely. "Of course, while she's here, you will have to sleep apart from me. It wouldn't be seemly. But it will be all right."

But it wouldn't, Elizabeth knew that. She shrank from even

175

the idea of Annunciata's scorn and rage, let alone the reality. She would be sent away for sure, and Ralph would not lift a finger to save her. She'd be cast out, and an unmarried woman, alone, and with child, would be in a terrible plight. In desperation, therefore, she was turning to the only place she knew for help. She did not yet know what she would ask, but perhaps the wisewoman would know without being told.

In the sunlight the hovel looked more shabby than frightening, and in the black mouth of its door a tabby cat was lying on her side, licking her paws and blinking in the sunshine. The old woman (surely not a witch?) was also outside, sitting beside the doorway on a stool, her hands in her lap flicking the web of growing lace back and forth. In her voluminous black clothing she looked shrunken, but her eyes were still as bright and dark as a snake's. She looked up at Elizabeth's approach, but did not speak until Elizabeth had dismounted and hitched her pony to the tree stump and come close.

"Well?" she said.

"I came to see you," Elizabeth began hesitantly.

"So I see. I have few visitors. Will you take a little buttermilk? It's all I have to offer, but it's cool from the well."

Elizabeth knew that to eat or drink with a witch gave her power over you. "No, thank you," she said hastily, and then, realizing how rude it sounded, added, "I am not thirsty, thank you."

They looked at each other in silence for a while, and then the old woman said, with amusement in her voice, "Well, mistress, what do you want?"

"Your potion worked," Elizabeth blurted out. "I am with child."

"You are happy, then."

"Yes. No. Oh, mother, please help me. I am afraid. Tell me what to do."

The old woman looked for a long time, and then sighed and put down her lacemaking. "Give me your hands," she said, and her voice sounded resigned as if to an unmerited fate. "Kneel here before me."

Elizabeth knelt on the packed earth before the door, shook

back her sleeves, and offered her hands, palms upward, eagerly. The old woman took the tips of the fingers in her sharp, hard ones and stared at the palms for a long time, and then traced the lines along one palm with a fingernail, making Elizabeth shudder.

"Yes, one you are afraid of I see," she said at last.

"You see that?" Elizabeth cried eagerly. "Oh, tell me what to do."

"No, I can't tell you that. But your fates are intertwined, you and her. One strand winds through you both, and when it is tugged . . ." She paused for a long time and Elizabeth grew restless. Then she looked up and fixed Elizabeth with her cold, bright eyes. "One of you must die," she said. "Both will not live—that is not possible."

Elizabeth's mouth was dry as her mind strained to understand. One or the other of them must die. "Mother," she whispered, "give me something."

She stood up, and after a while the old woman got up, too, slowly and painfully, and hobbled into the house. Elizabeth waited, watching the cloud shadows run across the ground. The cat got up and disappeared, and a little cold wind began, and she felt more alone than ever in her life, as if she were the only person left in the world. Then the old woman was there beside her, so suddenly and silently that Elizabeth was startled. She held out a small bag of white linen, tied at the neck.

"Burn these in your hearth fire in three parts, on three evenings following each other. Do it covertly, tell no one."

"What—what will happen?" Elizabeth asked, her eyes huge.

"Who knows?" the old woman said, turning away as if she had not the strength to be interested any longer.

"But—you said—"

"Life is a shadow, and each of us casts our own shadow, as long as we are. And the ending of it—who knows? Mostly, what you really want happens. The trick is to know what you really want."

"But what you told me—is true?"

"That's true. The death of one is the life of the other—that's written. Good day to you, mistress." She went back into the house without another word, and Elizabeth felt strangely bereft, as if the old woman had cast her off. She put the bag away inside her gown, and turned back to her tethered pony.

Annunciata had remained in Oxford only a few days. Chloris had used her wits and sent word to Prince Rupert, and he had ridden at once to Oxford and persuaded Annunciata to come back with him to Windsor, where he was still staying with Peg and the children. At Annunciata's request he also arranged for the body to be taken to Windsor, and thus it was that on September 19, 1678, George Edward Cavendish, second Earl of Chelmsford, Baron Meldon, was buried at Windsor by private funeral, his title dying with him.

Annunciata stayed another week with the prince, whose silent sympathy and genuine grief were balm to her. Hugo was with her, a Hugo grown strangely mature, quiet, and gentle, and in her bewildered sorrow Annunciata leaned on him and took comfort from him. Clovis came from London for the funeral, and brought Birch with him for Annunciata, while Chloris remained at Chelmsford House with Arabella. Poor Birch went about her duties in a daze, more in need of comfort even than her mistress, for she had always loved George best, idolized him and set him above Hugo, and now his death left her bereft, and suddenly grown older.

George's servant Michael had been sent home to Morland Place with the news of his death, and he arrived back at Windsor shortly after Clovis with Ralph's letter of sympathy and his request that Annunciata come home.

Clovis read it to her—she was too listless to make even that effort for herself—and said, "You should go. It would do you good to get some fresh Yorkshire air, and you could rest there until you feel well again."

"Home?" Annunciata said musingly. It was tempting, of course, the idea of going home; it seemed, as always, to offer the prospect of everything being all right again. She had fled death and grief and disillusionment once before to seek the balm of home; but then Mother and Ellen had still been alive, offering her the possibility of being a child again. Now she was the mother, and there was no human agency to whom she could take her pain to be eased.

"I will take you, if you like," Clovis said. "Everything can be arranged. You need not bestir yourself at all."

"You are kind," she said. "Perhaps I will go home."

But at the end of a week she was feeling restless again, and the idea of home was more remote to her, less tempting. Besides, there was Elizabeth, and her impending birth: that was a real barrier. Even here at Windsor the peace was impaired, for try as she might to conquer her feelings, she was still horribly jealous of Peg Hughes, and the presence of Peg's daughter Ruperta, who was five years old now, disturbed her deeply. Ruperta was a lively, pretty, forward child, who often made Rupert laugh by the quick way she answered her mother back. She was the image of her father, with his long, fine face, dark curls, and brilliant dark eyes; she looked the image of Annunciata at the same age, and Annunciata could hardly bear to be in the same room as the child who was her sister.

So she cut short her visit and returned to London, arriving on the twenty-seventh. Chloris greeted her with hugs and tears before she remembered her station and drew back into her dignity. The sight of her touched Annunciata anew, for she looked so pale in her mourning black, and her eyes were shadowed with crying. She busied herself settling Annunciata with hot bath, fresh clothes, and spiced wine, and though she had from time to time to dash the tears away from her eyes, she had wit enough to distract all three of them with chatter about the Court and London news.

"Lord Berkeley was here yesterday, my lady, with that young Captain Morris who has been running after Miss Arabella like a spaniel."

"At such a time . . . ?" Annunciata began, shocked, and Chloris shook her head.

"Oh, no, my lady, they didn't come a-courting, of course not. It was all most proper, although I could see young Captain Morris all agog at the sight of Arabella in black, for the color suits her, though I shouldn't say so. But she behaved perfectly, and so did the gentlemen, of course. Came to pay their respects and offer their services. Lord Berkeley asked if he might have the honor of waiting on you today but I thought tomorrow would be better. Are you thinking of staying here, my lady?''

"Ralph wants me home, and I thought of going. Perhaps you can send a letter, Chloris, to say I will come home in a day or two. I somehow can't bring myself to write to anyone yet. Clovis has said he will write to Edmund in St. Omer, so that is one burden the less.''

"St. Omer!'' Chloris said. "Of course, I had forgot Master Edmund was there. You will not have heard the latest scandal, I suppose, my lady, about this fellow Oates and his Popish Plot?''

"Oh, not another plot,'' Annunciata said wearily. "There seems to be one every summer, and there is never any substance in it. Who is Oates?''

"Well, my lady, it seems he was at the seminary in St. Omer back in the spring, living there for some months, though the word is he got thrown out for bad behavior. He has a very poor character, my lady, and they say he's no gentleman, though I've not seen him. But he's saying that while he was at St. Omer he found out about a Popish plot to kill the King and put the Duke of York on the throne and bring the country back to Rome.''

"The usual nonsense,'' Annunciata said wearily.

"Oh, yes, of course, my lady, they always are, but you know what Londoners are like.''

Jane Birch, who was a Londoner herself, looked offended. "Londoners remember the Gunpowder Plot,'' she said shortly. "There was no fantasy about that, my lady.''

"Well, at any rate,'' Chloris said, diplomatically ignoring the issue, "there's so much talk and rumor around the town that Master Danby has agreed to let him put his case before the Council tomorrow, so that should be the end of that. Now, my lady, what will you do for supper?''

"I'll take it here in my room. I think I will go early to bed, and you can read to me, Chloris, if you will. Birch, will you see that Hugo and Arabella eat here and then remain in their rooms quietly? They can come in after supper to say good-night to me.''

Arabella observed her twin's changed demeanor with silent amusement as they went in to bid their mother good-night. Gone was

the turkey-cock strut, half arrogance, half defiance, the surly
scowl and jutting lip. Hugo walked softly and meekly, his face
wreathed in tender sympathy, and he bent his head for his
mother's kiss in a gesture that was both submissive and protective.
When they were outside again and the door was safely closed,
Arabella said, "Would you like to take some wine with me?"

"Wine?" Hugo asked in mild surprise. Arabella nodded briskly.

"I have suborned Gifford, and he gets me anything I want,
within reason. It's a disgrace that I have no maid of my own. As
well try to move the Tower of London as corrupt Birch; but
Gifford enjoys the excitement of treason."

"Why, Ara, how hard you sound," Hugo said.

"Why, Hugo, how meek you sound," she parodied him. "Is
the wolf become the lap dog at last?"

"You shouldn't speak so when your brother is so recently
dead. It isn't proper," Hugo said.

Arabella smiled tightly at him. "Don't add hypocrisy to your
other sins. You know you hated him." Hugo was silent, redden-
ing angrily. "God knows, he was inoffensive enough, poor boy,
but you always hated him. I wouldn't be surprised if you hadn't
killed him yourself."

Hugo flared up. "That's a wicked thing to say!"

Arabella turned away. "Ah, well, you've got your wish now—
there's no one to come between you and our mother. I hope you
enjoy your new situation. Are you coming to drink wine with me
or not?"

Hugo hesitated, torn between pique and loneliness, and then
capitulated. "All right," he said. "I'll come."

On the following day Annunciata went to Whitehall to pay her
respects to the Queen, and discovered that all the gossip was
about the supposed Popish Plot, which that day was being laid
before the Council in the privy chambers behind locked doors.
Just before dinner time Annunciata came upon the Earl of
Rochester, just up from his bed, to judge by his looks, and she
tucked her hand under his arm and invited him to dine with her in
her apartments. Rochester raised one eyebrow smoothly.

"My dear, dear Countess, don't tell me I have at last reached the top of your list? Can my fortune have changed so radically?"

"Now, John," Annunciata said severely, "I shall withdraw my invitation if you talk such nonsense."

"Is it nonsense to adore you? Cruel Annunciata, forbidding me to speak my love! Would you cut out the nightingale's tongue?"

"You know perfectly well that all you poets prefer your mistresses to reject you, otherwise you have nothing to write about."

"True. Loving women is a damned insipid passion," he said cheerfully. "Come, then, we'll go together with disdainful looks, and glare at each other across a snowy nap and a jug of claret."

"And you shall tell me the news, to divert me."

"Ah, yes." Rochester's face grew suddenly gentle and serious. "I had not failed to observe the black clothes. I heard the sad news—poor young man. You must miss him greatly." Annunciata pressed his arm gratefully, and they went on toward her apartments.

For propriety's sake, Annunciata invited Lord Berkeley, who had sought her at Chelmsford House and followed her to Whitehall, in the dinner invitation, and Hugo and Arabella joined them for the meal, which she had sent in from a tavern nearby which had a celebrated French cook. The talk was naturally enough about the Council meeting, and between them Rochester and Berkeley had many more details to give Annunciata.

"Oates is an out-and-out rogue," Rochester said. "A dreadful fellow altogether. His father was a dissenting chaplain in a Roundhead regiment, but young Titus sniffed the wind in time and got himself ordained into the Anglican church when it was clear there would be more profit that way."

"But I thought he was a Jesuit? Was he not, then, at St. Omer?" Annunciata asked, cracking another oyster. It was Michaelmas Eve, and therefore a fast day, so there was only fish on her table.

"Oh, yes, he was at St. Omer, and at Valladolid before that—dismissed from both. He took to Rome a year or two back when he thought that would serve him," Rochester said.

"He's no more nor less than a paid spy and informer," Lord Berkeley added. "I hate the breed, but I suppose we must have 'em, or how would the law be served? But I must say this Oates fellow is worse than most. And I don't like his companion any better.''

"Who is that?"

"One Israel Tonge, a fanatic pamphleteer," Rochester said, holding out his glass as Tom passed his chair with the wine. "Between them they've cooked up a fine mess of half-truths and downright lies, salted, I regret to say, with a list of names culled from Oates's time at St. Omer.''

Annunciata felt the first chill of fear. Edmund was at St. Omer, and Edmund was a Morland. "What names?" she asked lightly. Rochester cocked an eye at her.

"All the Jesuit priests known to be in England, all the Roman Catholic peers, and all the leading citizens sympathetic to Rome,'' he said. There was a brief silence, and then he added, "But it is all such nonsense, it will come to nothing.''

Berkeley shook his head. "I don't know. The Whigs might well seize on it—a public panic would be to their advantage. It is Shaftesbury's dearest wish to have an election called, and this might prove the lever he needs.''

After dinner, when Berkeley had departed, Rochester held back for a private word with Annunciata.

"Would it not be a good time to visit your family in Yorkshire?" he asked softly.

Annunciata's bright dark eyes held his gaze. "You think I might be in danger? But I am no Papist.''

Rochester shrugged. "My dear lady, anyone who is not a strident Protestant is a Papist to the mob. Besides, there is the matter of your relative in St. Omer, is there not? Even your name is suspect. Better your mother had named you Meg or Dorothy. A country visit might be prudent.''

"I'll bear it in mind," Annunciata said. "I had intended going home anyway, but I'll not be frightened away.''

"As you please, of course,'' Rochester said. "But one other thing. I should stay away from St. James's Palace for the time being. The Duchess of York is a dangerous friend to have at the moment.''

Annunciata decided for herself that Rochester was exaggerating the danger, and determined to pay her respects to the Yorks on the following day, for not to do so would be slighting to her former master and the godfather of her son. But that evening before the hour of supper one of the King's personal servants came to her apartments and asked if she would come privily to the King's chamber by the secret stair to speak with him. It was a device he used to avoid the tedious Court etiquette that would have delayed and encumbered easy meetings between him and those he accounted his intimate friends, and so she came at once without thinking anything of it. But as soon as she entered his apartment and saw his tired face, she knew that the trouble Rochester had hinted at was real enough.

"Your Majesty," she said, making a deep curtsey. The King nodded to the servant, and when they were alone he came forward to take her hands and raise her, and kiss her fondly.

"My dear—I am glad to see you. I heard that you were back in London. Rupert told me of your family tragedy, of course. You have my deepest sympathy."

"Thank you, sir." Annunciata surveyed him. He was in his shirt-sleeves, and had removed his wig, and she noticed for the first time how much gray there was in his dark hair. His deeply lined face looked tired, and there were shadows under his eyes. "But how is it with you? You look troubled."

"I have been all day with the Council and that villain Oates," he said, sitting down on a long seat and drawing her to sit with him. He loved the easy informality he could have only when alone with his family, and he accounted her one of his family. "It sickens me that such as he should flourish, a greasy, smirking liar. He blunders and contradicts himself so that he would be a laughingstock if he had any matter other than Popery to display. If it were left to me, I should have dismissed the whole thing from the beginning as nonsense."

"Could you not, then, sir?"

Charles shook his head. "The times are difficult. James is an avowed Catholic, and my heir. Shaftesbury and his brisk boys are hungry for power. Danby wanted the whole matter publicly crushed in order to spike Shaftesbury's guns, and that meant holding some kind of inquiry. And Oates had deposited a copy of his accusations with a magistrate—Edmund Godfrey, the only incorruptible magistrate in London, I truly believe—and told every member of Parliament he can find that he has done it in case the Council tries to stifle the matter. Jamie has also been to me to demand a public clearing of his name, so there is no hope of the thing quietly dying in a corner.''

"There is danger, then, sir?'' Annunciata asked quietly. The King gave a grim smile.

"Why are people so afraid of Catholics? I don't know. But the people of London in particular are convinced that Catholics are a secret and bloodthirsty army waiting for the chance to rise up and slaughter Protestants to a man. Look at the Great Fire—the moment it began the Londoners said it was started by Catholics.''

"I heard the Gunpowder Plot mentioned today,'' Annunciata said.

The King nodded. "And the Irish Massacre—they remember what they want to remember. Well, I shall do what I can. The hearing goes on tomorrow—the damned rascal has assembled a huge document with eighty-one sections and a forest of names, so it will take us days to get through it all. But''—he paused, and his face grew graver—"he has the first sheaf of warrants in his hands this moment, and he has gone out with the Council's authority to arrest leading Jesuits.'' Annunciata stared in horror. "My hands were tied, I had to allow it. Pray God I can keep them from ever coming to trial. But I wanted to see you to bid you be careful. Keep out of the public eye, my dear, and avoid the company of Catholics. There are so few of my family left and I do not want to lose you. Perhaps it would be better if you went to the country for a while.''

"I will take care,'' she said, "but I will not go just yet. You will surely want your friends about you, sir—and Her Majesty—''

"Bless you,'' the King said. "I would not ask you to risk yourself, but thank you for wanting to.''

The Plot grew at mushroom speed. The initial hearing went on for three days, and each evening there were more arrests of Jesuit priests, and on the third day permission was given for the private papers of the Duchess of York's secretary Edward Coleman to be seized. His official papers were innocent enough, but the searchers discovered a box hidden in the chimney of his room which contained treasonable correspondence with a papal nuncio and with the King of France's confessor, and the last hope of stifling Oates was lost. When the news broke, London grew hysterical and it was impossible to find anyone who did not believe wholeheartedly in Oates's accusations. A full public inquiry was inevitable.

Then on the fourteenth of October Sir Edmund Godfrey was discovered to be missing from his home, and on the seventeenth his mutilated body was found in a ditch on Primrose Hill.

"I've never seen such panic, my lady," Chloris said when she returned from an outing with Tom and Gifford to the 'change. "People are barricading themselves into their houses. All the talk is that the plot to kill Protestants has begun, and the poor gentleman was the first victim. There was hardly anyone at the 'change. I tried talking to one young woman, but all she could say was 'The Catholics are coming, the Catholics are coming.' "

"God save us, the people are so ignorant," Annunciata said, looking pale.

"Well, my lady, the notices are out calling the trainbands to arms, so they'll be patrolling the streets every night. Tom says the shopkeepers are all mortally afraid of fireballs in the night, that being the way they think the great fire was started. They keep great buckets of water by their bedsides. And every citizen is warned to arm himself if he goes out on the street. In the 'change there was one stall selling little muff-pistols for ladies. You never saw such a commotion."

"My lord Rochester says it is the Whigs who are stirring up the panic, spreading stories wherever people seem inclined to dismiss the plot," Annunciata said. "I think I had better write to Ralph and warn him. Father St. Maur may be in danger."

Parliament met on the twenty-first, and soon afterward Annunciata had another private speech with the King. He was looking more harried than ever.

"I cannot hold it," he told her. "Berry's murder has made even Danby's pensioners panic, and no one in either House dares publicly doubt the plot for fear of being named by Oates on the next bulletin. Parliament has decided unanimously that there is a plot, and all trials and documents must be in the hands of Whig members, since anyone in the Court party is automatically suspect. They want the militia called out and all Catholics imprisoned. God knows what will happen next. You must leave London my dear.''

''But, sir—''

''No, no. I know that you wish to stay by me, and I am grateful for it, but I shall have in any case to agree to send all Catholics out of London—the Ten Mile Act is to be revived.''

''But I am not a Papist,'' Annunciata said. The King took her hands.

''They will not care about that. You are a Catholic in their eyes. I beg you to leave now and make yourself safe in Yorkshire.''

''Very well, sir,'' Annunciata said. ''I would not willingly add to your troubles. I will go in the morning.''

''Thank God,'' the King said, and closed his eyes wearily, and Annunciata realized that he needed most of all to be alone. She withdrew her hands and moved quietly to the door, and the King said, ''God bless you,'' without even opening his eyes.

At Chelmsford House none of the servants was surprised at the abrupt order to begin packing.

''We leave first thing tomorrow,'' Annunciata said. ''We must work quickly and get everything done tonight.''

''Better you had left weeks ago, my lady,'' Chloris said.

''I was not to know how things would be,'' Annunciata rebuked her. Everyone had warned her, from Rochester onward, but she had never really believed the Plot would threaten her. Her eyes were stinging from the memory of her interview with the King. ''Do you know what to pack?''

''We have had everything in readiness for a long time, my lady,'' Birch said. ''We expected to have to go.''

She met her mistress's eyes accusingly, and her look was eloquent. ''I have Miss Arabella's things packed and ready.''

''Very good. Then go and tell John Wood to pack for Hugo. He is to go back to Oxford. He will be out of mourning in a few days, and he will be safe enough there. Chloris, come with me. We must write out the orders for the servants who are staying.''

In the middle of the organized turmoil of packing, however,

there came a thunderous knocking on the great door below, which made some of the maids scream in fright. The street outside was filled with torchlight, and the knocking was repeated to the cries of, "Open, in the name of the King."

"Who is it, Chloris?" Annunciata asked as Tom went to answer the summons.

Chloris was at the window, peering down from behind the curtain, but she shook her head. "I don't know, my lady. I can't see past the light of the torches. But it's soldiers, thank God, not the mob. Oh, for Jesu's sake," she added impatiently as the knocking was repeated yet again, "cannot Tom hurry and answer them, before the noise attracts every night-lounger?"

In tense silence the women waited, and at last there came the sound of booted feet mounting the stairs. The door was opened, and Annunciata's breath rushed out in a sigh of relief at the sight of Lord Berkeley in his scarlet uniform.

"Berkeley, thank God it is you," she cried. "Why are you here so late? Have you news? Tom, some wine."

But Tom did not move, and Berkeley did not respond to her smile of welcome. His face was strained, and he held himself stiffly. Behind him were two frightened-looking ensigns, and behind them four armed soldiers.

"My lady," Berkeley said in a voice unlike his own, it was so strangled, "I have a warrant here for your arrest."

"What!" Annunciata cried.

Berkeley avoided her eyes, holding out a rolled document as if it might speak for him. "I have a warrant for the arrest of the Countess of Chelmsford on a charge of Popish recusancy and treason. I have a guard here and am ordered to escort you to the Tower."

Birch let out a strangled cry at the terrible words, and Chloris stepped close to her mistress to support her, but Annunciata, though deathly pale, did not faint.

"Berkeley," she said dazedly, "are you sure?"

"My lady, forgive me. You know that I would not willingly see you in jeopardy. But I am ordered to do my duty."

"But you are my friend," Annunciata said, her voice high like an incomprehending child's.

"My lady, better me than another. At least I can see to it you are treated with respect."

"But what are the charges? What are the grounds?"

"You have been named by—by Master Oates," Berkeley said, aware that any of his soldiers might be a spy or informer, and that if he spoke slightingly of Oates or the plot it would eventually get back to those who could do him harm. "You have a cousin, a Jesuit priest, in St. Omer. You are a known Catholic and have corresponded with the said cousin frequently and secretly."

"Of course I have!" Annunciata cried, outraged. "But not secretly, never secretly. I have written to him as a member of my family, no more than that."

"My lady, you will have ample opportunity to answer the charges at your trial."

"Trial?" Chloris cried. "Oh, dear God preserve us."

"I am the King's loyal subject. I am no traitor," Annunciata cried.

Berkeley stepped forward and spoke more softly. "For God's sake, madam, I know, I know." He glanced over his shoulder and said harshly to his men, "Stand off, stand farther off." Reluctantly they did so, and Berkeley said rapidly in a low voice, "There is nothing I can do. I have to take you to the Tower, and the way things are you will be better off there. I have come as fast as I could to take you, but the mob will not be far behind when the word is out, and in truth, madam, nothing could protect you here. Catholics all over London have had their houses attacked and burned down. In the Tower your life will be safe at least, and I doubt not you will have a fair trial."

"And my family?" Annunciata asked. "My children."

"So far you are named alone. Come with me quickly, and let your servants get them out of London. None of you are safe here."

He stepped back from her, waiting for her decision, but still she hesitated, unable to accept what had happened.

"Treason," she said dazedly. "To be accused of treason. Sweet Mary!"

"Madam, you must come," Berkeley said, and now his voice

was harsh and official. He had his own skin to protect. Annunciata was suddenly stirred into action.

"Very well, I am ready." Chloris stepped forward, and Annunciata shot her a quick glance. "No, Chloris. I will have Birch with me." She turned her body to shield her words from the soldiers, and whispered rapidly to Chloris, "Get the children away—I trust you for it—and for God's sake, get word to the King."

"Madam—" Berkeley said warningly, and Annunciata turned to him.

"Yes, I am coming," she said calmly. "Birch, my cloak. How are we to travel, my lord?"

"The tide will serve us, but we must be quick. It is on the turn."

"The river?"

"It is quicker and safer. The streets are seething," Berkeley said, but Annunciata was trembling. To go to the Tower by river meant to pass in through the water gate, which Londoners called Traitor's Gate, and so many who had passed in through Traitor's Gate had never come out again.

Hugo and Arabella and the servants rode straight for Yorkshire. They thought to be safe enough there, for Yorkshire was not a stronghold of fanatics, and Ralph was justice of the peace, and therefore in a strong position to protect the family. He heard the news of Annunciata's arrest with horror, yet ironically it was his decision long ago to conform with the Test Act, the decision which had caused his estrangement from her, that was now his strength; for had he not taken the oath, he would not now be justice of the peace.

It was necessary to hide Father St. Maur, for not all the Morland tenants were wholeheartedly Catholic, and at Chloris's suggestion her father, the carpenter Moleclough, was brought in to make a secret room for the priest. The spiral staircase which led from the chapel to the priest's room and on up into the servants' quarters in the loft was sealed off at the top, and false paneling was put in to convert the upper section of the staircase into a secret room. It would make cramped quarters, but was undetectable. Having seen her charges safe at Morland Place, Chloris returned to London and her mistress, but the day after her departure a warrant for Hugo's arrest arrived, having followed him from the city. It was, of course, for Ralph to serve it, and he was therefore able to delay matters long enough for Hugo, with John Wood and Michael to escort him, to make a hurried departure for Ireland.

"You can take passage from there easily enough for France," Ralph said, seeing him off with horses and money. "Go to my brother Edmund. He will take care of you. I will get word to you when it is safe to return."

"My mother—" Hugo said, seizing Ralph's hand.

"Everything will be done that can be done. Look to yourself, and pray for better times."

CHAPTER ELEVEN

The guard opened the door for Clovis, and when he had entered, locked it behind him again. No dungeon, this, he thought, but bleak enough. One large room and a small closet was all that Annunciata had been granted, and though the tiny slit window looked out onto the green and the church of St. Peter-ad-Vincula, the river smell was strong, and the room was cold, dark, and dank, and moisture trickled down the walls where they were exposed.

He tried to put on a cheerful face, however. Annunciata was sitting near the window, a piece of work in her lap, but her hands were idle, and she was staring blankly at nothing. Birch sat nearby, sewing diligently but clumsily, for the cold and damp had made her fingers stiff, and she put the work aside gladly to rise and greet Clovis. Annunciata looked up, but did not rise, and Clovis was torn with pity. She looked so pale and thin and haunted, and though her eyes were bright and there was a touch of color in her cheeks, it was feverish rather than healthy.

"Have you news?" she asked eagerly, and drawing her breath in made her cough. Birch looked at her anxiously, and Clovis answered, "Nothing yet. No order yet for your release. But do not give up hope—the King will not let you remain here much longer."

"He has let me remain here two weeks already," Annunciata said bitterly when she had regained her breath from the coughing fit. "In God's name, must the innocent suffer for the villainy of fools?" Clovis spread his hands, hopeless of an answer. "Is there any news of Hugo?'' she asked in a moment. Clovis sat down on the stool Birch had vacated for him and drew it nearer to Annunciata. She looked shrunken in her gown, and wore a thick blanket like a shawl around her shoulders, a disregard of her appearance that told him more than any words how badly she felt.

"Nothing more. He got safe away to Ireland, as we know. Edmund will take care of him, but he will not be able to send a message yet; to do so would only be to compromise you more. Tell me, now, how are you? Is the cough no better?''

She moved her head restlessly. "It is just the same. It hurts me—here''—she pressed the heels of her hands against her breastbone—''when I breathe. For God's sake, when will the King release me?''

"As soon as he can," Clovis said, trying to sound reasonable. "He has so much trouble, and he is all alone, trying to protect his family and his subjects and his throne. He will not forget you, you know that.''

"I am forgotten. What is it that delays him?'' Annunciata said, peevish with the fever in her veins.

"Parliament is still in session, and they are discussing the matter of the succession now,'' Clovis said. "Shaftesbury has gathered the hungriest of the lords about him, and they have moved to exile the Duke of York, and others want to exclude him from the succession, too.''

Annunciata moved her hands wearily. "Oh, that is old news. There have been those who wanted a Protestant succession before, ever since the Dutch marriage.''

"Ah, but now Shaftesbury and his supporters are parading young Monmouth around the streets, drinking toasts to him to the mob from the balcony of the King's Head and Monmouth—''

"Loves it all, of course, conceited young fool. They will ruin him, and when the trouble is over they will lose their heads and take him with them for their treason.''

"But there is another move afoot—to try to persuade the King to divorce the Queen and marry a Protestant princess. There is talk now of Queen Catherine being involved in the plot to murder the King—''

"Dear God," Annunciata said, disgusted, "surely not even the mob would believe that. Why, she loves him to distraction."

"The mob believe in Oates as their protector and savior. And speaking of protectors, it's my belief that if the King agreed to the divorce, Shaftesbury would abandon Monmouth. After all, if the King got a son, he would likely die while the child was still under age, and then a Lord Protector would be needed—"

"And Shaftesbury would be the man for the job, he thinks?" Clovis saw that his plan had worked; that in her anger Annunciata had, at least for the moment, forgotten her misery and fear. "He and all his tribe are fools. They do not know the King. The one thing he cares about above all others is his throne, and his throne depends on a legitimate succession. He will not divorce the Queen, nor legitimize Monmouth, nor exclude the duke, not if he were to die for it."

"You may believe so," Clovis said.

"I know so," Annunciata broke in.

"But there is not a Whig in London who would agree with you."

There was a silence then, at the end of which Annunciata made a sound that was half sigh, half groan. "Oh, Clovis," she said wretchedly, "when shall I be out of here? What will come of me? Shall I die?"

Birch drew a sharp breath, and Clovis said quickly, "Of course not. Come, you must not be gloomy. You will be safe in time. You must simply endure until the King has you freed."

Annunciata refused to be comforted. "You know," she said casting her eyes upward, "that above me is the room where Anne Boleyn spent her last hours. Sweet Mother, this place is so dreary. I look out of the window and I think I see her execution, and I wonder—"

"You must not," Clovis broke in firmly. To speak words was to give the thoughts power.

Annunciata began to cough again, and when she stopped she seemed worn out. She sank a little in her chair and said, "How is Chloris? Is she looking after my dogs? Do they miss me? Clovis, tell her—"

But at that moment the guard opened the door to say, "Time's up, master. You must leave now."

Clovis rose, and Birch accompanied him to the door to whisper, "Her health is not good, master. I'm afraid if she stays here much longer she may never recover it."

"I'll do what I can. Look to her," Clovis said.

Elizabeth lived in terror, starting at shadows. The weight of guilt on her mind was so great that at times she thought it must actually be visible, that people would look at her and see a mark of Cain on her brow. Again and again in her thoughts, she relived the moment when she had thrown the herbs on the fire and allowed the forbidden thought to form in her mind. Three times she had done it, each time compounding her guilt and blackening her soul, now she was an outcast, she could never be forgiven. She wept hysterically at times, at others moped apathetically, staring at nothing. For she had ill-wished Annunciata, and Annunciata had been arrested for treason, had passed in through the dark portal to the Tower, and was languishing there, awaiting her trial. Ralph said it would never come to trial, that the King would rescue her; but Elizabeth knew better. She would never be tried, because she was dying of a fever in her damp cell.

She kept to her room, not even venturing out for meals. The servants thought little of that, for she was large with child, and it was more seemly for her to hide herself. But they gossiped among themselves when she did not attend chapel. She longed to go, longed to confess her guilt and be absolved, but she knew it was impossible, that her crime was too great. So she stayed in her room, pacing the floor, weeping, wringing her hands, staring out from the window at the gray, leaden November sky.

Her child was due in a matter of weeks, and then what would become of her? How could she live with the knowledge of her crime? Her mind revolved helplessly around the same questions, until gradually the answer began to crystalize. The witch had said—and she was a witch, that was evident—that the death of one was the life of the other.

But her child, her child!

One strand winds through you both.

Ralph, and her child!

One of you must die. The death of one is the life of the other.

She found paper and pen, and sat down, slowly and reluctantly, on the window seat, resting the paper before her. Life had been sweet once. The new, sweet air of spring, the green grass, the sun drying the dew. But she must expiate. God would judge her, He would give her justice, her and her child. She drew the paper toward her, feeling the child stir heavily in her belly.

Annunciata's trial took place in December. The guilty Coleman and a number of innocent Jesuit priests had already suffered the extreme penalty, but Annunciata, after six weeks in prison, was too weak both in body and spirit to be much afraid. A kind of lethargy had settled on her. She had not expected ever to be brought to trial—she had thought the King would arrange for her release in some way—and the fact that she was now facing her judges made her believe she was doomed. She felt haunted by the ghost of Anne Boleyn, for the story was well known in the family of how Nanette Morland had attended the fated Queen at her trial and upon the scaffold.

"Anne Boleyn was innocent," Annunciata said to Birch more than once, "and yet she died upon Tower Green."

Clovis had not been idle, however, during those weeks. The King had not been able to have the countess released, but he had put help and information in Clovis's way before the trial to help him prepare a defense, and Clovis was confident of an acquittal, although he could not persuade Annunciata out of her gloom, which he knew was largely due to her state of health.

Annunciata was feverish when she entered the hall, and it was to her like a scene out of hell; she felt as if she were in a nightmare. How could she be here, on trial for her life, charged with treason against the King who was her friend and kinsman? She saw Oates for the first time, a hideous creature, moon faced, slack mouthed, puffed up with his disgusting pride, an ape in man's clothing. He seemed to gloat and lick his lips as he looked at her, as if he were tasting her blood, and she shuddered and felt her knees weaken. She must not appear too faint, she thought, gritting her teeth. She would be thought afraid, and fear was an admission of guilt. She stiffened her spine, and held her head up, and walked forward to the seat that had been placed for her, facing the judge and jury.

Thin and white as a wraith she looked, and there was a stirring of pity for her along the bench, for she was still in mourning for her son, and the stark black made her look younger and more beautiful. She stared straight ahead of her as the charges were read out—that she had conspired with her cousin, a Jesuit priest, to aid the Jesuit Congregation in their plot to assassinate the King. Then Oates jumped to his feet and began his deposition.

Much of what he said was rambling and irrelevant, but he spoke rapidly and fluently and with a kind of ecstacy in his tone that swayed mobs with the sound, regardless of the words. He told how the countess was an avowed Catholic; how she had entered the service of the first Duchess of York at the time of her conversion and with the duchess had helped her cousin Edmund to enter the seminary at St. Omer. This, Annunciata supposed, he had had from Edmund, or at least from associates of Edmund's at St. Omer.

The countess had continued to serve both the Yorks after their converson and had attended Masses with them. She had left her husband because he had refused to become a Papist also. Annunciata heard this with relief, thinking that at least Ralph and the rest of the family would be safe.

Oates went on to describe the countess's depraved character, how she was a woman of loose morals, easily given to all kinds of heinousness. She lived wickedly at Court, had been the mistress of innumerable men, including the King and Prince Rupert. She had kept up a regular correspondence with her Jesuit cousin and mixed freely with other Catholics.

On the second day he came to the plot—it had been hatched at the Jesuit Consult which was held on April twenty-fourth of that year in London, and Oates himself had been present, he said. The countess had not been present, he admitted reluctantly, but her name had been prominent, and it had been stated that she was one of the main means of communication with the Jesuits of St. Omer, and had pledged money to help arm the Catholic soldiers. She had connections with Ireland, through her son Ballincrea, and would help raise the Catholics of Ireland when the time came. She was known to be the King's natural daughter, and was jealous of the Protestant princesses, and hoped for glory under a Catholic regime which she could not hope for otherwise.

Eventually the outpouring of poison ceased, and Oates retired in glory to contemplate another victim. Annunciata was unable to speak for herself, but Clovis rose on the third day to speak on her behalf, primed with his questions and armed with witnesses, the fruit of his labors those past weeks. He was hopeful, for Oates's testimony had been full of contradictions. One by one he brought up his points, and one by one they were cut down. He had brought witnesses from the Low Countries to swear what was well known among the informed, that Oates had been at St. Omer on April twenty-fourth, and therefore could not have been at the Consult. The witnesses spoke well, but when they had finished the judge dismissed their evidence on the grounds that they were Jesuits, and therefore their oath could not be trusted—they would lie in the cause of their church.

"My lord," Clovis cried, "the man Oates has given a testimony so full of contradictions that it must be plain to all that *he* is lying." He stared at Oates, who grinned, not at all perturbed. "My lord, he deposed that her ladyship was the King's mistress, and then later deposed that she was his natural daughter. How could this be?"

There was a stirring of interest in the jury, but Oates jumped up and cried, "This evil woman would not even stop at incest, my lords. That is proof of her terrible wickedness!"

"He says the countess had connections in Ireland, through her son. This is untrue. Her son does not own any land in Ireland—that is a fact, and can be proved."

And Oates said, "She hoped to regain that very land that her son has been denied—that was to have been one of her rewards for helping the cause." And he added smugly, "I can bring witnesses to prove it. And I myself heard at the Consult how they would give her the land around Rathkeale that she has been asking for in vain these ten years!"

Then to the letters. "The countess adopted the young man into her household when he was orphaned, at which time he was a chorister in the chapel royal, long before he was converted to Rome. The substance of her letters to him and his to her was merely family news. How should she not write to a young man she regarded as her son?''

"Let him produce the letters from St. Omer," Oates demanded with a grin. Clovis could not—those that had not been destroyed in the normal course of things had been stolen. Oates grinned wider still. "Aye, that they were—stolen by an agent of mine, acting on the King's instructions.''

Clovis's heart rose. If the letters were to hand, they would prove innocence of the correspondence. "Unfortunately," Oates went on, "they were later subject to a most lamentable accident—they fell into the fire and were burned to ashes. Fortunately my agent read them before they were destroyed, and is here to swear that the contents were treasonable.''

Of course, thought Clovis, he would swear anything, for a price. But the oath of a witness in Court was trusted absolutely by everyone except the witness himself, if he were a Protestant. He despaired, and prepared to launch, hopelessly, his last weapons.

"My lord, the countess is a Catholic, but not a Papist. This man has deposed that she is the King's mistress as well as his daughter, and reaps great rewards from her sinful actions. How, then, could she expect greater rewards if the King, her protector and patron, were dead? How could a Roman Catholic successor help her?''

But before Oates could answer, there was a commotion at the back of the Court, and Clovis saw one of the King's personal servants entering, wearing a cloak and boots, much travel-stained, as if he had come straight from his horse to the Court.

"My lord," he cried, "I have new evidence pertinent to this trial. I beg leave to enter it.''

"What manner of evidence?" the judge asked, raising his voice through the clatter of comment that rose on all sides.

The servant, a man called Browning who was one of the King's secretaries and also a recorder for the Privy Council, said, "I have here, my lord, the original letters sent by the Countess of Chelmsford to Edmund Morland at the seminary of St. Omer." And he raised his hand, showing the tied bundle of papers.

"Forgeries," Oates bellowed. "They are forgeries. I'll bring you a witness to swear they are not genuine."

"And I, my lord," Browning said firmly, "will swear that they are."

The judge had to call for silence, and when the noise subsided Clovis said, his voice lifting with hope, "My lord, this is a *Protestant* witness!"

The judge nodded quietly. Browning was well known to them all, and the fact that the King had evidently dispatched him to St. Omer to fetch the letters back was the clearest indication that the King knew Lady Chelmsford to be innocent and wanted her acquitted. He turned to the jury.

"If these letters are genuine, then it invalidates the evidence for the prosecution. You may disregard the whole of the accusing deposition."

Clovis lifted his hands in triumph as the jury, with no alternative, acquitted the Countess of Chelmsford on all charges; then he hurried forward to help Annunciata, who was close to fainting. He and her women helped her from the court under the eyes of the crowds waiting outside.

"What verdict, sir?" a well-dressed tradesman called as they came out.

"Acquitted, sir," Clovis cried triumphantly. "Acquitted on all charges." An interested murmur came up from the crowds, not unsympathetic, for Annunciata was beautiful, which always helped, and was known to be generous to the poor. "He saved you," Clovis said to her as he helped her to his carriage. "The King saved you. In his own way, and in his own time, but I knew he would not let you suffer."

But Annunciata was close to collapse, and he doubted if she heard him. At Chelmsford House he helped her women to take her upstairs, and then waited outside while they undressed her and put her to bed, and then he came back in for a few moments more to speak to her.

"The acquittal of Hugo will be a matter of course," he told her. Her eyes were heavy, and he did not know whether she understood what he was saying. "I shall talk to Browning about it; he will get word to Hugo safely. And I'll take care of everything else, so you need not worry about anything now. As soon as you are well enough, I'll take you home to Morland Place."

She was too weak to take in more, he knew, but sometime soon he must find a way to tell her the news he had been keeping from her for her peace of mind, news from Morland Place: that Elizabeth had had a terrible accident. She had been found at the foot of the great staircase, apparently having fallen down the whole flight. She had gone into premature labor, and both she and her baby had died.

It seemed that Christmas as if the nightmare would never end. Annunciata, having taken to her bed, stayed there, like a frightened animal in its burrow. At Court the King kept up an appearance of normality which was his best defense against the hysteria of London, but Chelmsford House was silent, its great rooms unlit, the door closed to callers. In her room Annunciata dozed and woke, read a little, ate next to nothing, and in her feverish dreams relived again and again the horror of her trial and imprisonment. Chloris slept in the bed with her, to quiet her when she woke sweating and crying out because she had seen again in dream the bloody and headless figure of Anne Boleyn beckoning her toward the block. She grew yet thinner and paler, and her cough hardly improved, and Birch, in terror of a consumption, begged her to consult a doctor. Annunciata refused, but at length the King sent his own physician, whom she could hardly refuse to see. The doctor examined her, shook his head, and said that she must have rest and nourishing food, but that her complaint was not hectic.

Outside in the streets the trainbands marched past every night, their feet ringing on the frosty cobbles, and citizens went armed by day and locked themselves behind their shutters at night, for the madness that had seized London did not soon die away. And from time to time there would be torchlight processions of ardent Protestants carrying an effigy of the Pope to be burned, or of drunken Whigs, sporting their green ribbons, cheering for the Duke of Monmouth and booing at the name of the Duke of York.

Alone of the household Arabella was unconcerned by the events outside, and she fretted with boredom, forbidden to leave the house and deprived of company and entertainment. Clovis visited every day, but he was the only person admitted, and her only permitted exercise was to walk her mother's dogs in the garden each morning. When Berkeley and Morris called they were politely sent away, and Arabella sulked furiously.

"They came to see me," she raged at Birch. "Why cannot I see them? I am out of mourning. Am I to be shut up here like a nun forever?"

"They were told your mother is ill," Birch said severely.

"*I* am not ill," Arabella interrupted. "They could have taken me out riding."

"Don't talk such nonsense. Riding, at a time like this?"

"The King goes walking and riding and fishing every day as if nothing had happened—Clovis said so. And if we had been at Court I could have gone to all the parties and suppers and balls—"

"Never mind, your turn will come," Chloris said more tactfully, for she felt some sympathy for Arabella.

"Not if *she* has anything to do with it," Arabella muttered.

After Christmas Annunciata's health began to improve, and with it her spirits, though as she returned to a more normal state of mind her interrupted mourning for George returned, and she had fits of grieving for him. Then, a week after Twelfth Night, the first visitor was most reluctantly admitted by Birch and came, travel-stained and anxious, to her ladyship's bedside.

"Annunciata! Oh, God, I am so glad to see you. I have been worried almost sick about you."

"Kit, oh, Kit, what do you here? I did not think to see you this winter." Annunciata gave him her hands, and his own were icy-cold and trembling. He sat on the edge of her bed as if his legs would not hold him up any longer, and she could see by his strained face how worried he had indeed been.

"I wanted to come before—I would have come as soon as I heard the news," he said. "You can't imagine how I felt when I heard you had been arrested . . ."

"Don't speak of it." Annunciata shuddered. "I don't want to think about it anymore."

"But I couldn't come sooner. Cathy was so close to her time—she had a son on Christmas Eve. I couldn't leave her."

"You could have done no good," she said. "And it has been dangerous here for everyone."

"I should have been near you. There must have been things I could have done."

"Clovis was here—he took care of me. There was little anyone could do. But I am glad to see you now."

He kissed her hands fervently. "I am glad to be here. But how are you? You look so pale."

"I have been ill, but I am mending now. I want most of all to get away from London. When I am strong enough to travel I shall go into the country."

"Will you go home?" Kit asked. "Things are so troubled there, but you could rest safely."

"You have been there recently?"

"On my way down. I could hardly pass and not see Ralph, grieved as he is—"

"Grieved?" Annunciata said.

Kit looked surprised. "Did you not know about Elizabeth?"

"What about Elizabeth?" she asked apprehensively.

Kit told her. "Ralph has taken it badly, I'm afraid. I think he felt guilty about her. And then, of course, this Popish plot has had its consequences there as everywhere. He has been forced to preside over the trials of many people whom he regards as friends, and commit them to prison."

Annunciata was shocked, but also she felt a stirring of pity toward her husband. His position was not enviable.

"Did he mention me?" she asked in a small voice.

Kit looked at her oddly. "Of course he asked me to call on you and see if you needed anything. I think he would have asked me to bid you come home if he thought there was any chance that you would come."

Annunciata was thoughtful. "He helped Hugo to escape," she said, and it was almost as if she was asking a question.

"Of course," Kit said. "He is very loyal."

It seemed odd to her that Kit should say so, so soon after

mentioning Ralph's mistress. Where did loyalty lie for a man? Yet she was still Ralph's wife, and loyalty was her duty, too.

At the end of January the King, in a desperate attempt to save lives and buy time, dissolved Parliament; and Annunciata, escorted by Clovis, and accompanied by her household, went home to Morland Place. She parted from Kit in London, and though nothing was said between them, he knew that if they met in London again next winter, it would not be as lovers.

On a gray February day Annunciata rode into the yard of Morland Place. Ralph was at the door to greet her, and she was shocked at the change in him, for since she had seen him last he had grown suddenly old: his shoulders had an old man's stoop, his face was lined and troubled, and his silver-fair hair had gone quite gray. He did not come forward to lift her down from her horse as he once would have, though his eyes never left her face as he stood motionless in the doorway. It was Clem who hurried forward to hold her horse's head and shoo away the troublesome hound pup who had taken the place of Bran and Fern, and whom Ralph would once have had well trained by that age. His eyes met Annunciata's anxiously as he said, "Welcome home, my lady. We have all missed you."

"Thank you, Clem," she said, understanding from his look that things were as bad with the master as they seemed. Tom hurried forward to help her down, and she smoothed her dress and cloak and walked forward to meet her husband. They looked at each other for a long time, each seeing in the other not the changes that had taken place, but the old and familiar betrayals. There had been too much done for words to heal now.

At length Ralph leaned down to place a formal kiss on her cheek, which she accepted as formally, and he said only, "Welcome home," and stepped aside to allow her to pass. He followed her into the hall, and then added, "I am glad you are safe."

"Thank you," she said. Father St. Maur was there, with tears in his eyes, to kiss her and thank God for her safe return, and Daisy was there, grown very tall and solemn now that she was the only woman of the house, and Dorcas, half laughing, half crying, to tell her that the children were beside themselves with excitement at her return. There were familiar faces of servants, waiting to greet her and receive orders, and her own servants crowding in, bringing luggage and looking around them with relief and pleasure. Clem restored order with a few brisk, quiet commands, and came forward to relieve her of her cloak.

"Thank you, Clem. Where is Martin? He seems to be the only one missing."

"He is gone into the city on business, my lady, but he will be back by dinnertime. We did not expect you so soon." He paused, and surveyed her face carefully. "Shall I have your things taken up to the great bedchamber, my lady?" he asked quietly. Annunciata had been aware that this choice must come, but had not known until she saw Ralph how she would feel. But seeing him, seeing his absent expression and the marks of grief in his face, she knew that, reasonably or unreasonably, she could not share with him the bed he had shared with Elizabeth.

"No," she said finally. "I'll have the west bedroom."

The morning passed in a flurry of unpacking and settling in, but it was not until Martin came home that Annunciata really felt she had arrived. He came straight up to her bedchamber, where she was directing Chloris in the disposal of various belongings, and when she turned and saw him standing in the open doorway, watching her with an expression of warmth and satisfaction, she flung out her hands to him in a gesture of spontaneous pleasure.

"You have made good time," he said, kissing her hands. He did not release them, but stood before her looking her over searchingly. "I am sorry I was not here to greet you. You are well? We have all been so worried about you."

"I am better, and will be better still soon," Annunciata said. She flung Chloris a sharp look, and Chloris dropped what she was doing and hurried out. Alone, she and Martin continued to survey each other, both of them smiling more warmly than they thought. Martin was twenty-two now, a man and more mature than his years, with a frank, open countenance which spoke of responsibility and authority. He would never be tall—slight as he was, he was hardly bigger than Annunciata herself—but there was power in his slender, wiry body, and with her hands in his

Annunciata felt with a distant shock his enormous magnetism. She could not think of him as her stepson: she felt more equality with him than with Ralph. "You have had your troubles here, too," she said.

"Ah, yes," he said, his face growing grave. He released her hands and walked to the window, thinking hard for a moment. His position was delicate, and there were many things he wanted to ask and to tell, without knowing quite how to do it. He turned at last and said, "You have seen my father, of course."

She nodded. "How is he? Tell me frankly. He seems to me to have changed greatly."

"He is dazed by what has happened, I believe," Martin said. "It has gone very hard with him to condemn his friends, and yet he could not resign his commission when it was the very thing that protected us all—you in particular, he felt. He hoped that his status and reputation would count in your favor, and when it did not—" He paused and shook his head. "He is very withdrawn. I suppose you must have guessed by now that it is I who run the estate and all his business. He concerns himself with the horses, but little else."

"He is lucky to have you," Annunciata said. "It must have been hard for you, doing everything all alone. But now I am here I will help you all I can."

"You help just by being here," he said, and his sudden smile was like sunshine. "The children have been so excited that you were coming home. Have you seen them?"

"Not yet—there has been so much to do."

"Will you come now, then? There is time before dinner. Come, put them out of their agony." He held out his hand, and she laughed and took it, feeling suddenly younger than she had for a long time.

In the schoolroom her boys were doing their lessons with Father St. Maur. She had not seen them for so long, and she felt a pang of sadness that they were almost strangers to her. They stood up at her entrance, but were restrained by shyness and their strict upbringing from rushing to her, and when she called them to her, they came awkwardly and red faced, looking up at her with a mixture of awe and longing that both amused and touched her. Rupert, the eldest, had grown tall and thin, and would be handsome one day when he had grown into his long features. His dark hair was worn in long lovelocks, his dark eyes were enormous, and he made her a courtly bow with his hand on his sword hilt: he had put on his best clothes in her honor. He was nearly nine years old.

Charles and Maurice, who were seven and six now, were still very much children, sheltered by their brother. Maurice looked like a smaller version of Rupert, but Charles had taken after his father, and was very fair, with a round, sweet face, all smiles. Annunciata wanted to gather them all up and hug them, knowing how close she had been to never seeing them again, but they were still too shy of their long-absent, illustrious mother, so she contented herself with questioning them on their lessons, and then left them, to get ready for dinner. There would be time to make friends with them later, when they had got used to her presence.

The first few days passed busily for Annunciata, for her own estates needed her attention, and between occupation and fresh air she regained her appetite and her spirits, and had no time to fret over the past. She slept well at the end of each full day, and Chloris and Birch watched with satisfaction as her cheeks regained their color and her face and body began to put on flesh. She saw very little of Ralph, and that was to the good, for her relationship with him would have perplexed and upset her if she had had time to consider it. But Ralph spent most of his time at Twelvetrees about his horses, frequently not even returning to dinner. Annunciata quickly got into the habit of regarding Martin as the master, and it was evident that the servants already did so. It amused her to see that that attitude extended even as far as the three boys in the schoolroom, who called Martin ''sir'' as if he were their father, not Ralph.

Daisy was a great help to Annunciata in settling in, and it was clear that she had taken over much of Elizabeth's role in running the house. Annunciata was rather saddened on her behalf, for at nineteen she should have been married, but there seemed to be no suitors, and no attempt on the part of either Ralph or Martin to find her a husband. Ralph barely seemed to notice Daisy, and while Martin evidently still adored her as much as ever, he seemed to regard her as a child, his little sister to be petted and protected. The time would come, Annunciata thought, when she would have to speak to Martin about that. Meanwhile she encouraged Daisy to abandon her housewifely duties and accompany Arabella in walking and riding: she hoped that Daisy would influence Arabella's less-than-perfect manners, and that Arabella would awaken Daisy to the desirability of getting married.

One day, when Annunciata had been at Morland Place almost a week, Chloris came to her with a very grave expression and asked for a private interview with her. Annunciata was in the winter parlor, going through the accounts for Shawes with her steward, and seeing how serious her woman looked, she bade the steward at once to wait outside. When they were alone she said, "Why, Chloris, what is the matter? Michael isn't ill, is he?" Chloris's delighted reunion with her son had been a joy to witness.

"Oh, no, my lady," Chloris said, and she drew out from the pocket of the apron she was wearing a folded piece of paper. "You know that I have been clearing all Miss Elizabeth's things out of the west bedroom, and when I took her prayerbook out of the wall cupboard by the fireplace, this fell out of it. I think you should read it."

Annunciata took the piece of paper and unfolded it and smoothed it out. The rambling, hysterical, and tear-blotched confession was pitiful to read, and for the first time in her life Annunciata was forced to view Elizabeth as a real person, with a real and inward life of her own. She had never troubled herself to wonder what Elizabeth thought or felt about anything, but now the tormented woman's voice called to her from beyond the grave, compelling her pity and her forgiveness. She looked up at length and met Chloris's eyes.

"What should I do with it, my lady?" Chloris asked. "Do you think we should . . . ?"

"Burn it," Annunciata said decisively. "Tell no one."

"But, my lady, reading this it occurs to me that she might not have fallen down the stairs by accident."

"And who would be the better for knowing that?" Annunciata said. "Ralph? Martin and Daisy?"

"She has been buried in hallowed ground," Chloris pointed out quietly. Ah, that was the problem, of course. If she had killed herself, that was a sin which barred her from burial in sacred ground, and if Annunciata concealed the fact, she was sinning, too. But the voice was still strong in her ears. If it was a sin, her soul was strong enough to bear it: she owed Elizabeth something for never having loved her.

"Leave matters as they are," she said finally. "I take full responsibility. Burn this letter, and never mention it to anyone, do you understand?"

"Yes, my lady," said Chloris. "Yes, I do understand."

CHAPTER TWELVE

When Hugo learned that his mother had been acquitted at trial, he often thought that a six-month incarceration in the Tower would have been infinitely preferable to the rigors of fleeing the country in winter. That endless ride from York across country to Liverpool, through rain, sleet, and snow, along roads which, where they were not in appalling condition, ceased to exist at all! He had thought of England as being a civilized country, but he was not twenty miles from home when he changed that opinion. The inns at which he stayed were warm and the food was plentiful and cheap, but, oh, the filth and the smells, the fleas and bedbugs and lice, the rotting mattresses, the stinking rushes on the floor, the scratchy blankets: no sheets, of course! After the first night he learned not to undress, for the rough fibres tore his tender skin. That first night, too, he had been awakened by a rat running along the bedhead, and had been almost too afraid to sleep any longer.

He had thought himself quite a horseman, but riding eighteen hours a day, day after day, taught him otherwise. His only comfort was that his servants were even more saddlesore than he was, and hated the inns quite as much. Then at Liverpool they had found a ship going to Ireland, and had bought passage on it when they learned that the skipper thought it would be a smooth crossing and that it would sail that night. It was a nightmare crossing, and took three days, and hour after hour as he lay shivering and vomiting between two damp smelly blankets he prayed that he might die there and then and be spared any more torture. On the second day he was quite sure that he *was* dying, and when he was awakened by a rat running over his face, he was too apathetic and miserable to care.

In Dublin their money ran out, and they had to sell the horses to pay for their passage to France, and even then they had to borrow from a sympathetic Catholic gentleman, who offered the money on the strength of Hugo's name, and a promise to pay an extortionate rate of interest. The journey to France took two weeks, for the winds were dead foul most of the time, and the ship had to beat about for days at a time waiting for it to change. Hugo toyed with the notion of throwing himself overboard, since he was sure to end up drowning anyway, and it would end the torment of seasickness and the hideous swooping movement of the ship hove-to; and was prevented only by the lack of strength to get to his feet, let alone to struggle as far as the open deck.

However, once the actual journeying was over, he really rather enjoyed his exile. He had not made the usual "grand tour" that most of his contemporaries at Oxford had done as a matter of course, and apart from his three months in Paris, this was his first experience of a foreign country. Thanks to Father St. Maur his French was excellent and his accent comprehensible to the natives, and where his French could not get him by he did very well in a mixture of Latin, Italian, and gestures. Being an exile gave him a certain distinction, and being a victim of the Popish Plot made him something of a hero, and he was well treated everywhere. He thought the food mostly very poor, but the wines excellent, the girls ugly but willing, and the clothes extraordinary but, once he was used to them, very becoming. Edmund, when he finally reached him, greeted him with open arms, seemed to be a very good sort of fellow. Hugo stayed for a while in the guest quarters of the seminary, which, though bare, were very comfortable by comparison with his journey, and then got himself lodgings in the town, where his movements would not be so restricted.

His fear for his life and his mother's safety were at first a terrible obstacle to his enjoyment, and he could only wonder if he would ever be able to enjoy again the sensation of having her call him "my son" and smile at him. But once he learned that she had been acquitted, and had gone back to Morland Place, and that his own recall would surely follow, his only fear was that the recall would come too soon. For the rest, he got the news from England almost as soon as he would have at Morland Place: that the King had dissolved Parliament and sent the Duke of York to Brussels for his safety, that the new Parliament had again moved to exclude the Duke from the succession, and had been prevented from passing the Act first by its own internal disagreements and secondly by the King's dissolving it. The Queen's physician had been accused of plotting to poison the King as part of the Popish Plot—an attempt, of course, to remove the Queen to make way for a Protestant marriage—but had been acquitted; a sign, it was hoped, of the waning of Oates's power.

Edmund was surprised and worried that the army dispatched to deal with rebels in southern Scotland had been placed under the command of the Protestant Duke of Monmouth, the Whigs' darling and the alternative heir; Hugo was surprised and worried at the discovery of the beginning of a bald patch on the crown of his head.

"It's putting a firebrand into the hands of a petulant child," Edmund said anxiously. "If he does well, it will increase his popularity among the people, too. What can the King be about?"

"If it gets any bigger," Hugo muttered, "I shall have to become a monk."

Then in July came the news that the Duke of Monmouth had triumphed over the rebels, won the love of Scotland by his clemency, and had marched back south like a conquering hero; and by the same dispatch came Hugo's long-expected recall. He was almost sorry to have to leave, but the fact that his mother was so eager to see him that she was going to Windsor, where the Court was spending a few weeks, in order to be there when he arrived, made him disinclined to delay. The prospect of his mother eager to see him was one which almost defied his imagination.

The journey back to England was a very different one from his flight nine months ago. He traveled inconspicuously, but in much greater comfort, laden with letters and gifts, his pockets replete with money sent to him by his stepfather's agent in Calais. The weather was good and the crossing calm, and when he reached

Dover he stayed in the best inn for three days while he had new clothes made and sent John Wood out to hire horses that wouldn't shame them, before setting out for Windsor.

It was plain that Monmouth had arrived in Windsor, for Hugo found the town full of soldiers telling stories of their courage and prowess and drinking the health of their brave and noble commander-in-chief. It made Hugo very nervous, and he kept his safe-passage document at hand until he was safely inside Windsor castle, and making his way at last toward the Royal Apartments and his mother's welcoming embrace.

Annunciata woke, and for a moment did not know where she was. It was hot and the bedcurtains were open and through the gap she could see a stone wall and a number of paintings, and she stared at them until gradually the recognition seeped into her mind. This wakening moment of confusion was a legacy of her nightmare period in the Tower, but it was gradually growing less. Of course, she was safe in her own familiar quarters in the Round Tower, the rooms she always had when she was at Windsor. Windsor Castle had been badly damaged during the Civil War and equally badly neglected during the Protectorate, but once it became the principal residence of Prince Rupert, he had begun the extensive repairs needed, and added a number of improvements of his own devising. The King loved Windsor, too, and so was happy to find the money needed, and the Round Tower was now both comfortable and beautiful.

Outside the sun was shining, and it must be almost time for chapel, but she remained as she was, staring at the wall opposite and enjoying the sensation of contentment. The King and Rupert were both here, and later that day she would go riding with them along the new ride Rupert had planted, and that evening there was to be a ball—with so many soldiers in the town it was a waste not to dance—and she had a new gown to wear. Hugo was back, and was so much improved of late. He seemed to have gained some experience while he was abroad, and talking to him was sometimes now an actual pleasure. Arabella was also behaving herself, although at Windsor, where she spent most of every day riding, there was nothing to prompt her to behave badly.

And Ralph was coming next week, for the races at Datchet, bringing Barbary with him and two young colts of whom he had great hopes. Annunciata found that she was looking forward to seeing him again: their relationship had improved since the winter, for being at home had reminded her how much of her life he had shared, and time had begun to heal his mental scars. He still left the running of the estate to Martin, and had fits of abstraction, but during the spring he had enjoyed involving her with his plans for his horses, and they had even gone to Wakefield together for three days for the horse fair.

If only George were here, it would be perfect, she thought, and then shied away from that train of thought. She didn't want to be sad today, and to distract her mind she was preparing to get up without waiting for her women to call her, when the door opened somewhat unceremoniously and Chloris came in.

"What is it? What's the matter?" Annunciata asked at once, sitting up. She could see by her woman's expression that something had happened.

"My lady, the King has been taken ill."

Annunciata's heart lurched. "What? How? Is it serious?" Chloris stood beside the bed clasping and unclasping her hands.

"It was very sudden, my lady. You know what an early riser he always is. His man got him out of bed, and he collapsed. The doctors are with him, and the prince. They are trying to keep the news, but of course it will be out in no time." While she was speaking she was helping Annunciata up and sorting through the clothes that had been left ready last night. "You won't be riding, of course—I'll get Birch."

"No, wait, tell me more first," Annunciata said quickly. "What do the doctors think? Have you found out that much?"

Chloris paused as if she had far rather not speak the words, and then said reluctantly, "My lady, I have not heard the official pronouncement. But they must think it is serious, for they have sent for the Council, and I heard my lord Shaftesbury was seen going in great excitement toward the apartments of His Grace of Monmouth."

Annunciata stared, her eyes widening. "They are apprehensive for his life?" she whispered. Chloris did not answer, but the two women read the same thoughts in each other's face. "Fetch Birch," Annunciata said at last. "And send for Hugo and Arabella. I want to see them as soon as I'm dressed. And take the dogs out, will you?"

By the time Annunciata was dressed more news had come in: the King had had a seizure and was apparently in a coma, and the doctors despaired of his life, although that had not been made official. Hugo brought her that news when he was admitted to her presence. Despite the earliness of the hour and the haste with which he had been summoned, he was fully dressed right down to wig and patches: his sojourn abroad had made him as clothes-conscious as any Court gallant.

"The castle is in a ferment," he told his mother when he had made his bow and received her kiss. "It cannot be long before the whole town knows, and then there will be trouble."

"With the castle full of Whigs and the town full of soldiers," Annunciata said grimly, "who knows what will happen? Is it true that Shaftesbury has been to see Monmouth?"

Hugo nodded. "It could hardly be worse, could it? Monmouth victorious and still officially commander in chief of the army, and the Duke of York out of the country. Madam, do you really think that the Whigs will—"

"We must pray that the King recovers," Annunciata said firmly. "It is our only hope. We will go to the chapel at once. Where is Arabella?"

Hugo looked uncomfortable, and glanced back at Birch, who reddened.

"Birch," Annunciata said sharply, "where is Miss Arabella? Answer me at once."

"My lady," Birch said reluctantly, "I do not know. She was up early and I dressed her for riding before you called for me. When I came back from taking the dogs out, she had gone."

"Gone? What do you mean, gone? Gone where?"

"My lady, I do not know. Her room was empty, and I cannot find her. I think she must have gone out riding before hearing the news about His Majesty—"

Annunciata bit back the furious words that sprang to her lips, for no good would come of exposing either her anger or her fears. When she had her voice under control again, she said quietly, "Go and find Tom and Gifford and search the castle for her. Look everywhere. And if she is not in the castle, search the gardens and the grounds. Ask at the stables—discreetly—if she has taken a horse. Find her and bring her back here. Hurry."

Birch curtseyed and left, and Hugo said, "Madam, shall I go, too? I can more easily make inquiries at the stables than a servant. If she has gone out, I'll take a horse and go after her."

"Yes," Annunciata said gratefully, "yes, do that. Thank you, my son."

And Hugo, his heart glowing from those words, went, too.

The hours dragged by. Annunciata waited in her rooms for news, walking up and down, fretting, sending Chloris out every few minutes to glean what talk she could from the corridors. A message came for her from Prince Rupert by one of his most trusted servants soon after Hugo left her, giving her the bare news that the King was ill, and Annunciata begged him to come again when there was more news. An hour later he came to say that various remedies had been tried but to no avail.

"The prince is remaining by His Majesty's beside, my lady, and begs you to excuse his not coming to you himself."

"Of course, of course"—Annunciata waved this away—"he must stay there. But tell me"—she lowered her voice—"what is happening? What have the Council said?"

The servant stepped instinctively closer and murmured, "My lady, the situation is very dangerous. There is talk that the Whig leaders intend to keep the Duke of York out of the kingdom by force of arms, and place the Duke of Monmouth on the throne, trusting on His Grace's new popularity and the hatred of Popery to gain the support of the people. And if that happened . . ."

He did not need to say more. Civil war, violent and bloody, would be the result. Monmouth, as a puppet of Shaftesbury, would soon be challenged by other would-be kings, while those who were loyal to James would take arms for him, and James himself would raise a French army to invade his own kingdom. The prospect was too terrible to contemplate.

Birch came back to say that they had been unable to find Arabella in the castle, but that Hugo had taken out a horse and ridden off toward the woods, so presumably he had learned something of Arabella's movements. "Shall I send Tom to ask the grooms, my lady?"

Tom sent back word that one of the grooms had seen a red-haired young woman riding off with a Guards officer, and that he had told the same thing to Viscount Ballincrea.

At the hour of dinner, when Birch was trying to persuade Annunciata to eat something, Chloris came in with the news that the King had regained consciousness and had told the chief members of his Council—Halifax, Essex, and Sunderland—to summon the Duke of York at once from Brussels. Annunciata felt numbed by the news: it meant that the King thought he was dying, too.

The final bad news came when Hugo returned. He had traced Arabella easily as far as Eton Wick, but then she and her companion had ridden away across the fields and he had no idea where they had gone.

"You don't think she has been abducted, do you?" Annunciata asked as the thought suddenly came to her.

"Oh, no," Hugo said hastily, and then stopped.

Annunciata looked at him in surprise. "You know whom she is with, don't you?"

Hugo nodded reluctantly.

"Who is it? Tell me. Not that puppy Morris? I'll wager that's who it is. He was always sniffing around her."

"No, madam, not Morris," Hugo said, and, avoiding her eyes, said, "It was Lord Berkeley."

Arabella stood before her defiantly, and even through her anger and worry Annunciata noted with pride and also with a strange pang that, in her own way, Arabella had grown beautiful of late. She was a tall girl, taller than Annunciata—she had inherited her grandfather's height—and she held herself superbly. Her face was flushed and glowing from the open air, and the touch of color became her otherwise rather harsh features; her tawny eyes were bright as a wildcat's; her red hair, coarse as a pony's mane, was drawn back to the crown of her head and fell straight and untamed down her back. She had that imperious look that had always reminded Annunciata of her mother.

Berkeley, on the other hand, looked anything but defiant; he was abashed, nervous, apologetic, and desperately worried. Annunciata ignored him and addressed herself to Arabella.

''Where have you been? And what explanation do you have of your infamous conduct?''

''Madam—'' Berkeley began, but she rounded on him like a whiplash.

''Be silent, sir. I will speak to you later. Arabella, answer me.''

''I have been to Dorney. We dined at Dorney Court with my lord Castlemaine. James is a great friend of his.''

Annunciata was struck speechless for a moment by the enormity of it, and the instant realization of the scandal that would ensue if it were known that Arabella, an unmarried girl, had accepted an invitation to dine as Berkeley's companion. The fact that Castlemaine was the husband of the King's most notorious mistress would not help matters, either. Roger Palmer was an odd man, reserved, almost a recluse, and seeming completely indifferent to his wife's notoriety, even to the point of continuing his friendship with Berkeley, who, it was well known, had been one of Barbara's lovers some years ago.

''How could you do such a thing?'' Annunciata cried at length. ''Don't you realize what you have done?''

''I did not expect to be found out.'' Arabella shrugged. ''We didn't intend to go as far as Dorney, but when we found we'd gone farther than we intended, James suggested we call at Dorney, and the earl bade us stay to dinner, so we did. Otherwise I'd have been back in time not to be missed.''

''My lady, we did not know, of course, about the King's illness,'' Berkeley blurted out. ''Had we done, of course I should never have dreamed—''

''I am glad to know you have some principles,'' Annunciata said cuttingly, ''though it seems you have as few as my daughter. She, it may be hoped, will learn better as she grows older, but for you there is no excuse. You will regret this day's work, believe me. As for you, Arabella—''

But Berkeley had summoned up his courage, and interrupted her. "Madam, I beg you to believe that I had no improper designs on your daughter. I wished only—"

"You do not think it improper to risk a young woman's reputation in such a manner?"

"It isn't James's fault, mother," Arabella said. "It was I who suggested going riding this morning."

"You?" Annunciata said in disbelief.

"I've done it before," Arabella said defiantly. "When we were in London I often slipped out—"

"Be silent!"

"James never wanted us to meet like that," Arabella went on unabashed.

Berkeley added eagerly, "Madam, it's true. I agreed out of my damnable weakness, but I wanted everything to be correct. I wanted to marry Arabella, but she said you would never agree, and made me promise not to speak to you. But now that everything is discovered, I beg you to let me ask for her hand."

Annunciata said furiously, "How dare you, how dare you even think of it? Do you imagine for a moment that I would allow my only daughter to marry a reprobate like you, a man without any moral principles, a man so sunk in infamy that he forgets his duty so far as to ruin a young woman's character in this way? To say nothing of the breach of my confidence in you. I would sooner see her hanged at Tyburn than married to you."

"Mother—" Arabella said warningly, but Annunciata continued.

"Be silent! Lord Berkeley, leave us at once. You are no longer welcome in my presence. Go!"

When they were alone together, Arabella turned on her mother angrily.

"You should not have spoken thus to him," she said.

"How dare you criticize me?" Annunciata cried. "You should be begging for forgiveness, but you seem to be quite shameless."

"Mother, if you let me marry him, we may be able to cover up the scandal. Let me marry him, and I'll say we were secretly married last winter in London. It won't seem so bad then that we dined at Lord Castlemaine's—"

"I'll cover the scandal, leave me alone for that! As for you, I shall never let you out of sight again. You will be watched every minute, since you cannot be trusted alone. You will never see or speak to Berkeley again, do you understand? If you try to communicate with him, I'll have you sent to a nunnery abroad. How I could have raised a daughter so shameless I cannot understand.''

At that Arabella lost her temper. Her face reddened and she shouted, ''Perhaps she learned from her mother! Shameless, am I? Have you considered your own behavior? But of course not. You call James a reprobate, but that isn't why you won't let me marry him—or why you're so angry now.''

''Be silent, Arabella!''

''You won't let me marry him because you're jealous! Because you wanted him for yourself! Because he used to be your lover, and now he doesn't want you anymore, and you're jealous—oh!''

Her voice cut off abruptly as Annunciata hit her so hard on the side of the head that she staggered backward. The silence that followed was the more terrible by contrast to the raised voices before. Arabella put her hand to her wounded face, and the two women stood staring at each other in horrified silence.

''Go to your room, Arabella,'' Annunciata said at last in a low voice, and without further comment, Arabella went. Annunciata watched her go, feeling sick. It was monstrous, but there was a grain of truth in what Arabella had said, and the discovery chilled her. That tall eighteen-year-old girl was her daughter, and yet in her heart Annunciata was no more than eighteen herself, had never yet grown out of being the new arrival at Court, the Yorkshire heiress, young, beautiful, desirable, able to take her pick of suitors.

She went to the table and picked up her hand mirror and looked at herself. She was still staring in the mirror when Chloris came in, and as the woman came to stand beside her in silent sympathy, Annunciata said, ''I'm thirty-four, Chloris. I've never really thought about it before.''

''You are more beautiful than ever,'' Chloris said. ''The glass should tell you that, my lady.''

''Perhaps. But I am a woman, not a girl any longer.'' She put the mirror down and turned to her friend. ''What on earth am I going to do with her?''

"It will blow over," Chloris said comfortingly. "It seems important now, but in a day or two it will be forgotten. Besides, there are bigger matters to fill people's minds just now."

"God forgive me, I had forgotten for the moment. Is there any more news?"

"Nothing yet. We must simply wait and pray."

"Of course. Nothing else matters beyond that," Annunciata said. "If the King should die . . ."

But the King did not die: his recovery was as sudden as his illness had been, and by the time the Duke of York arrived at Windsor, the King had resumed his normal health and good spirits.

"Poor James," the King said to Annunciata on one of their morning strolls soon after the Duke's arrival. "He was terrified, as well he might be, thinking he would have to fight his way into the castle against Shaftesbury's troops; or slip in disguised as a servant, I suppose." He chuckled. "Did you ever see such a poor hand at disguising himself? Even if his height and that great Stuart nose didn't give him away, the enemy would have known him by the knocking of his knees."

"We all had a terrible fright, Your Majesty," Annunciata said severely. "I must ask you never to do it again."

"Oh, and the poor Whigs," he went on, still laughing, "so crestfallen when I rose from my bed, crowding round me and saying, 'We are so happy, Your Majesty,' with faces as long as a Scottish mile. To have the kingdom so nearly in their pockets, only to have it snatched away again! I swear it was almost worth the administrations of the doctors to see their faces!"

Annunciata shuddered. "Don't, sir. You can't imagine how terrible it was for us, waiting and wondering—"

The King drew her hand through his arm and pressed it. "My poor Countess! But comfort yourself that it has done the Whigs a great deal of harm. Realizing how close they've been to civil war will shake some sense into my people's heads, and they won't be so eager next time to listen to them. All the same," he added thoughtfully, "I think I shall be happier without my loving son for a while. I'll send him to Holland, and he can dance with his cousin and forget politics with a little flirtation. If the rest of the Dutch courtiers are like Prince William, the ladies will flock round him.''

"As they do here," Annunciata said. "Lord Monmouth is a charming young man.''

The King looked at her shrewdly. "You don't think him charming at all.'' He sighed. "If only we could combine his manners and religion with James's birth and rectitude, we'd have a perfect heir. And speaking of the heir, I think I can do without James's company for a while, too.''

"You won't send him abroad again, sir?"

"No, not abroad. That would be dangerous. He's too far away to get back quickly. No, I think Scotland should have him. They're a grim people up there—they'll enjoy James's frivolity. And just to remind people that the Stuarts are still a dynasty, he can take his wife with him, and his daughter.'' They turned at the end of the walk and began strolling back toward the castle, and the King, after musing for a while said, "I wonder, now, whether that might be the solving of your little problem, my dear.''

"My problem, sir?"

"That tall, wicked daughter of yours. God's fish, Countess, don't look so surprised! I have my own ways of hearing things, you know.''

"Browning," Annunciata said, smiling. "Every time I look for my woman Chloris, I find her deep in conversation with Browning. I thought he had designs on her virtue.''

The King roared with laughter. "Browning—of all people!" he said. "No, no, you need not fear for your woman, not from that quarter, anyway. But your daughter—from what Browning tells me she's your Monmouth!''

"She hasn't killed anyone yet, sir," Annunciata retorted, nettled by the King's amusement. The King smiled.

"Well said, my dear. But as to young Mistress McNeill, how would you like to send her to Scotland? My niece will have to have her own household up there, and I could easily appoint your daughter a Lady of the Bedchamber. It will get her out of harm's way, and she'd be under supervision, what with Anne's lady governess, and James and his wife. Besides, I defy anyone to get into trouble in Edinburgh—it's too cold and damp."

"Thank you, sir. I am most grateful to you, and I'm sure it is a very good plan," Annunciata said. "My cousins at Aberlady could keep an eye on her, too."

"It shall be done, then. And now, what do you think about the racing this morning? I liked the look of that colt of your husband's, but Frampton assures me that he can't possibly beat my colt Cadogan. What do you say to a small wager on it?"

In May of 1680 the whole Morland family was gathered together at Morland Place for the first time in twenty years. Ironically, the occasion concerned one who was a Morland only by courtesy, but Ralph had needed only the excuse. At forty-nine he had begun to feel the cold hand of age upon his shoulder, and he wanted to call his family around him once more while he still could. He had always been a lover of family, and the odd circumstances of his upbringing had left him feeling like an orphan and had given him a hunger for kin that was all but insatiable.

His mother had died in giving him birth, and his father had been so alienated from the family that Ralph had never been able to feel filial toward him. His grandfather Edmund and his stepgrandmother Mary Esther had brought him up, but they were long dead now. Losing his first wife and three oldest sons in quick succession had increased his hunger, and marrying Annunciata had done little to abate it. The sense of being an orphan was, oddly, one of the things that he had in common with Annunciata; but as Ralph had never been skilled in communicating his feelings, neither was much aware of it.

Annunciata had been negotiating the terms of the marriage of her son Hugo all winter, and there were times when, in a blaze of temper, she declared she would call off the match, for the old Marquess of Ely was a difficult man, very poor and very proud, an uncomfortable combination. But in February the old marquess had died, and his son Masseldine succeeded to the title, and any doubts that the new marquess had about the match were outweighed by his personal friendship with Lord Ballincrea. The betrothal was announced, the contracts drawn up, and the wedding fixed for May. And then Ralph had asked if it could be held at Morland Place.

"After all, he is my stepson; and Shawes will be his, I suppose, when we are gone, so he should be married where his tenantry can see him."

Annunciata had imagined a wedding in London, at Westminster perhaps, but in a rare moment of kindness toward her husband she agreed, and Masseldine had no objections to spending a month or so enjoying the hospitality of Yorkshire, and so it was agreed. Ralph delightedly issued the invitations and spent five thousand pounds on the occasion, besides paying for the bride's trousseau, since Masseldine was not only penniless himself, but was burdened with many debts that his father had left him.

Annunciata had many second thoughts about agreeing to the Yorkshire wedding, but she had to admit that Ralph stinted nothing. The house was cleaned from top to bottom, every piece of plate and crystal polished to brilliance, the servants decked out in new uniforms, flowers banked in every room. In the great hall Ralph had miniature trees in pots set here and there, and the walls were decorated with green boughs and garlands of flowers so that it was like the Garden of Eden. Among the boughs were silken banners displaying the arms of the Morlands, the McNeills, and the Boveries, and over the great fireplace a huge representation of the black lion sejant of the Morlands and the unicorn of the Boveries, linked with a golden chain.

The food for the wedding feast was laid out in lavish array, the centerpiece being a gilded peacock and four huge gilded pies, the piecrusts being built up into the shape of castles, and the claret and champagne were served out of four great silver tubs. A twelve-piece orchestra played for the entertainment of the indoor guests, while outside a second feast was served to the tenants and villagers from long trestles.

Annunciata met the bride-to-be for the first time when she arrived with her brother a week before the wedding. Lady Caroline Boverie was certainly a beauty, and had for a long time been one of the toasts of the Court, although her poverty had prevented her from making a match before now. She was nineteen, with a well-developed figure, fair hair, blue eyes, and very regular features. Wissing had painted a portrait of her dressed as the goddess Diana, and Rochester had written a poem to her addressing her as Phoebe. Most of the Court gallants had paid her attentions, and in the case of some of them scandal had been narrowly averted, and when Rochester wrote his poem and seemed inclined to follow it up with a more personal adoration her father had removed her to the country out of harm's way. A month or two later Hugo had come to stay, and met her for the first time.

Annunciata spent most of the week before the wedding in her company, and decided that apart from her beauty there was nothing to her. She found her sentimental and dull, reminding her very much of the young princesses, but there was no harm to the girl, and Hugo was evidently charmed with her. She wondered how long the enchantment would last: Hugo was used, in his own family at least, to women with more education and a great deal more spirit. However, in her gold brocade wedding-gown, the skirt sewn with tiny pearls, the sleeves and bodice clasped with rubies, she certainly looked magnificent.

Annunciata's gown was of midnight-blue silk, over a stiff cloth-of-silver petticoat, and she wore the fabulous black pearls around her white throat, and the white pearl headdress in her black hair, and she was satisfied that she looked far more beautiful than the bride, especially when she noticed that Martin, in common with many other of the male guests, could not take his eyes off her. As they were going in to the chapel he came up quietly behind her to whisper, "It's hardly fair, you know. This is poor Lady Caroline's one chance to shine, and our eyes are all so dazzled we can hardly see her."

Annunciata pinched his hand in reproof, but her smile lasted all the way through the ceremony.

Ralph, too, was smiling, and to Annunciata looked more like the Ralph of her youth than at any time since Rupert's christening. He held himself upright and his gold-gray eyes shone, and his mouth curled in a smile that made his face look young again. There all around him was what remained of his family—his son Martin, of whom he could be justly proud, his daughter Daisy, a tall, handsome, serious girl whose air of gravity, oddly, made her seem younger than silly, frivolous Caroline.

Beside Daisy was Ralph's brother Clovis—hard to believe he was almost thirty—and Ralph's three surviving sons by the countess. Then there was the party from Northumberland—Sabine and her husband Crispian, and fat breathless Anne. That marriage had been a happy one, except that it was childless. Sabine had had two pregnancies that ended in miscarriage, and since then had not conceived again. She had grown very thin, while by contrast Crispian had grown rounder than ever, his short neck seeming to disappear into his meaty shoulders. But Sabine was full of stories about the wonderful life they led at Emblehope, and it evidently pleased her still to be the queen of that tiny kingdom, with Anne doing all the real work and deferring to her so humbly.

And then there was his sister Cathy. He had not seen her since that summer when he had run away from Annunciata, and he thought with some distress that she had aged greatly in that time. She was the same age as Annunciata, but looked at least ten years older, and she had never been a beauty. The harsh life in Scotland and continuous sorrow had made her gray and shapeless. Kit looked much as he always had, although he seemed indefinably ill at ease. With them they had the only one of their children to have survived, the nine-year-old girl Hero, whose twin brother had died only last year. She was a delicate, spindly child, and Kit seemed to watch her with as much pain as pleasure. With them also was Arabella, released from the princess's household for the occasion.

Hugo, in a sky-blue silk suit and a new wig of hair several shades darker than his own, was making his vows in a confident, ringing tone, and Masseldine was producing the ring—a broad gold band studded with diamonds which he had gone into debt to buy—and soon afterward the new-wedded couple was walking toward the chapel door to a fanfare of trumpets. Ralph caught Annunciata's eye and knew what she was thinking: that the ceremony seemed strangely short and bare without the Mass. For once he agreed with her; but the bride was a Protestant, and in view of the troubled times Masseldine had stipulated that the shorter Protestant rite should be used.

But if the service was short, the celebrations were long, and after the couple was put to bed in the somber dignity of the Butts Bed in the great bedchamber, Ralph wondered a little irreverently whether Hugo listened with envy to the noises of merrymaking coming from below him as he savored the joys of marriage with the lovely Caroline. It was late before quiet fell on the house, and everyone had gone to bed except for Ralph and Annunciata, Clovis, and Cathy, Kit, and Arabella. Annunciata and Kit had been talking about their childhood together at Shawes, and Annunciata had been telling him about her renewed plans to modernize the house, while Cathy, who looked as if she longed for her bed, listened with grim determination not to be left out. Clovis and Ralph had been talking horses, and Arabella had been listening with interest, but at last even their conversation dried up, and a silence fell over the group.

"Well, perhaps we had better go to bed, too," Annunciata said, though without conviction. She looked around the group and seemed to change her mind. "I must have something to drink first, however—I have such a thirst upon me. Ralph, will you call? I'll have some tea."

The boy waiting outside the door of the long saloon to take messages had actually fallen asleep standing up, like a horse, and Ralph had to speak to him quite vigorously before he could get him to understand his task. When he came back into the room Annunciata was talking to Arabella.

"Now, miss, I have had no chance to speak to you yet. Tell me how you liked Edinburgh."

"Not at all," Arabella said curtly. "Did you expect me to? I did not think people were exiled for their pleasure."

Ralph remembered that moment long afterward. It seemed etched on his memory with the clarity of the last seconds before a storm breaks, when the world is still, holding its breath for the lightning flash. Arabella looked somehow dangerous to him, tall, lean, her great mass of red hair glowing like burnished copper framing her white face. Round her throat she wore the Queen's emeralds, lent to her for the day by Annunciata, and they glittered in the candlelight like green cat's eyes. She seemed as tense as a creature poised to spring, making Annunciata seem relaxed by contrast. The candlelight had taken all color from her dress, and she was all black and white; beautiful, but the older woman, strong with authority, the white queen, very much the prince's daughter.

"I will not have you speak to me like that," Annunciata said. "Answer me civilly, or—"

"Or what?" Arabella broke in. "You have no power over me. You have done to me all you can do. You have separated me from my lover and sent me into exile. I suppose not even you can actually take away my life. So what more can you do to punish me?"

"I have no desire to punish you," Annunciata said, and though she was angry, she sounded more puzzled.

"Then why did you send me away?"

"For your good."

"Because you hate me," Arabella answered herself. "Yes, my lady, I know it, and I hate you, too, quite as much as you can hate me. As much as *she* does"—and she flung a gesture toward Cathy.

Ralph was afraid, though he did not know of what. He said, "Arabella, don't—" and stopped as she turned to him and cried, "You fool! Would you defend her still, that *wife* of yours? Don't you know she cuckolded you?"

"No, Arabella," Ralph said again, feebly protesting. He did not want to hear.

"Yes, yes. She made a fool of you gladly. Even when he was bringing your message to her after the trial—most convenient, wasn't it?" she said, turning to Kit, who was watching white faced with horror.

"Arabella, be silent!" Annunciata commanded, but she could not be stopped now.

"And you," she went on to Cathy, "didn't you wonder, year after year, what took him to London? What he did there? So much business to do, so little done. She made fools of all of you, and no one ever knew. No one but me. But then the young men started to prefer me to her, and she couldn't bear that. I took one of her lovers, and she was jealous, jealous—''

She stopped abruptly as Annunciata slapped her, looking more surprised than hurt. In the horrible silence, Clovis took her arm and wheeled her gently but firmly about and led her to the door. Cathy was staring at Kit with a sick expression.

''Is it true?'' she whispered.

''Cathy—'' Kit began wretchedly.

''*Is it true?*'' He made no answer and she thought for a moment and said as if to herself, ''That was the Christmas I was with child. I suppose I should be grateful you waited until I had given birth. You were in London, with her, when the baby died. And all the other times—''

''Oh, Cathy,'' Kit said hopelessly, reaching out a hand to her. She removed herself from his reach.

''No,'' she said, quite calmly. She was looking at Annunciata now. ''All your life,'' she said slowly, ''all your life, you've had everything you wanted. And the men—you had to have them all. At parties, when we were young, they must all ask you first, even the ones you didn't like, before they came to Elizabeth Hobart and me. You took everything from me. It must have gone hard with you when Kit married me. So you had to take him, too. Are you satisfied now? He's the only man I ever loved, but you had to have him, too, just for your amusement.'' She half-closed her eyes, as if in pain, and in a low, clear voice that barely trembled she said with great force, ''*Damn you.*''

No one spoke. Cathy turned and walked out, a gray, shrunken figure and yet at that moment one of great dignity. Kit avoided their eyes and went after her, leaving Ralph and Annunciata alone.

It was a long time before either of them spoke. Annunciata stood as she was, very upright, staring ahead of her like a soldier. Ralph watched her, his heart bruised. After a long while she turned and met his eyes and said quietly, ''I am ashamed. And yet—''

''And yet?'' he prompted her at last.

''She blamed me. Not Kit. No one will ever blame Kit. Why?''

Ralph could not answer—the question was incomprehensible to him. She had wronged him, but most of all at that moment he pitied her. The image came into his mind of a tethered eagle, and he did not understand why.

"Do you hate me, Ralph?" she said at last.

He stared. There were tears on her face. He could not remember when he had last seen her cry. He shook his head, wanting to speak, but his lips were numb.

"For God's sake," she began, but the protest seemed to have no conclusion. He met her eyes, and took half a step toward her.

"It seems," he said slowly, "that we have to forgive each other, you and I."

CHAPTER THIRTEEN

In December 1680 Prince George Louis of Hanover visited England, looking for a wife. He was the eldest son of Prince Rupert's sister Sofia, who had married the Elector of Hanover, and though nothing had been said officially it was understood that he had come to look at the Princess Anne, now nearly sixteen and ready for marriage.

Princess Anne was at Whitehall again, having left her parents in Scotland, and Arabella was still in her household. Hugo and Caroline were at Court, too, while Annunciata and Ralph were spending Christmas at Windsor with Prince Rupert, and so when the young prince rode to Windsor to visit his Uncle Rupert, Hugo took the opportunity to ride with him to see his mother.

Hugo found his mother very distracted, for the prince was confined to his bed by a sore in his leg that troubled him from time to time.

"His health is not what it was," Annunciata told Hugo when they had exchanged greetings. "He is cheerful about it—he always is, of course—but the trouble recurs, and he suffers from terrible headaches, too."

"Don't worry, Mother," Hugo tried to comfort her. "If he was really ill he wouldn't be able to see the prince, would he? And he sent for him first thing."

"I suppose so." Annunciata frowned.

Ralph thought it prudent to change the subject. "What do you think of Prince George, Hugo? We haven't seen him yet, though from what we hear he is very fond of his uncle, which speaks well.''

Hugo chuckled. "Oh, dear, never was there such an ill-famed visit. When he arrived at Greenwich, no one seemed to know he was coming, and there was nothing prepared for him, no lodgings, no welcoming committee.''

"So much we know," Annunciata said. "He wrote to Prince Rupert asking for help. Rupert seemed to be of the opinion that someone at Whitehall had bungled.''

"It would not surprise me at all," Hugo said. "How anything ever gets down there I don't know. And the King is so secretive—I never could discover whether he knew Prince George was coming or not. When Prince Rupert's letter came, he sent word to Greenwich that Prince George must lodge at Whitehall, ordered an apartment for him, and went off to play tennis.''

"But what is he like?" Annunciata asked. "You still have not told me.''

"Well, I didn't see much of him, but Arabella didn't like him," Hugo said. "She said when he was brought before Princess Anne his face fell several inches. Princess Anne was mortally offended, Ara says. He's no courtier, I know that—a good soldier, so they say, but uncouth. Ara says Princess Anne will never forgive him: he took one look at her and cut his visit short.'' He chuckled at the memory.

"Is he handsome?" Annunciata asked.

Hugo looked at his wife. "Let Caroline answer that. How can I say what women think is handsome?''

But Caroline only blushed and would not answer. Annunciata gathered that Hugo teased her a great deal, and she was never sure if he was serious or not.

"Well, we shall see him for ourselves tomorrow," Ralph said. "Prince Rupert insists we do not confine ourselves because he is confined, so we are to hunt with Prince George and show him some sport.''

Annunciata answered her own question the next morning when the large party assembled for the hunt: Prince George was not a handsome man. He was small and stocky, with a soldier's carriage, and fuzzy, pinkish-blond hair, but his face was heavy, with lackluster eyes that reminded Annunciata of a cod's, and a wide loose mouth like a frog's.

"Frog and cod, and no courtier," Annunciata said. "No wonder Anne did not like him. I suppose he must take after his father. There's nothing of Rupert in him, sure."

Hugo, having spent a blissful evening in his mother's company, was now obliged to ride at the front with the prince and the gentlemen, leaving his wife to ride behind with the ladies. Annunciata was riding a new colt which Ralph had bred for her, and was content to ride behind, rather than up with the first flight as was her usual custom, and after the first gallop Ralph dropped back, too, and, with a smile, rode beside her.

"Won't the prince think you are slighting him?" Annunciata said.

"I can always plead my age," Ralph said, checking Oryx's long stride to keep him alongside the curveting youngster. "Unlike poor Hugo, who would far sooner ride with you than royalty."

By the time they reached Eton Wick they were the last in the field, but they made no real attempt to keep up. Since Hugo's wedding, they had found a kind of peace with each other: by tacit consent neither mentioned the past troubles, and Ralph had resumed his half-fatherly, half-brotherly role toward her. For Annunciata it was a relief, like a return to childhood, and he was once again her companion and protector, as he had been before there had been any thought of marrying him.

"What do you think of him?" Ralph asked suddenly as they picked their way across a stream, on their way to draw a new wood.

"What, the prince?" Annunciata asked, startled out of a reverie.

Ralph smiled. "No, Hugo, of course. You are pleased with him, I think."

"Oh, yes, he is much improved. Marriage suits him. I think Caroline must have more to her than I suspected."

"I don't think he cares a jot about Caroline," Ralph said. Annunciata looked at him, startled, and he went on, "The only person in the world that he loves, apart from Hugo, is you, and now that he is your beloved son, and first in your confidence, he is happy."

"Ralph, what nonsense you talk," Annunciata said briskly. "I like him better because he behaves better."

Ralph shook his head, smiling more broadly. "He behaves better because you like him better. He was always jealous of George, you know. Even I could see that." A shadow crossed her face, as always at the mention of George.

"I wish he were here," Annunciata said in a low voice.

But Hugo does not, Ralph thought, and then he spoke aloud. "I can never really think of you as Hugo's mother. You still seem too young to me."

She smiled happily at the compliment, and they rode on after the hunt. When they drew a blank and rode on toward Dorney it put Annunciata in mind of Arabella, and her smile faded to a frown.

"I can never rest easy, even when she is behaving herself," she said when Ralph asked her why. "I can never be sure what she's going to do next, and when she's quiet, that's when I feel the need to worry most. It's generally because she's planning something terrible."

"Like the time she put a dead mouse in Birch's pocket?" Ralph asked.

"I'd forgotten that," Annunciata said, and then began to laugh. "Oh, poor Birch! I never heard anyone scream so loudly. It must have felt dreadful."

"It was a very dead mouse," Ralph agreed.

"Birch never forgave her."

"Birch never forgave her for having hair that wouldn't curl," Ralph said. "She wanted your daughter to be like you. Well, perhaps she is, after all—not in looks, but in character. Don't you remember the beatings you got as a child?"

"I never did such terrible things as Arabella does," Annunciata said hotly, and then, seeing Ralph's amused look, reflected and wondered. "Not quite as terrible, anyway. But, Ralph, what on earth am I to do with that girl?"

"Marry her," Ralph said. "Once she has a husband and a few children it will quiet her down. Don't you remember that red mare of mine that no one could ride?"

"Do you mean Oriflamme? Yes, of course."

"And in the end I had to mate her. Three lovely foals she dropped me, and she was as quiet as an old plough-mare after that."

"Well enough as a theory," Annunciata said, "but it's finding a husband that's difficult."

And Ralph answered easily, as if it were the most obvious thing in the world, "Marry her to Martin."

The bedcurtains were pulled around the Butts Bed with a firm hand, and the candlelight and footsteps and murmuring voices retreated. Someone laughed; silken skirts rustled against the doorframe; someone said something that ended in "more wine;" and then came the sound of the door closing with a terminal click. The darkness seemed suddenly close and listening. Arabella could hear Martin breathing, and the fact of his closeness impinged upon her body far worse than if he had actually been touching her. Her skin seemed stretched tight and screaming, and a growing pain in her chest made her realize only then that she had been holding her breath.

It came out in a rushing sigh, and as if that had been a signal, Martin stirred toward her. She could not see him in the dark, but she felt the sheet move on top of her and the mattress under her, and his breathing seemed hot and menacing. She was as terrified as a rabbit that has bolted by mistake into a fox's hole.

"Don't touch me!" she squeaked. The movement toward her checked and began again.

"Arabella," he began in a reasonable voice, but she was beyond reason.

"Don't touch me! If you touch me I'll—I'll—kill you!" Her voice rose with hysteria, and Martin lay very still.

"All right," he said gently. "I won't touch you. Be calm, Arabella. I won't move. Calm down now." He lay still and listened in the dark for her breathing, which panted like a spent hare's. Gradually it slowed, though he could feel the tension like lightning in the air. After a while he said, "Won't you tell me what's wrong?"

The sound of his voice was familiar to Arabella, and as he spoke she saw his face with her mind's eye, knowing exactly

what expression accompanied that tone: the curve of the mouth
into a half-smile, the crinkling of the corners of the eyes in faint
amusement. It was the way he looked at her mother sometimes
when she was being outrageous; the way he used to look at his
half-brother Charles—always now called Karellie—when, before
he learned to speak, he would come trotting up to Martin chattering in his own burbling language. The voice and the face were
familiar and unfrightening; but the situation was menacing. In the
dark he had become a huge, powerful presence, a male creature,
dominating, punishing, obliterating.

"I don't want you," she whispered, and Martin heard the
genuine terror in her voice. It surprised him, for having spent a
lifetime with horses, Arabella must know the facts of life: why,
then, should the notion frighten her? And yet he knew she was
frightened. He tried to project himself into her mind, but drew a
blank. Arabella was thinking of horses, too: she remembered the
stallion Kingcup covering mares; she remembered his hugely
muscled body, the raw power of him, the way he seized the
mares by the back of the neck with his teeth, forcing them to
accept him, remembered how they rolled their eyes and squealed
as if in pain. At the back of her mind, a thing she was trying not
to remember, was the time Kingcup had mated a very young,
small filly, and the weight of the great stallion had broken the
filly's pelvis and Ralph had had to put her down.

"But you consented to marry me," Martin said gently. "That
was your choice—no one forced you to."

No, she had not been forced to. She had enjoyed the wedding,
the beautiful gown of white cloth-of-gold and silver lace, the
King's diamond necklace that her mother had lent her for the
day, the feast and the dancing.

"When Father St. Maur said, 'I now pronounce you man
and wife together,' you turned and smiled at me," Martin
reminded her, still gently and as if half amused. His intention
was to make her talk, knowing that talking would relax her.

"Yes," she said. "I was thinking—" she paused, not able to
tell him that at that moment she had turned and smiled at him
because she had thought, "Now *I* shall one day wear the black
pearls." When she did not go on, he prompted her.

"What did you think when you wanted to marry that captain of yours, Lord Berkeley? Did you not think then what it would entail?"

"Yes, I suppose so," she said reluctantly, and then, "no, not really. I just thought . . ."

"Yes?"

"I just thought, well, that we'd be married, and I'd be Lady Berkeley."

Martin chuckled softly at the thought. Oh, Arabella, child of your mother! "Well, now you are married, and you are Mistress Morland," he said. "Unless you want to call the whole thing off?"

"What do you mean?" Arabella asked, startled.

"The marriage is not binding until it is consummated," Martin said gently. "If you like, you can get up now and walk away a free woman."

The silence fairly rang with her startled thoughts. Would he really not force her? Was the choice really hers? A free woman! But then, not really free. Sooner or later she would have to marry someone. And the scandal! Her mother's scorn! The laughter and pity of the gossips! It was not possible.

"If I've got to marry someone," she said reluctantly, "it might as well be you, I suppose."

Now he laughed aloud. "And why the distinction, I wonder? Am I so handsome, so desirable? I'm fairly rich, of course—"

Arabella was uncertain why he was laughing, and said cautiously, "Because I know you, I suppose." He moved toward her and she went instantly rigid again.

"Look, Arabella," he said firmly, "this is my bed as well as yours, and I do not intend to spend the whole night frozen into immobility because you are terrified whenever I move."

"But—"

"No buts, my girl. I am going to put my arm around you, and hold you, and you are going to lie comfortably with your head on my shoulder, and we are going to go to sleep."

"Is that all?" Arabella said hesitantly. Unseen in the darkness, he smiled.

"That's all. Come here, child. That's right. Be easy now. Nothing will happen to you that you don't want to happen. Trust me."

And he gathered her against him, and settled her in his arms, head on his shoulder, and folded his arms around her. After a while she sighed, and he felt her relax.

"Are you comfortable?" he asked her.

"Yes," she said in a very small voice.

"Good. Then, go to sleep."

In the morning she woke as soon as it grew light enough to see. Outside the birds were singing the dawn chorus, and the peacocks were shrieking as if in protest at being woken by it. She had a stiff neck—she was taller than Martin, and it was not entirely comfortable sleeping on his shoulder—and it was that that alerted her to her situation. With a smothered gasp she pulled herself away from him and sat up, and then cautiously, as he did not seem to wake, she looked down at his face.

It was composed in sleep, the lips lightly together, the long dark eyelashes brushing his brown cheek. Without the blue, bright gaze of his eyes, his face looked somehow abandoned and defenseless. His hair was tousled. Carefully, not to wake him, she touched a curl of it. He had the finest, silkiest hair she had ever known, and it fascinated her, her own being so coarse and stiff. His skin was smooth, too, a wonderful honey-brown in color, and such a texture! It reminded her of the fairy story in which the prince was known to be of a superior birth by the delicacy of his skin.

Studying him, she could not be afraid of him. His lips looked firm and silky, and staring at them she experienced a strange and thrilling feeling that started at the back of her neck and ran all the way down her spine to settle in a place she was not accustomed to feeling with. And then he opened his eyes, and smiled, and without even thinking about it she smiled back.

"What were you thinking?" he asked after a moment.

"That you look like a prince," she said shyly.

He put his hands to her shoulders. "You look like some wonderful, untamed wild animal, a great cat, perhaps." He pulled her very gently toward him. "Lioness." He smiled. She smiled, too, and went down into his arms, and gave her lips to be kissed. The touch was tender and electric at the same time, and she was so astonished and excited that she simply went on kissing him, pressing closer to him to go with the sensation. At the back of her mind she knew that something was going to happen, but it had become something she wanted—wanted at least to know about.

His arms were strong and loving about her, and when he rolled her over to her back, his silk-skinned hands were gentle, and seemed to know all the places to stroke her. She remembered watching him once absently caressing the brindled stable-cat, remembered how the cat had arched gloriously to his touch. I wish I could purr, she thought distantly, easing new places under his fingers. She kissed his neck, which was close by her mouth, the warm place just behind the ear, and it was silky, too, and when she heard him groan with pleasure she thought in her pleasant confusion it was her.

Not Kingcup and broken-backed mare, was her last thought, but prince and lioness.

Annunciata went down to London in October of 1682 accompanied by Hugo and her son Rupert, who was twelve, in order to present the latter at Court. At least that was the excuse: in fact she wanted to get away from Morland Place, where she was beginning to feel hemmed in and bored. "Everyone has become so domesticated," she complained to Chloris. "Nothing but the company of dull women and old men. I shall go mad."

Chloris wisely said nothing, but she eyed her mistress with sympathy, knowing something of the causes. Hugo's Caroline had just had her first child, a son, born in August, whom they had named Arthur. Birch, who liked Caroline as much as she had always disliked Hugo, insisted on referring to the baby as "Little Lord Rathkeale."

"As if," Annunciata remarked softly to Chloris, "she can't wait for Hugo to die so that Arthur can have the other title, too."

But Little Lord Rathkeale was Annunciata's grandson; and Annunciata was approaching forty, and she could not endure the idea of growing old. She wanted amusing men around her, to flatter her and flirt with her and make her feel young again. Ralph was companionable and kind, but he was not her lover, never would be again. Caroline and Daisy she found as dull as most modern women—she often declared she would sooner spend a year in Chloris's company than an hour in her daughter-in-law's. Martin, who was always good to be with, was so preoccupied these days with running the estate that she hardly saw him, and Arabella, who had always been stimulating, if nothing else, had grown intolerable since her marriage.

"You'd think no one before her had ever been wed, that she invented the state for herself," Annunciata said in disgust. "That mixture of smugness and arrogance!" Arabella was no less forceful in her character, but now she felt she had authority, and used her forcefulness in bullying Daisy and the servants and giving unnecessary orders. Since Ralph was growing too frail to do everything with the horses, Arabella had taken over much of his work at the stud farm, which at least kept her out of Annunciata's way for part of each day. Chloris and Birch both shook their heads over it, however.

"All that riding, bumping about in a saddle every day," they said. "She'll never get pregnant that way."

"I can't imagine she wants to," Annunciata said, but Chloris shook her head, knowing better. She had seen the way Arabella followed Martin with her eyes, and how she had looked at Caroline's baby. "Anyway," Annunciata said, "she would be impossible if she were pregnant. I'd probably wring her neck in sheer desperation."

And Chloris knew that Annunciata didn't want Arabella to be pregnant and present her with another grandchild, and she was not in the least surprised when her mistress announced she was going to London for the Season. Hugo promptly offered to accompany her, and she accepted the offer without interest. Hugo had been delighted with his son, but he had no real interest in babies or in Caroline, and was glad of the excuse to get away. He had a number of disreputable friends in town, with whom he frequented coffeehouses and taverns, and there was a fascinating girl at Madam Bennett's who could do the most extraordinary things.

Though it was better than the Country, the Court was not the most cheerful place. The King was much as he always was, except that even he had settled into a pattern, and was almost domesticated with his principal mistresses behaving more like wives than courtesans. Louise de Kéroualle had never been a favorite of Annunciata's, and now she thought her both bossy and dull. She had grown very fat lately, and was obsessively interested in her son, and could talk for hours about him. Hortense Mazarin was even more boring, being disinclined to talk about anything to anyone, and spending her life, so it seemed to Annunciata, lying on a sofa eating sweetmeats. Nelly Gwyn, whose house in Pall Mall made her a close neighbor of Annunciata's, was always amusing, but even she had her two sons for whom she eagerly sought titles and pensions.

The reaction against the Whigs which had set in at the time of the King's illness at Windsor had gathered pace, and the Duke of York had been able to be recalled to Court in May. His duchess had recently had another child, a son, who had lived only a few weeks. Her six pregnancies had all ended in failure, and it began to look more and more as if Princess Anne would one day come to the throne, for her sister Mary, married to Dutch William, had miscarried of her first pregnancy in 1678, and had never conceived again. The idea of Princess Anne—whose only two passions in life seemed to be playing cards and her lady-in-waiting, Sarah Churchill—one day ruling the Court made Annunciata feel extremely depressed.

She amused herself with the round of parties and balls and theater-going, and interested herself in her son, Rupert. She presented him to the King, who was very kind to him, talked to him, showed him his laboratory, and promised him a title one day, and took him to Hammersmith to see Prince Rupert. That was a good day, which Annunciata remembered afterwards with a great and wistful pleasure. It was one of those beautiful blue-and-gold days of October that made her think of an heraldic blazon, azure and or. The sun shone in a winter-blue sky, and the sunlight was deep yellow like butter. The trees were all turning, and the leaves of the great beech trees in the garden where they walked were like gold coins.

"You could buy the world with such riches," Annunciata had said, throwing back her head and feeling the sunlight like a warm, caressing hand on her face. She and Prince Rupert were alone, strolling round the walks he had laid out in the ground of the house, and her hand was on his arm, and he had closed his other hand on top of hers. Peg Hughes was not there, she had gone back to her former trade of actress and was in London rehearsing a new play. Dudley was at Windsor on business for his father, and Ruperta, whom Annunciata could never like, was playing with Rupert somewhere in the house.

The prince had greeted Rupert kindly, and spoken with him for some time, and then had suggested that Ruperta take him away and play with him. There had been one moment of unpleasantness during the morning, when a dispute had broken out between them and Ruperta had spat at Rupert, and the nurses had sent to her father for discipline. The prince had spoken to her solemnly, and she had listened with her head on one side and then reached up to kiss him, and had been instantly forgiven. The prince was charmed with her, and thought her an angel, but Annunciata privately thought her impudent and spoiled, though she would never have said so to Rupert.

So she and the prince had dined alone, and spent the afternoon walking in the garden and talking desultorily. Late in the afternoon the children had come out to them, friends again, and in a more subdued mood, and they had watched like fond parents as Ruperta sat on her swing and Rupert good-naturedly pushed her.

"You must bring the others next time, too—Karellie and Maurice," the Prince said. They watched the children for a while. Ruperta was demanding to be pushed higher and higher, and Rupert was looking doubtfully toward his mother, wondering whether it were safe or proper. The prince smiled down at her, and Annunciata looked up into his eyes, and her stomach clenched with the old, forbidden love. His head was framed by the dazzling sky; he looked to her exactly as he had always done, older, but no less lovely, and she arched her neck, aching to be kissed, though she knew it would not, could not, be done. He reached his hand tenderly and brushed a thread of dark hair from her brow where the little breeze had disturbed it, and his hand lingered against her head, cupping it a little, and she leaned her face into his palm.

"You are very, very beautiful," he said. The afternoon seemed strangely still around them, the children's voices far away and unimportant like the chirping of birds that you ceased to notice, and the sunlight soft and heavy so that they seemed held in a golden bowl.

"And so are you," she said. He stooped his head and kissed her forehead, and as his lips lingered there, she closed her eyes, feeling the ache in her throat. The two children called to each other and chattered, near and far away, the children, in that moment, of both of them together; she seemed separated from her natural relationship with him only by the thinnest and most transparent pane of glass. Yet the barrier was absolute. It was as if she placed her palms to the glass and he placed his against hers, always with the pane in between. It was almost twenty years since they had been shut out irrevocably from each other, but nothing, nothing had changed.

Later, when he saw her to her coach, he said, "I have to come to London at the end of the month, for the meeting of the Hudson Bay Company. That's on the twenty-fifth. Will you come with me to the theater on the day before, and see Peg, and sup with us afterwards?"

"Of course, I'd be delighted," she said. "Give my greeting to Dudley when he returns. I'm sorry to have missed him."

"He will be sorry, too. God bless you, my dear. Good-bye, Rupert. I shall see you again soon."

As they drove away, Rupert said, "Mama, tell me again about the prince and the seige of Breda."

But Chloris looked at her mistress's averted face, and touched his hand lightly, shaking her head.

The supper party at Prince Rupert's house in Spring Gardens, close by Whitehall Palace, was a cheerful one. They had been to the theater and watched Peg in her latest role, and they had been joined in their box by the Duke and Duchess of York, and by Rupert's son Dudley, who had returned from Windsor and was once more resident at the Tower of London, where he was studying military engineering under Sir Jonas Moore. He greeted Annunciata with respect but much affection, and she responded warmly. He was a charming youth of sixteen, having something of his father's features, the same dark eyes, but a mass of soft golden hair. His nature was sweet and frank, just as his father's had been, though he did not have his father's temper, and he was universally liked. Annunciata thought it amusing but a little inappropriate that Rupert so evidently intended him for a military career: he seemed too gentle to associate with killing.

After the play they waited for Peg to change, and then went back to Spring Gardens, Dudley traveling in Annunciata's coach with her, and there had supper, after which Peg sang for them until she complained that her voice was tired, and they got out the cards. Peg loved gambling, which seemed a universal vice among actresses, and so Annunciata obligingly lost a few guineas before begging to be excused. The prince, she thought, looked tired. She made her adieus, and Dudley saw her to her coach.

She stayed late abed the next morning, for Nelly Gwyn was giving a party that day to which she had accepted an invitation (the King was to be there, and Madam Kerwell had graciously said she would call in for a little while, and Annunciata could never resist the prospect of watching Nelly bait Madam Kerwell), and she was dozing peacefully among her letters and dogs when Chloris came in, with Birch behind her, and Hugo behind Birch; and she knew, with a sickening lurch of her heart, that something was wrong.

"My lady," Chloris said, holding her eyes steadily, "a message has come from Spring Gardens. Prince Rupert is ill."

"Peg tells me you refuse to be bled," she said, holding his hand tightly. His face was flushed with fever, and taut with pain, and her heart was pounding all over her body with the shock of realizing the truth.

He smiled faintly. "I know that bleeding is supposed to cure everything, but I don't believe in it."

"Will you take the medicine the doctor has prescribed?" she asked. "Peg says it is all good herbs, nothing else."

"For her sake, I will take it," he said, and she pressed his hand harder, knowing that he did not hope for life.

"Please," she said, "please—" Her voice failed, and she tried to swallow the knot of tears in her throat.

"My dear—" he began. "Annunciata—"

"Please don't leave us," she said. "How can we live without you?"

The fever came and went, leaving him weaker each time. He had pleurisy, and an old head-wound gave him severe pain. Lord Craven came, his old, old friend, and on the second day he made his will, appointing him executor and trustee. Lord Craven was in tears, his old eyes dim and red with crying.

"I promised your mother, so many years ago, that I would look to her family," he said. "I never thought that I would outlive them all."

On the twenty-eighth he was plainly sinking fast. Annunciata stayed near all day, watching over him along with Craven, Dudley, and Peg. Rupert and Ruperta stayed away in another room, and all day visitors came to the door to ask for news. He was still rational when he woke, but he spoke little, for he was very weak. When he did open his eyes, he would search around him for the faces he loved, and if any was missing, he would ask where they were. When night fell and he seemed quieter, Annunciata and Dudley persuaded Peg, who was exhausted, to sleep for a while. She refused at first, but when Dudley had a bed made up for her in the adjoining dressing-room, she consented. She slept at once, heavily, and woke just after midnight on Wednesday the twenty-ninth. She came back into the room, rubbing her eyes at the candlelight. The prince was sleeping still, unmoving. His breathing was very light, the fever having left him for a while. She obliged Annunciata to rest in her turn and, like Peg, she did not think she would sleep, and slept at once.

She woke to candlelight; Dudley was standing in the doorway; he looked very young, very alone. She struggled up, and their eyes exchanged question and answer which they could not speak. At last she said, "What time is it?"

"Just before six," he said. The pain in her throat was terrible, and she turned her head away from him, toward the window. The blackness outside was very black, unrelieved by any promise of morning. It was November, nearing the shortest day.

He had been no Catholic, but she knelt by his bedside to pray in her own form, to a God who must love him best of all men, who had been always so faithful, so loving, so upright. She did not want to look at him, to see him dead; she wanted to remember him alive, as she loved him, and when she closed her eyes and prayed he seemed still near in the darkness.

"God receive him, and let him be numbered in the glorious communion of saints. . . ."

Outside the window the first blackbird sang a broken phrase, inquiringly, heralding the dawn.

On Christmas Eve Dudley came to Chelmsford House. The Court was still in mourning, and the house looked shut up, but he was admitted at once to the countess's audience chamber. The countess was sitting on the window seat. There was a piece of work in her lap, but her hands were folded over it, and she looked as if she had been still for a very long time, staring out into the garden. It was one of these gray December days that hover dimly between dusk and dusk, never seeming to grow fully light, and the sky was low and tangible, like mist. The countess was in plain black, with her hair loose, and wearing no jewelry; her face was very white, and she looked very young. She turned to him as he came in, and for a moment seemed not to know who he was. She looked so like his father that it made his chest ache. He remembered the portrait of his father taken in 1642 by Gerrit van Honthorst, that hung in his Aunt Sofia's palace: she could have been that portrait's twin. He wondered again, as he had wondered since the first time he saw her, what she was to his father; and he knew that he would never find out.

She got to her feet now, and came forward to greet him, and as soon as she spoke, her eyes brightened with tears. Close to, he could see how she had wept, and it threatened his own control. He wanted to be gone, quickly.

"I have been going through his things, helping my Lord Craven. I came across this—I thought you might like to have it."

She took the velvet bundle and laid it on her palm and un-wrapped it. Within a circular frame of gold was the miniature tablet of ivory on which was painted, by Samuel Cooper's delicate hand, the likeness of a very young Annunciata. She looked up at Dudley questioningly.

"I think he would have liked you to have it," he said.

She looked at it for a long time, and then closed her fingers over it, and the shadow of a smile touched her lips. "Thank you," she said.

CHAPTER FOURTEEN

In the drawing room of Chelmsford House Rupert Morland tried to take his mind off his discomfort by counting the pearls in the hilt of the sword, which was very nearly all he could see. It was almost impossible not to fidget, and when he did his mother would say reprovingly, "Rupert, be still," and Master Wissing would sigh as if his patience were being hard taxed. His mother seemed to have no difficulty in keeping still, but then of course she was standing, which was easier. The portrait would show her standing with one arm negligently leaning on a pillar while he knelt at her feet offering her his sword, hilt first. On the other side of her his mother had asked Wissing to paint in the two spaniels, and he had agreed. Lucky spaniels, Rupert thought, not having to pose. He took his mind off his knees for a few minutes more by wondering how one would get two spaniels to pose, and deciding that it would be impossible to paint them other than sleeping if it were necessary to draw them from life.

His mother interrupted his reverie by saying, unexpectedly kindly, "Never mind, my darling, it won't be much longer. Once Master Wissing has the sketch, he will not need to have you kneeling anymore, will you, sir?"

"I think, my lady, that we have enough now, if the young gentleman would care to rest," Wissing said. Rupert heaved a sigh of relief and tried to get up, and found his feet had gone to sleep, and Annunciata, laughing, reached down and helped him up, and together they went to look at the sketch.

"Yes, yes, I think it will do very well," Annunciata said.

"Don't you think so, my darling?" she added, kissing the top of Rupert's head. She did not have to stoop very far to do it now—Rupert had grown since Christmas. "You may run along and change now, child." Rupert bowed to his mother and to Master Wissing and left.

As he went out of one door of the drawing room, Gifford opened the other and said, "My lady, Master Morland has arrived."

"*Which* Master Morland?" Annunciata asked, amused.

"Master Martin, my lady."

"Alone? Ah, I suppose he has ridden on ahead. Show him in, Gifford—and perhaps you would see Master Wissing to his carriage at the same time. Will you need to come again, Master Wissing?"

"Not for a day or two, my lady. I will send round to you next week. There is a great deal to be done, as you understand—"

"Yes, of course."

He left, and Annunciata had just time to throw off the ermine-lined cloak she wore for the portrait before Martin came in. He paused at the door to look at her, and his mouth curved into the familiar grin which made her suddenly homesick. He made a formal bow, but she held out her arms to him.

"Martin! Oh, it is good to see you. Come embrace me, quick."

He crossed the room and held her hard, smelling of the fresh air. His arms and hands were strong, his hair was silky soft under her mouth. When at last he put her back from him, there were tears in her eyes.

"How now, what's this?" he said gently, touching her cheek with his finger and bringing it away wet.

"Your hair smells of leaves," she said inconsequentially. "I've missed you."

"You should not have stayed away. My poor lady, how sad you have been, and all alone here. We all thought you would come home after the prince—" He did not complete the sentence, not knowing how she would find the word.

"I intended to, and yet somehow I just couldn't leave. But I wasn't entirely alone, you know. I had young Rupert, and Clovis came from time to time, and—''

"In the way that counts, you were alone," Martin said.

His sympathy was too acute, and she felt the need to break this intimacy with him. She said cheerfully, "How comes it you are here alone? Have the others perished on the way?"

"They will be here soon. Clovis is traveling in the coach with Daisy and the two children, but I discovered my horse simply would not lag. He must have known he was bringing me here." He grinned.

"You almost burst in upon my sitting," she said. "That was Master Wissing who passed you in the hallway."

"Ah, I wondered who it was that was scurrying away so fast," he said, eying her with humor, and she found herself blushing.

"Sir, please! Curb your tongue. It is merely a new portrait for the east fireplace."

"Good, you are taking down that one of you on horseback. I never liked it."

"Did you not?" Annunciata raised an eyebrow.

"It made you look too hard. The horse was good, though."

"It is to go into my bedchamber, so you need never see it again," Annunciata said unthinkingly.

He took her hand and pressed it to his heart and said, "My lady, what cruel words! A savage blow, so casually given."

"Oh, stop it!" Annunciata said, trying not to laugh, and looking at once much younger. "Will you have some wine? I am longing to hear all the news."

"Let's go into the garden and walk, shall we? I find it very hot in here, despite your wonderful long windows."

It was a little cooler in the garden, under the shade of the trees. June had been hot, but July was stifling, and in other years the houses of the great would have been deserted by now, their owners retreating to country estates. But great things were afoot, and so Annunciata had sent for Karellie and Maurice, and Clovis had offered to go up and fetch them.

"Now tell me, why is Daisy coming to London?" Annunciata asked. "It cannot be for her health, in weather like this."

"Give me your arm, first. I do not feel comfortable without a woman on my arm. Good, that is better, now we can stroll at ease.'' He glanced at her, and his eyes seemed to be a brighter blue than ever, as if they took color from the intense summer sky. ''You are very comfortable to walk with, you know. We are exactly of a height. Arabella and Daisy are both taller than I.''

''I don't want to talk about Arabella,'' Annunciata said, pinching him. ''Answer my question.''

''Very well—it is for her health in a way, although I would sooner have sent her to Harrogate or Scarborough, but I know well she would not go. I told her she was needed to bring the children, and that I had to come and did not wish to go alone, and so eventually she agreed. But she is working much too hard, and I had at all costs to get her away. She is never out of the house, you know, working and worrying from morning to night.''

''Does not Caroline help her?'' Annunciata asked, but she knew the answer already.

''Caroline is not accustomed to running a household,'' he said tersely. It was not his place to say so, but Caroline tended to treat Daisy like a maid, bidding her send for this and pick up that, read to her or entertain her. ''And now that Arabella is pregnant it is even worse'' he went on. ''Before, she was out of the way most of the time, but now she is confined to the house she bullies and scolds Daisy all the time.''

''Pregnancy has not improved her temper, then,'' Annunciata said, as if to herself. ''So you thought to give her a rest from her domestic cares by bringing her here.''

''Daisy is looking very pale and thin these days,'' Martin said. ''I am afraid her health will suffer.''

''It is your fault, you know,'' Annunciata said.

''Mine? How is it mine?''

''Because you should have got her a husband long ago. Leaving her at home unwed has caused her troubles.''

''It was for my father to get her a husband,'' Martin said, but even as he spoke the defensive words, he knew that as he had taken over all his father's other duties, so he should have taken over that one, too.

Annunciata said more gently, ''I think I understand. You are very fond of her, and to you she has always been your little sister. It was hard for you to realize she had grown up. And I am to blame, too. I am Mistress of Morland Place, and I should have arranged for a housekeeper in my absence, not left matters to chance. Well, I shall make amends if I can. You shall leave Daisy with me, and I will find her a husband. If we do not get her wed here at court, never trust me.''

"Thank you, my lady," Martin said, though he looked as though his gratitude were not unmixed. Daisy was his own special property, as the countess had guessed. "So you are not coming home yet?"

''I did think to come home in August for a month or two. Why? Is something wrong.''

"My father—he is not well. Oh, it is nothing specific, but he hardly moves from his chair anymore. I would be happier if I knew you were not to stay away much longer."

Annunciata looked at him anxiously. "You don't think—" She bit her lip.

"Madam, he is an old man," Martin said gently.

"He is but fifty-two. The King is a year older."

"To some men, fifty is not old. But my father is an old man.''

They walked in silence for a few moments, and then Annunciata said, "Tell me the rest of the news. Is there anything good? It has been such a winter of deaths." Prince Rupert in November, and in January Anne Symonds, and in February Cathy and Kit had lost their last remaining child, their sickly daughter Hero. Then in April Caroline's second child had been born a month early, and had lived only a few hours.

"You have heard, I suppose, that Cathy is with child again?"

"No, I had not—she does not write to me," Annunciata said. "I am delighted to hear it, though at her age—" She stopped abruptly, remembering that Cathy was the same age as she was. "When is the child due?"

"In November or December, so I understand. Pray God that poor woman has a happy issue of it. What else now? Ah, yes, Karellie won the Founder's Prize at St. Edward's. I went to hear his discourse, it was remarkable. I wish you had been there to hear it. We were so proud of him.''

Annunciata looked at him oddly, for he spoke as if Karellie

were his own son: he really did sound proud of the child. It gave her a strange feeling of duality. Martin was her stepson, and husband of her daughter, but at the same time she felt toward him—abruptly she closed her mind to that.

"Well, that is good news. And our good news at Court is that the Whigs are utterly confounded, and the King may rest easy again. Pray God he has some peaceful years now. We were all much afraid when the Rye House Plot was revealed—you know that Monmouth himself was involved in that. It is said he was to deal the blow himself as the King rode past on his way back from Newmarket. Of course, when all was made known, he ran to his father to beg forgiveness and swore that he had not been told that the plan was to kill the King, but only to change the succession."

"It would be too terrible to believe that the duke would murder his own father, surely?" Martin said.

Annunciata looked grim. "So you may believe if you do not know the duke. But others came forward to say that they and the duke entered the plot only to prevent the blow being struck, so that they must have known the King's death was planned. The duke is so utterly spoilt and lacking in principle that I believe he would murder his father without a second thought."

"Surely not, madam." Martin was shocked.

"Ah, you are too good, and cannot believe in real infamy. But the King believes it. He told the duke he forgave him, and would not punish him, but he banished him from his sight, and when the duke would kiss him, he put him away and said that he had grave doubts as to whether he was the duke's father at all. Monmouth turned quite white at that. There have always been stories about his mother." She shrugged. "But at least it discredited the Whigs, and the leaders of the Green Ribbon Club are all dead and Monmouth in disgrace, and the Duke of York is restored to the Privy Council, and so we have peace again."

"And young Rupert is to have a title," Martin concluded for her, smiling. "You must be very happy. What a pity Hugo will not be here for the ceremony. He is still in Brussels?"

"No, he has gone on to the Hague; Dudley is there, the prince's son, and he will stay with him, and then come back via St. Omer." She hesitated. "He does not know yet about Rupert's title. I am glad enough he will be out of the country. Your father said . . ."

"What?"

"I don't know if it seems as foolish to you as to me, but there may be some truth in it. Chloris says it, too, that Hugo was jealous of George because although he was younger, he took precedence, having the higher title."

Martin only looked at her, for it was impossible to tell her all he had observed through her children's childhoods. Eventually he said, "Hugo is older now, with a wife and son of his own." He did not mean anything in particular by it, but she seemed to take comfort from it.

"You are right. I did think it was foolishness, and so I told Chloris. Ah, here is Gifford, looking for us. The children must have arrived. Shall we go in?"

It was in May that the King, fresh from the perils of uncovering the Rye House Plot, had met with the envoys of the King of Denmark, to discuss a possible marriage between Princess Anne and the Danish king's younger brother, Prince George. An ill-omened name, Annunciata thought, remembering the visit of George of Hanover; but the miniature of the prince that was sent as a present for Princess Anne showed a pleasant, if rather plump, face with large innocent blue eyes and a great deal of curly blond hair. Besides, the princess, now eighteen, was anxious to be wed, far more so since her beloved friend and lady-in-waiting, Sarah Churchill, was the mother already of a large brood of children and spent less and less time at Court. Annunciata had learned a little more about this curious relationship, for since Prince Rupert had died she had often played cards with the royal ladies, the Queen, the Duchess of York, and Princess Anne, and while she did so, Chloris always put her time to good use by gossiping with the waiting-women.

A wedding was finally agreed on for July.

"Then the princess will soon be leaving us?" Annunciata had said to the King when he told her during one of their morning strolls. He smiled.

"Oh, no. She and her prince will live here, at Whitehall."

"Then she is uniquely lucky among princesses," Annunciata commented. "I suppose—"

"You suppose correctly, my dear. Unless the Duchess of York has a son, which looks extremely unlikely, Princess Anne will one day be Queen of England, and she must not on any account, therefore, leave England."

"How will that please her husband, do you think?"

The King shrugged. "It is all part of the bargain, which he must know. It can never be easy to be Queen of England in your own right, but I shall not be here to see how she deals with the problem."

Annunciata thought of Queen Elizabeth, and of Mary, Queen of Scotland, and how they had to face the problem of what status a husband of a queen would have. It depended a great deal, of course, on what kind of a man the husband was.

"Do you know anything of the Prince of Denmark's character?" she asked.

"I know no harm of him," the King said. "He is a good soldier, and a keen huntsman."

Annunciata remembered the plump, fair face. It seemed to hold no guile, if the artist had not lied.

"Perhaps," she said cautiously, "he will prefer the outdoor life to one of Court gossip and intrigue."

The King smiled. "Exactly what everyone will hope. I am engaged to play tennis with James—come and watch me win. It will not be a long game."

They turned toward the tennis house, and the King said, so casually that at first Annunciata thought she had not heard correctly, "I thought of giving your son Rupert a title. How would an earldom suit, do you think?"

"Your Majesty—" Annunciata stammered in surprise. She had brought Rupert to Court in the hopes of preferment, but the King had never spoken a word about it, and she had almost forgotten her plans. He looked apologetic.

"I should have done something long ago. I hope you will forgive me. When my dear cousin died, I meant to have the patents drawn up at once, as a tribute to him, but other matters intervened. The wedding will be a good excuse. I shall create some new courtiers to intrigue after I am gone, in case the new prince *does* prefer the outdoor life.''

"I am very grateful to you, sir," Annunciata said, and the King pressed her hand and smiled down at her.

"It is only what I should have done long ago. Your continued presence at Court will be my reward. I like to have my family around me. I have so little left.'' His eyes were sad, and for a moment, as the animation left it, his face looked lined and old. Then he smiled again, and was again the King everyone knew and loved. "Now we shall have to think what earldom to give him. There are one or two I have in mind.''

"Sir, if you have no preferences yourself, there is one title more than any other that is valuable to me.''

The King nodded, understanding her at once. "Of course, I should have thought of that. Your son was a very good gentle young man, and much missed. I shall recreate the Earldom of Chelmsford.''

So Annunciata had sent for her other children, hoping to catch the King in a giving mood and get titles for them, too, though as Nelly Gwyn, who made a neighborly call of congratulation as soon as she heard the news, said, "I hope you have better luck than I have, that's all. The King's been promising me a duchy ever since Squintabella got hers, but promises come cheaper than actions. If he offers you anything for your pretty boys, you get it in writing. I don't nag him enough, that's the trouble. Charles will do anything for a quiet life. Still,'' she went on, eyeing Annunciata with interest, "he is mortal fond of you, and that's a fact. Is it true what poor Rochester used to say about you, Nan?'' Rochester had died two years ago, it was said of syphilis, though Nelly said he had died "of living.''

"I don't know what Rochester used to say,'' Annunciata said blankly, and Mrs. Gwyn smiled.

"It probably is true, then. Well, if you get my duchy, remember I wished you well.''

Annunciata was sure the children would make a good impression on the King. Maurice looked very like Prince Rupert, although he was still very slight, small even for his ten years.

Annunciata remembered that Rupert had grown suddenly and thought that Maurice would probably be tall. He was the quietest of the children, and rather solemn, but with a sudden smile that brought the prince painfully to mind. Karellie, who was approaching twelve years old, was very like Ralph, a big-boned, fair child, blond haired but with startlingly dark eyes. His sweet expression matched his merry good-humor. He was the clown of the schoolroom, often in trouble for his pranks, for he was full of high spirits. He was very quick to learn, and excellent at his studies, and seemed likely to go far. His mother was sure that the King could not fail to ennoble such potential greatness. He greeted the children kindly when she introduced them to him, evidently liked Karellie's charm and frank intelligence, but did no more than murmur something along the lines that he would see what he could do for them.

Chloris's son Michael was also brought to London, on Annunciata's instructions, and there was a tender reunion between him and Chloris and an even more touching one between him and Rupert, who had missed his playmate and companion even more than his brothers. Michael was a nice boy, though not handsome, being sandy haired and freckled and not looking at all like his beautiful mother. Annunciata caught herself thinking that she must see what she could do for him, and then laughed at herself for echoing the King's vague words.

Annunciata was much afflicted with guilt when she saw how ill Daisy really did look, white and tired, with an anxious frown that had quite marked her previously smooth brow, and she determined that she would do something to rectify that situation at once. Daisy was now nearly twenty-four, and the cares of her life had somewhat marred her beauty, but Annunciata decided if she was rested and well fed she would soon plump up again, and with good clothes, the right company, and a large enough dowry, she would be married in no time. She determined that Daisy should have some fun at last, and planned to involve her, in the week or so before the wedding, in as much of the gaiety that London could offer as she could cram in. Shopping, driving in Hyde Park, strolling in St. James's, morning visits, dinners, theaters in the afternoons, supper parties, balls and masques—she

should taste everything. And first of all, Annunciata thought with
relish, she would send for Mrs. Drake, and Daisy should have
new dresses. With the right clothes and a little paint, Daisy could
still challenge most of the Court ladies for looks.

The wedding took place on July twenty-third—St. Anne's day.
The chapel at St. James's Palace was crowded and stiflingly hot,
for it had been a burning hot day, and even now as dusk gathered
outside the windows there was little relief. It was very different,
Annunciata thought, from the wedding of Princess Mary, when
the rain outside had only been surpassed by the water being shed
inside. Princess Anne looked radiant, extremely happy and therefore prettier than she had ever been. She was no great beauty, but
her plump shoulders were very white, her lips were very full and
red, and her dark hair and eyes shone with youthful health. She
reminded Annunciata very much of her mother in looks, though
Anne Hyde's face had expressed the excellence of the mind
within, while Princess Anne's was more often than not quite
vacant.

She was evidently well pleased with Prince George, who seemed,
from the little Annunciata had seen of him since he arrived at
Whitehall a week ago, a charming enough man. He was very tall
and strongly made, with a well-fleshed look that Annunciata
guessed would easily turn to fat on such a big frame if he were
not careful of his habits. His features were handsome, his hair
abundant and golden, his carriage graceful and his manners
impeccable, and even the telltale fullness around his jawline was
not unbecoming of his youth. But the blandness of his expression
and the wide, empty blue stare of his eyes accorded with the
generality of opinion about him, that there was very little in his
head. So much the better, Annunciata thought briskly: he would
be less likely to resent being merely the consort if Anne ever
came to be Queen.

The King gave the bride away with a great deal of merriment;
Annunciata thought that he had always found his nieces rather
comic, and was deriving some unholy amusement at wedding
Anne to such a dullard—and a Lutheran to boot! The Duke and
Duchess of York stood just behind him as the Bishop of London,

who had been preceptor to both princesses in their childhood, performed the ceremony. Behind them the rest of the leading figures at Court crowded in, while those who could not fit into the chapel filled the passages outside and had the scene passed back to them in whispers. In the silences between the bishop's words and the responses, the sound of Prince George's breathing could be heard, for he had an unfortunate tendency to asthma, which the airless conditions in the chapel exacerbated. Mulgrave, the Court rake and wit who had two years before caused a scandal by trying to seduce the Princess Anne, had already remarked rather sourly that Prince George breathed heavily because he was afraid if he did not he would be taken for dead and removed for burial.

But the wedding was popular with the people, and when the ceremony was done, and the bells were rung, and the conduits in London flowed with wine, the Londoners made merry all night, drinking toasts to the new-wed couple and thanking God that she had been married to a Protestant, even if he was a Lutheran. The King gave Princess Anne the Cockpit at Whitehall as a wedding present, and there she and her husband settled down with the nation's blessing.

A fortnight later came the ceremony that made Rupert Earl of Chelmsford. It took place in the presence chamber at Whitehall and was witnessed by the King and Queen, the Duke and Duchess of York, Princess Anne and Prince George, and most of the people who had crowded into the chapel at St. James's two weeks before. Young Rupert in a suit of crimson velvet looked quite grown-up as he walked slowly across the room toward the dais where the King sat, smiling genially. He was very serious and Annunciata, watching proudly, thought he looked as if he was afraid he might trip over his sword and fall halfway there. He was attended by his two brothers, and by the Earl of Feversham and the Earl of Craven, who were presenting him.

Rupert reached the dais and knelt before the King, bareheaded, his head bowed displaying his beautiful, luxuriant long curls, and the King read out the words of the patent.

". . . We therefore do make, create, and ennoble the said Rupert Morland to be Earl of Chelmsford and Baron Meldon, and by the putting on of a mantle and the setting of a coronet of gold upon his head, we do truly invest this name and title unto him and to his heirs male.''

The mantle was laid about Rupert's shoulders, and the Bishop of London handed the earl's coronet to the King, who placed it gently on the boy's head, settling it on his brows, and then raised him up and kissed him on both cheeks. To Annunciata, as well as she could see through her tears, it seemed that he looked at the boy with a tenderness that was almost wistful, and she wondered if he were thinking what it would be like to have a son like this.

Rupert's voice trembled a little as he said, ''I humbly thank Your Majesty,'' and then he retired backwards, making three deep bows as he went. There was a banquet afterward at Chelmsford House, to which Annunciata had invited everyone of any consequence at Court, and after the banquet was a ball, to be followed by a private supper-party which the King and Queen had consented to attend. It was an exhausting, but delightful, day.

The following morning visitors began to arrive early, and the courtyard was already thronged with tradespeople wanting the new earl's custom before the countess had even come out from the chapel. All day there were carriages drawing up and driving away, and it was not until after two o'clock that the countess was able to sit down with her family to dine. In the afternoon Martin and Clovis disappeared into the city on business, and in the evening they and Annunciata and Daisy went to a masque at the Duchess of Cleveland's. Annunciata noticed how attentive Clovis was to Daisy all through the evening, and how Daisy, blushing prettily, liked his attentions, and thought it was a pity that their consanguinity prevented Clovis marrying Daisy. They would make a pretty couple, she thought.

It was after midnight when they arrived back at Pall Mall and the countess's big black coach pulled up outside Chelmsford House. Daisy stumbled slightly as she descended from the coach, though Clovis caught her and prevented her falling, and Annunciata said, ''You must lie along abed tomorrow, Daisy. You are not quite strong yet, and we have had some very busy days.''

The great door was swung open at their approach, and as

Annunciata swept through she did not notice the expression on the footman's face. Her eyes went at once, however, to the cloaked figure before the empty fireplace, and as he turned she said in a quiet voice that knew the answer, "Why, Clement, what are you doing here?"

He had ridden post from Morland Place to tell her that Ralph had died three days before, quietly, in his sleep.

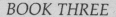

BOOK THREE

CRANE IN
ITS VIGILANCE

So I will court thy dearest Truth,
When Beauty ceases to engage,
And thinking on thy pleasing Youth,
I'll love thee on in spite of age:
So Time itself our transports shall
    improve,
And still we'll wake to joys, and live to
    love.

> Matthew Prior:
> *Verses by Mr. Prior*

CHAPTER FIFTEEN

"Now, Arabella, you must stop screaming, and work a little," Chloris said.

Annunciata, restraining her urge to slap her daughter, added from the other side of the bed, "Caroline didn't make all this fuss, did she?"

"I can't help it. I'm going to die. I know I'm going to die," Arabella groaned, and then began to scream again. It was warm for March, so the great fire that was essential in a birth chamber made the room insufferably hot. In addition to Annunciata and Chloris there was Caroline, holding Arabella's hand sympathetically, Daisy biting her lip anxiously, Birch curling hers in contempt, and Dorcas chatting quietly in the background with the midwife and her girl. Annunciata was aware that there was sweat running down her body inside her dress, and that at any moment she would begin to show wet circles at her armpits, and she felt she would die without a breath of air. She put the cloth with which she had been mopping her daughter's brow into Chloris's hand and stalked out, shutting the door behind her with a bang.

Downstairs the male population had shrunk since she went upstairs, and there was now only Martin and Father St. Maur playing chess in the drawing room, though judging by the number of casualties on both sides they were not playing with much attention. They both looked up anxiously as she came in; even down here Arabella's screams could be heard, hardly muffled at all by the intervening rooms.

"Is she all right?" Martin asked. "What's happening?"

"Her suffering must be terrible, poor child," St. Maur added with a shudder. He had seen, in the course of his duties around the estate, what tortures childbirth could put women through. "The screams—"

"It's sheer naughtiness," Annunciata said shortly. "That girl is nothing but temper and a desire for attention. Really!" She stalked to the window and pushed it open, fanning herself with her hand and feeling the blessed air cooling her burning cheeks.

"Should we not call in the doctor?" Martin asked. Annunciata glanced over her shoulder at him, and repressed a smile. She guessed that he was feeling guilty, a sentiment common enough to men at the time of their wife's bringing to bed, though no less puzzling for being so common. His relationship with Arabella, now she had had time to observe it, seemed an odd one to her: he treated her more like a wayward daughter than a wife, and though he was undoubtedly affectionate toward her, there was nothing of intimacy in the affection. Annunciata had found that she was glad about that, although she had not been able to decide why.

"Lord, no, there's nothing wrong with her. As soon as she decides to work at it, all will be well. At the moment I think she fancies herself at Drury Lane. Perhaps I should not have taken her to see so many plays when we were in London."

She was rewarded by a faint smile from Martin, and followed it up with a smile of her own.

"Come, be easy—Arabella, like a pig, squeals out of all proportion to the hurt." She saw Father St. Maur about to protest at her likening her daughter to a pig and hurried on, "But where are the others? Have they deserted you in your hour of need?"

"Ely said he couldn't stand it anymore," Martin said, "and one can hardly wonder, since he lost his own wife that way. I don't think he expected to be subjected to this when he came here."

"No, he expected no more than free board, lodging, and entertainment." Annunciata smiled. "I swear he spends so much time here I sometimes wonder if he's not another brother of yours."

"He comes to see his sister," Martin said reasonably. "He's fond of her."

"He wasn't so fond of her when Hugo was in town, and he could spend all his time eating and drinking at his brother-in-law's expense," Annunciata said.

"Well, he was fond of Hugo, too," Martin said.

"If he was that fond of him, why didn't he go with him to Morocco? No, Martin, he's fondest of all of his comfort."

"So are many men, child," St. Maur said quietly. "And many women, too."

Annunciata smiled at him, but would not look contrite. "Of course, Father. And I don't mind in the least that he practically lives here. I was only trying to divert your minds a little."

She turned her head quickly, not to miss Martin's look of amusement at this blatant untruth, and continued, "So where has dear Ely gone?"

"He persuaded Ailesbury to go for a ride with him. I think they've taken guns up to the Whin, so we might have some pigeons for dinner, and they've taken Karellie and Maurice with them."

St. Maur looked contrite. "I could not concentrate," he said, rolling his eyes toward the source of the screams, "and I thought it better to have them out of the way, in case—"

Annunciata nodded understandingly. "Don't worry, Father, it will all be over soon, and we shall have a pleasant—and peaceful—dinner." At that moment the screams rose to a pitch that shook the glass in the windows: Arabella was finding her range now. Annunciata's brows drew together.

"No, this is really too bad," she said, and with a haste that ruffled Martin's hair as she passed, she strode from the room. In the great bedchamber she marched to the bed where Chloris and Daisy, one on either side, were trying to restrain Arabella, who was sitting up, flailing her arms, and screaming deafeningly, her eyes quite blank to anything but her own performance; and drawing back her hand she put all her power behind it and smacked Arabella's face. The blow made a sound like the crack of a whip and the latest scream was cut off abruptly in a curious little squeak. Arabella's eyes focused on her mother, and her mouth, open already, sagged a little wider with sheer surprise.

"Now, listen to me, Arabella," Annunciata hissed furiously,

"if you make another sound I shall whip you until you can't sit down, and don't think I wouldn't. If you behave like a naughty child, I'll treat you like one. Now, lie down, be quiet, and get to work. You've a baby to deliver, and if it's not here by dinnertime, I warn you we'll all go away and sit down to our dinners in comfort and leave you to get on with it by yourself."

In the dead silence that followed Arabella lay down on her pillows, her startled eyes never leaving her mother's face, and from behind her Annunciata heard a soft chuckle of appreciation from the midwife.

"Eh, that's t'way, mistress—ah must remember that one: if all else fails, beat th' bairns out of 'em!"

At all events, it worked, for half an hour later Arabella was lying back on her pillows looking sweaty and unbearably smug, while the midwife's girl was sponging and wrapping a long, thin boy child. As soon as he was bundled up in his cloths and shawl, Annunciata took him from the girl and showed him to Arabella, who smirked with pleasure and croaked unintelligibly, having lost her voice from her previous vocal exertions.

"He's a healthy-looking thing," Annunciata said judiciously. "And he's got a lot of hair. You've done well child. Rest now— Chloris shall bring you some wine and a good dinner to build up your strength. I shall take the baby down to show to his father."

It was almost the kindest address Arabella had ever heard from her mother, and she was touched, even though she did think she might have been allowed to hold the baby for a little before it was taken away. However, she was in no condition to protest, being voiceless, and in any case Dorcas was there with a basin of warm water and was proposing sponging her clean and dry, and the idea was almost too delicious to bear.

Both men jumped up when she came in to the drawing room, and Martin said at once, "Is all well? Is Arabella all right?"

"Perfect," Annunciata said, smiling. "She's lost her voice— serves her right—but otherwise she's no more discommoded than after a good hunt. They'll get her something to eat and drink now, and then you can go and see her if you want. Meanwhile—" She stepped forward, the baby in her arms, and Martin came to her and looked down, drawing the shawl back from the baby's face with a careful forefinger.

"Lord, but they're ugly when they're just born," Martin said softly, but the tone of his voice belied the words. "Is it a boy?"

"It's a boy," Annunciata said. As well as a long body, the child had very dark skin, and a thatch of black hair that seemed quite surprising on such a tiny thing. His eyes were shut tight, and every now and then he pursed his lips and raised his hairless eyebrows as if he were wondering where he was, and disapproving of the change in his circumstances. "He's going to be dark as a corsair, and to judge by the length of his legs, as tall as the King himself."

Martin ran his forefinger over the pink plush silk of the baby's cheek in wonder, and said, "He's bigger than I expected. He's a better baby than Hugo's, isn't he?"

"Oh, better in every way." Annunciata laughed at him. He looked up and their eyes met, and they both laughed, the warmth of the moment filling them so that just for the instant they forgot everything else.

Then St. Maur said, "Well, it seems there is no hurry to baptise him—we can all have a glass of claret first, to drink his health. And may God bless him, and make him a joy to his parents."

The moment was past. "Amen to that," Annunciata said. "Now I'd better take him back upstairs, and Tom can go and take word to the wet nurse." At the door she paused and turned back to say, "I told Arabella that if she didn't produce this child by dinnertime, we'd all go and leave her to it. Marvelous how the threat of hunger can inspire people." And she left them laughing.

The baby was christened James, after his father, and Matthias, because he was born on St. Matthias's Day. Annunciata had not wanted James, because Cathy's baby, born on the last day of the old year, had been called James, but that was an objection she had not been able to voice, and she could not think of another, and so James it was. The wet nurse was a cousin of Chloris's, a girl of fifteen called Flora, whose husband had died only a month after they were wed, leaving her pregnant and destitute. Annunciata was glad to be able to do something to help the girl, who seemed a decent little thing, only rather pathetic. Her own baby had died, but once Annunciata had ascertained that it was not from any catching disease or insufficiency in the mother's milk, she hired her willingly. Flora moved in to the nursery under Dorcas's stern eye, and baby James flourished.

Arabella recovered indecently fast. While she was confined to her bed, she was fascinated by her baby, loved to hold him, longed to do things for him, even complained that her station in life prevented her from suckling him herself. That made Birch retort that she would not talk so shockingly, and heralded two whole days during which she babbled about the simple pleasures of the shepherdess who nursed her child among the ewes in the open air.

But once she was out of bed, the glorious spring sunshine beckoned to her, and in two days the novelty of the baby had worn off. She barely glanced at him when Flora brought him to be seen by his mother each day, fretted that she was not permitted to ride for another month, and when Martin's blue hound-bitch whelped she rapidly discovered that puppies were far more interesting than babies. Martin and Annunciata observed this process with amusement; Caroline, who had lost her second baby last year, with amazement. She adored her own little Arthur, and spent most of her time in the nursery or out in the gardens with the babies, until Dorcas remarked that Master James was never likely to want for mother-love, Lady Caroline making no distinction between her own child and her sister-in-law's.

A month later, on Annunciata's birthday, they celebrated the marriage of Daisy to John Ailesbury.

After Ralph's death, when Annunciata came home to Morland Place, she determined to do her duty by the household and sort out the problems that her absence had largely caused, and generally set her own life and everyone else's in order. The first thing she did was to find a housekeeper, and this caused some problems, for the task of running a household like Morland Place was a large one, needing intelligence and energy, but eventually she hired another of Chloris's many cousins, a brisk young woman called Dorothy Clough, and placed her under Daisy's charge, with a very small girl to help and, incidentally, to learn. Mrs. Clough had quickly taken the reins out of Daisy's hands, and within three months she was running the house entirely, with the very small girl, Dora, as her mercury. Daisy was at first disconcerted to find she had nothing to do, but soon discovered she could pass her time pleasantly with walking, riding, gardening, sewing, playing with the children, and visiting neighbors with Arabella and Caroline. The removal of responsibility from her shoulders unbent them so rapidly that she seemed ten years younger, and rediscovered the ability to romp and laugh, which brought a wistful smile to Martin's face and an astonished stare to Arabella's.

There were other changes to be made. Clem had retired, and his grandson Clement had taken his place, but though he was honest and hardworking, Clement had not Clem's ability to combine the offices of steward, butler, bailey, and agent, and many of the tasks Clem had done without seeming to stir himself were being neglected.

Annunciata discussed the matter with Martin, who, naturally, was attempting to do everything left over as well as his own business.

"You will exhaust yourself," she said firmly.

"I am the master, after all," he replied.

"Then, as master, your duty is to hire people to do these tasks for you, so that you can be free to make the important decisions."

So between them they decided to make Clement the steward, with Ralph's manservant Arthur under him as butler. Annunciata found a man called Bankes to take over as bailiff for the Morland Place estate, and put him under her own bailiff, Parry, to train. Father St. Maur had been doing the accounts for many years, and since Karellie and Maurice were at school now at St. Edward's, he had plenty of time to perform the tasks as Martin's agent as well as his priestly duties.

So the household settled down to a smoother flow. Rupert went up to Oxford, to Christ Church, where he had the same quarters that Hugo had occupied during his time there. Chloris's son Michael went with him as his manservant, although the relationship between them was more that of close friends, and Rupert, before he left, assured Chloris that everything he learned he would pass on to Michael, so that her son should have the benefit of the same education as his master.

Hugo was still abroad, and seeming unlikely to return. He had struck up an unlikely but, to Annunciata, gratifying friendship with Dudley Bard, Prince Rupert's son, and the two of them were at present fighting Turks as volunteer officers in the Polish army. Annunciata had found it hard to believe in Hugo as a mercenary, especially with the example of his friend Ely before her, who talked enviously of the excitements and hardships of a soldier's life, while sprawling at his ease before a large fire, with a glass of claret in one hand and a stinking pipe in the other.

But the wandering life was in his blood, she recollected, even though his father, in exile, had earned his bread with the dice rather than by fighting. Caroline, who tended to be weepy after her miscarriage, wailed that she would never see him again, that he would die under the walls of a Moroccan stronghold, leaving her a widow, not even knowing where his body lay.

Annunciata retorted, "Better that than to die of the clap, like poor Rochester, or in a drunken tavern brawl like his father," and was surprised when Caroline took no comfort from her words but only howled the louder.

With the practical matters of the household arranged, Annunciata turned her energies to finding Daisy a husband.

"Since it is obvious you will not stir yourself to do it," she said sternly to Martin.

"I don't know anyone good enough for her," Martin said, and when Annunciata looked about her, she had to agree with him. There was no one among the society of York that was both eligible and satisfactory. Ely had one or two bachelor friends but Martin said he would sooner see her wed to a poor and virtuous man than a rich rake who would break her heart, and though the men at Court that Annunciata knew of were often poor, they were hardly ever virtuous, and so they had to look farther afield.

At that time Annunciata was also busy with her own estates, which had been neglected to some extent over the last few years. Among the properties she owned there was a house in Kendal which had belonged to Rob Hamilton, a Morland cousin, and had been given by him to his daughter Hero as her own property. This house Hero had left in her will to Annunciata's mother Ruth, in thanks for Ruth's having looked after her and her son ever since the Scots drove them out of Watermill. Hero, of course, like everyone else at that time, had expected her son, Young Kit, to marry Annunciata when they both grew up, and so even if he did not regain the Watermill estate, he would have all Annunciata's wealth, and the house in Kendal would thus have come back to him after Ruth's death. In the event, of course, he did not marry Annunciata, and the fact that the Kendal house passed to her on Ruth's death was another of the things Cathy felt bitter about when she cared to think of it.

The tenant who lived in the Kendal house and farmed the small estate there died, and the question of what was to happen to it was serious enough to require a visit from Annunciata in person, and since she did not care to go to what she thought must be a primitive place alone, she wheedled Martin into accompanying her, and he, in his turn, insisted that Daisy needed the change of air, too.

The trip turned out much better than Annunciata had feared. The weather was remarkably mild, and the journey was accomplished pleasantly and easily, and when they arrived at their destination they discovered that the people there, though simple and unsophisticated compared with those in London or even York, were kindly, hospitable, and by no means ignorant of the comforts of life. They stayed at the house of the High Constable of Kendal, one George Browne, a recently rebuilt farmhouse at Townend, near Windermere. The Brownes had been wealthy farmers who had recently, through judicious marriages, raised themselves to the status of gentlemen, and the rebuilding of the house into a small but comfortable mansion was a sign of their newly acquired place in society.

George and his wife Elinor were almost embarrassingly excited at playing host to the Countess of Chelmsford, gave her the best bedroom, which they called the State Bedroom, to her amusement, and arranged a continuous round of social activity for fear that she should grow bored, so that Annunciata found it quite difficult to fit in her business. George Browne was very helpful to her, however, since he knew everyone and every piece of land in the ward, had a shrewd head for business, and, through his position as Constable, some influence.

It was at one of the dinners which he and Elinor arranged for the countess's entertainment that they first met John Ailesbury. He was thirty, a widower without children, who lived alone in good style at Staveley, between Kendal and Windermere. Ailesbury was a shy and reserved man, who found the countess too dazzling to speak much to, but Daisy obviously fascinated him, and so the idea was put into Annunciata's head. She made discreet inquiries, discovered the amount of Ailesbury's fortune, ascertained that his character was stainless, observed that his manner was kindly and courteous, and prodded Martin into speaking to Ailesbury before they left.

Martin, to her amazement, insisted on asking Daisy for her opinion first; Annunciata thought it folly to ask a girl what husband she wanted, but Martin pointed out that Daisy, though unmarried, was twenty-four and had a right to her own views. Daisy liked Ailesbury, was flattered by his attentions, and longed for her own establishment, and so the thing was decided; and the more both Martin and Annunciata knew of Ailesbury, the more they felt it was a very fortuitous meeting, and that the match would be a good and happy one for Daisy.

So Daisy was wed on a bright, sunny spring day, and paid her bridal visits, and rode off with her John to her new home in Staveley.

"She'll be near enough to visit, often and often," Annunciata said, trying to comfort Martin as he watched them ride away, and he smiled and shook his head.

"I know. It isn't that. It's foolish of me but—she's not my little sister anymore."

"A good thing, too. You are too old to cling to the poor girl like that. Besides, if you want company, you have me now."

And Martin gave her that sudden, brilliant smile of his, and said, "Yes, that's true. I have you now."

With the wedding over, and Arabella returned to her normal pursuits, Annunciata settled down to enjoy the spring and approaching summer. Martin had given her one of the blue hound pups as a birthday present, to replace her spaniels, who were both dead now. She called him Fand, and took great delight in training him. She also had a new horse, a colt named Banner, one of Kingcup's descendants, for she much preferred the Morland chestnuts, though Barbary's progeny were splendid. The golden spring grew into a delicious, vibrant May; Martin had more time to enjoy himself now that business was running smoothly; the children were amusing, and Rupert was doing well at Oxford and would come home for a visit at harvest time; and she revived her plans to rebuild Shawes, which was showing signs of long neglect. The days passed swiftly and happily; she did not miss London and Whitehall at all.

Martin arrived back from Leeds, where he had been for several days on business, a little before dinnertime on Candlemas. The weather was extraordinary: after a long golden summer, there had been a short, hard winter, and the thaw had come in the middle of January, to be followed by such balmy weather that it might have been spring. He was too hot in his riding cloak, and Mab's neck was sweaty, though he had not been riding her hard.

He found the countess alone in the drawing room, sitting in the window seat reading a book, with Fand asleep at her feet, and he came in so quietly that she did not at first hear him, and he was able to look at her unobserved for a moment. Fand woke, and smiled at him, but did not move or speak, like the well-trained dog he was; he was looking very elegant in the jeweled collar that had been one of Martin's New Year gifts to Annunciata. Then the dog yawned hugely and beat his tail softly on the floor, and Annunciata looked up and saw him. The reaction was gratifying.

"Martin!" she cried, her face lighting to a smile, and she jumped up, putting her book aside, and ran to him, and he put his arms round her and kissed her on both cheeks, and she hugged him, hard. "I did not expect you back today."

"How does my lady?" he asked. "All alone? Where are the girls?"

"Visiting the ladies at Beningborough Hall—had you forgotten? They won't be back for another week."

"Ah, yes, I had forgotten. So you have been alone all day?"

"Alone, and bored," she said, making a face. "How I have missed you!"

"And I have missed you," he said, taking her hand and leading her back to her seat in the window. "I always forget how dull the rest of the world is."

Annunciata smiled wickedly. "What, dear Sir John, and Lady Parker? Were they not kind to you?"

"Kind, yes," Martin said. "No one could be kinder. But after dinner Sir John fell instantly asleep, and Lady Parker had but one story to tell, of how her maid had burnt her best chemise with the goffering iron. I expressed my sympathy a hundred and thirty-two times in all. I counted them."

"But the young ladies—they have three very handsome daughters, do they not?" Annunciata said casually.

"Do they?" Martin said. "I didn't notice. I expect they were well enough, for those who have not a higher standard of comparison."

"But I dare swear *they* were kind to you?" Annunciata said.

He lifted her hand to his lips and kissed it. "One giggled, one sang—out of tune—to her own accompaniment, and one played at basset, and lost all her allowance in the first hour. I longed for some conversation! I wonder if I have not lost the faculty? But if I have, a quarter hour with you will restore it. How have you amused yourself while I have been gone?"

"Writing letters. Making plans. Playing with the babies. I have no great hopes of Arthur's intellect, you know, but my guess is that he will make a great sportsman. He was trying to ride on Fand's back yesterday, so I took him out and put him up on Banner, and he wasn't the smallest particle afraid. Dorcas came running out in a perfect panic when she found what I was doing, and Birch sent her back indoors, saying that little Lord Rathkeale couldn't learn too early how to ride like a gentleman." She laughed at the recollection. "Birch is such an amusement to me. I wouldn't part with her for worlds, though she's so poor-sighted now she's as like to put my dresses on me backwards or upside down."

Martin smiled at her. "You're happy," he said. "It suits you to be happy. It makes you look very, very beautiful. But you know that.'' The strange unseasonable sun shone through her black, glossy hair, giving it a golden nimbus; and fringing her brilliant dark eyes, her eyelashes were golden, too. It was impossible to remember or believe that she was thirteen years his senior: she looked no older than he, and he felt so protective toward her that she might even have been younger.

''If ever I am like to be too happy,'' she said, laughing, ''sure Karellie will do something outrageous to put it right. What are we to do with that boy, Martin? He'll kill himself one day, if some outraged squire doesn't kill him first.''

''It's only high spirits,'' Martin soothed her. ''He will grow out of it, when he has something to occupy him. He finds his lessons too easy, and he has too much energy left over, and so he gets himself into mischief. But there is not an ounce of harm in him.''

''Oh, I know,'' Annunciata said, ''and he does make me laugh so, that I can never get angry with him. You are so good with him, Martin—I could never reprimand him as you do, so gently and seriously.''

Martin grinned. ''Some of the things he does!''

''Like bringing the ox and the ass into the chapel at Christmas for the midnight Mass?'' Annunciata suggested.

''How we ever got the donkey out again I shall never know,'' Martin said, remembering. ''It very nearly broke Father St. Maur's leg with that last kick.''

''And the smell still hasn't gone,'' Annunciata said. She sighed. ''I suppose I ought to send him to Oxford soon, to be with his brother. That would ease his restlessness. But I don't want to part with him. Once he goes to Oxford, he will begin to be a man, and not my Karellie anymore.''

''Now you are beginning to understand how I felt about parting with Daisy,'' Martin said.

''That was different,'' Annunciata said quickly. ''She was much older, and only your sister. Anyway, she is very happy. Her letters are full of 'her John,' and he evidently spoils her terribly.''

''Nothing could spoil Daisy,'' Martin said firmly. ''Now, my lady, are we to have dinner, or must I ride down to the Hare and Heather for a sixpenny ordinary?''

She jumped up at once. ''I'll hurry it along. I am so glad you arrived to rescue me from the horrible fate of dining alone. And this afternoon you will ride with me—''

''Ride?'' Martin groaned. ''I have ridden all day every day for the last week.''

''Never mind,'' she said firmly. ''I must have your opinion about the new house at Shawes, whether to build it on the same spot or further toward the stream.''

''I don't believe you will ever build the new house,'' Martin teased her. ''But I suppose I had better continue with the fiction.''

They arrived back from Shawes well after dark to find the children back from school, the candles lit, and the fires well made up, which combination made a warm welcome. Karellie and Maurice greeted Martin joyfully, and Annunciata thought how good it was that they were so fond of him, and respected his authority. They hardly missed their real father at all, accepting Martin easily in his place, and Annunciata remembered how Hugo, in his childhood, had adored Martin, too—the only aspect of Hugo's character that had given her any satisfaction.

''How did you happen to come home together?'' Karellie wanted to know. ''Mother didn't go to Leeds today, did she?''

''I came back this morning, and we have been looking at the site of the new house at Shawes,'' Martin told him solemnly. ''Your mother, having begun her career as architect with a pigeon cote by Wren, is now eager for a bathing house in the baroque style, perhaps by John Webb. The rest of the house can wait, though it will be a mortal long way to go for a bath.''

''I shall have it, too,'' Annunciata said, laughing. ''*With* fountains. Karellie, what have you done today?''

''Nothing, madam,'' Karellie said hastily. ''Maurice was commended for his Greek translation, though.''

Annunciata was thus diverted, and the evening passed pleasantly, with supper, and then music, before bedtime.

The next morning Annunciata persuaded Martin to go with her to Shawes again, and they left early, returning at lunchtime to discover a deputation awaiting them in the hall. There was the governor of St. Anne's school, the usher from St. Edward's, and two private gentlemen, and from the expressions on their faces, in which indignation, embarrassment, and apology were equally mixed, Annunciata guessed what was coming.

"My lady, we are sorry to disturb you at such an hour, but an outrage occurred yesterday at St. Anne's school, and the identity of the perpetrators has only just been discovered. We deeply regret to have to tell you—but there is no doubt about it, my lady—"

And Annunciata groaned. "Karellie and Maurice. You had better come into the drawing room, gentlemen, and tell me about it."

When the indignant gentlemen had left, Annunciata looked at Martin and bit her lip.

"It's disgraceful," she said.

"Absolutely," Martin agreed. "It can't be allowed to go unpunished."

"But you'll have to speak to them for me," Annunciata said. "I know I should laugh."

Karellie and Maurice, wearing clothes borrowed for them by one of the more high-spirited inmates of the school, had disguised themselves as serving wenches, sneaked into the servants' hall at dinnertime, and actually served two tables of young ladies before being discovered. In the haste of their flight they had knocked down the trestle leg of the high table, and several dishes had tipped their contents into the laps of the governors, who were dining in the school as they did four times a year, on Candlemas, Holy Rood, Lammas, and Hallowmas, a most solemn occasion.

"It was all my idea, sir," Karellie said. "I made Maurice do it. He's not to blame."

"I had already assumed you thought of it," Martin said. He had spoken most seriously to Karellie, who had hung his head with seemly shame. "Though *how* you thought of it escapes me. But you do see, now, how wrong it was, don't you?"

"We didn't *mean* any harm," Karellie said cautiously. "We just thought it would be funny."

"And so it would be, if it weren't for the implication of the young ladies. But you must be very, very careful where the reputations of young ladies are concerned."

"Oh, *they* didn't do anything, only lent us the clothes. And *we* only served them their food—"

"I know that, and I don't believe you meant harm. But rumor and fame are cruel to ladies' reputations, and once they have pointed the finger, the stigma is never lifted. So you must be more than careful—you must be absolute in propriety. Do you understand?"

Karellie looked him levelly in the eyes. "Yes, sir."

"Very well. You may go now, and send Maurice in to me. I will think of an appropriate punishment for you both." As Karellie reached the door, Martin said softly, "And one day, when all this is forgotten, you must repeat the performance for the benefit of your mother and me. I warrant you made a pretty wench."

Karellie turned, his eyes shining with mirth. "Maurice made a prettier, sir! I swear I would have wed him, if we weren't kin!"

Annunciata was almost sorry when the end of the week came, and Gideon took the coach out to drive to Benningborough for the young ladies, for there had been such an uncluttered peace in those few days with Martin and the children. She persuaded him to come out with her for one last time alone, and they took two grooms and two pair of greyhounds and went out to the north fields to look for hares. They were riding back through Ten Thorn Gap, intending to turn north in the Beck Field and look once more at the possible site for the new Shawes House, when they heard a halloo behind them, and turning in the saddle saw Karellie riding hotfoot toward them.

"Why, what is he doing here? He should be at school," Annunciata said. "Pray God he is not in more trouble."

Karellie reached them, breathless, and his face was red with some suppressed excitement, though not a joyous one.

"Why are you not in school?" Martin said sternly.

"We were sent out at once, to go home, when the news came," he gasped, but his eyes were on his mother. "There is a messenger at home waiting for you, madam. In the King's livery." And to their surprise, he burst into tears.

"What is it, child," Annunciata said more gently. "What is wrong?"

And Karellie, the tears running down his dusty face, said, "Oh, Mother, the King is dead."

CHAPTER SIXTEEN

The coronation of King James and Queen Mary took place on April twenty-third, and the strength of the reaction against the Whigs and their exclusionist policies was seen in the joyful celebration even of the Londoners, who had always been the most Protestant and republican of communities. There were feasts and fireworks, parties and pageants, bonfires, balls, and church bells ringing almost nonstop for a week. London was crowded with up-country gentry, come to show their loyalty to the Crown, and lodgings could not be got for man nor horse in a ten-mile radius of Whitehall.

One of the pleasant consequences of the Coronation was that Hugo came home from the wars, bringing Dudley Bard with him, and both stayed at Chelmsford House. Annunciata found Hugo much improved from his experiences abroad. The fat had been stripped from him and turned to hard muscle, and his tanned face wore an expression of intelligence and responsibility which became it far better than its former arrogance and petulance. He talked sensibly about the situation abroad, and told about his part in the campaigns amusingly and modestly. It had been quite a shock to her to see him for the first time, for he arrived without a wig, and his short-cropped hair and his growing bald patch prevented her from recognizing him at once.

Rupert also came to London for the coronation, of course. He was now fifteen, and heartbreakingly like his grandsire in looks, so that Dudley looked from him to his mother with increased speculation. As Annunciata had expected, he had grown handsome as he grew tall, and when she saw him dressed in his robes for the coronation itself, she felt a kind of awe that she could have had anything to do with the creation of such a wonder. Rupert had done well at Oxford, and was universally popular, and his manners were so unassuming and friendly that both Dudley and Hugo took to him at once. Annunciata thought Michael much improved, although in comparison to Rupert he was an ill-favored thing. But he had grown a little taller, and he had a gentlemanly bearing and a frank, easy manner which made him pleasant company.

When the official celebrations were over and London had cleared a little, Annunciata settled down to a round of more informal visits and entertainments. She had not been to London since Ralph died, and had much to catch up on. Daisy and John Ailesbury, who had come up for the Coronation, left after a week, for Daisy was pregnant and her husband did not want her to be in London during the hot part of the year, and Annunciata entrusted the younger boys to their care to be escorted back to Yorkshire. To her surprise and secret amusement, Hugo insisted Caroline go back to Yorkshire, for the same reason, and she guessed that he had things to do in London that would be hindered by the presence of his wife. Caroline, understandably, was not eager to part from her husband so soon after a long separation, and he had to promise to come home himself before the end of summer and bring Ely before she would submit to his will. Arabella decided to go with her—riding and hunting in London were dull compared with home—and so Annunciata found herself sole woman in a household of men, a situation she had always relished.

She paid her formal visit to the Princess Anne and Prince George and found them playing cards with the Queen Dowager. Anne was the proud mother of a new daughter, named Mary, and was evidently well pleased with married life, and evidently also adored her husband, whose health she fussed over continuously. Annunciata thought the prince looked materially sadder since she last met him, and decided it must be boredom with the London life, which gave him so little scope for the things he was good at—riding and soldiering. He was also materially fatter, and all the time she was there he picked continually at a bowl of sugared almonds on a little table beside him.

The princess talked a great deal about her friend Sarah Churchill and her friend Sarah's children and her friend Sarah's husband, and when she was not talking thus a profound silence fell on the company, for neither Prince George nor the Queen Dowager had anything to say. Annunciata stretched her visit to the appropriate length, for Princess Anne was second in line to the throne, and vastly more important now that King Charles was dead, but when she finally left she felt such a wonderful relief that she almost skipped to her carriage.

Parliament met in May, called by King James to settle certain financial matters. It was a most meek and loyal Parliament.

"It is hard to believe," Annunciata said one afternoon at dinner to her assembled menfolk, "that they have settled the King's income upon him for life. The only reason the King would ever have to call Parliament would be to raise money, so they have just ensured they will never be called again."

"It may not be enough," Hugo suggested. "Kings seem always to be short of money, don't they?"

"Ah, but he'll have the revenues from the custom houses, too, and since trade is expanding all the time, that should be more than enough," Clovis said. "As long as he avoids going to war."

"I doubt he'll be such a lavish spender as King Charles, either." Martin smiled. "Did he not clear the palace pretty effectively of all the hangers-on? I understand he even sent away Mistress Sedley."

"A few horses, a few dogs, they will not cost much," Annunciata agreed, with private amusement. It was well known at Court that, try how he might, King James could no more curb his appetite for women than could the Duke of York, and almost every night some cloak-wrapped figure would be bundled up the backstairs by the King's chamberer. It made the Queen weep, and the King would be racked with guilt, and the courtiers were thus given endless material for amusement. Catherine Sedley, his present mistress, the daughter of Charles Sedley the poet, was so plain that she professed herself amazed at the King's devotion, and

Annunciata remembered how the King had once said that James chose ugly mistresses for a penance. It was a fact also that he always chose Protestant ones, and Annunciata wondered if he did so for the same reason.

"All the same," Annunciata went on, "it is an amazing thing that Parliament should be so meek toward a Catholic King."

"He did promise them the very first thing that he would uphold the Church of England," Dudley pointed out. "If he keeps his religion as a private thing as he did before—after all, he and my father were ever the greatest of friends, and my father was the staunchest Protestant."

"Yes, that's true," Annunciata said kindly. She did not mention what she had learned the day before from the Princess Anne, that King James annoyed her by leaving, in her apartments, Catholic pamphlets urging her to convert every time he came to visit her.

"Besides," Clovis said briskly, "even though King James is a Catholic, he is fifty-one years old, and the situation is purely a temporary one. The next heir is Princess Mary, and she is Protestant and married to a Protestant, and next after her is Princess Anne, of whom the same is true. That's why London greeted the succession so cheerfully. The legitimate succession, for which King Charles fought so successfully, ensures a Protestant monarch after King James."

"Unless the Queen has a son," Annunciata said, merely for wickedness' sake, and Clovis fixed her with a stern and kindly eye.

"The Queen has not been pregnant for three years, and for the sake of peace in England you had better hope that she does not conceive again. Everything is happy and prosperous at the moment, trade is booming, the Pool of London is crowded with ships laden with the produce of the four corners of the world, the people are quiescent—"

"King Louis has swallowed up Strasbourg and Luxembourg and is moving inexorably toward the Rhine," Dudley put in quietly. There was a brief silence, and then Hugo clapped his friend on the back.

"Never mind, we'll go back soon and fight, and push old Louis back to Paris. With good soldiers like us, Europe will be made safe for Protestantism, never fear.'' Dudley began to grin unwillingly. ''Didn't we drive the Turks and Barbarians away? Just as soon as I've had my fill of pleasure, we'll be off again.''

''If you have to wait for him to have his fill of pleasure,'' Rupert murmured, ''you may grow old here.''

''Sharp words, little brother,'' Hugo said as everyone laughed. ''Engendered by envy, no doubt.''

Annunciata, looking at her younger son, saw that it was true. Rupert was envying the soldier's life that Hugo and Dudley had been describing for the past few weeks, and a sudden sharp fear touched her. ''You have no immediate plans to go away, surely, Hugo?'' she asked, trying to sound casual. ''I had hoped to have you home, if not for good, at least for a year or two.''

From the corner of her eye she saw Martin give her a look of sympathy. Hugo said, ''We have come a-begging, Dudley and I. He wants his house back, that his father left him, which has been stolen away, and I want my Irish lands, that Cromwell stole away. The new King may be feeling generous and give them to me. Then I shall have a little luxury and pleasure, and then''—he tried to look apologetic and failed—''I shall have to go back. The campaign is not over. We are needed—''

''You want to go,'' Annunciata said flatly.

''We'll stay a month or two,'' Hugo said placatingly. Clovis was giving her warning looks, and Martin reached out subtly and touched her hand, and she made herself smile.

''That will be good. We shall enjoy having you here—and Dudley, you will stay here, I hope? You are welcome for as long as you wish.''

''Thank you, madam,'' Dudley said. ''I should be honored to be your guest.''

Then, mindful of her duty as hostess, Annunciata turned the conversation to lighter things.

Hugo and Dudley were recalled to arms sooner than they expected. In that same May the Duke of Argyll, who had a personal grudge against King James and had been in exile for many years, landed in Scotland with a band of mercenaries to raise an army in rebellion against the King. It was an ill-judged plan, for the recruitments were unstable and fickle, and the royal army in Scotland hemmed Argyll in, scattered support, crushed the rebels, and captured and executed Argyll.

But even as this news was being celebrated in London, it was learned that the Duke of Monmouth, who had been in exile in Holland for two years, had landed at Lyme Regis on June eleventh, and was raising the peasantry of Dorset and Somerset for the purpose of deposing James and placing the crown on his own head. Owing to the prompt action of two loyal and resourceful men, the news was known in London only thirty-six hours later, and the King, whose life's experience had made him the best administrator in the country, acted at once, sending word to the Lords' Lieutenant and militia commanders of Devon, Dorset, Somerset, and Gloucestershire that the militia was to be called out at once, and that the principal towns were to be guarded and no one allowed in or out without their showing good reason for their movement.

Chelmsford House was a scene of comings and goings all day. Clovis came in with the news that Parliament was loyal to a man, and had at once voted taxes on imported wine, vinegar, tobacco and sugar, for war expenses for the King.

"They have voted six hundred thousand pounds," he told Annunciata, "and it should hardly take more than that to crush the rebels."

"Is it true what they are saying in the streets, that Dorset and Somerset has flocked to Monmouth's banner?" she asked. "If so, it will hardly be enough, I fear."

Martin, who had been out and about that morning, too, said, "There is some truth in it, but it is only the poor people—laborers and poor craftsmen—who are for him. Mostly the Puritans and Dissenters who have suffered under the penal laws. The gentry are for the King, and it is the gentry who command the militia."

"The militia will fight for him, then?"

"I have no doubt of it," Clovis said. "The King is moving fast, and will have them marching before they have any thoughts of rebellion. Monmouth has been away too long—he has not understood the temper of the country. He may gather an army of ploughboys, but what will they know of fighting? I doubt if he will even have arms for them.''

Later came news that Parliament had passed an Act of Attainder against Monmouth for High Treason, condemning him to death and offering a reward of five thousand pounds for his body, dead or alive. Monmouth had issued a Declaration at Lyme Regis, of which some copies had reached London, and Parliament had ordered all copies of it to be burned by the public hangman, for it was treasonous and vile. Clovis had seen a copy.

''It begins well enough, and is fairly written, talking about the purposes of government. But then it goes on to accuse the King of every imaginable crime, not just the usual tyranny. It says he started the Great Fire of London, was responsible for England's alliance with France, started the war against Holland, fomented the Popish Plot, and arranged the murder of Sir Edmund Godfrey.''

''An appeal to the ignorant,'' Annunciata said. ''Well, I suppose the fanatics will believe it all.''

''But that's not all,'' Clovis said, an expression of disgust crossing his face. ''It finishes by saying that King James was so moved by the bloody designs of the Papists and his own desire for a crown that he murdered King Charles by poisoning him, so Monmouth is come to revenge him.''

''Dear God!'' Annunciata exclaimed. ''There will be no mercy for Monmouth when he is caught, and he surely deserves none. None but the ignorant and opportunist will follow him after that.''

It was late when the three young men arrived back, and they were all in a state of great excitement.

''Churchill has been made brigadier,'' Hugo said. Lord Churchill was the husband of Princess Anne's friend Sarah, and a fine soldier. ''The regular troops are being called, and the first of them are to march off to Salisbury tomorrow.''

''The King is lucky to have the Tangiers men home—they are the best fighters in the world,'' Dudley added.

''You're right,'' Hugo said, grinning. ''We should know, Mother, we've commanded them.''

Understanding began to dawn on Annunciata.

"What troops is Lord Churchill to command?" she asked.

"Four of Lord Oxford's Horse," Hugo said, "two of the King's Dragoons, just back from Morocco, and the five veteran companies of the Queen Dowager's Regiment. The rebels will have no chance against those men, especially with experienced officers to command them."

Annunciata looked steadily from Hugo to Dudley. "You have been given a commission? You two?"

"How could we refuse?" Hugo grinned. "By God's precious Blood, I'm looking forward to a scrap. It gets confounded dull spending one's days in drinking and gambling and whoring!"

Dudley, though expressing it more quietly, was equally pleased. "I suppose Monmouth is kin of mine, too," he said, "and I know he is a great favorite at the Court of Holland."

"And he's a Protestant," Annunciata said quietly. Dudley nodded.

"But King James is my father's cousin, and his dear friend. I'll fight any rebel who raises a hand against him."

"For a Morland, the matter is simpler than that," Martin said. "King James is the rightful King. Nothing else matters."

"So, Mother, we must get busy," Hugo said. "We must do our packing and get us gone, to join our men. I've already sent John Wood to see to my bags, and Daniel is seeing to the horses. They say the rebels have managed to steal fifty horses from somewhere, but how they'll get their pitchfork-carrying laborers to sit them is another matter. Now, Dudley—"

"First," Annunciata said firmly, "we will all kneel and say a prayer for the King and for the success of the expedition. Yes, you, too, Dudley—we pray to the same God, even if we use different forms."

A few minutes later Hugo and Dudley had dashed off to chivy their servants, and Rupert, who had listened to all this in silence, approached Annunciata, where she stood watching the closed door with a thoughtful expression.

"Mother—" he said doubtfully. He usually called her madam, and the use of the more affectionate term sharpened her wits. She turned to look at him, and his dark eyes asked for understanding.

"What is it?" she asked sharply. "Rupert, not you, too!"

"Mother, Lord Feversham has been made commander-in-chief."
Lord Feversham had stood sponsor to Rupert when he was
ennobled. "They are raising more cavalry, to follow after the
detachment under Lord Churchill."

"Rupert, you are only fifteen years old," Annunciata said,
trying to sound reasonable. "You have no experience at all of
soldiering."

"Lord Feversham has offered me a commission in Lord Oxford's
Horse, Mother," Rupert went on. "I am a good horseman, and
of course I would have experienced men around me, and I learn
quickly." His eyes yearned into hers. His fine face, eager, high
colored, made her think of a whetted blade. It was in his blood,
along with loyalty; she must not dampen his fires with her heart's
concerns.

"You will make a fine officer, I am sure. It is a compliment
that Lord Feversham should have asked you."

"Well—I asked him," Rupert admitted shyly.

Annunciata forced herself to smile. "To be sure. You had
better go and pack, had you not? I suppose Michael will go with
you. Ask Tom for anything you want. I suppose you will want to
be off tonight as well?"

Rupert nodded, and then flung his arms quickly about her. She
closed her eyes and pressed her lips against his neck. Once she
could have kissed his hair, but he had grown tall now; her tall
son, her prince.

"God bless you, darling," she said, and he was gone, whirling
through the door, calling for Michael as he went. Now she was
alone but for Martin—Clovis was still at the Old Palace—and he
watched her in sympathetic silence.

"He is only fifteen," she said at last, a break in her voice.
"He will be killed, sure."

Martin said nothing, but came across the room quietly and
took her in his arms, and she leaned against him, resting her head
on his shoulder and staring past him at the closed door, as if she
was afraid to move again until that door opened to admit her
children again, safely returned.

*   *   *

Monmouth had himself proclaimed King on June twentieth, in Taunton, and at once sent letters to two of his old drinking-companions, inviting them to come to him in Taunton and sample of his mercy. One was the Duke of Albemarle, commanding the Devon Militia, and the other John Churchill, who had arrived with his cavalry at Chard a few miles away the previous day. Albemarle's reply was to send an amused refusal of the invitation, telling Monmouth that he would have done better to leave the rebellion alone and not to have put the country to so much trouble. Churchill's reply was to send out a patrol to reconnoiter Taunton's defenses which, meeting with a rebel patrol, engaged them in a brisk skirmish and drew the first blood of the conflict.

The Tangiers veterans, marching hard, reached Chard on the following day, while the King's artillery had reached Dorchester, and reinforcements were on the way. Lord Feversham had reached Bristol and was reviewing its defenses, for Bristol was the key city to the West Country, and full of Dissenters and Quakers. The King's forces, though their numbers were smaller than the rebels, were superior in weapons and training, and there would be no doubt of the outcome if they engaged, and Monmouth seemed to have realized it, for in the early hours of the twenty-first, he marched his rebels out of Taunton, heading for Bristol.

The fair weather turned foul, and teeming rain began to fall as Monmouth's army marched toward Bristol, with Churchill's never very far behind. The rain favored Monmouth, for the King's army was behind and having to march on routes churned into quagmires by the rebels ahead of them. Lord Feversham had inspected the defenses at Bristol, and retired to Bath on the twenty-third to meet up with a troop of Lord Oxford's Horse and two troops of dragoons, and to receive reports from reconnoitering officers, and on the twenty-fourth Monmouth's rebels reached Keynsham, just a few miles from Bristol, and during the night crossed the Avon by the bridge there. Bristol, full of Dissenters, and guarded only by the militia, which was unreliable and likely to run away sooner than risk its life, lay before them.

At midnight on the twenty-fifth, Lord Feversham was still receiving reports, and had sent off a letter to the King assuring him the rebels had no chance, being surrounded on all sides with veteran and well-armed forces which were inexorably closing in. Taunton and Lyme had been retaken, and at the latter the rebel's ships and their supplies had been seized. And it was then that the report arrived that Monmouth was about to attack Bristol.

All night they marched, reaching Bristol at dawn to find it still standing, and no sign of the rebels. The rain poured steadily down as Feversham formed up his small force and set the men to filling in the ditches around the city to make a better ground for battle if it were needed. Scouts reported that the rebels had crossed the Avon, but no one knew why they had not attacked.

"Surely it is madness, not to press home their advantage," Rupert said to a veteran ensign as they stood to all day in the pouring rain, waiting for the rebels to move. "The longer they leave it, the stronger we'll be. What can they be about?"

"Why, my lord," the ensign said, "they aren't soldiers at all, so who can tell what they would be doing? There's a squire come in, who's been wandering about their camp quite unchallenged, and he says they've at least half their men armed with nothing more than a stout stick, and all their shoes are falling to pieces with this rain. Perhaps the duke is waiting for nightfall before attacking. They do say he likes a night action. Covering his wickedness with the darkness, I suppose."

"Well it doesn't do any of us good to stand about all day in the rain," Rupert said.

"Don't you worry, my lord," the ensign comforted him. "Our men don't mind a bit of a wet. Makes a change after the desert."

In the evening, as it was growing dusk, orders came for Rupert to place his men under Captain Parker for a surprise attack on the village of Keynsham. Lord Feversham had told of three hundred horse and, Rupert thought, had not forgotten that it would be a good occasion for his protégé to gain some experience. Captain Parker was a ferocious fighter and a fierce Royalist, who was famed for having in the course of one fortnight taken on seven Whigs in duels, and beaten them all. Rupert tied his sash, mounted his horse, and took his place somewhat nervously for his first encounter with battle.

"It probably won't come to anything," Michael told him,

having been talking to some of the veteran troopers. "The men say that no one can stand up to a cavalry charge if they haven't been trained to it. His lordship's idea is to scare 'em off, if possible without fighting. It seems he gave orders to destroy the bridge, and if it had been done, they'd not be where they are now. If we can recoup the situation—"

In the growing darkness they swam their horses across the Avon, and as soon as they had reformed, Parker gave the order for drums and trumpets, and making as much noise as possible, they rode forward toward the village from the west side. The sound of the drums and trumpets, the muted thunder of the horses' hooves, was thrilling, and Rupert thought that if he were a rebel he would be terrified. Half of him wanted the rebels to stand, however: his first battle! He was named after the most famous cavalry leader of all time, was his godson, and he wanted to be worthy of his name.

It all seemed to happen so quickly. Suddenly the village seemed to spew forth horsemen, who were galloping toward them from an angle, where they had crossed the bridge on the south side of the village. In a moment the orders shrilled out, Rupert and his men whirled their horses round, and they were charging head on toward each other, swords out. Rupert found himself yelling, without having been aware of it. His horse seemed to fly under him, and as they drew nearer to the rebels he saw that the force they faced was twice the size of their own. But we are the better soldiers, he told himself; and then they clashed, and he was fighting for his life.

Cut and thrust and parry, men screaming, bewildered faces coming and going before his eyes. He had not thought what *hot* work it would be; soon sweat was running into his eyes, and his hair was sticking to his hot forehead. He had no sense of time, for he was stretched in every nerve to see and hear the next blow, and every moment was occupied to the exclusion of everything else with the fighting. Horses locked shoulders, bit at each other, snorting; some of the rebel horses panicked and tried to run away. But if a cavalry charge did not break its opposition, the larger force had the advantage. Rupert heard the trumpets sounding the retreat to reform, and he knew a thrill of fear.

From behind the enemy horses there was musket fire, and occasionally Rupert had heard a ball flying past. Now as they were pressed back he risked a look behind him, and saw the cheering sight of reinforcements charging the rebels from the bridge-side, and clearing a way through them. Now the rebels were falling back.

The trumpets called the attack off, and the two forces fell apart in the gathering darkness. Rupert, panting, found Michael beside him, and only then realized that he had not seen his friend since the charge began.

"Are you all right?" Rupert asked him anxiously. "There's blood on your face!"

"Not a scratch, my lord." Michael grinned. "This is the other man's blood."

And Rupert began to grin, too. "Our first battle!" he crowed.

"Hardly a battle, more a skirmish. Still, we sent 'em off! Did you see 'em run, with their tails between their legs, like the curs they are!"

"Jesu, I'm thirsty," Rupert said, licking his lips. "As soon as we get back to camp—"

"Aye, my lord," Michael said, and laughing, the two young men turned their horses to rejoin their troop, for the moment well-pleased with life.

As Martin came out from the Old Palace, he saw the little black-and-crimson chariot with the Ballincrea arms painted on the door—Hugo's chariot—which Annunciata had been using these past few days, standing at the door of the Cockpit Palace. Annunciata, of course, would have been visiting Princess Anne. The princess, through her friend Sarah, was in touch with John Churchill, and Annunicata thought it worth exposing herself to the boredom of playing basset and crimp with the princess, or of admiring Prince George's new model ship, or of deciding which of her parents the infant Princess Mary resembled most, in order to receive the earliest news of "the children."

Gifford saluted him gravely as he approached.

"My lady should not be much longer. Would you like to sit

inside, sir, or will you go in? She never stops above an hour and a half.''

"I'll wait. I have some news for her,'' Martin said, and opened the carriage door.

"About the young gentlemen, sir?'' Gifford asked eagerly.

Martin smiled gently. "Nothing as to them, which is good, for we would know if there was anything amiss.''

It was a formula he had had to offer Annunciata again and again, for she had an unreasonable fear that something was going to happen to Rupert. She had no fears for Hugo and Dudley, though Martin thought they were more likely to be in danger than Rupert, whom Feversham would surely keep by his side.

He had been waiting only a few minutes when a servant came out to alert Gifford that his mistress was approaching, and Gifford jumped down from the box, took off the horses' nosebags, and folded down the step, and a moment later Annunciata came through the door in her light summer cloak and hood of gray, edged with swansdown. A slim hand came through the folds of the cloak to lift her dress; a black ringlet slipped forward as she bent her head to see the step; a long, narrow foot in a neat green morocco shoe came from under the hem of the skirt; Martin smiled, moving back on the seat to make room for her, for she was so dainty, so feminine, that unless you knew her it would be impossible to guess at the tough and agile intellect within.

She did not notice him until she was stepping into the coach, and then her face lit up in a way which made his heart jump.

"Martin! How you startled me! But I am glad to see you— another minute of the company in there and I should have gone mad. Thank you, Gifford. I'm sorry you had to wait so long.'' She settled herself and turned to Martin to say, "It was impossible today to bring them round to the subject, and when eventually I despaired and asked directly what news, they said nothing, nothing at all.''

She made an exasperated noise, and Martin laughed and said, "Well, I have something for you, not much, but a little.''

She turned a little pale and reached out an involuntary hand.

"Martin, not—''

"No, my lady." Martin smiled and took her hand and shook it reprovingly. "Do you think I would sit and smile so if there was such a piece of news? You must stop worrying so—the children will be all right."

Annunciata, smiling to hear him call them "the children," a habit he had caught from her, yet said, "I have a feeling, that's all, a bad feeling. But what is your news?"

"Only that the King's pardon to all who would lay down their arms has had some good effect. Many have turned themselves in, and they bring reports of the poor state the rebels are in. Monmouth is in despair, they say."

Annunciata was thoughtful. "So many of the men against whom he is fighting now are the same men he commanded in so many battles. Poor young man—"

"You have sympathy for him?" Martin asked, amused. "For this rebel who is endangering the lives of so many—including your own kin?"

"I know"—she sighed—"and yet—he has been badly brought up, badly advised all his life, spoiled by indulgence. He could have been a good and useful man—"

"And it so happens that he is extremely handsome," Martin added drily. "If he was as ugly as Cromwell, he would attract as little sympathy from you."

Annunciata began to protest, but then reluctantly admitted the truth of it. "Still, God made beauty for us to love, did He not?" she said.

"He made yours, that is certain," Martin said quietly. Annunciata looked at him, her eyes widening as if some sudden realization were reaching her, and then she blushed a little and turned her head away.

"And is that all your news? That Monmouth's heart is broke?"

"Almost all. The best is that he has turned west again, and so we have him hemmed in. He seems to be marching from town to town to no purpose, although he is gathering supporters in places where he has never been before. Feversham thinks he may be intending to try to get to Cheshire, where there are malcontents who may rise for him, but that would be a long and weary march. At all events, turning west has lost him the initiative—so the tacticians think.''

For a moment Annunciata was silent, imagining the scene. Through her childhood she had heard stories of the former civil war, of the marching, the camping, the hardship, sleeping on the stone floors of cold churches, tramping through mud and penetrating rain, dining off hard bread and cold salt meat, standing-to all day while generals decided your fate, whether to fight and die, or march on in ignorance for another day. Her own imagination provided the other things, the poor clothing and equipment of the rebels, their ignorance, their fear; she saw Monmouth, in despair, issuing orders whose efficacy he doubted, marching back the way he had come because there was nothing else to do.

She shivered. She did not want to feel anything for the rebels; she had enough of her own sorrows and anxieties to occupy her mind; she did not want her thoughts peopled by the sad and tattered sinners.

''Martin,'' she said abruptly, ''I cannot bear to go back to Chelmsford House. I want to get away from it, to get away from everything that reminds me.''

''Well, we have a coach at our disposal, and a fine day,'' Martin said reasonably. ''Let us go somewhere else. Where would you like to go?''

She shut her eyes, screwing them up like a child asked a difficult question, and it made him smile.

''We could have dinner in a tavern somewhere, if you liked it,'' he added, and at that her eyes flew open and she smiled happily.

''Yes, yes, that's what I want. Tell Gifford to turn around and drive to Hammersmith. We can have dinner there, at the Dove, by the river. The best dinner they can provide. I'll put on my mask, and we'll go incognito, and no one in the world will know where we are.''

''Very well—it shall be just as you wish,'' Martin said, reaching up to knock on the chariot's ceiling to attract Gifford's attention. It would be hard for the Countess of Chelmsford to be incognito, he thought, even masked and hooded, when she was riding in a coach with her son's coat-of-arms boldly painted on the door: but he did not mention that. For the price of the sort of dinner they were likely to order, the landlord of the Dove would fail to recognize the King of England himself.

CHAPTER SEVENTEEN

The Dove was a pretty tavern, so close by the river at Hammersmith that the spring tides generally made its kitchen unusable for a week. There had been a tavern on that spot for as long as there had been men in the world, and the present one had become a fashionable place when courtiers had taken to escaping London's heats and plagues in the summer in this little village on the river. Many of the great and famous had their summer houses here; here it was, of course, that Prince Rupert had bought a house for his mistress to settle down in; even King Charles himself had patronized Hammersmith Spa, and had dined at the Dove in the company of Mrs. Gwyn in the early days of their friendship.

When they arrived, Annunciata remained outside in the carriage while Martin went in to speak to the landlord. The landlord, who had spotted the arms on the chariot before its wheels had stopped turning, and was rubbing his hands at the thought of the profit to be made, assured Martin that he could provide the best dinner he had ever eaten, along with finer wines than he would get anywhere outside of France.

"And I have a lovely room, sir, a sweet dining room, with its own balcony looking over the river, as nice as even her ladyship could desire, all ready and aired for you, sir," he added.

"Excellent," Martin said, and added in a lower voice, "of course, her ladyship is incognito, you understand? It will profit you and all your servants not to recognize her."

"Oh, yes, I perfectly understand, sir," the landlord said, looking just a little puzzled. "I will warn the maids, sir, don't you worry. I'll send them up now to open the windows, sir, if you would like to ask her ladyship to step in?''

Martin returned to the carriage, and found to his amusement that she had evidently come to some conclusions herself, for she was telling Gifford to take the chariot away and find somewhere in the village to put up the horses and make himself comfortable.

''I will send you word when I want you,'' she said. ''But I do not intend to hurry my dinner, so you may as well enjoy your own.''

''Yes, my lady,'' Gifford said impassively. ''Should I send word to Chelmsford House that you will not be dining there, my lady?''

Annunciata frowned with annoyance. It was impossible, of course, for someone in her position to be completely free from restraints. She had gone to Whitehall without attendance because it was so close to home and so safe, and she was in her own coach with her own coachman; but if she did not return, there would be likely to be an outcry, and they would wonder at Chelmsford House if she had been abducted or murdered. It was on the verge of being improper, in any case, for her to be here without a servingwoman; she supposed she must send them word. But it should be done in her own way.

''I will send a boy from the Dove, Gifford. You need not trouble yourself.'' And she gave him a sharp look, which was intended to warn him to be discreet, a look which he received expressionlessly. With a sigh, Annunciata took Martin's arm and went in to the tavern.

''Yes, my lady, come in, my lady, most honored. The best room, my lady, of course—this way, my lady,'' the host bowed them in, backing before them toward the stairs. There was an agreeable smell of food about the place, overlaying the less agreeable smells of the taproom.

''Mrs. Freeman, landlord,'' Martin said solemnly. ''You have not had the honor of seeing Mrs. Freeman before.''

''No, sir, of course not. This way, my—madam. I think the room will be to your liking.''

It was. Annunciata did not speak, merely nodding her acceptance to the landlord, but the room was excellent. It was a long, low room with a fireplace at one end, and all along one side were French doors opening into the balcony, beyond which could be seen the river, dancing and sparkling in the sunlight, and the green bank beyond, lined with noble trees, and the watermeadows where cattle grazed peacefully. War and treachery seemed a hundred thousand miles away.

The room had been recently redecorated, and the furniture was old and solid and well cared for. There was a dining table and chairs with new red plush seats, a sideboard and a long chaise, and a door which led through into the bedchamber. Even as they stood inspecting it, the first of a train of servants came in bearing the snowy cloth, and vases of flowers, sweetly scented white stocks and vivid, sky-blue flax, and sheafs of sweet peas. The flowers were a nice touch.

Annunciata smiled at Martin, and the landlord said, "What may I bring you to drink madam, sir? I have some delicious white Rhenish, which perhaps might be to her ladyship's taste? Or some champagne?"

"Bring champagne," Martin said, "and your best claret with dinner."

The champagne was brought, with silver goblets to drink from, and when they were alone again for a moment, Annunicata at last removed her cloak and mask, and threw them onto the chaise, and held out her hand for her goblet, laughing.

"It is so hard for the poor man to pretend not to recognize me! What did you promise him?"

"You guessed?" Martin said. They clashed their goblets together and drank. It was very good champagne.

"Well, whatever you promised him, I don't care," Annunciata said, wandering round the room, touching things, smelling the flowers. "It is worth it. I suddenly feel released from all care. How heavenly the flowers smell. I'm glad it wasn't roses—it could so easily have been. Martin, am I wicked, or mad? I suddenly feel fifteen, and as irresponsible as a goosegirl."

He did not answer, merely stood still in the center of the room, turning with her to watch her as she moved about. Her gown was of apple-green silk, so fine it blew lightly around her as she walked, and her hair was drawn up to the crown of her head so that the long ringlets just brushed her neck. She was vividly beautiful, the essence of summer.

"Do you ever want just to run away from everything? I am rich, and titled, and well connected, received at the Court of the King of England, and can have anything I want—except the freedom to run barefoot through the grass in summer. Do you think the bare-legged girl who watches the sheep in the summer meadows all day, and then walks, alone and unwatched, with her swain by moonlight, knows how lucky she is?"

"In summer, perhaps," Martin said gravely, to conceal his amusement. "But in winter when her bare legs are chapped and her bare feet swollen and cracked with chilblains, and she searches in the freezing rain for a lost sheep, and her swain is hanged for stealing food because he is hungry—perhaps then she envies you."

Annunciata stopped still and opened her eyes wide. "Why, Martin, I never heard you speak like this before."

"We were never alone, like this, before," he said, stepping toward her. Her heart began to beat uncomfortably fast, but the door opened again and the landlord ushered in the servants with the hot dishes, and they moved apart to take their places at the table. Now they were restrained by the presence of the servants, and while the dinner continued, they talked only of neutral subjects, as they ate the delicious food. The landlord had indeed provided a handsome meal: there was fresh carp, broiled crisp, with a bitter orange sauce, roast duck stuffed with cherries and almonds, a treacle-cured ham so moist and fragrant that as it was carved the scent of it made their mouths water, shrimps in puffed pastry—since it was July and no oysters could be eaten—with a dish of asparagus, fresh raspberries and strawberries in a tart with custard and cream piled over them, and a delicious pudding with pureed apricots at its heart. When they had finished the champagne they turned to the claret, which was nearly as good as the landlord had said it was.

And all the time they talked, animatedly, interestingly. They had so many memories in common, their educations were similar, and their minds had been trained into the same channels by the same teacher, and their temperaments were similar, and they had always found it easy to talk to each other. For years now Annunciata had thought of Martin with great affection as her closest friend and most satisfying companion. But now she was aware, underneath their accustomed ease with each other, of a tenseness, brought about by the awareness that for some time, perhaps unnoticed by either of them, their relationship had developed a deeper tenderness. Annunciata remembered the many teasing kisses; the readiness with which he took her hand or gave her the permitted embraces; the assurance with which she went to him for comfort when she was afraid or unhappy. Their eyes were bright as they smiled at each other across the table, but the brightness had in it something of inquiry and calculation.

When they had finished eating, they sat for a long time over their wine. The flow of talk was slowing now, not drying up, but merely going underground, and the tension in the air was like a silently swelling bud that would sooner or later burst into flower. Annunciata suddenly had an extraordinary feeling of peace. Time seemed to stretch away on all sides of her, acres of it, to be used at her pleasure. She was rich with it, confident in it, she could spend and squander it with complete ease.

"I want to walk," she said at last.

"Where?" he said, acquiescing to her will with a simplicity that told her better than anything that he shared her sensation of contentment.

"Along the river. I just want to walk in the fresh air, and watch the water pass, and the sky change. No, not the mask. Just the cloak. I want to feel the air on my face."

And they did exactly that. For longer than either of them had the means of measuring, they walked along the riverbank, arm in arm, sometimes speaking, sometimes silent, and when they were silent, their thoughts kept pace. They passed the summer houses of the rich, and then there were green fields only, grazed by cows, summer-fat. Duck and snipe rattled up from the reeds of the river as they passed, and where the bank was clear, swans drifted along beside them, eying them with interest.

"People must picnic here—they think we will feed them," Annunciata said. They walked, and eventually, without either speaking, but in complete accord, they turned and walked back.

The heat was draining from the day; the nights, though it was July, had been cold recently, and here by the river dusk brought a smell of dampness, and they were glad to find that the landlord had had fires lit in the two rooms they had hired. Annunciata felt that the decision had been taken from her, and she was glad. They had not asked for fires, but the landlord had lit them, and so they must stay.

"You must send word to Chelmsford House," Martin said reluctantly, as he took off her cloak for her: reluctantly, because he was afraid of spoiling the mood. But she only smiled at him, a strange, remote smile, and called for paper and ink. He stood by the window while she wrote two notes, folded and addressed them, and with her customary briskness handled the sealing wax and candle herself, using the seal that she always carried with her. One for Gifford, he thought, and one for Chelmsford House. He did not want to ask what she had said, though he wanted to know.

When the servant had departed, and they were alone again, she stood up and came to join him by the window.

"How different the river smells at night," she said. "All day it smells of grass and mallow and St. John's wort, a sort of peppery smell that makes me think of ducks. But at night it smells sad and secret. It is getting its night-smell ready now. Close the windows, will you?"

He did so, drawing first one closed, then another, and turning up their catches, concentrating on the task to try to shut out from his senses the nearness of her, her faint, delicate scent. As he turned the last catch, she placed her hand abruptly over his, stilling him. He turned his head carefully to look at her. Her whole body was trembling lightly, and her eyes seemed enormous.

"I told them we were not coming back tonight," she said. "Was that right?"

Very carefully, as if neither of them knew how it was to be done, he took the hand that restrained him and turned away from the window and gathered her into his arms. She came, not reluctantly, but with a kind of weight, as if pulled against something, and when she was close he gazed down into her face, which was passive with some mysterious suffering. He could have understood it, but did not want to: his mind walked safe between two screaming abysses, shut out only by a fragile wall of glass. She closed her eyes, and her eyelids trembled, so that her dark lashes moved like little fans against her cheeks. He felt love and desire surging up in him resistlessly like the tide, that would break any barrier placed against it. Slowly, very slowly, he bent his head and placed his mouth against hers.

Ah, the smell of her, the taste, the texture of her lips was so familiar, as if they had kissed a hundred times. Her lips parted, the soft, bruising pressure increasing, their tongues searched and touched each other, and then the restraining silken knot snapped, and they were pressed together fiercely, their bodies crying to be closer. They kissed and kissed, and stopped to hug, laughing with a kind of breathless joy as if they had found again a loved one they had thought dead, and then kissed again.

They had no hurry, no haste of desperation, no thought of pursuit. They walked together, arms about each other's waists, to the bedchamber, and undressed each other, slowly, laughing at the unaccustomed exercise, puzzling, amused, over each other's strange laces and awkward buttons. He took down her hair for her, seeking the pins with his sensitive fingers, pulling the mass of it with his loving hands so that it fell like a silent, weighty mist down her back, and drew off her last thin white shift, and then they were naked.

It was as though nakedness were their privacy; as though the clothes had been witnesses, and now they were truly alone with each other. Time held them softly, lapping them like the high tide that is too full for sound or foam; they knew their richness. She looked at his body in wonder, how silken and brown-skinned, how perfect. She lifted his hands and kissed them in pure passion, turning them, mute, in her own, for they were delicate and strong, their power quiescent. She touched his face, traced the line of his nose and mouth, ran her fingers along the clean line of his jaw to his small, perfect ear, drew his silken black hair through her fingers.

"Oh, I love you," she whispered, in wonder and awe, for he was perfect, and beautiful.

He lay down with her, and before him the matchless kingdom

of her white body stretched, unimaginable and remote, and she looked up at him with her fathomless eyes, patient under the burden of her beauty, from which he alone could release her. He touched her, running his fingers quietly over her skin, and the feeling was so light and smooth it seemed there was no difference between the touching and the touched, and all their sensations were one. He kissed her eyes, and her cheeks, and her lips, her long throat and the delicated shadowed hollows below it, her round breasts, her long flanks, the curved secrets of her thighs, and she trembled under him with love, waiting for him to deliver her.

And when at last he moved upward, and slid at last, at last, into her, they both cried out, softly, with their unbearable desire, and the movement seemed outside them, a thing possessing them, without will of their own, as if they were born by that same great dark tide, far, far away to a place of unimaginable ecstasy.

And as they lay quiet in that clean, dark water, he felt her tears running freely and without effort, wetting his face.

"It is not like knowing love," he said at last, "it is like *being* love."

And she said, "All my life, I have looked about me, searched, and said in my heart, 'Is this all? Surely there must be more.' " She moved her head under him, pressing her cheek more closely to his. "And now I have found it. I have found you."

By the fourth of July the rebels had reached Bridgewater, and the intelligence coming in was that Monmouth had sent out for provisions and for laborers and carpenters and tools, as if he were preparing to stand siege in the town.

"It would be madness," Feversham said. "It would be the end of him."

"It is a deception," Lord Churchill said. "He is also collecting horses, and saddlery. The siege preparations are intended to deceive. He will hope to slip away while we are not watching, to the North."

"This letter would seem to confirm that," Feversham said. It was a letter from London saying that Lord Delamere had ridden off hotfoot to Cheshire, probably to raise men there for Monmouth. "A breakout to the North. Well, we have the better cavalry, so that would favor us. And if they do try to hold Bridgewater—" He shrugged: such a course would be suicide. Either way, the rebels had no chance. "We'll march on to Weston Zoyland and camp there. It is open ground between the village and Bridgewater."

By three o'clock on the afternoon of the fifth, the royal army had made camp on the flat ground before the village, facing Bridgewater, three miles away across a flat peat-moor called Sedgemoor, with a deep drainage ditch, called the Bussex in front of them. The six infantry battalions camped here, leaving a hundred yards between them and the ditch. The artillery were placed beside the road which led to Bridgewater, and the cavalry were billeted in the village. Orders were to keep the horses saddled and bridled, for it was expected that the rebels would try to break out either during the night or early in the morning, and as soon as they broke, the cavalry would be needed to pursue them.

Rupert saw his horse comfortable and fed, and then, with Michael, went down to the camp to walk about, and to speak to Hugo and Dudley if they could find them. The first battalion they came to, nearest the road, was that of the Moroccan veterans, under Colonel Kirke—known as Kirke's Lambs because their emblem was the Paschal lamb, but also perhaps with irony—and they watched the soldiers pulling off their boots and making themselves comfortable, and then sought out Dudley and Hugo.

"Well, little brother," Hugo greeted him, clapping him on the shoulder. "How is cavalry life suiting you? I must say I never thought to see you in uniform, but it certainly becomes you. If only there were some girls in this damned village, I warrant they'd say so, too. But all there is, is cider."

"Not to be despised," Dudley added. "The cider they make in these parts is to be treated with respect. Pray God we keep our Lambs from it this night, Hugo."

"Ah, they're all right, the lads." Hugo waved a hand. "What's more to my concern is what we're going to get to eat in this godforsaken place. What's your billet like, Rupert? Can the goodwife cook?''

"I haven't discovered yet," Rupert said. "I just put up the horses and came to see what was happening."

"Nothing, that's what's happening."

"The rebels will probably make a break for it at first light," Dudley said. "Word is that they lost a thousand men today, who went off to pay a Sunday visit to their wives and families and simply didn't come back. The duke won't want to risk losing more. Now he's rested them, he'll march them off as soon as he can."

"Then you'll play your part," Hugo said, clapping Rupert's shoulder. "Well, now, we must part from you for a while, get the men settled, and then find ourselves a billet. Come and eat with us later, when all's done, hey? You, too, Michael. We'll down some of this famous cider, if our bellies can stand it."

Genially dismissed, the two young men wandered on, along the line of the camp. To their left was the drainage ditch, deep and wide and lined with the very black mud of that place, looking rather sinister. There was a crossing place, called a plunge, at each end of the camp area, marked with stones, and sentries had been placed there, just in case. To their right were the other battalions of foot, Trelawney's, which was the Border regiment, alongside their sister regiment, the Coldstream Guards; then the First Guards, then at the right end of the line, Dumbarton's, the Scots regiment. They could be told apart at any distance by their white breeches and cuffs, and they were known as the most disciplined of all regiments. Even now, while in the other parts of the camp men were chattering cheerfully as they lit cooking fires and prepared their evening meal, the men of Dumbarton's were marking out the ground before their tents in case of a night turn-out.

They stopped and asked one of the men whose orders that had been, and the man said, "Why, sir, our Captain MacIntosh: he says he'd put money on it that the duke will attack by night, sir, and so we're marking up our stands."

"But the commander-in-chief does not think there will be an attack?" Rupert said, with a faint query in what was meant to be a statement. The burly soldier spat on the ground, which may or may not have been a comment: Feversham, though a good soldier, and in Rupert's experience a kind of pleasant man, was not liked by the common soldiery because he was a Frenchman, even though he had lived in England almost all his life.

"Don't know about that, sir," the Scot said indifferently. "I take my orders from Captain MacIntosh."

Rupert and Michael walked on, passing the second of the plunges, and then turning back behind the camp to pick up the mud track back toward the village.

"I'm beginning to feel hungry," Rupert said. "I suppose it's seeing those fires being lit. Shall we go back to our billet, and—" He stopped as a trooper saluted him.

"My lord, I've been sent to fetch you to Weston Court."

This was the place where Feversham had set up his headquarters, and when the two men reached it, it was still a ferment of activity. They asked one or two men they knew who were passing in and out, and learned that the plans were unchanged, that the army was staying put, but that scout patrols were being sent out in case of a night breakout. A few moments later Rupert was heading for his billet, not to eat, alas, but to fetch his horse, for he had been detailed to join Captain Crompton's patrol, which was to consist of two troops of Lord Oxford's Horse and a troop of dragoons, to guard the village of Chedzoy, which was halfway between the camp and Bridgewater. A small group of horsemen under Oglethorpe went farther north to guard the crossroads of the Bath and Bristol roads.

Rupert grumbled as he grew hungrier. "Why are we needed here, if the rebels are going to break out to the North? Am I to lose my dinner and my sleep for nothing?"

"Never mind, my lord," Michael said, "where there's a village there's an inn, and once we're in position I'm a Dutchman if I don't find us something to eat, even if it's only cheese and bread."

"This campaign is not going to be something we'll be able to tell our children about," Rupert continued to grumble. "When you remember some of Hugo's stories—and all I've got to tell is that one skirmish. I don't think we're ever going to have a battle. We'll just keep marching about the West Country until the rebels all desert, one by one, and leave the duke on his own to surrender."

"Well, never mind, my lord. There'll be other campaigns."

Though there was a full moon, and the night should have been clear as a bell, a strange, thick mist had come down, muffling all sounds, deadening the senses, hiding everything that was more than a pace or two away. Rupert felt as if he were swimming in a sea of milk, and it gave him a strange sensation of timelessness. It would have been frightening, he thought, if he had been alone, but a man with a horse has a sure guard and guide. Samson, his mount, could see as little as his master, but his nostrils fluttered, seeking scents in the strange white air, and his keen ears would hear danger sooner than Rupert's. While Samson was content to doze, cocking one foot and then the other, Rupert did not need to be afraid, even in the dead of night.

The clock of Chedzoy church struck one, a muted sound, away behind him. All the ground around Chedzoy was enclosed, right down to the banks of another rhine, the Langmoor, and Rupert was glad of it, for at least the hedges would prevent him from stumbling into the ditch in the mist and darkness. The Langmoor was no bigger than the Buzzex, but it had water in the bottom of it, and there was no knowing how deep that water was, or how much mud it concealed. There was a crossing, away to his left, beyond the hedges, marked out with stones, and four troopers were standing sentry near there, four of his own men.

It was time, he thought, to go and inspect them, make sure they had not fallen asleep. He was almost asleep himself, and he knew how easy it would be for a man out of sight and touch with every living being but his horse, to fall into a doze. Besides, the mist was damp and his feet and hands were growing numb, and moving might warm him up. He woke Samson and rode down toward his sentries.

Then it happened—a sharp crack penetrated the mist, making

Samson flick his ears forward. What could have made a sound so sharp that even the muffling mist could not damp it? Surely, it must have been a musket shot? Or a pistol? One of his sentries was in trouble, sure. He kicked Samson into a trot just as a dark shape loomed through the mist toward him, a man on a horse going fast. His hand had gone to his sword when he recognized his sentry.

"Manyon, what is it?" he called, instinct making him keep his voice down. Manyon started at him with wide eyes, and then dragged his horse to a halt.

"Sir, my lord, the enemy—crossing the Langmoor! Thousands of them!"

How in the name of God had they got so far without being discovered?

"This damn mist," Rupert muttered. It would obscure anything. But that they had not heard them either! There was no time for wondering. "Ride as hard as you can for Captain Compton, Manyon. I'll alert the camp."

"My lord!" Manyon cried, evidently about to demand the other role himself, to keep his officer safe.

"Ride, damn you!" Rupert cried, and whirled Samson in the darkness back into the enclosure. He had to keep to this side of the enemy if he was to get to the camp without running into them. There was a bridge across the rhine a bit farther along, and he rode beside the hedge until he came to it, and swung Samson across and onto the moor. Then he galloped. Samson's hooves made no sound on the soft, dry ground, and with a distant part of his mind Rupert registered that this was why they had not heard the rebel troops marching. They were away to his left somewhere, thousands of them, heading for the sleeping camp. Their numbers were greater than the royal army, and with surprise on their side! It did not bear thinking about. And Captain MacIntosh had been right. Rupert remembered how at Bristol they had thought Monmouth might try a night attack, and had said that he favored them. Well, it was a bold move by a desperate man, the only chance of success he had had, and Rupert felt a twinge of admiration for the duke.

The mist was thinning as he left the Langmoor behind him. How long 'does it take to gallop a mile? Three minutes? Five? Suddenly the Buzzex was in front of him, and beyond it the dark shapes of the tents and the village rising behind it, silhouetted against the moonlit sky. Samson skidded to a halt at the dyke's edge, his hooves sliding in the dry peat, and Rupert swung him round to gallop along the edge of it, yelling with all his might.

"Beat your drums, beat your drums! The enemy is coming! Halloo, there! For God's sake, beat your drums!"

For a moment nothing seemed to happen, and then there was movement beyond the ditch, and first one then another, then dozens of infantrymen came tumbling from their tents, and the drums started, their sound raising the hair on Rupert's neck. Seasoned men, all, they were falling-to without panic, seizing their weapons, and all along the bank he could see tiny points of light starting up and whirling round as the musket men swung their slow matches to brighten them. The drums rattled on and on: in the village the troopers would be tightening their girths, even before the trumpets began to sound for them.

From behind him Rupert heard the sound of horses and he whirled Samson round hard, to see the rest of the patrol under Captain Compton riding down toward the rhine, while beyond them the first of the enemy cavalry appeared, their courses converging. There was a rattle of shots exchanged between the patrol and the enemy, and Rupert, heart in mouth, saw men fall before the patrol drew off. He pushed Samson into a gallop again after them, and reached them as they crossed the rhine at the upper plunge.

"Where's Captain Compton?" he called breathlessly to an ensign.

"On ahead—wounded," the man replied, and added, "my lord," when he saw who it was. Rupert pushed past him, plunged Samson through the ditch, and saw the captain up ahead, being supported on either side.

"Captain!" he called, riding up beside the group.

Compton's face gleamed with sweat in the moonlight, but he nodded to Rupert. "Yes, well done, you did right. God knows what would have happened. Get back to your men now. Our business is here, covering the right flank."

Rupert halted his horse and let them draw ahead of him, and looking back toward the rhine, he saw a strange thing. The rebels had reached the rhine farther down, and they all halted at it as if they had not known it would be there and were milling about on its bank in disarray. What could they be about? he wondered. What was a cavalry charge for, if not to charge? The rhine was dry, and though they had missed the plunge, they could have ridden through it, or even jumped it, if they had gone at it hard. But they looked utterly confounded, and in a moment he saw their officer raise his sword and order them to ride along the bank, away from the plunge, toward the heart of the royal infantry. One of the Dumbarton's sentries challenged them, evidently not sure whether they were rebels or the scout patrol, and then another challenge rang out. Someone answered, and the royal army opened fire.

Rupert heard the horses screaming, some with pain, where they were hit, but most with panic. They were not cavalry horses, and wanted only to flee. That will scatter them, he thought, holding Samson, who was made restless by the noise. But then he had no more time to think. One troop of the rebel horse had turned the other way, and found the plunge. Compton was gone from the field, and Captain Sandys had taken his place at the head of the three troops which had formed the scout party.

"Form up, lads—we'll take them. Trumpet!" Rupert heard Sandys's voice clearly through the moonlit darkness. So this was it, he thought. He was to have his battle at last! The trumpets sounded, and the horses began to snort and dance with excitement. Rupert looked about him to his men, and they were grinning fierce elated grins, and he realized his own lips were drawn back likewise, so that he could actually feel the night air cold on his teeth. Extraordinary! he thought. The rebel troop was coming for them, looking more like soldiers than the others who had gone the other way. Perhaps there were some veterans among the rebel horse. Then the trumpets sounded the *charge*, and all thought was swept away as Rupert drove his horse toward the enemy.

*　　*　　*

As the light strengthened, the rout became obvious. The Duke of Monmouth was nowhere to be found: he and his lieutenant Lord Grey had presumably anticipated the defeat and fled.

"Pity," Lord Churchill remarked as he formed up his men to march them back to Weston Zoyland. "Still, with five thousand pound upon his head, he won't get far."

For the rest of the morning there was the task of collecting and numbering the dead, and dressing the wounds of the survivors, and for the officers, writing reports. Lord Feversham gave orders for the militia, who had been waiting in reserve in Middlezoy, a few miles back, to take on the task of counting the rebel dead, and rounding up the rebel prisoners, who were brought in to Weston Zoyland church to be confined. By noon they had brought in near two hundred and fifty, of whom about one in six was wounded, and the church was gradually filling with the moans, screams, and stinks of the defeated men.

The dead from the rebel side were to be gathered and buried in pits out in the cornfields, but the dead from the King's army were to be properly buried in the churchyard at Weston Zoyland. Most of the casualties were from Dumbarton's regiment, where all the officers but four had fallen, and a hundred ordinary soldiers, half of the total casualties on the King's side. The other group to suffer severely had been the cavalry who, with Dumbarton's, had borne the brunt of the attack in the dark.

Dudley and Hugo did not see each other for most of the morning, each busy on his own tasks, and it was near one o'clock when Dudley sought Hugo out where he was laboring over a report. Hugo looked up and wiped the sweat from his brow, and grinned at his friend.

"I hope you've come to force me to stop for dinner, for my health's sake," he said. Dudley did not smile. Beside him was a very young trooper, his head roughly bandaged with what looked like the leg of a pair of breeches, his face very white, perhaps from loss of blood, or from sheer exhaustion. Hugo's grin faded as he stared from one to the other.

"Don't tell me," he said at last, flatly. "Is it Rupert?"

"And his friend, Michael," Dudley said. "I'm sorry, Hugo. They've only just found them. There were a lot of bodies there, and a lot of horses. It must have been where the fighting was fiercest."

Hugo nodded, knowing Dudley was offering that as a comfort— they died in the thick of the battle. But he was remembering his brother's face, alight with the first excitement of soldiering. He found his hand trembling, and put down his pen. "Well," he said after a long time, "at least we won."

CHAPTER EIGHTEEN

The day was still and hot and sunny, and over everything there brooded a great and golden silence. The house was like an empty ship anchored on the glassy waters of a harbor: all the servants had gone to the midsummer fair at Camberwell, and Annunciata and Martin were alone. The windows of the great bedchamber were fully open, but no breeze stirred the hangings, and the air that crept in from the garden was hot with the scent of roses. Fand lay just below one of the windows, stretched out on his side with his belly toward the open air, to get the maximum cooling effect, and he snored a little as he slept; that, and the occasional drone of a fly, were the only sounds, for in that golden June midday even the birds were silent among the motionless leaves of the beech trees.

The summer hangings of the bed had been tied back, and they had stripped off all the covers and lay naked on the white undersheet. Martin lay on his back, his hands folded under his head, staring up at the canopy. Annunciata was prone, her head turned to the side, one hand resting on his flat belly. After a while she sighed, and he looked down at her inquiringly.

"I was just thinking that this time last year Rupert was still alive," she said. "He was marching toward his first engagement in battle, so young, so proud of himself." Martin freed one hand to stroke her hair, and she continued, still staring at nothing, her eyes introspective, "I still can't think of him as dead. It's as if he were simply away somewhere, as Hugo is, away for a long time, but still in the world. I suppose it's because I never saw him

dead, as I did George. I mourn George every day of m̶
Rupert—'' In her mind he smiled at her, his image as f̶
close as if she had seen him last only a moment before̶
reached up and caught Martin's hand and brought it to her lip̶ ̶
kiss the palm. ''Don't worry,'' she said. ''I'm not sad. How
could I be when we are alone together at last?'' She turned onto
her side and put herself into his arms, resting her head on his
shoulder. He bent his head and kissed her long and tenderly, and
then they were silent for a while, and when she sighed again, it
was a contented sigh.

''Privacy is the greatest luxury in the world, and no amount of
wealth can buy it,'' she said. ''Why can't I feel guilty about
loving you?''

He stroked her flank from shoulder to hip, a long, hard stroke,
as one might stroke an animal.

''Do you love me?''

She smiled. ''You know I do. Do you want reassurance? I love
you, with all my heart. But I don't feel guilty.'' He continued to
stroke her, his mobile mouth curled at the corners in his habitual
half-smile. She caught his hand. ''You do, don't you?''

''Yes,'' he said. ''Sometimes. A little. Not now, when we're
alone, but—''

''At Morland Place,'' she finished for him. He grunted. ''I'm
jealous, you know.''

''Of your own daughter,'' he mocked. ''You needn't be.''

She considered for a moment. ''I know she had not conceived
again, but that might be—'' She could not finish. It was a
delicate area, one she could not with propriety ask him about,
and in any case, only half of her wanted to know. She went on,
''She doesn't seem to mind your going away.''

''It is not her business to mind,'' Martin said firmly.

''I know, but—''

''She is happy enough,'' he said, turning his head to fix her
gaze. ''She likes nothing better than to ride and hunt and hawk,
and she has Caroline for company. If I feel guilty, it is not
because I think she suffers in any way.''

She returned his gaze. She was his stepmother, and what they
did was forbidden by every church in the world. Deep and

unspoken went the knowledge that she had lain with his father, that her children were half-brothers to Martin; it was that which engendered the guilt. The further complication of her being his mother-in-law was as nothing beside the fact that their relationship was incestuous. She cupped his face in her hand.

"We are the victims of an accident, my dear. Your mother might have married someone else, and if she had, you would have had a different father, and we might have met and fallen in love with perfect propriety. It is not our fault."

He smiled. "That is a strange logic, stranger still for a Catholic. Sin is for us to resist—"

She placed a finger to his lips, stopping him.

"Don't," she said. "Don't call it sin."

"You know that it is," he said gently. Yes, she did, of course she did; but she could not repent it, nor confess it; she could not take the Mass anymore, was cut off from her religion, her mainstay, but still she could not repent it. "It is sin, and we will be punished."

"Do you want to stop, then?" she asked in a small voice. He rolled over, turning her onto her back and leaning above her on one elbow.

"No," he said gently. "Whatever the price, I will pay it." He pushed the hair from her forehead, and ran his fingers over her face, tracing its lines lovingly. "You are so beautiful, lying there in the tangle of your hair; like a young roe-deer caught in a thicket. You look up at me with such an expression! A faint apprehension, mingled with trust and desire—it turns my heart to water."

"Can you love me so much? I am thirteen years older than you," she said.

"You look no more than sixteen," he said. "You look like a child grown suddenly woman on her wedding night." He kissed her forehead and then her eyes, and she felt him stirring against her, and held him in wonder that she could move him so readily to passion. Her mouth sought his out, and they spoke between kisses as she ran her hands over his hard-muscled back.

"I feel like a bride with you," she said. "Every time is like the first."

"I love the touch of you," he said. "You want me now?"

"Always," she said. "Now and always."

They made love, and it was unlike anything she had called by that name before. She had thought herself in love before, with her first husband, with Edward, with Ralph; but looking back she knew they had all been part of the searching. She had been preparing herself to know this feeling when finally it came to her, a love so profound that it seemed to move the very foundations of her being. They loved, and her soul seemed torn open by something so piercing that she could not cry out, though she were to die of it. She had been wife and mistress to other men, but it had not touched more than the surface of her, and to Martin she brought an offering more precious than her life—her innocence.

Afterward they lay quietly for a long time. Martin turned his face in to her neck, and she folded her arms around him, and they drifted between sleep and waking. Time seemed to pause that still day. Annunciata knew that by the very nature of things their time together must come to an end, but now, as at first, she had no sense of hurry. In one year, she thought, I have lived ten lifetimes in your arms, and if we have no more than one year left, I can live another ten. There was no counting such riches. She drifted away a little, and dreamed that they were walking in a garden, and the sunshine was soft on their bare skin; they looked at each other, and smiled at their nakedness, and walked hand in hand through the silent, sunlit garden; she felt the grass under her feet, and it was softer than velvet.

They were apart sometimes. He had business to conduct—his excuse for being in London. Clovis visited often, dined or supped with them, and Annunciata thought he sometimes looked curiously at them, though he never asked anything. Once Daisy and her husband came to dinner, Daisy looking thin and unwell since her second miscarriage. On that occasion Annunciata noticed a wistfulness about Clovis, and wondered whether, if their relationship had not forbade it, he would have liked to marry her. In her happiness she wanted everyone to be happy, and wondered many a time whether the consanguinity laws were God's, or merely made by man. To forbid love seemed to her now a worse sin.

She paid visits around the Court, sometimes with Martin, sometimes alone. The Princess Anne had had another daughter, whom she named Anne-Sofia, and paying her respects to mother and daughter were her excuse for being in London. Sometimes she discussed soldiering with Prince George, a relief at least from small talk and cards. Hugo and Dudley were once again fighting Turks in the army of the Emperor, and Prince George liked to discuss the campaign with her, as if she understood any of it. They had been gone almost a year, for they had left England as soon as the Monmouth crisis was over. Hugo had not even gone to see his wife; Annunciata thought he forgot for most of the time that he had one.

She visited the Queen's apartments out of duty, but her visits were short. She felt less at home in that deeply Roman Catholic atmosphere, especially now that she was cut off from her religion. She had some sympathy with the King, for his principles were sound, and he had a genuine desire for freedom of conscience for all denominations, but she could not enjoy his company, and remembered how the irreverant Nell Gwyn had dubbed him "dismal Jimmy." There were some mutterings up and down the country about the fact that he had not dismissed the large army that he had raised to put down the rebellion last year, nor dismissed the Catholic officers he had appointed, despite the Test Act. In November Parliament had refused to repeal the Test Act, and demanded that the King dismiss the Catholic officers and his newly chosen Catholic ministers, and the King had responded by proroguing Parliament. But on the whole, though people grumbled, they were content. The country was prosperous, and now that Monmouth was dead, beheaded on Tower Green for his treason, it was certain that Protestant Princess Mary and her husband would be the next rulers of England, so it was only a matter of waiting.

Once she and Martin visited Oxford, where Karellie and Maurice were both at Christ Church. Maurice seemed quieter than ever since the death of his brother, but he did not seem unhappy. He was studying music, for which he seemed to have inherited some of the talent of his ancestor, William Morland, and

Annunciata intended to try to persuade Henry Purcell, the Court musician, to take him on and teach him composition. Karellie, now of course Earl of Chelmsford, was the same as always, bold, bright, innocently wicked, laughing his way through his studies and excelling effortlessly. There ought to have been a brilliant career waiting for him at Court, but she could not imagine Karellie in the sober, gloomy Court of James, or imagine what sort of Court either of the Protestant princesses would rule. Perhaps his future lay abroad, at one of the Courts of Europe, a diplomat, or a soldier, like Dudley, in other rulers' armies.

The large standing army of the King had a permanent camp now on Hounslow Heath, within sight of London, and some of the bright life of Court had transferred itself there. In the rows of white tents, parties and banquets were held, and ladies strolled with the red-coated officers as once they had strolled with courtiers through the Privy Garden or in St. James's Park. Annunciata was invited there once, and accepted only because Chloris was being courted by a soldier whose acquaintance she had made because he had been in Rupert's troop and had seen her son Michael fall. He had come, of his charity, to tell her what he knew, and had fallen in love with her. Annunciata thought he probably wanted to marry Chloris, but how Chloris felt she did not know. She had adored Michael, but as far as Annunciata knew she had been interested in no man since Michael's father abandoned her. She thought that Chloris only accepted the trooper's attentions in the hopes that he might tell her more about Michael's last days.

But for the most part, Annunciata and Martin were alone together, either staying at Chelmsford House, or driving out to Islington or Vauxhall or Hammersmith alone. They did not entertain, and refused the few invitations they received, wanting nothing but each other's society.

"What shall we do when winter comes?" she asked him once, thinking of last winter when they had endured the frustration of living in the same house without being able to touch each other, or even speak freely.

"We'll think of something. We'll find some way to be together," he said, and she accepted his words, trusting him in a way that made him seem the older of the two. There had been no urgency to her question: the summer seemed endless to them.

Then in August, quite unexpectedly, Hugo came home. He arrived late one afternoon when Annunciata and Martin were sitting in the garden seeking the cool shade of the bower. They were eating cherries, Annunciata sitting on the stone bench, Martin on the grass at her feet, both of them dressed in *déshabillé;* Annunciata's feet were bare, and her hair was carelessly piled on top of her head for coolness. Had Hugo been in a more normal state of mind he might have wondered at such informality from his mother; as it was, he merely thought she looked astonishingly young and beautiful, and feasted his eyes on her with a soldier's hunger for his home's women.

He arrived hot, dusty, and very worn. Annunciata was shocked at the sight of him, for he looked years older. He was very thin, his face burned dark brown, and much lined; war, fatigue, and the desert had aged him, and now sorrow had wearied him.

"Hugo! What are you doing here? You did not write—I did not expect you," she cried as he came into the garden unannounced. Martin got quickly to his feet as Hugo came towards them. He had a soldier's gait, but he looked bone weary. He had discarded his wig because of the heat, and his short-cut curly hair surrounded a bald patch like a tonsure, and his eyes were no longer a young man's.

"Mother—Mother," he said, and fell to his knees in front of her, taking both her hands. "I'm so glad you are here. I was afraid you had gone back to Yorkshire. I did not think I could endure another day without seeing you."

"But, my dear, are you ill?" Annunciata asked, staring at him in consternation.

"Dudley is dead," he said, and his shoulders sagged as though the news had been the burden he had braced himself to carry home to her. Annunicata heard it with a dull shock. She tried to draw back her hands but he held them fast.

"How?" she said at last.

"At Buda," Hugo said. "We had driven the Turks back and back and they had gone to earth at last in Buda. We laid siege to the city. Dudley conceived a plan to shorten the siege—our men could not hold out much longer. When we stormed the wall, he was in the forefront. I saw him fall. Literally fall—he was shot through the lungs when he was almost at the top of the wall.'' He stopped abruptly, as if the effort of telling had exhausted him.

"He was his father's son," Annunciata said. Her eyes were wide, looking beyond Hugo, seeing that desert place as if she had been there. Dudley—her brother.

"He was my friend," Hugo said. "After that—I could not stay. I lost heart in it. So I came home." He looked up at her face, devouring it with his eyes. "I had to come back. I had to see you, Mother." She did not look at him. She sat still, shrinking back from him, her mind far away from him. He did not add, You are all that is left, Mother, though the words were in his mind. He was very thirsty, and hungry, and tired, but he saw he had shocked her with his sudden news. He stood up, and turned to Martin, offering his hand to shake.

"I'm glad to see you here," he said. "She should not be alone. You have been taking care of her? But I can see you have. Bless you."

Martin concealed his embarrassment, shook Hugo's hand, and said, "You must be very tired. Shall we go in, and find some refreshment for you?"

At his prompting Annunciata stood and followed them in, but this dusty, sunburned, balding soldier was a stranger to her; she did not want to acknowledge him as her son, and she resented his intrusion into her life.

He came home in more style than he went away, with John Wood and Daniel and a black servant in addition, a train of horses and a great deal of luggage, and a pet monkey, which Fand attacked on sight, driving it to refuge at the top of the drawing-room curtains where it sat jibbering at the maddened dog until the black servant, Casimir, rescued it and took it away. Hugo was a little feverish, and it made him restless, and while he ate and drank, and for a long time afterward, he talked, an endless, rapid stream of words, telling them about the campaign and the siege and his life as a soldier. Most of what he told was incomprehensible to his listeners, and afterward the evening took on an air of unreality in their memories. They sat in silence as the words flowed over them, broken from time to time by an exclamation of "Oh, how good it is to be home!" or by an inquiry about some other member of the family—"How is your sister Daisy? Is she well?"—though he never waited for an answer. Annunciata watched him in growing hostility, this grown man who insisted on calling her mother, who smiled at her with such proprietory fondness, who had brought to her the death of her only brother and taken from her her privacy. When at last he had talked himself into silence, there was nothing left to do but go to bed, and Annunciata and Martin, with a regretful glance toward each other, parted at the top of the stairs for the first time in two months.

Hugo was eager to go home to Morland Place, and now that he had interrupted their idyll, Annunciata and Martin acknowledged that it was time they went back, too. It was a strange homecoming: Hugo, who had found it difficult to remember that he was married, fell upon his wife's neck and matched her tears of joy with his own, and blessed his four-year-old son with a look of profound and tender emotion, though little Arthur, who did not recognize his father, wriggled with embarrassment. Arabella, who was pleased to see Martin, and not indifferent to the return of her brother, took exception to Casimir and swore she would not have him in the house.

"If Hugo wants him, let him go and live at Shawes," she expostulated. Martin pointed out gently that Shawes was not yet Hugo's, and besides, it was no longer fit to live in.

"I don't care," Arabella said. "I'm mistress of this house, and—"

At that point Annunciata entered the argument. "While I live, *I* am mistress of Morland Place," she said, freezing Arabella's tongue with a look, "And I shall say who is to be permitted to stay here, I or the master, no one else."

But after the initial disturbance, the household settled down well enough. Hugo seemed to be seized by a strange lassitude, interrupted by attacks of the same low fever which made him restless and garrulous. Father St. Maur said that it was an illness many men suffered who had sojourned in the eastern deserts, and

that in time it would work its way out of his system. Most of the
time Hugo was content to sit about the house, or in the garden,
talking to Caroline or playing with his son. Occasionally he
would ride out with his wife or his sister, but hunting tired him,
and if he went out with a hunting party he usually returned alone
after an hour. When the restless fits were upon him he sometimes
indulged in violent activity, and his temper could be very uncertain,
and was inflamed by wine to the extent that Martin gave discreet
instructions to Clement that if possible wine and Lord Ballincrea
were to be kept apart.

Arabella was at first fascinated by her brother's stories of
soldiering, but when he reached the end of his repertoire and
began to repeat himself, she abandoned the role of listener and
returned to her normal occupations, though deprived now of
Caroline as a companion. Martin was, as usual, preoccupied with
the business of the estate, and her mother was absorbed with
Karellie and Maurice home from Oxford for the summer recess,
and she had never cared for the pleasure of the nursery, since
James Matthias was still too young to teach to ride, so she was
forced to amuse herself for the most part alone.

At the end of September Karellie and Maurice went back to
Oxford, and the Marquess of Ely arrived for a visit. Hugo was
delighted to see his old friend, and became almost like his old
self for a while, his strange lassitude seeming to fall from him
almost visibly. Ely had always had a fancy for Arabella, and so
the four of them did everything together, rode, hunted, walked,
danced, visited, attended assemblies, spent evenings playing cards,
gambling, or playing charades.

Martin looked on at all this activity with mild amusement. He
found Arabella's tentative devotion irksome, and was glad to see
her so fully and so safely amused, but it occurred to him that
anyone acquainted with the household would be forgiven for
thinking that Martin and Annunciata were married to each other,
and Arabella and Ely as much a couple as Hugo and Caroline.

Deprived of her sons as occupation, Annunciata turned her
attention to Shawes and actually hired the builders to begin the
work she had planned for so long. The outer, defensive wall of
the old house was in poor condition, and the gatehouse was in the

process of falling down, so she gave instructions for it to be demolished and the stone used to begin building. She spent much of her time there, and Martin often rode over to see her there, partly as a means to see her in comparative privacy, and partly because he was interested in the realization of a scheme he had long thought to be mere moonshine. To his amusement she gave instructions for the bathing house to be built first.

"It will be a test of skill, you see," she explained to him. "If they do well by the bathing house, I shall know I can trust them with the main building."

And Martin smiled knowingly, and said, "You know that is not the real reason. Now confess, it is because you crave quick results, and have not the patience to wait for years to see your plans come to life."

"Well, and if it is, I can gloat over my bathing house, and refuse to let anyone use it who annoys me."

"You would never refuse to let anyone use it who might be relied on to marvel at it and tell you how clever you were to devise it," Martin said.

When the foundations were laid, she led him over the area of it and described exactly how it would be.

"There will be two rooms, you see, the bathroom here, and the dressing room here. There will be windows all about, glazed with private-glass, so that it will be full of light inside, and the floor will be covered in black-and-white tiles, and there will be a fountain in the center of each room. In the bathroom, here, there will be a great bath of white marble. In the dressing room I shall have a long French chaise, covered in white brocade, with gold cords, and all around I shall have trees growing in white marble pots, bay trees and orange trees. And *here* there is to be a firehouse, to heat as much bathing water as one could want. And *here*, above the bath, there is to be a great marble rose on the ceiling with a series of holes drilled in it, and above it in the roof space a cistern of water, so that when a lever is pulled the water comes through the holes in the rose, and falls upon you like a shower of rain. Look, I will draw it for you."

Martin walked after her as she darted from place to place, pacing out the dimensions and describing the devices with flourishes of her hands. She was so eager, and looked so young in her enthusiasm, and he smiled with private pleasure. Fand also trotted after her, and pushed his inquisitive blue nose into the places she paused at, trying to discover what it was about them that so excited his mistress. But when the October weather turned wet and cold, her enthusiasm for visiting the site of the building waned, and she preferred to observe the progress by report from the comfort of Morland Place.

The closing in of the weather and the consequent curtailing of outdoor activities brought frustration, and it grew harder week by week for Annunciata and Martin to live in such close proximity and keep their love secret. She cast him burning, beseeching glances, and in November he devised a scheme, which he told her about one morning when they were alone in the steward's room.

"There is a house," he said, "on North Street. It belongs to Kit, but I've been acting on his behalf in having it restored and repaired. The builders have finished with it now, and my next task will be to find a suitable tenant for it, again on Kit's behalf. But until I do, it stands empty."

He paused, and their eyes exchanged messages, questions, and answers.

"It would be dangerous," she said at last, "but—"

"But it is better than nothing," he finished for her. "There is no reason why I should not go there at any time, but you will have to arrive separately, and masked. We will have to be careful, of course—"

She nodded, and felt her heart pounding with the sudden anticipation and fear.

"Chloris will have to know," she said, "but I can trust her."

"Very well. Then. . . ?"

"Let it be *soon*," she said fiercely.

The house had little to recommend it, apart from the view from the upper windows over the river. Martin had it furnished with a few essentials, and they began to meet there whenever they could. Their precautions were elaborate and, to Annunciata, faintly ridiculous, but she had to admit that they were necessary.

Chloris purchased a cloak and mask from a secondhand clothes shop in York where the gentry sometimes disposed of garments they no longer thought fashionable, and with these Annunciata disguised herself. They would leave their horses at the inn on Micklegate, opposite St. Martin's Church, and walk through the back ways to the house, the part of the journey Annunciata dreaded. She had never in her life before walked through the city of York, and she soon discovered that it smelled even worse at ground level than it did from horseback. Martin would always arrive before her, approaching it from the other direction, muffled up in a cloak and wearing a wig of hair lighter in color than his own, which he hoped was sufficient disguise, and if all was well he would tie a scrap of ribbon onto the door handle, sign that she could come up. Chloris waited in the living room below, reading a book or doing some sewing and keeping guard against intruders.

"Years ago," Annunciata said one day when she and Martin were alone in the room that she came to call "Sanctuary," "I would have thought it all an adventure. Now I resent it as a trammeling of our love."

"Do you want to stop meeting here?" he asked. She had been standing at the window, watching the first light snow drifting down from the gray sky to the green river, and she turned swiftly at his words, her face lighting with that eagerness that so moved him.

"Oh, *no*!" she cried. "It is life to me! I only wish . . ."

"What do you wish?" he prompted her, coming across the room to stand beside her, putting his arm around her waist and looking out with her at the gray-and-white day.

"I wish that we could go away together, away from here, forever, and just live together simply, as man and wife, in some place where we are not known."

"Would you leave all your wealth and your position behind?" he asked, half amused, half touched by her words.

"Oh, yes. Wealth and position would mean nothing to me without you. But of course it is not only that," she added sadly.

"No," he agreed. "There is also responsibility."

She turned to look at him, at his dear, gentle face that had known responsibility for so long. He was nearing thirty; the gap between them was lessening year by year. "You have always been older than your years, Martin," she said. "You seem to me never to have had a chance to frolic."

He laughed. "I was not a frolicsome child, even before I put on manly-clothes. Perhaps if we ran away together I would learn to be light. As it is, we must make do with this."

They turned on the same impulse to look at the bare little room, the mattress on the common, rough wood frame, the tripod with its washing bowl, the crude three-legged stools, and the flat-topped chest over which their clothes were flung—all bought cheaply and at secondhand to furnish their sanctuary with the barest essentials.

"It doesn't look much like Paradise, does it?" he said.

"It doesn't look like anything," Annunciata said. "It is a place out of time. Here we are safe from the world."

"Until the world follows us in," he said, and kissing her tenderly, walked with her back toward the bed. "Sooner or later I suppose it must."

"Then we shall go somewhere else," she said.

"But where?"

"Well," she said, "I suppose there is always London."

Hugo was delighted, but somewhat surprised, that his mother remained at Morland Place for Christmas: he had expected her to take the opportunity to go to London. But she threw herself into the celebrations with a will, organizing a large party to ride out on Christmas Eve and fetch the holly and ivy and mistletoe and bay to decorate the hall, and to drag back the Yule log. The day was sharply cold, dry and crisp; snow had been falling for a week, but on that day the skies cleared and were wide and curved and blue as a robin's egg, and the snow glittered like diamond dust, and crunched and cracked beneath them with a noise like dry twigs. The sun shone down on them, pale, brilliant and heatless, and their voices rang and echoed as if the sky were as close as it looked. It was a day of brilliant, contrasted colors—

the bitter white of the snow, the heraldic azure of the sky, glassy green holly, red holly-berries like fallen drops of blood in the snow. His mother wore a cloak of kingfisher blue, and its folds hung vividly across the burnished copper of Banner's rump. She was laughing all the time as she exhorted them all to greater efforts; Maurice found her a pheasant's tail-feather, and she stuck it into her hair as if she were wearing a hat, and Hugo remembered how it swung against the blue sky as she turned her head this way and that.

When they reached home the servants ran out with cups of hot spiced wine, and Clement brought the brand preserved from last year's Yule log, with which the new one must be fired if good luck was to come to the house. The log was dragged indoors in procession while everyone sang the Yule-log carol, and was put into the hearth in the great hall; Clement lit the brand and Father St. Maur blessed it and Martin fired the new log. There was a breathless silence while everyone watched and waited, and as the first smoky crackling flames jumped up a great cheer rang round the hall and set all the dogs barking madly. The cups were refilled, and everyone stood round drinking and laughing and talking. Annunciata crouched down by the hearth like a child to rescue the little creatures driven out of the log by the heat, and Martin teased her gently for her tenderness.

It was a lovely Christmas, twelve days of freezing sunshine, and the house filled with the smells of delicious cooking and the sounds of merriment. Great fires burned in every room, and at night there were enough candles to light the house as bright as day. The house was full of people, too: Maurice and Karellie were home, of course, and Daisy and John Ailesbury came for the season—Daisy was pregnant again, as was Caroline, so they had plenty to talk about. Sabine and Crispian came, too, and they joined in cheerfully with everything, although Hugo thought that Sabine looked rather wistfully at the two women whose bellies were full, and at the two babies, Arthur and James Matthias.

Hugo had never known his mother in such a mad mood, and when Martin named Karellie as Lord of Misrule, he and his mother seemed to conspire to make it the merriest Christmas ever. Each of Karellie's pranks was wilder than last, and Annunciata urged him on to still more lunacy, until Martin protested that they would not reach Twelfth Night without some broken limbs. Karellie had acquired a long, striped cat's tail from somewhere, and had it sewn to the seat of his breeches, and he wore odd-colored hose, one leg white and one yellow, "To show my authority," he said.

Then, when everyone was exhausted with playing games and dancing and charades, there would be music and singing. Martin played to them, and Daisy and Maurice sang, and they all joined in the carols that everyone loved, *"In Dulci Jubilo,"* and *"Quem Pastores,"* and "Green Groweth and Holly," and "There is no Rose." On Christmas Evening there was a special surprise for them all: Maurice had written a piece of music especially for Christmas night, and over the past week had taught Martin the second part, and they played it together on two cornetti for the assembled family. It was very beautiful: the cornetto was thought to be the instrument that most closely resembled the human voice in its range and flexibility, and Maurice played it exquisitely. Martin had never played a cornetto before, though he could play any reed instrument, but the second part was simple, and he managed it extremely well for his one week of tuition. When Hugo closed his eyes, it sounded like two voices, distant and pure, twining one around the other—it made him think of angels singing out in the clear dark night. He opened his eyes again and looked across at his mother. She was sitting in the high-backed chair by the fireplace, gazing into the leaping flames, and as he watched he saw tears on her cheek. He thought that she was weeping for George and for Rupert.

There was only one thing that puzzled Hugo that Christmas. His mother, usually so punctilious in her religious observances, did not publicly receive the Sacrament of the Mass. She attended Mass in the chapel, and often went there alone at other times, but she did not receive the Body and Blood of Our Lord, and he wondered what private crisis of conscience she was suffering. But he noticed, after Christmas, that she frequently went out, alone except for her waiting woman, on some mysterious errand,

and he thought perhaps she had had a disagreement with Father St. Maur, and was taking the Sacrament at some other church. After Christmas, when the guests had gone and things had returned to normal, he noticed, too, that she seemed to have something weighing on her mind, and he resolved to find out what it was that was troubling her. She was the one thing in the world he loved, reverenced, and valued, and he would give his life to make her happy.

CHAPTER NINETEEN

The thaw came early, at the beginning of March, and Annunciata would have liked to be off to London, but the pox was still raging there. It had struck Whitehall in February and carried off Princess Anne's two daughters, Mary and Anne-Sofia, within one week, leaving the princess, who had suffered a second miscarriage in January, once again childless. Then her beloved husband George had taken the sickness, and for a time his life was despaired of, and it was reported that the princess in defiance of advice had sat by his beside hour after hour, holding his hand, while they both wept at the prospect of being parted. He recovered, but it began to look as though the Stuart line was destined to peter out, for Princess Mary in Holland had not conceived again since the first year of her marriage, and the Queen was now thought to be past childbearing, since she had not been pregnant for five years.

With Maurice and Karellie back at Oxford, Annunciata turned her energies to bullying the builders, and by the end of March the bathing house was finished, and she took everyone in triumph to see it. It was quite charming, and they had managed everything exactly as she had wanted it. The floors were black-and-white marble, laid in a checkerboard pattern, the walls were plastered, with beautiful and elaborate moldings on the ceiling and friezes, and Hugo's Chinese paper hung in panels. The marble bath was in the shape of a huge scallop shell, and had cost a small fortune, though Annunciata thought that was rather a joke.

"It's even more splendid than my ebony bath," Hugo said generously, and his mother frowned.

"As I remember, *I* had to pay for that ebony bath," she said. "I think perhaps I'll have a second bathroom built on to the side, and furnish it all in black and silver, and put that ebony bath in there."

"Where is it, anyway?" Hugo asked, not sure if she was joking.

"Rupert had it, and now Karellie," Annunciata said. "It is in your old rooms at Peckwater Inn—and far too good for them."

They looked at Shawes, which was growing more and more unfit to live in because it was *not* lived in. Hugo was concerned that the stones for the bathing house had been taken from the outer wall. "Houses have a way of disappearing when they are once breached," he said. "People come secretly by night and steal the stones to build sheep pens. I shall be left with nowhere to live."

And that angered Annunciata. "You should have done something about making your own fortune, and then you could have bought yourself a home, or had one built. But you seem to feel you need not stir yourself, as long as I can beg pensions for you. How long are you going to stay at Morland Place? What are you going to do with your life?"

Hugo was a little taken aback. "I thought you liked to have me here," he said.

"I don't know why you should think that," Annunciata said, and closed the conversation by walking away. Hugo was upset, but reasoned that his mother's sharpness was probably due to her secret worry, and he decided that the next time she slipped out on one of her mysterious errands, he would follow her and find out where she went.

It was difficult to keep out of sight, but he managed it, though he nearly lost her at Micklegate Bar. That was because as soon as she was inside the bar she changed her cloak and put on her vizard, and Chloris bundled the spare cloak into a saddlebag. He spotted her by the horses, and was more than ever intrigued that she needed to disguise herself. Had she, he wondered, by any means become reconciled to Rome? Was she on her way to a secret Roman Mass? That would account for her not taking the Mass at home.

It was easier to follow them inside the city, for they moved more slowly, and he quickly abandoned his horse. He was surprised, even rather shocked, when the two women abandoned theirs—it was not right that his mother should walk through the filthy streets like any common person—but it made following simple. He kept half a street behind them, and they never looked back, until they came to the house on North Street. He watched as Chloris untied a piece of white ribbon from the door handle, and the two women went in, and then he retired to an alley off Tanner Row where he could watch the door from the shadows. A pieman came past, and he bought a hot pie and settled down to watch, but no other person came, so he assumed that she was the last to the Mass, or whatever the meeting was.

Up in the tiny chamber Annunciata put back her cloak and flung off the mask and went quickly into Martin's embrace. It was two weeks since they had met here, and for a while all they wanted to do was to hold each other close.

"It's cold in here," she said at last, pulling back just enough to look at his face.

"I could not get here early enough to light a brazier. I was only here a few minutes before you."

"Oh, I hate all this subterfuge," she cried, pressing herself against him again as if she could hide in him. He folded his arms tightly round her, wishing he could protect her against all sorrow.

"It's like living in the shadow," he said.

"Such a long shadow," she said bitterly. "When will we ever come out into the sunlight?"

"When we die," he said gently. "Perhaps not until then. We must endure what comes to us, since we choose to love where we should not."

"But why must it be forbidden to love?" she cried passionately. "How can what I feel for you be wrong? How can what is good and warm and tender not come from God?"

"My lady, I don't know," he said softly, lifting her chin with one finger. She was like a wild bird, beating its wings against the bars of a cage; he longed to free her, he who was as strait imprisoned as she. "You ask me what no man knows."

She was still. "I know," she said. "I'm sorry. You suffer, too, perhaps even more than I. Oh, Martin, I want to live with you openly, not hide our love." Her eyes were like dark fire, burning into his. "Perhaps the time will come when we have to run away. We could go to Antwerp, or to Heidelberg, anywhere so that we could begin again—"

"And leave your children?" he said.

"Karellie and Maurice would come with us. They would be happy enough there. Karellie could make a career for himself in the Emperor's court, or the Elector's. His kin are there. And Maurice—Maurice could go to Leipzig, and study under Johannes Pezel. He is almost as great as Purcell. And you and I—"

"My lady," he said, "I am master of Morland Place—"

"King of your small kingdom," she said bitterly. He stroked her hair and kissed her forehead, as if soothing a pain.

"We must not tear at each other, my heart's love. You know that it is not the glory I want. But people depend on me— servants, tenants, villagers, those of the Old Faith who have no one else to defend them, quite apart from the family. Can I desert them?"

"Can you desert me?" she countered. She drew a long breath, and reaching up, placed her lips against his, closing her eyes, leaning against him for a long, quiet moment. Then she stood back, taking his hands, and looking levelly into his eyes, she said quietly, "Martin, I am with child."

He did not say anything for a long time, and in the end she thought that the silence had gone on too long, and that neither of them would ever be able to break it. Then, at last, he said, "How long have you known?"

"Since Christmas," she said. "But I could not be sure until last week."

"Since Christmas," he repeated, sounding rather dazed. Then he smiled his sudden, white smile, and said, "I thought you were acting strangely then. You were so elated, so uninhibited, like a happy child enjoying her first Christmas. I never thought—"

"It could have been my last, you see," she said, "so I made

sure it would be the best. And it was, wasn't it?'' She pressed his hands and laughed, ''Martin, I am with child! I am to bear your child! Now you see that God cannot condemn us, or he would not quicken me. This is his blessing on our love. Men may condemn us, but God sees our hearts, and this proves that he knows our love is good, and honest.''

Martin did not reply, less sure than she was of the workings of God's justice. He only saw that this changed everything. There would be no concealment now.

''Then,'' he said at last, ''I suppose we shall have to run away after all. God may love us, but as you say, men will condemn us. Oh, my lady, I don't want to darken your happiness, but you must know what people will say. They will regard the child with horror, and us with reviling, as unnatural monsters.''

And she faced him fiercely. ''I don't care what people say! I love you, and I'm glad, glad, *glad* that I have your child in me!''

She flung herself into his arms, and he held her closely, and after a moment felt her tears soaking into his shirt. She would fight, she might cry defiance, but she knew as well as he did what faced them. He kissed her hair, and stroked her head, and held her against him, and when her tears eased, he led her to the bed, and they undressed and made love with an overwhelming tenderness, and also a strange sensation of freedom, as if, now that the worst was upon them, they need fear no more.

It was a long, cold wait, but Hugo stuck to his resolve, and at length the door opened and the two women came out and passed along the road, going by him so close that he could smell his mother's perfume. He remained in his hiding place, watching the door for the rest of the congregation to leave, but no one else came out. Then after a long time a man came out, a man in a cheap cloak and fair wig, which he assumed was a disguise, as his mother's was, and locked the door behind him. The man walked away down North Street, and Hugo, puzzled, fell in behind him. Who could his mother have been meeting in secret? Was it an assignation? Anger stirred in him at the idea—he wanted no one to come between him and his mother, he wanted to be first with her, and now that she had no husband, he, as eldest son, must be first in her heart. If she had a lover, why, he would—

He did not finish the thought, but his hands balled into fists of their own volition. Stealthily he trotted after the man in the fair wig, who walked briskly along North Street and then turned into an alley. Hugo darted after him, in time to see him pull off the fair wig before reaching the other end of the alley, revealing dark, soft curls that looked disturbingly familiar. Then as the man turned out of the alley at the other end, Hugo caught a glimpse of his profile against the sunlight, and recognized him, unquestionably, as Martin.

His first feeling was of relief, that it was not an assignation after all, that she did not, then, have a lover. His second was of puzzlement. Why should his mother meet Martin in secret? They saw each other every day at home, what more could they have to say that required a clandestine meeting in a hovel in the city? He toyed for a moment with the idea of religion again, that perhaps they had both become reconciled to Rome, and met there for a secret Mass. But of course if that were the case there would have to be a priest, and there had not been, unless Martin locked him in that house each time he left. No, it must be some piece of business they were transacting together—Martin ran the large Morland estate and Annunciata the Shawes and Chelmsford estates, and between them they conducted a great deal of business—but why it should be secret he could not puzzle out. He abandoned his pursuit and retraced his steps to the place he had left his horse and rode home.

The family reassembled for dinner, except for Martin, who was still said to be in York on business. His mother seemed thoughtful but not unhappy, and she ate with a good appetite. Once or twice she looked around the table with an abstracted air and once Caroline had to repeat a question to her before she realized that she was being addressed, but these things would be consistent with a difficult business transaction to think about.

Martin came home shortly after dinner and went up to the nursery to see his son, spent some time talking pleasantly and kindly to Arabella about her horses, and then disappeared. Hugo went to look for his mother, assuming that she was upstairs in the Long Saloon; her work was there, but she was not. A servant passed and Hugo asked him where her ladyship was.

"She went into the garden a while since, my lord. I have not seen her come in again, so perhaps she is still there. Shall I send to find out?"

"No, it's all right—I'll go and find her myself," Hugo said. It was chilly out of doors as the sun grew low: he would go and exhort her to come in, for fear of the cold. That would give him a reasonable excuse for disturbing her, for she was likely to be short with him if he merely sought her out unasked.

The Italian Garden was her favorite, for she had never liked roses, so he sought her there first. Perhaps, if she was in a gentle mood and did not take him amiss, he might ask her where she went on those lone trips, and gradually coax her confidence. He turned the corner of one of the tall, dark hedges, and saw his mother and Martin standing together in one of the hedged alcoves.

The knowledge came to him like a blinding flash, its truth unquestioned as light. They were standing facing each other; he noticed, as one notices small things in moments of drama, that they were exactly of a height, and so similar in build they might have been twins; they were holding each other's hands as they talked, but it was not that which made him understand. It was the way they looked at each other, a kind of look that passes between those who have been lovers, and once recognized can never be mistaken again; there was an air about them of belonging.

As Hugo saw all this, they perceived him, and both turned their heads to look at him at the same instant. Their hands parted, though they did not otherwise move. Hugo did not see Martin's expression, for he was looking at his mother, and she for a fraction of a second looked startled, afraid, before her face darkened with a frown. It was that fear that tore his heart. His first impression had been right, she had gone to meet a lover. His mother, to go on foot through the streets of York! His mother, to go to an assignation in a nasty little hovel, like any common trollop. Anger welled up in him, not against her—how could he ever feel anything for her but longing and love?—but against the man who had betrayed both of them. Martin, who had been his friend and champion, had brought his mother to this!

"I would not have believed it," he said slowly, "if I had not seen it with my own eyes." He looked at Martin now, and Martin's face was set, wary, though he said nothing.

His mother said, her voice high with anger, "Seen what? What do you suppose you have seen?"

"I followed you today, Mother," he said, not taking his eyes from Martin's face. "I was afraid you might be unhappy about something, I wanted to help you."

"How dare you follow me?" she said in contempt, "how dare you sneak like a thief behind me? Am I to have no privacy?"

He ignored all this. "I followed you to a house. I thought you were going to hear a Roman Mass. Then I thought you were going to meet a lover. It seems that I was right the second time."

He took a step toward Martin, and his anger boiled over. "You cur, you stinking cur, to dishonor my mother! You have befouled her! When I think of you pressing your lecherous attentions on her, and she your stepmother! Have you no shame? No decency? To see her on foot, walking alone in the streets—my mother! The Countess of Chelmsford—and you a mere nothing. How dared you even think to look at her? I'll have your life for this!"

He drew his sword. Martin's face was blanched, his nostrils wide with distress, but still he had not spoken. Annunciata put herself between them, furious, but afraid, too.

"No! Put up your sword! Hugo, you fool, would you murder your brother?"

"My brother!" Hugo's voice cracked on a rising note, and he stared at her with something approaching hatred. "You remind me who he is, madam—did you forget it before? Your stepson, madam—incest! And you, you were my friend, so I thought," he want on across her to Martin. "How long have you designed against our peace? Did you always wish to destroy us? What was it, jealousy? Jealousy that she had taken your mother's place? Unsheathe your sword, unless you are a coward as well as an adulterer and a thief!"

"No. I forbid it! Martin, you are not to fight!" Annunciata cried. "Hugo, I forbid it!"

"Stand aside, Mother," Hugo said through his teeth. Martin's hand was on his sword hilt now, and his face was composed and sad, as he saw the inevitable before him. "Stand aside and let me defend your virtue and your honor, though you hold it light." At that she froze, and drew herself up in fury.

"It must be," Martin said quietly to her. She looked at him, wild eyed.

"Stand and fight," Hugo said, "or I will cut you down where you stand like the cur you are."

"No! No!" Annunciata cried again, but Martin put her gently out of the way, and drew his own sword.

"It has to be," he said again. "He will not stop now."

"You will be killed," Annunciata cried, and neither knew which one she was addressing.

"Keep out of the way," Martin said tersely, watching Hugo and feeling his ground. Annunciata looked about her wildly, wondering if she should shout, or go for help. Surely someone would come and stop them? But she could not bring herself to go, when the bright sword-blades were gleaming in the sun, holding the life and death of two men in the balance. She stepped out of their way as they circled each other, wide eyed with horror, her hands at her throat, her frightened breath tearing harshly at her breast.

Hugo's face was dark with anger, so that he looked deranged; Martin's was set and white. He would be careful, he would try not to harm Hugo; but Hugo would try to kill him. Their circling ended as Hugo lunged in a flurry of strokes. Annunciata choked off a cry. Martin parried, grimly. Hugo was a professional fighter, had fought for his life on more than one occasion, while Martin had never drawn his sword in anger, had learned fencing as an art. But Hugo's anger would tell against him; Martin was cool and watchful. Another flurry, the sharp clash of the blades ringing in the confined space between the dark hedges. In alcoves all about the white statues gleamed like impassive watchers.

Martin, watching for the next attack, stumbled slightly, regained his balance, and saw Hugo bare his teeth in contempt and rage. I must wound him, Martin thought. Nothing else will stop him. But I must not kill him. If I can wound him in the arm . . .

He prepared to lunge to the left, making his preparation obvious enough so that Hugo would have time to get out of the way—it was not meant to be a fatal stroke. But Hugo had fought hand-to-hand both in hot and cold blood. Martin could not know the half of it. Seeing Martin move so obviously, Hugo took it for a feint, to draw him: the real blow would be to the right. All this he calculated instantly, instinctively, with his body rather than his mind. Martin lunged and Hugo jumped toward the stroke instead of away from it, and the blade pierced him through.

Annunciata screamed, a high inhuman note. That was when Hugo knew he was struck. For a moment all movement was frozen, like a tableau. Hugo stared at Martin in shocked disbelief, aware of the blade inside him, though there was no pain, afraid to move for fear of what it would do to him. Martin stared at Hugo in sick horror—this had not been intended to happen! He was aware of the weight of Hugo's body on his sword, was afraid to move for fear of what it might do to his victim. Annunciata stared at them both, almost mad with shock and fear. She could see the point of Martin's sword sticking out of Hugo's back.

Then in a swift movement Martin put his hand against Hugo's chest and drew the sword out. Hugo made a horrible choking noise, and crumpled to the ground, his own hands going to the wound. He felt dissolution and wetness and cold, but no pain, only the terror of knowing he had been dealt a fatal blow. Annunciata ran to him, reaching him as he reached the ground, and he felt her hands on him, searching for the wound, for something to do. She made no sound, though he could hear her sobbing breaths. She did love him after all! he thought in confusion. She turned him, lifting his head, and he strained to look at her. Now the pain was beginning, warming up inside him as though it had been frozen away in a block of ice, a living, feeding pain that would eat his life away.

"Mother!" he whispered, and the effort of speaking made him cough. In distress he saw he had coughed a gout of blood onto his mother's hands and skirt.

"Hugo, Hugo, are you badly hurt? We must get help," she cried. "You were mad to do it, mad!"

"Mother, listen, I have to tell you—" He knew he was dying. Already it was growing darker, she was receding into shadow, and he was growing dizzy. He must tell her, he could not die with this on his conscience. "Mother . . . George, my brother George . . ."

She thought he was raving. "George is dead," she said blankly.

"You always loved him best," Hugo gasped. "I couldn't bear it. I killed him. Mother, I poisoned George."

She stared at him in horror, drawing back her bloody hands. His own came scrabbling after them. "Why?" she whispered.

"So that you'd love me best," Hugo said. He coughed again, spattering her dress, coughing his life away. "You do, don't you? Mother?" His voice was fading. "Mother, say you love me—" His body convulsed, and blood spouted from his mouth with a horrible gulping sound, and he collapsed, his eyes going blank. He was dead. Behind her she heard Martin putting up his sword. He must have wiped it on the grass, her mind offered her irrelevantly.

"Dear God, dear God, dear God," she whispered. There were noises, servants coming, alerted by her scream.

"He's dead," Martin said from behind her, and it was half question, half plea. Suddenly she was revolted by the thing she held. She pulled herself away sharply and got to her feet, turning to Martin, not knowing how she looked, spattered and smeared with her son's blood. Martin's face was white with horror.

"I didn't mean to kill him," he whispered. "He jumped the wrong way. I meant to miss, just nick him to bring him to his senses. He jumped on to my sword."

"Martin—" Her mind was reeling with horror, too much to try to take it all in now. He was trembling with the shock of it, and she knew he must not break down now. "Martin, I know you didn't mean to kill him. But he's dead. You fought a duel and he's dead. You must get away—they'll put you in prison, maybe hang you. You must escape."

He shook his head, not in denial but as a dazed man will, trying to clear his vision. "What? Where?"

"You must flee the country. I will find a way to get you pardoned, and then you can come back. You must run." Even as Hugo once did, she thought. "You must get a boat to Holland. From there you can get to Hanover. The Electress Sofia is my aunt. She will help you. I will send you word when it is safe to return."

"But what about you? What about our child?"

Annunciata stood firm, though her heart was breaking. "I would slow you down. Besides, I must stay here to take care of things, and to get your pardon."

"Yes," he said dazedly, understanding the inevitable. They had planned to run away together—ironic now that he must run without her. He gathered his strength together, for she must not be alone with hers. He took her hands, bloody as they were. "It won't be for long."

She tried to smile, and agree with him, but she was gulping for air as the tears streamed down her face, and he cried out, "No, I can't leave you alone, with all this. I'll stay and face it out. Perhaps—"

She shook her head frantically, and gasped between tears, "No, no! They'll kill you! I don't want you dead. You *must* run."

She could manage no more. He took her in his arms, felt her shaking even as he clutched her. They embraced one last time, hard, taking the impression of each other that would have to last them through the terrible time to come, and then he left her, and she sank to the ground beside her dead son, sobbing hopelessly.

Sometimes she thought it would never end, the horror of it. Afterwards she knew that the only thing that kept her sane was the necessity of concealing the reason for the duel. That would have been one thing too much, but though Chloris might guess, no one else need know. It was not until a long time afterward that she had the leisure to think about Hugo's last words, and mourn again her lost son George. She remembered his bouts of sickness, how they had stopped when Hugo went away to Oxford: Hugo had been poisoning him slowly for years. Had George guessed?

Her heart rocked for her son, suffering so long, killed so point-
lessly for Hugo's insane jealousy. For Hugo she felt no pity, no
remorse.

Martin was gone within the hour, taking with him money,
jewels, and nothing besides. Clement went with him as far as
Hull Port. He begged to accompany his master overseas, but
Martin denied the request. Between directing the servants and
trying to calm the hysterical Caroline, Annunciata had no time to
notice Arabella. She managed to get Caroline to lie down on her
bed at last, and as she came out of the bedchamber Arabella was
waiting for her in the hallway.

"Well, madam, what have you to say for yourself?" Arabella
said harshly.

"What do you mean?" Annunciata asked wearily.

"What do I mean? Hypocrite! Murderess! God, how I hate
you!" Arabella hissed. "You never liked either of us, but I
thought you would stop short of murder."

"What are you talking about?"

"You murdered my brother, all the kin I ever had since my
father died." Arabella glared at her. "And you've stolen my
husband away. What next? Will you murder me?"

"You are being hysterical," Annunciata said in a vain attempt
to calm her daughter. "You must not throw such wicked accusations so lightly. And Martin is not gone forever—he will come
back as soon as—"

"You stole him long ago," Arabella said. "Did you think I
did not know? Ah, that touches something in you! You thought
you had got away with it, that no one knew. You disgust me,
madam! I am ashamed to call you my mother. No mother was
ever so unnatural. My husband, and my brother, the only two
people I ever loved, and you—"

Now Annunciata lost her temper. "You, love? You don't
know the meaning of it. You never cared a jot for Hugo, and as
for Martin—"

"How do you know what I feel? What have you ever known
about me, or what I cared for, or didn't care for? You have never
loved me, since I was born. You wanted only to be rid of me

without trouble. That's why you married me to Martin in the first place, to be rid of me. And now, don't you regret it! I hope it burns you, madam, with a steely point of fire for the rest of your life, because I am his wife, and you can never be! I hope you suffer torments, knowing that he and I are man and wife, and that I am with him and you are not, and through your own wicked fault!''

"What are you talking about? How are you with him?'' Annunciata said.

Arabella stared at her in triumph. "I am going after him.''

"No, no, you can't.''

"Who is to stop me? I am his wife, and have the right to share his exile. And if I have anything to do with it, we shall never come back here, never, never, never! You've looked your last on him, madam.''

"Don't be ridiculous, Arabella,'' Annunciata said coldly. "He doesn't want you. Besides, he is gone, and you can't follow him alone. You'll never find him.''

"I can, and I will,'' Arabella said. "He has gone to Hull Port, Clem told me so, and I can ride faster than him. I'll catch him, all right.''

"You stupid girl, you can't go out alone. I forbid it.''

"You can't stop me. If you try to, I'll tell everyone the truth.''

They stared at each other, Annunciata sickly, Arabella in malicious glee.

"What about your child?'' Annunciata said, trying one last card.

Arabella turned on her heel contemptuously. "You have him,'' she said. "I can get plenty more.''

Clement came back in the early hours of the morning. Annunciata was in the chapel, keeping vigil over Hugo's body. She had not slept.

"We found a boat, my lady,'' he told her, swaying wearily from his long ride. "I saw him on board. They seemed civil people, though a little rough. They will have sailed at first light. He sent me straight back—he would not have me wait. He sent this to you by my hand." He drew a crumpled note from his breast and gave it to her.

"Did you see Miss Arabella?" she asked. "Did she catch up with you?"

Clement looked bewildered. "Miss Arabella, my lady?"

"She went after you on horseback. She said she'd catch you up."

"I didn't see her, my lady," he said. "Perhaps she will have got there after I left."

"Yes, perhaps she will. We must send out to look for her, however. Don't worry about it, Clement. Go and get some food and sleep. I will see to it."

"Yes, my lady." He paused as he was about to go, and said, "My lady, will you not sleep?"

Annunciata shook her head slowly. "I cannot. Go now, leave me alone."

He went away, and for a while she sat motionless, seeing the light grow outside the chapel windows. Her heart was a long way away, seeing the gray dawn over the gray sea, and a small boat beating bravely against the choppy waves, white-topped, and a cloud of seagulls wheeling silently around the masts. She remembered his saying, "Whatever the price, I will pay it." This is the price, she thought, this anguish of being apart. The days stretched long before her, to be used up somehow. She became aware of the feeling of paper between her fingers and remembered his letter.

It was hastily written, but his handwriting was familiar to her. It was hard to read, her eyes were so clouded, and she had to stop again and again to wipe them dry.

"My lady," it began—long, long ago a very young Martin had chosen to call her "my lady," meaning it from his heart—"I have found a boat, and will be safe away to Holland as you read this. I place my son in your care until I come home again. You must keep my kingdom for me. I cannot write much, but to tell you what was yours is still yours, will always be. Keep faith, keep courage. I will never be far from you. Pray for me, as I for you, daily, hourly. God keep you, my lady."

She folded the letter again, and sat for a long time just holding it. The pain had eased a little. The gray light grew golden, and the birds were singing outside and the candles within the chapel had grown dim by contrast. She looked toward the statue of the Lady, with its serene face and slender offering hands, and she prayed, Holy Mother of God, take care of him, keep him safe, bring him back to me at last. She was crying again without having noticed; her vision blurred and wavered and in the flickering candlelight it looked as though there were tears on the Lady's face, catching the light.

CHAPTER TWENTY

On a still, damp, hot day in September Annunciata gave birth to her child. It was the eighth of September, the Birth Feast of Our Lady, and appropriately enough the child was a girl; a small, wizened creature, however, with a thick pelt of dark hair, and strangely dark skin. Annunciata gazed at her apathetically when they placed her in her arms. She was so small and strange, looking like neither parent, a changeling baby. Exhausted and weak from her labor, Annunciata cried, and when the tears dropped on the baby's head, they took her away. Chloris tried to comfort her.

"She'll look prettier by and by," she said. "God knows it was a long labor for her, too. You are tired, my lady. Rest now."

"Who will feed her?" Annunciata said through her tears. "You are too old, Chloris. I am too old to be her mother. What will become of her?"

"Hush now, hush, all will be well. You are tired. It's been a long, hard year. We'll find a wet nurse for the poor little creature."

Outside the bedchamber the house was silent, seeming deserted. Chloris moved quietly about the house, seeing that things were in order, looking in at the nursery, where Dorcas reigned serenely over her four charges—the new baby would make it five. Apart from James Matthias, and Arthur, who had had his fifth birthday and would outgrow the nursery soon, there was Caroline's second child, a son she had named John after her brother, and Daisy's baby. Daisy had died of the childbed fever—one of the many things that had made that year so long and so hard, Chloris thought—and John Ailesbury had sent the little girl, Mary Celia, to the safety of the Morland Place nursery until she should be a little older, or he married again. Chloris couldn't remember who had first dubbed the baby Clover, but the name had stuck, and suited the fuzzy, dimpled little thing better than her stately true name.

For the rest, the house was deserted, with Hugo dead, Martin in exile, and Arabella missing. Nothing had been heard of her since she left the house that night, and though Annunciata had sent out party after party to search for her, they never discovered any sign or heard any word of her. There were so many ways in which she could have perished, but the countess, oddly enough, would not believe she was dead, and persisted that Arabella was simply lost somewhere abroad, having missed the ship that took Martin away and somehow getting on board another.

"She will turn up one day," Annunciata would say. "You'll see."

Martin was in Hanover, where the Electress Sofia had taken him in, and he repaid her kindness in some measure by teaching English to the children. He communicated through Edmund at St. Omer, which was the safest way for the time being, Jesuits being now familiar faces at Court. The King had refused to pardon him, but Annunciata intended to renew her request at intervals until he did, and the tone of her letters to Martin was always cheerful. At home, as Chloris knew only too well, her mood was not so sanguine. She brooded darkly through that terrible year, sending people away as if to ensure her isolation. She had sent Karellie to Europe to do his Grand Tour with Father St. Maur, and Maurice, as she had planned, to Leipzig to study under Pezel at the university there, and she had persuaded Caroline, as soon as the baby was born, to go home to her brother's house for a visit, to regain her health. Chloris thought she was hoping that pretty, silly Caroline might soon wed again, and never come back. It was as if she wanted to be alone.

The mystery of her pregnancy had been much canvassed among the servants and throughout the society of York, but if anyone had a depraved enough imagination to guess at the truth they had more modesty than to air their opinion. All the same, the stiffer elements of society ceased to invite the countess to their functions, and those who cared more for popularity than propriety and continued to invite her were refused. She went nowhere, hardly ever leaving the house, and when she did, going no farther than the gardens, except on the occasion when she went to London to plead for Martin to the King. Growing larger with child, she had moved like a ghost about the silent house. With Father St. Maur gone, there was no Mass said in the chapel, though the sanctuary light still burned, but the countess spent many a long hour in there, not kneeling or praying, but just sitting, as though it eased her.

Chloris guessed that being cut off from her religion was the hardest thing the countess had to bear, harder even than being parted from Martin, for she knew that Annunciata believed they would be reunited one day. But she could take no comfort from the thing that had been her mainstay all her life, unless she confessed to her sin and asked for absolution; and she could not, would not, regard it as sin. The dichotomy was worse than anything, and when she sat hour after hour in the Lady Chapel, looking at the statue of the Holy Virgin, Chloris wondered if in her mind Annunciata continued a long argument with Her.

Some of the servants had left after Hugo's death, not caring to be associated with the crime, or perhaps not being able to bear the atmosphere at Morland Place. To those who remained the countess was distant but unfailingly polite and kind, and it broke Chloris's heart to see it. She drove herself hard, taking care of all the business, running the Morland estates, the wool and cloth business, the Shawes estate, and the Chelmsford estate, overseeing the house, and the bringing up of the babies. But when she was not working, she walked like a ghost, or sat motionless, looking at nothing. If she would only be as kind with herself as with others, Chloris thought.

Having seen that everything was well with the house, Chloris went back to the great bedchamber, and found that Annunciata had fallen asleep. Birch was sitting with her, watching her as she slept. Birch was fifty-five now, and to Chloris's eyes had not changed one whit in ten years; she was neat and precise and grim-faced as ever. She looked up as Chloris came in.

"She has gone off at last. I thought she would never stop crying."

"You should get something to eat while she is asleep," Chloris said.

"What about you?"

"I couldn't eat, not yet." She went across to the crib to look at the sleeping baby. "Poor little thing. We must find her a nurse."

Birch looked at her oddly. "She said she wants to call it Aliena," she said. The two exchanged glances of sympathy.

"Not such a bad name for her, I suppose," Chloris admitted, stroking the baby's cheek with the back of her finger. Birch stirred restlessly, and Chloris saw that she was about to make a rare excursion into the realms of intimacy. Birch never spoke about feelings, hers or anyone else's, and she must have been deeply moved to do so now.

"What I can't understand," Birch said, "is what could have brought her to do it." Chloris looked inquiringly, not sure how much she knew. Birch returned the look firmly. "You know what I mean. With the master. I mean—her of all people."

"I think I understand," Chloris said, "though it's hard to explain. But I think it was just because of that. She really loved him—the prince, I mean—and it was a terrible shock to her to realize he was her father and therefore she *shouldn't* love him. And what was worse, even after she knew he was her father, she went on loving him, deep in her heart, just the same. That was why she couldn't love anyone else, though she searched and searched. And being cheated of him, I think she couldn't rest until—"

"Don't," Birch said. Chloris stopped. "Don't go on," Birch spoke even more quietly. "I don't want to hear it. God forgive her!"

"God pity her," Chloris amended. She left the crib and went to the bedside to look down into the exhausted, sleeping face. Asleep she had always looked so much younger than her years. Now anxiety and grief had made her thin, and with the falling away of her flesh, her years had settled on her. No one would ever take her for a child again, nor yet a young woman.

"Whatever her misdeeds," she went on, "she has paid for them, and will go on paying. Don't judge her."

Birch stood up. "If you'll watch her, I'll go and find something to eat," she said. "Shall I bring you something up? A little bread and cheese?"

"If you will," Chloris said, and Birch went away. Chloris sat down by the bed and wondered what would happen next. Morland Place was like a house besieged, and Annunciata the lone captain, keeping it for her King. Guardian now of so many estates for so many young babes, keeping a lonely vigil, when would she sleep? And the new baby, too—what of her?

"Aliena," Chloris thought, and a smile crossed her tired face. "Trust you to think of that, my lady," she murmured.

While Annunciata was giving birth, the King and Queen were in the West Country where the General Pardon issued in March had released thousands of Dissenters from the prisons, as well as some former supporters of Monmouth. The West had been thoroughly subdued after the rebellion; now it was to be cheered. In April the King had issued a Declaration of Indulgence, and everywhere in the West Dissenters of every persuasion were able for the first time publicly to celebrate their religions. But as Annunciata wrote in her December letter to St. Omer:

"No one seems inclined to thank the King for his generosity. In fact, I believe the Dissenting community regard him with more suspicion than they do those who persecute them. I think the King is the only man in England who really wants to extend toleration at all."

She had more exciting news than that, however. While he was on his progress in the West, the King had visited the Well of St. Winefrede, which had a reputation for granting miracles, and had prayed there for a son. Within two weeks the Queen was pregnant.

"It was certainly a miracle—the Queen has not conceived for five years, and the fact that it happened so immediately afterward proves that it was by direct intervention of God. Perhaps for that reason the King is convinced that the child will be a son. The Queen was more reserved in her joy, no doubt remembering her previous unsuccessful endeavors."

The Queen had always been quieter, in any case, an intensely reserved and pious woman. She had refused to receive Annunciata while the latter was pregnant, and when Annunciata went to Court again in December to renew her request for Martin's pardon, she received her on the King's instructions, but was cool, seeming ill at ease with her. As Annunciata had hoped, the King in his elation was more inclined to be indulgent than before, but he did not at once grant the pardon, indicating, without precisely saying so, that if Annunciata embraced the Church of Rome, Martin would be permitted to return home.

"You are a Catholic, I know," he said, "but you do not go far enough. Yours is a compromise, a halfway religion. Why should you not give yourself entirely? A religion is nothing without authority, and there is no authority to be trusted other than Rome. Yours is a faith without a leader—look to the leader God appointed, the Pope."

Annunciata was cautious, seeing the pardon dangling just out of reach.

"Sir, if I could only be sure . . ."

"You *must* be sure. The Truth is all around you. Let me send you someone to instruct you."

And thus it was that when Annunciata returned, her mission unsuccessful, to Morland Place, she was accompanied by a young Jesuit priest, Father Cloud, and the Roman Mass was once again celebrated in the chapel at Morland Place. In its form it was little different from the Anglo-Catholic mass, but there were those among the servants who stayed away, and others who, though attending, yet complained. After a week of it, Annunciata asked him to desist. He held the Mass in his own room for those who wished to come to him there and receive it, and offered instruction in the Roman faith. Annunciata enjoyed talking to him, and they spent many hours arguing cheerfully; he was an energetic, sensible young man, with a great desire to convince but no desire to bully. But it did nothing to make the countess more popular in and around York.

To her surprise, when a letter came back from St. Omer, it did not contain any enthusiasm for the news of the Queen's pregnancy. Annunciata had been glad for the King and Queen merely on a human and personal level, because childlessness was a tragedy for a married couple, and because they were her kinfolk. She had not considered the political implications.

"The very worst thing to hope for is a son. Prince William has many friends in England who inform him of the spirits of the people, and they have said if there should be a son they would look to him to protect the Protestant religion. Do you understand what that means? King Louis is pressing on the borders of the Palatinate as well as Holland, and no one in Europe will support a Catholic prince who might join forces with Louis, against a Protestant prince who has resisted the French for a decade. We have heard that the King requested the return of the Anglo-Scots regiments which are in Holland helping Prince William, and that they refused to go home. They are four thousand of the best soldiers in Christendom, and they now give their allegiance to Prince William. My lady, take care! You may be in more danger than I."

The letter shook Annunciata—"friends in England," and look to him to protect the Protestant religion? Did she know what that meant? Yes, she thought—there were those in England who were pledging support to William if it became desirable for him to invade; and with the Anglo-Scots regiments behind him, he could invade without foreign troops, which would make him more acceptable to the people. It was a dangerous letter. She finished reading it—it told little more other than that Karellie and Father St. Maur had spent Christmas with Martin at Hanover, and that the boy had been a great favorite with everyone, especially with Sofia, and had probably broken the heart of every woman under twenty—and then burned it carefully.

She thought about her own danger, and she felt very alone. If it should come to an invasion, what should she do? She had no man in the house, and if Martin did not come home by then it would be for her to hold Morland Place—against, perhaps, "four thousand of the best soldiers in Christendom." She shivered at the thought. Would she have the courage? She knew what happened to the women when a siege was broken. But if she did not resist, she broke faith with the King, that faith which was a subject's first duty, especially a Morland subject. As Martin said, a son would be the last thing to hope for—but she could not bring herself to hope for a miscarriage or stillbirth. To wish that on another woman would be to her as basic a crime as treachery to the King. She sought the silence of the chapel, not to pray, for she could not, nor for comfort, for there was none for her, but for the liberty to be still. She sat there, hour after hour, numb, not talking.

Things gathered pace. In April the King issued a second Declaration of Indulgence, differing from the first only in that it named, as proof of its sincerity, some of the high officers of state who had recently been appointed even though they were Catholic. At the end of April he ordered it to be read from every pulpit in the Kingdom on four successive Sundays, in order that everyone should know about it. While it might please the Dissenters and the Catholics, it could not please the Church of England clergy, whose privileges it removed, and so a meeting was held at Lambeth Palace, as a result of which seven bishops—Ely, St. Asaph, Chichester, Bath and Wells, Bristol, Peterborough, and the Archbishop of Canterbury—presented a petition to the King at Whitehall stating their refusal to read the Declaration. Their refusal represented the resistance of the Established Church to the will of the King, and the King responded by sending the seven of them to the Tower.

Copies of the petition were circulated in London, and in the hot June sunshine tempers began to seethe. The Queen was near her time, and Annunciata had come to London to be on hand; day by day Chloris and Tom went out to mingle with the crowds and bring back reports, and they did nothing to cheer her. Then, in the middle of it all, on the tenth of June, word came that the Queen had gone into labor.

"We had better go across the park, my lady," Chloris said, helping Annunciata with her cloak. "There are such crowds around Whitehall. They are saying it is all a trick."

"What can you mean, a trick?" Annunciata asked. "Surely they cannot still believe that she is not really pregnant?"

"They believe what they want to believe, my lady, and it is well known the Princess Anne has said she does not believe the

Queen is with child. They are saying that is why she has gone down to Bath at this time, to demonstrate her lack of belief in the pregnancy.''

"It is undutiful and wicked," Annunciata said angrily. "It is her duty to be here when the Queen is so near her time.''

"She claims it is for her health," Chloris said—Princess Anne had had a miscarriage in the autumn and another in April. "But that is not what the people believe. And now that the Queen is in labor before the expected time, they are saying it is all a trick, and that the Jesuit priests have a changeling baby all ready—a miller's son, they are saying, though God knows why, my lady—to smuggle into the birth chamber."

"Wicked nonsense!" Annunciata cried. "All the more reason for me to be there, and all other loyal people of the Court. Poor lady!"

The birch chamber was stiflingly hot, and crowded with people— almost sixty members of the Court watched and listened to the Queen's cries as she labored that morning to bring her child to birth, ten of them ranged along the foot of the bed where they had the best possible view of the proceedings. Princess Anne was conspicuous by her absence. Annunciata felt great pity for the Queen, whose pious modesty must have been outraged on these occasions, but there was no help for it, for royal births were always witnessed by any member of the Court who wished to see and could find room in the chamber. But her suffering, if great, was not protracted and just before noon among the green velvet hangings of the great bed the King had had made for her, the Queen gave birth to a healthy son.

The King was overjoyed, and ordered lavish celebrations, bonfires, fireworks displays, banquets; the bells of London were ordered to be rung, and the conduits ran wine, to celebrate the birth of Prince James Francis Edward, Prince of Wales. The people of London were never averse to a celebration, especially when it involved free wine, but Chloris and Tom reported that among the bonfires and feasts the rumors were proliferating like fleas.

"The favorite story seems to be that the changeling was smuggled into the bed in a warming pan," she told her mistress. "It would have needed a great deal of dexterity to get it out without anyone seeing the action, but they don't seem to mind that, my lady. Others say the Queen really did have a child, but that it was a girl, and was changed for a boy while it was being swaddled.''

On the eighteenth of June the trial of the seven bishops for sedition began, and talk of that mingled with the stories of the changeling baby. There was consternation at Whitehall by then, for the infant prince was ailing and looked likely to die, which would have pleased the London crowds mightily. Annunciata, on one of her daily visits to the Queen's apartments, discovered that the prince was unable to keep down the gruel he was being fed, even though it was enriched by currants, and remembering her own troubles with her baby Rupert, she begged the Queen to order her physicians to let the child be breast-fed.

"I am sure it will save him, Your Majesty," she pleaded. "My children, the three of them, died in infancy; the next three I had breast-fed, and they all lived to be strong healthy boys. The eldest, Rupert, fell at Sedgemoor, Your Majesty, as you may remember.''

The Queen, perhaps moved by the last appeal to her maternal instincts, said she would consider it. Annunciata did not know, of course, whether she had had any effect on matters, but the following day, after a prolonged examination of the baby, the Queen's physicians decreed that "His Highness should have the breast.'' Discreet servants went out to the outlying country districts nearest London, and in the evening a tile maker's wife was brought in from Richmond, a poor woman in old shoes and no stockings and shabby working clothes, but young and healthy with a fresh complexion. She was in milk from her own recent delivery, and the prince took to her at once. In a few days he was well again, and thriving. The King in his gratitude gave her a purse of two hundred guineas and settled a pension of a hundred pounds on her for life.

Chloris reported that the prince's rapid recovery was said in the streets to be firm proof that the tile maker's wife was his true mother, and that it was clear from the fact that the Queen also recovered so quickly that she had not given birth at all. The King in his exasperation ordered a public inquiry into the birth, to dispel all the rumors once and for all. The inquiry determined that there was no trickery involved; but in the streets the people said that had there been no trickery, the King would not have thought it necessary to have an inquiry at all.

Then on the thirtieth of June, the seven bishops were acquitted, and the streets were filled with rejoicing Londoners, whose unofficial celebrations were louder if not more lavish than the official ones for the prince's birth. The army, camped a few miles away on Hounslow Heath, celebrated so noisily that their cheers could be heard in London. Annunciata was thoughtful—the standing army was intended to be the King's strength, but if they rejoiced so at the bishop's acquittal, for whom would they fight if it came to a confrontation? She tried once more to achieve the pardon for Martin she needed, but the King only told her, more openly than before, that it depended on her conversion, and so in the middle of June she shut up Chelmsford House and went home to Morland Place to await developments.

Through August and September, the Prince of Orange amassed troops and ships in Holland for the invasion of England. News of it came to Annunciata through Edmund from Martin, along with the alarming intelligence that a number of notable men had signed a secret document asking William to invade and pledging support if he did.

"I do not know the names of these men, but the document undoubtedly exists. Think who would receive the greatest benefit, and there is your man."

Annunciata returned to London early in September in an attempt to alert the King to his danger. His own intelligence had informed him that troops were gathering in Holland, some from as far away as Sweden, but nothing that Annunciata could say would convince him that these troops were not being assembled for the repulsion of the French. Annunciata would not reveal the source of her information, for fear of what might happen to her family abroad, and so he gave it less credence than he otherwise might. He thanked her courteously for her trouble.

"You can go home in the knowledge that you have done your duty, and in the assurance of safety. No one, my dear Countess, would consider trying to bring an army across the Channel this late in the year. You have a sailor's assurance for that. It would be folly to attempt it, and my son-in-law, whatever else he may be, is no fool.''

She went home, more afraid than ever, and wrote begging Martin and her two boys to come home. To Martin she said, ''Your exile has been long enough, and I am convinced the King would protect you. If you gave him your services, he would have no other choice, and you are needed here, more than I can possibly tell you.''

There were rumors flying around the north of the support that would be given to Prince William if he landed, and Annunciata was no longer sure who she could trust. She did not mention this in her letter, in case it should be intercepted; she began, discreetly, to make preparations for holding Morland Place if it should be necessary, and blessed the long-ago decision to build a priests' hole where Father Cloud might hide when the time came.

In the beginning of October copies arrived in England of the Declaration made by Prince William, stating his intention to invade England, but claiming his sole purpose was to call a free Parliament so that England's laws and liberties might be sustained. The King finally believed in his danger, and began to prepare his defenses. He called in regiments from Ireland and Scotland to strengthen the army. Feversham was again made commander-in-chief, with Churchill as second-in-command, and the generals Kirke and Grafton were again appointed the positions they had held at the time of the Monmouth rebellion. Lord Dartmouth was given command of the fleet, and he assembled his ships around the southeast corner of England where he could watch for the Dutch fleet and hope to head it off. It was believed that the Dutch would most likely head for Yorkshire or some other place on the east coast, since the winds at that time of year were generally dead foul for the Channel; but the King did not dare send his troops to one place for fear of invasion in another, and so he kept them centrally, ready to march off in any direction, as required.

So October passed, and the country waited. Annunciata had had no further word from Martin or Edmund, and had no idea whether her last letter had reached them. She did not know where Karellie or Maurice were, and hoped that, if they were not coming home, they were remaining safely at some secure court or university; she wondered again and again what had become of Arabella, and wished her fierce daughter were here with her, for whatever her faults, Arabella would have fought like a tiger for her home, and would have been a good person to have beside her in that troubled time.

Toward the end of October the news came that Prince William had set sail, with thirteen thousand soldiers, two hundred troopships, and fifty warships, but had been driven back on the second day by a storm. Relief was short lived. On the first of November he set sail again, apparently heading for Yorkshire. Again on the second day out the wind changed, but this time it swung round to the east, trapping Lord Dartmouth's fleet on a lee shore, and the Dutch fleet changed course and sailed along the Channel, passing within sight of the helpless English ships, passing the white cliffs of Dover where a huge crowd of spectators watched them go by in silence, and on the fifth of November landed in the West Country, at Brixham. They disembarked, unopposed, in a leisurely fashion, formed up, and marched for Exeter, and on the ninth Prince William entered that city like a King, riding on a white horse; sensibly he put the English troops under his command in the forefront, led by the English Earl of Macclesfield, who had fought long ago for Charles the Martyr, and if he was not cheered or welcomed, Prince William was at least not resisted.

"What is the King doing?" Annunciata cried with frustration. "Why does he not make a move? There Dutch William sits, a huge foreign army is on English soil, and he does nothing."

"Prince William also does nothing," Chloris said, trying to comfort her. Everyone at Morland Place was nervous, for there were rumors everywhere about a rising, and no one knew what would happen next. Morland Place was like a ship aground, marooned in a sea of mud, and within its walls the servants and the children moved lightly and quietly as if afraid to attract attention to themselves.

"He is hoping, I suppose, to win the war without fighting a battle. It would not be good for him to have to spill English blood in order to steal his father's throne," Annunciata said bitterly. "All the more reason why the King should force his hand. The longer he waits, the more people will go over to the enemy."

Gradually they were fortifying themselves against the rising, if it should come. It was hard to get in supplies of food without attracing attention, and with trepidation Annunciata had sent out some of the loyal servants to markets farther afield than York in order to buy up food where they were not known. Father Cloud had been a great help, and had been quietly training the younger men in the use of arms, and his cheerfulness and confidence were keeping the servants together, but there were still those who could never forgive him for being a Jesuit. Jesuits were known to drink little babies' blood in order to keep young, and Annunciata was not sure whether his presence might not impair the loyalty of some of the more credulous servants.

On the eighteenth of November the news came winging that Lord Delamere, who was to have raised Cheshire for Monmouth, had now done it for William, and that the King had finally left London to join his army at Salisbury. The news sent a trickle of fear along Annunciata's spine. She knew the time had come. Quietly she ordered all the servants inside the house, and had the gates closed, and the portcullis, which had never been lowered since the Civil War, came down. Father Cloud held a special Mass to pray for God's aid in defending the house, and for once everyone attended, and the chapel was crowded. The candles burned softly, the murmur of voices rose to the arched beams, and all around the walls the effigies of former Morlands looked down benignly on the bent heads of the faithful. Four-year-old James Matthias, heir to Morland Place, watched with wide eyes from the safety of Dorcas's lap as six-year-old Arthur, Viscount Ballincrea, frowning with concentration, swung the censer, serving the altar for the first time in his life in company with Clement's second son Valentine. Nursery maids had the babies, Clover, John, and Aliena, in their arms, and took them up one by one to be blessed, as did those servants who had young children.

Annunciata sat in the master's place in the front pew, her face grave, her eyes remote, and she alone, when the moment came, did not go up to the rails to receive the precious Body and Blood.

Afterward, when the chapel was empty again and Arthur and Valentine had snuffed the candles and gone away, Annunciata came back, with Fand padding at her heels, his nails clicking on the stone floor. She went into the Lady Chapel, and stood for a moment looking at the statue. The gilded face, worn soft by time, looked back at the white face; suffering was in both; and then the living woman knelt beside the altar and felt along the paneling for the notch that worked the secret door. A sound behind her made her start violently to her feet, but Fand was trotting forward, head low and tail swinging, to sniff at the hands of Father Cloud.

"I have been positioning the men," he said, making no reference to the countess's unexpected posture. "They are fine lads, and will give good account of themselves."

"I'm sure they will," Annunciata said. "But what good can they do, armed with sticks and pitchforks, against men with guns? I wish to God we had more guns!"

"God will be our aid," the young priest said.

Annunciata looked bitterly at him. "Against cannon? If they bring cannon, we are done."

"We do not know that they will have cannon. We can pray to God for that." He looked tenderly at Annunciata, noting the hard lines that had deepened in her face over the past months. "My lady," he said, "I know that you are not reconciled to Rome, but when all your servants come to me, why do you not take the comfort I can offer? Why will you not receive the sacred mystery, the Host? I know you want it."

Annunciata looked away for a moment, and then back, and he saw she was weakening, that her eyes were bright with unshed tears.

"I cannot," she said. "I cannot confess myself."

"Let me beg you," Cloud said, moving closer. "Unburden yourself to me—you need not carry that terrible weight any longer. Trust me. Did not Our Lord say, 'Come unto me—'?"

"Please," she said, breaking in on him, "don't ask. I cannot—accept it."

"But I know that you want it, need it—won't you tell me why you cannot? There is nothing in the world so terrible that God cannot understand and forgive, if you truly repent."

"That is the point, Father Cloud," she said wearily. "You do not understand—I cannot confess, because I cannot repent. What I did, I would do again, gladly, willingly, with my whole heart, and rejoice in it, and though the Church condemns me, and shuts me off forever, yet I cannot in my heart say I am sorry that I did it."

"My child—"

"Please Father, say no more. Come, you must help me put away the precious things. There is a secret panel here, behind the Lady Altar. Bring the altar vessels and place them here. I will hide the family treasures, for safekeeping."

The priest obeyed her, dropping the subject, and together they put into the safe place the family treasures.

"There," she said, as she closed the panel again, "they will not find those, at least. Now, Father, if you will excuse me, I must send out my scouts, like a good general."

She went to pass him, and he caught her arm gently to stop her, and with his other hand made the sign of the cross upon her forehead.

"God *will* bless you," he said quietly. For a moment her dark eyes held his, and he saw some of the weariness leave them, saw her shoulders straighten a little before she detached herself finally, and without a word, left him.

CHAPTER TWENTY-ONE

The hardest thing of all was getting a boat. They finally managed to purchase the use of a fishing boat from Dardrecht and the services of her crew, but when Father St. Maur saw the vessel for the first time on a fine but windy November day he grew very quiet.

Karellie observed the change in his expression and said, "Cheer up, Father. You said you would rather die than desert the cause. God must have taken you at your word."

"I have changed my mind," the priest said. "I think I will do more good alive and on shore than by feeding the fishes somewhere out there." And he jabbed at the gray horizon with a quivering finger.

They went on board to wait for the tide, and at three in the afternoon they set sail. Once they reached the open sea, the full force of the gray English Channel seemed to be pit against them in an effort to tear their meager refuge into matchwood. So it seemed to them, at least, although the sailors seemed unperturbed and one of them even managed to tell Martin in his appalling mixture of bad French and worse German that the seas were surprisingly calm for this time of year and the weather clement. The four men, crouched in the smelly cabin and hurled now skyward, now plunging toward the seabed, found it hard to believe. There was no possibility for speech; an extraordinary cacophony of wind, sea, and boat noise dissuaded them from any but essential communications; they huddled in silence and communed with their thoughts.

Maurice, Karellie, and the priest thought mostly of the situation in England. The great army of Dutch William was marching eastward, away from Exeter and slowly but surely toward London, gathering support as it went. The King had spent some days at Salisbury with the army, and then, without offering either battle or explanation, had withdrawn back to London. Churchill, Kirke, and Grafton had all deserted and gone over to William, and when the King had reached London he had discovered that his daughter Anne, along with her friend Sarah, wife of Lord Churchill, had fled London to join William, no doubt by arrangement with Sarah's husband. Deserted even by his family, the King seemed to have no choice but to negotiate with his son-in-law.

Meanwhile the northern counties had been raised to revolt against the King, and while Lumley had taken Hull and Devonshire Nottingham, Danby, formerly the first minister of King Charles, had raised the northern part of Yorkshire and marched down to seize the city of York. Danby had been a friend of the Morland family in former times; he had known Annunciata at Court, and had been an acquaintance of Ralph Morland at home, and it appeared that he had done his best to ignore the fact that Morland Place was not joining the rebellion. But Morland Place was a conspicuous house, close to the city and at the heart of a large estate, and had long been the focus of Catholicism in that part of the country, albeit not Papism. But it was known that there was a Jesuit priest at Morland Place, and the time came when it was no longer possible for Danby to ignore the situation. On the twenty-seventh he had sent to demand that the priest be given up, and that any armed men should come and submit themselves to Danby's forces. Annunciata had sent back a defiance, and from then on Morland Place was under siege.

The news had met the exiles when they reached the Hague, looking for a boat, on the twenty-ninth; now, on the thirtieth, as they set sail for the east coast of England, they prayed they would not arrive too late. The boat heaved, and Martin sank his head in his hands, and Maurice, glancing across at him, guessed that his thoughts were not entirely on home, for it was when Martin had come to Leipzig to fetch him home that Maurice had been able, diffidently and, even then, unsure of whether he was doing the right thing, to give him news of Arabella.

Leipzig was a free city, and as well as a center of education and art, it was a flourishing center of trade and attracted many wealthy merchants. Johannes Pezel, under whom Maurice was studying, was professor of music at the university, but as well as being an outstanding musician and composer, he was a pleasant, jolly man of simple tastes, and he liked still to attend in person to his duties of town piper, which meant playing music for civic functions and important weddings. He wrote the music for the weddings of those wealthy enough to pay for it, and generally such music was played on two cornetti and three trombones. Pezel himself liked to play the first cornetto part, and it was now customary for Maurice to play the other. It was natural for Pezel to choose Maurice. In the time he had been there, Maurice had rapidly become Pezel's favorite and most promising student. Not only that, but he lived in Pezel's house, was adored by Pezel's wife, and idolized by Pezel's daughters. This beautiful young man with the perfect manners, the hint of royal blood, and the talent of an angel from heaven, was Leipzig's darling.

The merchant Finsterwalde, though not among the richest, was one of the keenest patrons of the arts, and was also a great traveler. He liked to gather, on his travels, things of beauty to bring back to his handsome house on the north of the town, and on his return from a visit to Prague he had brought not only a beautiful little Italian statuette, but a beautiful widow to be his bride. His first wife had died two years ago; the widow from Prague was said to be haughty, beautiful, and foreign, and had been supporting herself in Prague by dealing in horses. Maurice had caught sight of the Widow of Prague one day a week before the wedding as she traveled in Finsterwalde's coach with a servingwoman beside her on the way to the city warehouses to buy materials for her wedding clothes. Later that day Maurice had sought out his master and asked to be excused from playing at the wedding at St. Thomaskirche.

"But I have written such a pretty piece!" Pezel had protested. "And a part especially for you, Maurice. You cannot be serious.

The girls will be so disappointed! Herr Finsterwalde is a good man, very generous—"

"Please, Herr Professor, do not ask me," Maurice had said gravely. "There are very good reasons why I must ask you to excuse me, but I am not at liberty to tell you what they are. Ask Gregory or Thomas to play in my place."

Pezel regarded him affectionately. "You have good reason, I am sure, though I cannot for the life of me think what it can be. However, Gregory should be given a chance to play. He is very good. I will say only that you thought it right to give someone else the opportunity for once."

"You are very good to me," Maurice said. Pezel put his head on one side.

"Will you go and watch? Take the girls and Madame for me?"

But Maurice shook his head. There followed a week of terrible struggle with his conscience. He told himself he had been mistaken, but he knew he had not. He had only caught a glimpse of her, but the carriage had passed quite slowly, and he knew without question that the Widow of Prague was his half-sister Arabella. His plain duty was to expose her: she was about to commit bigamy, a most dreadful crime; she was still both legally and in the eyes of God wedded to Martin, who supposed her dead. He concluded that she had presented herself to the merchant Finsterwalde in some character other than her own and had won his trust on false pretenses.

But no matter how the idea troubled him, he could not bring himself to interfere. He had no idea what had happened to Arabella in the eighteen months since she disappeared, but he had no doubt that she had gone through terrible times, and had won through by a mixture of courage and audacity. If she did not go home, or declare herself, or seek out Martin; if she set up as a widow and accepted the hand of a wealthy merchant, she must have good reasons for doing it. It puzzled him, for he could not guess why she had left England if it had not been to join Martin, but instinct told him that to interfere would be the most painful course for everyone. So on the day of the wedding he stayed home and tried to think of other things.

He was glad when Martin came to summon him home—he could not hope to live for long in a city the size of Leipzig without bumping into Arabella; indeed, she must surely already have heard of the young musician, Maurice Morland, who lived with the Herr Professor and played at all the celebrations and functions. But Martin's arrival presented him with another problem of conscience, and this time the longing to be lighter of a burden was too strong. Let someone else make the decision. At sixteen, Maurice could be forgiven for wanting to pass on the responsibility, and in the short time between Martin's arrival and their departure together, he told him where he could find his erstwhile wife.

Crouched in the fish-smelling cabin of the boat, Martin relived that day in his memory. It had been a shock, of course, and at first he had naturally concluded that Maurice had been mistaken. When he was forced to accept Maurice's assurances that he was not mistaken, he could only wish with all his heart that the boy had kept his secret to himself. The situation in England was grave, and it was necessary for them to leave without delay, and deciding what to do about Arabella was something that needed days, weeks, of thought. He had assumed her to be dead. Annunciata had written to say she had gone off in pursuit of him on that day when he fled England, and that no trace of her had been found. Martin assumed that she had either met her death on the dark roads between York and Hull, or perhaps had hidden herself aboard some other boat and perished at sea; and though he had never wished her harm, it had been something of a relief to him to have one piece of his anxiety lifted. He had been carrying on an affair with her mother; by her death the enormous complexity of the situation was to that small extent simplified.

If she had survived and, surviving, had not sought him out, but had even married someone else, it was evident that she did not mean to find him or be found by him. He was forced to conclude that she had somehow found out about his relationship with Annunciata and had left home to escape that situation rather than to be with him. The conclusion eased him, and he made his decision swiftly and on that basis. If she did not want to be found, and he did not want to find her, then why should he do what promised only pain to everyone? He swore Maurice to secrecy and that evening he and the boy left for Heidelberg, where Karellie was waiting for them with Father St. Maur.

But before leaving he borrowed an all-enveloping cloak and a wide-brimmed hat and from Maurice's directions found his way to the Finsterwalde house. It was a large, handsome, modern house on a good street, with an imposing entrance. There was evidently a dinner party being held, for coaches were drawing up at the door from which were alighting the high society of Leipzig. Of course, he thought, the bridal celebrations would not yet be over. He watched for a while, and then, under cover of the crowds gathered to watch the arrivals, he worked his way round until he could see the door. Ah, now, here was a great coach with four liveried runners, some senior civic dignitary, without a doubt. For this guest the master and mistress of the house came to the door to receive.

He had never seen her look so beautiful. Her gown of blue satin over white brocade was trimmed with sapphires and ermine, the sleeves clasped with gold, and there were diamonds about her throat, and her magnificent red hair was dressed with diamonds and white flowers. Beside her, her "husband" in his white lace stock and scarlet sash and full-bottomed wig gazed at her adoringly and proudly as she received the civic dignitary with the haughty condescension of a queen, curtseying just sufficiently low to make the civic dignitary bow twice as deeply. It made Martin feel very strange to stand here in the crowd watching her, unseen, his young wife who had loved horses better than husbands and puppies better than babies. But as the Finsterwaldes moved back inside with their honored guests, Martin began to smile. It occurred to him suddenly that, had she been born a boy, she would have become a mercenary officer, as Hugo did, and could have left a wife and child with as much propriety to go and seek her fortune as Hugo left Caroline and little Arthur to go and fight the Turks. Arabella was unfortunate in being born a woman, when all her life she had craved excitement. Well, she had done the best she could, and though he could not know what adventures had brought her from York to Prague, he guessed she had used her feminine weapons to fight her way to this eminence.

She was a soldier of fortune; and unseen in the crowd, Martin saluted her as such. He drew himself to attention and as she turned away with her merchant prince, he raised his hand in a soldier's farewell, a little half-smile on his lips that, had she seen it, she would have recognized, even though she had never understood it.

The siege that began politely, almost reluctantly, grew more serious day by day, and by the end of the week the besieging forces were feeling frustrated. Morland Place was the only site of resistance in the environs of York, and they did not want to admit failure. Moreover the rumor that there was a Jesuit priest in residence had grown until the more fanatical elements were convinced that it was a thinly disguised seminary they were surrounding, and that there were twenty young men in orders within busy corrupting the Yorkshire servants.

In London the King had sent to William to ask his terms, but even as he was doing so, he was making arrangements for the escape to safety of his wife and son. Queen Mary and the Prince of Wales left England on the ninth of December, and the news drove the rebels in Yorkshire to a frenzy of anger against the deceitful Papists who said one thing and did another. There was a sharp attack on Morland Place that day, which almost succeeded. When the attackers drew off at dusk, Annunciata called her fighting men together in the long saloon.

"You see what our weakness is," she said. They all nodded wearily. The drawbridge had been replaced after the Civil War with a permanent wooden structure that could not be drawn up. It had then, of course, been considered impossible that the house would ever have to be defended again, and though the gates and portcullis had, fortunately, been left as they were, the moat was ineffective as a defense while the bridge stood. "We must destroy that bridge if we are to stand out," she said.

"It's very solid, mistress," Clement said, forgetting her title in the strain of the moment. "It would need blowing up, I should think."

"We've no explosives, and no chance of getting any," Father Cloud pointed out.

"The frame is solid, I grant you, and the piles, but I was not thinking of destroying those. As you say, it would take explosive material to move them quickly. But the planks, they could be levered up, could they not? Or splintered with axes? If they are removed, the frame will not do them much good. One man at a time may balance his way across, but we can easily pick off one man at a time, almost at our leisure. The important thing is to stop them making a concerted attack."

They listened and nodded, and Father Cloud said, "If it is to be done, it had better be done at once."

Annunciata nodded. "So I thought. They will not expect us to move so soon. They will be off their guard, making their supper, resting. It must be now—but you know it will be dangerous. I cannot tell any man to go out. Anyone who goes must choose to, knowing the danger."

"I will need four men," Father Cloud said at once. Annunciata had been expecting that.

"Not you, Father. You know what they would do to you if they caught you."

"I cannot allow that to influence me," he said.

"They want us to surrender," Annunciata interrupted him. "They want you to die. I cannot allow you to go. I need you here."

"I'll go, mistress," Clement said quickly.

"And me, my lady," Gifford added at once. Others spoke up after them, easily enough. Annunciata commanded the respect and devotion of her servants, especially the young men. She nodded and chose those who should work on the bridge and those who should stand guard and give covering fire if necessary.

"Remember," she said, "if it should be one man who comes, stumbles upon you by accident or from curiosity, kill him silently. Use a knife, not the guns. The best we can hope for is to get this done without attracting attention. We have few guns and little ammunition. Keep what we have for the last resort."

They nodded, and went to make their preparations. Annunciata and Father Cloud meanwhile went to the kitchen for a pot of goose grease, and then to the barbican, where with their own hands they greased the mechanism of the portcullis, the great black chains and wheels, so that it might be raised quietly. Annunciata put reliable men on the wheels, and took up her station in the upper room of the guardhouse. By and by there came what seemed like a deafening noise of squeaking and creaking though she knew that her nerves were exaggerating. A little way off she could see the dark shapes of the tents and the glitter of cooking fires as the besiegers made their supper. Many of them would be billeted in her own house of Shawes. She wondered what they had done to her bathing house, that small monument to her vanity. Others would be resting at Twelvetrees, and she clenched her fists at the thought of the horses there, which would have been stolen or taken in the name of Prince William to carry soldiers against their lawful King.

The portcullis was up, the gates open, and the men were coming out. Thank God the moon was not yet up. They could work as well in the dark, being in their own place, but the enemy would not know the ground as well, and would be night-blind from their own fires. As long as they had not set sentries—but they were rebels, not true soldiers, and she had good hopes they had not.

It was impossible, of course, for the work to be done without noise. She had chosen the strongest, and they were armed with axes and levers, and under her instructions were starting on alternate planks for the maximum effect. The noise seemed so loud in the still night she was sure the rebels must hear, and she clenched her fists so tightly that her nails drew blood from her palms as she stared with aching eyes into the darkness. There was a splash, and a muted exclamation: someone had dropped something, a tool perhaps. She had told them to pass the planks in as they freed them. There might come a time when they would need that wood, if the siege went on for long. Now there was a soft cry from one of the men keeping watch on the other side of the moat, and straining her eyes she saw some movement from the direction of the camp. Oh, hurry, hurry! She breathed anxiously. The men renewed their activities more urgently, and the noise was greater. Someone, in fear or frustration, started to hack at a plank with his axe. Now there was a shout, and then a scream, and almost simultaneously a musket shot. That must have been

Willum, she thought, judging by the direction, but whether he had shot a rebel or been shot by one she had no way of telling. But the alarm was given now. They were coming, shouting, and now there was a sparkle of firing. Six muskets, she judged. They would have to reload now. Her men had a few minutes more.

"Make your shots tell," she called down from her vantage point. She could see the shapes of her own men standing guard, but she could see nothing below her on the bridge—it was too dark. A flash, lighting up Tom to the left, and a cry from the darkness—he had got one of them. Then from the left, Gifford's musket spoke. But more of the rebels must have come, for there was another volley of shots, and under the covering fire the first-comers ran forward. There was hand-to-hand fighting down there now; more shots from her own men, and she called to them to retreat. All was confusion. She left her position and ran down, but Father Cloud was there and pushed her back.

"Keep away, there may be shots."

"Get them in! Call them in!" she shouted. "Stand by on the wheels, there!"

There were splintered planks under her feet, and now the men were coming in. The last of them was supporting a wounded man, and as he ducked under the portcullis it slammed down—the wheelmen in their anxiety almost decapitated the pair of them. The rebels were firing through the portcullis, and Annunciata heard a bullet whine past her without at once realizing what it was—it sounded like an enraged insect. But the great gates were being closed. A man cried out sharply; one of her own men fired through the narrowing gap and his victim screamed; and then the gates were closed. Up in the gatehouse she heard a few more shots being fired down at the rebels, and presently there was silence outside, for they would not risk their lives uselessly in the dark.

Clement was beside her, panting. In the dark she could smell his fear.

"We did it, mistress, nearly all of it gone," he said.

"Who was that wounded man brought in?" she asked.

"Tom, mistress—I think he's hurt pretty bad."

"There's another man here, shot in the arm," Father Cloud

said. That would be the man who had been shot while closing the gates.

"And we lost Willum," Clement said.

"What happened?" Annunciata asked. She realized there was a sharp pain in her hands, and forced herself to relax her fingers.

"One of the rebels ran him through, my lady." That was Gifford, coming up beside her in the dark. "He fired as he went down, but I didn't see if the shot told."

"That's one gun we've lost, though," Father Cloud said. She turned on him abruptly, angered by his callousness.

"Your duty is with the wounded, Father. Gifford, get us some light, for God's sake."

Willum was a shepherd's son whom she had been training as a footman, a handsome boy with a lock of barley-colored hair that would fall into his eyes in moments of stress. Did it fall into his eyes as the rebel knifed him? she wondered, following her men toward the house.

Tom had been shot in the belly, and died during the night. He had been with her for over twenty years. The other man's arm was broken at the elbow. Chloris and Jane Birch and Annunciata strapped it up after Father Cloud had got the ball out. If the wound did not gangrene, he would live, but the arm would be useless to him. When she had seen everyone comfortable, Annunciata went to the chapel, and sat there alone until dawn, when Father Cloud came in for the first celebration.

When they had been a day at sea the wind turned dead foul for them, and then blew up into a gale, and the ramshackle fishing-boat was driven north and east toward Texel. The fishermen knew their trade, and ran before the wind, not attempting to fight it, and made port safely, but they were farther from England than ever. There was no hope of sailing from that wild and windy place, and when they had waited a couple of days, the fishermen advised them to take horses and ride down the coast and try for a larger vessel from the Hague or some other large port.

"We are back where we started!" Karellie cried in frustration.

"Worse," Father St. Maur said tersely. His old bones had not enjoyed the knocking about they had endured.

"Is there any chance of the wind moderating?" Martin asked the fishermen, and they shrugged obligingly.

"With the wind, there is always a chance of change. One cannot predict the weather."

"If it moderates, will you take us out?" he asked. They nodded. They thought the gentlemen were ardent Protestants longing to get to England to help Prince William, and Martin had not seen fit to disabuse them. He considered for a while and then said, "I can't see the benefit in trying the Hague. We'll wait, and leave as soon as the wind moderates."

The same wind that kept them prisoner in Texel ran immoderate and unusual tides about the coasts, and one of these exposed a sandbank off the coast of Kent, onto which a certain customs hoy went aground. Some Kentish fishermen went to the rescue, well armed with pistols and swords, for they were looking for Catholic fugitives, and brought the passengers on the hoy back to Faversham, where someone recognized one of them as the King, who had fled Whitehall on the night of the eleventh, hoping to join his wife and child in France.

Two days later Martin and his companions, having beaten about the North Sea in vain for four days, trying to make port on the east coast, were dropped at the mouth of the Thames by the fishermen, who had had enough of the adventure. The first people they met on landing were Dutch soldiers, who regarded them with some suspicion and questioned them sharply, but soon let them go, for it was evident to them that anyone who was a Catholic synpathizer of the King's would be heading in the other direction, and Martin's story of wanting to help Prince William seemed acceptable to them.

"Come on to the inn," their corporal said. "It's a cold night, and we'll drink Prince William's health together."

Martin smiled and thanked him, trying to sound genuinely regretful, but said they must find some transport and get to London. He knew there was no way in the world to get Karellie or Maurice to drink Prince William's health, and in the warmth and bright lights of a tavern Father St. Maur would soon be revealed for what he was.

They found a boatman willing to take them to London for an

exorbitant amount, but the tide had only two hours to the turn, and they dared not wait to find another boat, so they hired him, and reached Whitehall steps in time to take breakfast in the Coffee House there. The early morning customers were full of the news of the King's return to London.

"Poor gentlemen," someone said, "it is a terrible thing to see him brought so low."

"It made my wife cry, I can tell you," said another.

"Think yourselves lucky, gentlemen," the proprietor said, "that he has come back, before the rioting and looting got too bad. There are some parts of the country, so it's said, where houses have been burned down and honest folk robbed."

"It's come of having so many soldiers about," said a third man. "England never was a merry place when there was soldiers to hand."

When they had eaten, the four men left quietly. Outside Martin said, "We've got to get some horses and get home. God knows what's happening there."

The siege had lasted nineteen days. They had run out of ammunition for their few firearms, and when the besiegers attacked they had to push them from the walls with poles, or throw stones at them. There were fewer of them out there than before, for they were no longer a proper army, more of a mob. Danby was still holding York, and his interest in Morland Place was only a side issue, but there was a hard core of fanatics who would not give up until they had seen the priest hanged and the walls reduced to rubble.

Inside Morland Place, Annunciata was struggling against growing despair in her people, her food was running short, and the news that the King had fled had made them lose heart. What possible hope was there for them if the King was gone? That would mean Prince William would take the throne, and *they* would be the rebels, not the mob outside. A deputation from the servants came to Annunciata to ask her to surrender. She argued with them and pleaded with them; just in time came the news that the King had returned to London—it gave her ammunition.

"But they say he's a prisoner, my lady," they said, "with Dutch guards by his bedside."

"He has been hearing Mass openly," she countered. "Does that make him sound like a prisoner? Besides, whatever he is doing in London, he is still the King."

She did not convince them, but they agreed to stay with her, more from love of her than of the King, who seemed now to have deserted them. But the next day the rebels launched another attack, and this time, they had cannon. She could not imagine where they had got them from—perhaps they had been released from some other siege in some other part of the country; or perhaps Danby had finally tired of hoping she would give in. The firing was erratic, and far from accurate, but the servants were terrified, and the children screamed pitifully at every new rolling crash of fire. They had no means of fighting back. If they had had guns, or grenades, they might have had some chance to pick off the gunners, but as it was, they had simply to wait helplessly for the next shot. They came to Annunciata and cried to her.

"We must surrender, my lady."

"It's no use, my lady. We must give in."

"Name of God, madam, we don't want to die."

"No," she said. The crashes, and the sound of breaking glass, and the ground shaking under her feet. They were concentrating on the gatehouse and barbican, but one shot had gone through the windows of the chapel—deliberately, of course. She could not think, her senses seemed battered.

"Please, madam, please—let us surrender before we're all killed."

Now here was Dorcas with Clover and Aliena in her arms, the babies screaming and she weeping incoherently.

"They're firing on the other side now," she cried. "They've smashed the schoolroom."

It was only a matter of time. Her will seemed paralyzed, and they clamored at her in vain. If only they would go away and let her be. If only there were silence. She gathered her strength.

"No," she said. "Never. God save the King."

"It is out of your hands," Father Cloud said quietly beside her. She heard the rending crashes even as he spoke. "They've broken down the gatehouse. They'll be in the yard next."

"The great door won't stop them," Clement said, and as he

spoke, one of the younger men cried, "Well, I'm not going to get myself killed, that's for sure. Come on, we'll hang a flag from the staircase window. Quick, before it's too late!"

And there was a rush for the door. Annunciata screamed at them, though she did not know what she said, or whether they had heard. They were going to surrender. She whirled round, her eyes going from one terrified face to another. "Father Cloud!" she cried. He nodded.

"Yes, I know," he said, and went quickly from the room. She hoped he had gone to his sanctuary. Now there were her women, and the children. "To my bedchamber," she said. "Oh, quickly!"

But it was already too late. Even as they rushed for the door, there was a tremendous noise downstairs as the great door, unlocked from inside, crashed back against the wall, and the hall was filled with shouting rebels and the glow of torches. They'll fire the chapel, she thought dully. There were the sounds of things being smashed, hoarse shouts and cries, somewhere a scream, a man's scream, cut off in the middle. Fury rose in her. She pushed the women toward the bedchamber, for what little safety that could offer.

"Hide in the closet with the children. Keep the door if you can," she cried. On the wall of the long saloon there had been a display of weapons for decoration, all of which had been taken down for use, except one, a child's sword, perfectly made and balanced for Ralph's eldest son when he was first breeched, and still bright, though the blade was not two feet long. She took it now, the last weapon to hand, and started down the great staircase.

To Martin and his companions it was a moment of great horror, that first moment when they saw the house, the gatehouse broken down with cannon shot, the windows smashed, smoke billowing out of the empty eyes of the chapel. They galloped their sweating horses, hearing even from a distance the noises of looting, though they were not to know that the worst was over by then. They saw even as they approached men making off with their loot; others were staying for the wanton pleasure of destruction.

The bridge was gone, all but the supports, and they had to

dismount and go across it on foot, which put them at a disadvantage, though the same disadvantage had stopped the looters from stealing their horses in the stableyard. In their frustration the rebels had killed or hamstrung about half a dozen of them before turning to other sport.

It did not occur to them afterward that they could all have been killed, not even to old Father St. Maur, who was not armed. They strode in, swords out, like the wrath of God, to the scene of hellishness in the great hall: there were bodies of dead and wounded men, smashed furniture and torn books, the smell of smoke and unwashed bodies, and a gaggle of men, yelling and brandishing their weapons. And on the stairs, armed with a slender blade more like a dagger than a sword, Annunciata stood, her hair streaming behind her, her face drawn into an unrecognizable snarl as she defied them all, holding them at bay by the sheer fury of her defiance as she bared her teeth like a maddened and cornered fox.

It was a short and furious fight. Some of the men recognized the master and slunk away, while the boldest were unnerved by the sight of three gentlemen of such distinguished appearance, armed with bright blades. Some of them crossed swords with the gentlemen, but when the first of them was run through the belly and two others wounded, they decided they had had enough. Karellie and Maurice, their eyes bright with vengeance, hunted through the house for more blood, while Martin ran up the stairs to where Annunciata stood, draggled and exhausted, her eyes wide, the sword, clutched now in both hands, hanging uselessly before her.

He put his arms round her, and her body was as rigid as iron, and she stared sightlessly before her.

"It's all right," he said, "it's all right, it's all over now. I'm here. Annunciata! It's all right."

Slowly, slowly she looked down at her hands, the knuckles white as they grasped the sword, and she opened her fingers one by one with a great effort, and the sword fell and slithered and clattered down the stairs into the hall, where Father St. Maur was looking to the wounded. Then she began to shake, and he gathered her into his arms and held her close. Her hair smelled of smoke. After a while she said, "Martin?"

She pushed back from him to look into his face. Tears were running down his cheeks, but she felt nothing, nothing, only a great weariness.

"Martin," she said. "I'm so tired."

"Oh, my lady," he said, and as she closed her eyes he took her in his arms again, and held her until he could stop weeping enough to take her upstairs.

They put out the fires, patched up where they could, buried the dead and treated the wounded, swept up the smashed furniture and broken glass, took stock of what had been stolen. They found the body of Father Cloud, hideously mutilated, floating in the moat, and buried him, too. They put down the hamstrung horses, and cut up the carcasses for dogmeat. They rebuilt the bridge with the planks Annunciata had had the forethought to save, and blocked up the broken windows until a glazier could be found to repair them. Most of the servants, who had fled when the rebels broke in, came back, though some did not. Martin set them to work repairing the damage to the house, and promised them all rewards for their faithfulness, and they looked at him, ashamed, because they had left the mistress to keep the stairs alone. Because the principal treasures were safe in the secret place, the losses had not been so great as they might have been, but Martin mourned the wanton destruction of his precious collection of books. Had Annunciata not held the stairs, and thus kept the rebels from the upstairs rooms, he would probably have lost every one.

He slept in the great bedchamber with her, and if any of the servants thought it strange, they did not say so. Karellie and Maurice exchanged puzzled glances, but then shrugged and assumed that he slept other than in her bed, simply to keep her safe. They slept in the nursery. The little children had nightmares and woke crying, and were reassured by the sight of their guardians, their rescuers, sleeping nearby.

All that took a week. Christmas was approaching, though it would be a strange sort of Christmas for everyone. Prince William and his army were still outside London, and the King was still at Whitehall with the Dutch soldiers guarding his bed. Mostly people thought William would kill the King: they saw him as a second Cromwell.

On Christmas Eve it turned bitterly cold, and with the windows broken it was hard to keep warm. Everyone gathered in the drawing room, and a large fire blazed in the hearth there with that strange brightness the cold brings. Annunciata, pale and thin, sat shivering, though she was wrapped in a cloak and nearest the fire. The shock of what she had been through had affected her nerves, and she could neither eat nor sleep well enough to regain her strength. Martin was reading aloud to try to soothe her while the other women sewed, and Karellie and Maurice played with the little boys.

It was after dark that there came the sound of a horseman, and Martin stopped reading and everyone froze. Annunciata started at the knocking on the great door, and Martin said soothingly, "It's all right, it is but one man. It must be news of some sort." And he got up at once and went out into the hall. Birch's eyes followed him, and Dorcas's. Chloris looked at her mistress, hunched in shivering misery by the fire. The master was so good to her, she thought, treating her more like a child than a grown woman, but what would happen when she was well again? *That* situation was no better than it had ever been, and Chloris could not see the ending of it. And what of the baby, Aliena, and what of the countess's two sons, who already wondered about Martin's care for their mother?

There was silence in the room, apart from the crackling of the fire, but the doors were thick and they heard nothing of what passed in the hall. Then at last Martin came in, alone. His expression was grave, and he looked at Annunciata with concern, and pity, but, underneath it all, some glimmering of hope. He came to her and knelt in front of her in the fireglow and took her hands, capturing her attention.

"My lady," he said, "it was news, as I thought. From London." Annunciata's eyes were on his unwaveringly. "The King has fled Whitehall. He is got safe away to France. It is said that Prince William arranged for the guards to be slack. It's all over.''

In the week since the rebels had broken in, she had remained dry eyed through everything, but now as comprehension came to her, tears filled her eyes.

''We failed him,'' she said at last. The drops welled over her lashes and dropped onto Martin's hands. He could not bear it.

''No,'' he said, pressing her hands. ''He has forsaken us, not we him.'' But he was glad at least that she was crying. There was healing in that. ''My lady, it's all over.''

There was silence in the room as each of them wondered what would happen next. Karellie and Maurice, their hands frozen above the merels board, looked toward that tableau questioningly, at their half-brother, Martin, kneeling at the hearth, gazing earnestly at their mother; and at their mother, her captured hands in her lap, her head bent forward so that her slow tears fell clear, shining in the red frost-light of the flames.

Dell Bestsellers

A CRY IN THE NIGHT
by Mary Higgins Clark $3.95 (11065-3)

STARVING FOR ATTENTION
by Cherry Boone O'Neill $3.50 (17620-4)

MAX
by Howard Fast $3.95 (16106-1)

THE G-SPOT
by Alice Kahn Ladas, Beverly Whipple,
and John D. Perry $3.50 (13040-9)

INDECENT EXPOSURE
by David McClintick $3.95 (14007-2)

THE ONYX
by Jacqueline Briskin $3.95 (16667-5)

REMEMBRANCE
by Danielle Steel $3.95 (17370-1)

STRANGER IN THE HOUSE
by Patricia J. MacDonald $3.50 (18455-X)

EDEN BURNING
by Belva Plain $3.95 (12135-3)

EDIE: An American Biography
by Jean Stein, edited by George Plimpton $3.95 (13003-4)

CONTROL
by William Goldman $3.95 (11464-0)

VICTIM: THE OTHER SIDE OF MURDER
by Gary Kinder $3.95 (19704-X)

DELL BOOKS

At your local bookstore or use this handy coupon for ordering:

Dell DELL BOOKS
P.O. BOX 1000, PINE BROOK, N.J. 07058-1000

Please send me the books I have checked above. I am enclosing $_____ (please add 75c per copy to cover postage and handling). Send check or money order—no cash or C.O.D.'s. Please allow up to 8 weeks for shipment.

Name _____

Address _____

City_____ State/Zip _____